COLLATERAL DAMAGE

City fraud, police corruption and personal tragedy – another ordinary day on the streets of London. Nick Shannon, still struggling to get his life back together after his sister's death, accepts a secondment to the Fraud Squad. On the point of collaring a small-time fraudster, Nick and his colleagues are left flat-footed when the suspect avoids arrest by defenestration. It seems he was part of a major financial scam set up by an ex-police officer, an erstwhile colleague of Nick's boss, Collins. Following a paper trail of fraud, Nick is determined to expose those at the heart of the corruption...

COLLATERAL DAMAGE

by

Paul Bennett

Magna Large Print Books
Long Preston, North Yorkshire,
BD23 4ND, England.

British Library Cataloguing in Publication Data.

Bennett, Paul
    Collateral damage.

    A catalogue record of this book is
    available from the British Library

    ISBN   0-7505-1654-2

First published in Great Britain by Warner Books in 1998

Copyright © Paul Bennett 1998

Cover illustration © Michael Trevillion by arrangement with
The Trevillion Picture Library and Little, Brown & Company

The moral right of the author has been asserted

Published in Large Print 2001 by arrangement with
Little, Brown & Company

All characters in this publication are fictitious
and any resemblance to real persons, living or dead,
is purely coincidental.

Magna Large Print is an imprint of Library Magna Books Ltd.

Printed and bound in Great Britain by
T.J. (International) Ltd., Cornwall, PL28 8RW

CHAPTER ONE

Perhaps I should have spotted the sucker punch and climbed from the ring before it had a chance to land. Maybe I should have recognised the sprats dangling from hooks – not swallowed them whole, mackerel-fashion. But I trusted Collins. It's what you tend to do when you owe someone your life.

Five cases he'd given me to date. Each one about as intellectually challenging as the nought-times-table. And as riveting as watching paint dry. In a dark room. With your eyes closed.

They were fiddles, not frauds. That fact alone should have set the alarm bells ringing in my ears.

Detective Superintendent Collins, head of 'C' Squad of the grandiosely titled 'Special Operations 6' (the plain old Fraud Squad to you and me) had pole position in the choice of cases. Yet he had fed me a stultifying collection of petty crimes only one step removed from raiding the stationery cupboard for a handful of ballpoint pens to take home for the kids.

Still, he was new to the job. Untrained, apart from the standard two-week crash course that all new entrants, of whatever rank, must undergo. He's simply finding his feet, I told myself. Taking it in easy stages.

So I gave him the benefit of the doubt.

Not exactly a judgement borne of pure altruism or a totality of trust, I must admit. Expedience was nearer the mark. As an ex-con you learn to take whatever work you're offered (or, more accurately in my case, pressganged into accepting). With a cheesy grin and a tug at the forelock.

'How do you cope with all this excitement?' I said to Walker as the lift climbed excruciatingly slowly towards the seventeenth floor. It was something to say, that's all. A piece of oral displacement activity intended solely to take my mind off the journey. Confined spaces aren't my strong point. The lift was currently giving a good impression of a car-crusher, the walls sliding in towards me like a scene from an *Indiana Jones* movie, or a chocolate orange commercial. But I was determined not to show my fear in front of Walker.

'What did you expect?' came the sharp reply. 'Weekly trips to Grand Cayman to follow the trail of freshly laundered money? Scuba diving off the coast of Africa to see if sunken ships really contained the cargo listed on the manifest?' Walker gave me a withering look. 'The Fraud Squad is five per cent complexity and ninety-five per cent paperwork. Now, you're the mathematician. You tell me how much that leaves over for electrifying thrills and cliff-hanging excitement?'

My sharply honed expert mind locked onto the complex calculation. Swiftly computed the only possible answer.

'I love you when you're angry,' I said.

She placed her hands on her skirt. Spread her

long fingers across her hips. Sighed deeply. Rolled her dark brown eyes skyward.

'You're beyond contempt, Shannon,' she said. 'I refuse to rise to the bait.'

The lift door opened before the smile could form on her lips. Or at least I hoped that was the case.

'Follow me,' she said, leaving me no alternative. She strode purposefully along the corridor, a conflicting picture of soft curves and hard, straight authority.

A black-helmeted, green-uniformed security guard, steel box chained to wrist, moved to one side to prepare to let us pass. His eyes flitted disinterestedly over me, and lingered a fraction too long on Walker. He got the withering look this time. That's one of the nice things about Walker. She shows no favouritism. Everybody receives the same treatment.

Walker pressed the button on the entryphone. The sign on the door said 'Van Damm Limited – Diamond Merchants'. Makes the heart beat, doesn't it? Were we here to put an end to a multi-million-pound fraud in uncut stones? Valuable gems leaving the premises secreted up the nostrils of shifty-eyed employees? Fake diamonds flooding onto the market in an effort to undermine the economy of South Africa? The hell we were, as The Duke would have said. Wayne that is, not Ellington.

We were here to arrest a small-time crook, a petty embezzler who had risked his career for a few thousand pounds. Well, to be perfectly accurate, the arrest was Walker's job. My role, as the humble civilian, was to secure the evidence before our man had a chance to tamper with it.

'Police. Open up,' Walker shouted into the microphone in that commanding tone used by all good cops on TV shows.

Nothing happened. Not exactly the conditioned response one has come to expect.

Through the small metal squares of the reinforced glass I could see a young girl perched behind a pale oak reception desk. She was talking animatedly on the telephone. Walker scowled irritably at her. The girl replaced the receiver in its cradle. And sat there, gawping back at us.

Walker tapped her foot.

I held my breath. And prayed to God that the receptionist wouldn't take out a nailfile, thereby inviting immediate incineration from Walker's laser-beam eyes.

After another minute, and a valiant attempt by Walker at the World Foot-Tapping Record, a small, heavily balding man appeared on the other side of the glass. He was in shirt-sleeves and braces, his trousers at half-mast below the convex curve of a large stomach. An eyepiece dangled from a black cord around his neck.

Walker scowled and pressed her warrant card against the glass.

The door opened.

'Sorry about the delay,' the man said, addressing me. 'Only you can't be too careful, you know. Not in our business.'

'Quite, sir,' Walker said, seething. 'I'm Detective Sergeant Walker. This,' she waved her hand casually in my direction, 'is Nick Shannon.'

I smiled confidently at him, hoping to suggest that Walker had absent-mindedly omitted the 'Special Agent' before my name. 'Go ahead, Walker,' I said, keeping up the illusion. I knew she'd make me pay for it later. But if you can't extract a little fun from the daily grind, then what's the point?

'Mendelssohn,' the man said.

I fought back the frivolous desire to say, 'I call your Mendelssohn and raise you a Bach and two Handels.' I was beginning to wonder if I was really cut out for this sort of work.

'Johan Mendelssohn,' he explained. 'Managing Director. What can I do for you?'

Walker explained the purpose of our visit. Mendelssohn's brow furrowed into more lines than a newly ploughed field. He led us, head shaking in sadness and disbelief, to the Accounts Department.

The offices had that ill-proportioned appearance redolent of having once been open-plan. They occupied half the top floor of this white elephant of a building. Finished at the height of the slump in property prices, Van Damm had probably picked up the premises for a song. On the right were a number of cubicles where narrow cones of light picked out a collection of serious men peering critically at small gems through identical eyepieces. On the left was a large, specially constructed strongroom, bricked off from more cubicles with even more men going through the squinting ritual. If this was what they did all day, then when they met as a group it must resemble the finals of a Patrick

Moore lookalike contest.

In the middle was an area where paperwork was being shuffled with little apparent enthusiasm across, and between, desks. Harsh fluorescent light shone down flickeringly on the unfortunate clerks. A gentle breeze from the air-conditioning drifted overhead, keeping the temperature exactly two degrees below what would have been comfortable: in a few months' time when summer arrived, I guessed with the cynicism of experience, it would be exactly two degrees above.

At the far end was a vertigo-sufferer's worst nightmare – a wall of windows from knee-height to ceiling. The thick, heavily tinted, blue-grey glass provided a surreal view of the skyline to the east of London, like looking at an eclipse through a negative. Today, the weak rays of the March sun had stretched the clouds into elongated bands of candy floss that brushed the top of St Paul's Cathedral. In the distance, I could make out Tower Bridge. Closer to hand was the unforgettable green dome of the Old Bailey.

I shuddered involuntarily. Six months I'd spent inside that monument to British justice. Six months during which the lawyers and expert witnesses pleading on my behalf failed to alter the predetermined course of the trial. Don't blame them, they did their best. Blame it instead on the antiquated laws of our land that insist on treating assisted suicide as a crime. And on the quarter of my blood that is Irish and rose uncontrollably to the surface in angry volcanic explosions against a judge who listened but would not hear. Okay, so maybe I didn't do myself any favours. But seven years in prison! Had I sinned that much? To me, the Old Bailey would never be the battleground of right and wrong. It was just the starting point of a long and painful journey that transformed a green-eyed, starry-eyed twenty-two-year-old into a battle-scarred ex-con and led, via a prison-acquired qualification in accountancy and a hefty prod from the fickle finger of Fate, to Collins's current hold on me.

Come on, Shannon, I reproached myself. Turn away from the window. And the past.

The 'Accounts Department' consisted of two desks. They were set apart in an open L-shape, each defended from encroachment by the other by a barricade of filing cabinets, the pair discreetly screened off from the main administration area. Our man, Redmond, sat with his back to the window. He looked up as we entered. In the lenses of his spectacles I could see the reflection of a spreadsheet on his computer screen.

A girl, early twenties, stared at the terminal on her desk, unnaturally anxious not to catch our eyes. She was probably considered attractive by those who go for maximum make-up and minimum clothing. Her hair was blonde and 'big', with waves that you could almost have surfed on: it tumbled down past shoulders bared by a tight halter-neck sweater and rested teasingly on the jutting points of twin peaks.

I'd seen her once before, and been equally impressed on that occasion. Her name, ill-fittingly, was Gloria. In the acronym-rich language of the sociologist or market researcher she would be classed as a SINBAD – Single Income, No Bloke, Absolutely Desperate. She had been Redmond's mistress until she'd realised there was no future in it. It was then that she'd turned informant.

I moved behind Gloria. Took the box of blank, ready-formatted diskettes from my briefcase. Set it down alongside the computer. We changed places, the aroma of her perfume wafting into my nostrils with all the subtlety of a jackhammer. She stood there, one ankle twisting nervously from side to side on the rapier point of a white stiletto, smoothing the creases from her short A-line skirt. And waiting expectantly for Walker to speak.

'Martin Redmond?' Walker said, on cue. She had the printed caution card in her right hand. The left was busy thrusting her identification towards him.

Redmond took off his glasses and laid them on the desk. He gave a tentative nod of assent.

While his eyes stared vacantly at her photograph, Walker read aloud, and without inflection, from the card. We all know the words by heart – the right to remain silent and all that jazz – but, believe me, when you're on the receiving end, the set speech takes on an ethereal, dreamy quality and the words float around your head without a single one actually sinking in.

I glanced up from my task of backing-up the accounts data from the computer's hard disk to the floppies. Redmond was standing now. He looked a lot older than his thirty-five years. Beneath the neat pinstripe suit his tall, well-built frame had contorted into a series of odd angles brought on by the rigidity that comes with fear. The skin on his face had turned that sickly shade of yellowy-white more often associated with victims of jaundice. He gazed with horror at Walker. His mouth gaped soundlessly open, receiving no directions from a brain that had shifted through shock into neutral.

Gloria took in the scene like a circling vulture. And failed to conceal a smile.

The blood returned to her ex-lover's face.

'You stupid bitch,' he said, spitting the words slowly and venomously at her. 'Why didn't you keep your big mouth shut? No-one need ever have known. I would have paid back the money.'

'Sure,' she said, raking her hair back with the long nails of her thumb and index finger. 'Remind me, Martin. What do you need now? How many twenty-to-one nags have to win to clear your debts? Five? Ten?' She was breathing hard. Her breasts rose and fell with emotion, testing the limits of her jumper's elasticity. She fixed him with a cold, pitiless sneer. Then turned her attention to Walker. 'Take him away, for chrissake. Before I puke.'

'You silly cow,' he said. The words, strangely, lacked bite. He shook his head despairingly. 'You don't know what you've done.'

I watched as Redmond's shoulders slumped. Saw the abject look of total resignation spread like a dark shadow across his face. And the swift movement as he grabbed the chair.

I leapt up.

Then wondered what to do next.

The desk was a frustrating obstacle between us. Should I take the slower path around? Or try a kamikaze vault over the top?

The metal legs of the chair were now pointing threateningly in Walker's direction. It was make-your-mind-up time.

I barged Walker roughly out of the way. Out of the corner of my eye I saw her collide heavily with the partition and send it crashing to the floor.

I fixed all my attention on Redmond. Tried to predict his next move. Prepared for a direct assault. Balanced myself to jump across the desk when a thrust or throw of the unwieldy chair had laid him open to counter-attack.

Then he made the only move I hadn't taken into account.

He turned his back on me.

And threw the chair at the window.

There was an ear-splitting explosion of shattering glass.

The chair went spinning into the void outside.

And, diving head first, Redmond followed it.

From seventeen floors up, as the Doppler effect played tricks on my ears, I heard the changing notes of his scream. Then it died, like Redmond, with a nauseating thump.

Walker was the first to recover.

I was still struggling with the vivid mental pictures being carried on the cold wind that blew through the enormous jagged-edged hole. And with trying to make some sense of the irrational act. *Why? Why? Why?* I repeated to myself, hoping that the mantra might provide solace, if not solution.

Gloria, meanwhile, was on her knees, loudly emptying the contents of her stomach onto the bright orange carpet-tiles – I'd always wondered why that hideous colour was so popular.

'Don't you ever do that again,' Walker shouted angrily at me, vigorously rubbing an aching shoulder. 'It's my job to protect you. Not the other way round. Is that clear? Do you understand?'

'So nice to be appreciated, Walker,' I said, gathering up the diskettes. I laid my briefcase on Redmond's desk so that it covered his address book. 'That's the way you want it, is it?' I said to the still-fuming Walker. 'Okay, then. If you *really* want to protect me ... *you* can be the one to tell Collins!'

'Shit,' she said vehemently.

'Exactly,' I said. 'And we're both in it. Right up to our armpits.'

CHAPTER TWO

In the turbo-charged climate of the City, the efficiency of information providers is measured in one-hundredths of a second. Compared to Reuters and the like, the police grapevine is a superhighway. News seems to circulate in milliseconds along its unofficial airwaves: bad news – especially when it is a rich source of embarrassment for one's peers or, better still, one's superiors – defies Einstein, travelling faster than the speed of light.

The offices of SO6 are situated above Holborn Police Station in High Holborn. In order to reach Collins's room we had to run the gauntlet past 'A' and 'B' Squads. Detective Sergeant Quinn – all moustache, mouth and monkey business – was leading a male voice choir in a bastardised version of the theme from *The Snowman*. 'We're flying through the air. Thud,' they sang.

Walker was used to being the butt of their juvenile humour. Much of it was pretty innocuous – the sort of innocent playground banter that goes on in any close-knit group. But some of the taunts were delivered in harder-edged tones that gave glimpses below the surface to the murky depths of prejudice. Out of 155 officers in SO6, only four were women. Given this sort of treatment, I was surprised it was that many.

Three years in the Fraud Squad had electro-plated a thin protective patina on Walker's skin. The gibes weren't exactly water off a duck's back, but she had soon learned that the best defence was to show no reaction. A blank expression provided no feast for their appetites.

She strode like Moses through the sea of jeering faces, looking neither, to right nor left. Only when we were outside Collins's office did I hear the faintest mutter of 'bastards' under her breath.

Walker knocked tentatively on the door. It shook within the badly fitting frame. Collins, refusing to join the other two squad leaders on the floor above, had insisted on a room near to his 'troops' – close to the action was probably more like the truth. And so this ten-foot square cell had been specially created for him. I'd seen better efforts come out of a first-form woodwork lesson. Great slabs of chipboard had been hacked unevenly into a rough approximation of the required proportions and sandwiched between inch-wide steel retaining clips. Breathe too heavily and the whole structure wobbled pre-cariously – the Three Little Pigs wouldn't have given it a second glance.

We shuffled inside – the only way to move about within its cramped confines – and took our seats in turn.

'Not the success of the century, by all ac-counts,' Collins said.

In the chair next to me, Walker bristled.

'It wasn't our fault,' I said quickly. 'How were *we* supposed to know he would jump? Jesus Christ, it was only a few lousy grand.' I shook my head and let Walker have her say.

'It was just a routine case, sir,' Walker said. 'I've had dozens like it in my time.' She paused so that Collins could not fail to understand the meaning behind the words. *I've been here three years, sir. You haven't even done three months yet. You're in no position to criticise me.*

'He was a nutter,' she continued. 'Must have been. Why else would he jump? You can't expect us to predict what a nutter will do.' She fixed

17

Collins with a defiant stare. 'If you'd been there, sir, the outcome would have been no different.'

Collins leaned back in his standard-issue leather swivel-chair (DS and above, bums for the use of). He swung his legs up. Placed his feet casually on the desk. The sole of one shoe had a hole in it, ruining the effect.

If we'd been standing up, I would have been three inches taller than his six-foot-nothing. But only strictly in terms of height, if you know what I mean. Where physical presence was concerned, he stood a good foot above me. There was an air of pent-up aggression about him. But so loosely controlled that it threatened to erupt at the slightest opportunity.

To go with the new job, and what was supposed to be a new image, Collins had bought two new suits – one dark blue, the other dark grey. Today it was the turn of the blue. It had a yellow egg stain on the lapel. If he had worn the grey one, then we would have been granted another view of the brown patch of dried ketchup. The new leaf had begun to shrivel in his first few days at the squad. Now, after a little over two months, he had regressed completely to his former self.

Collins looked pensively at Walker. Ran his right hand through his long ginger hair as if to check whether it *really* needed washing yet, or could it last a few more days before becoming unbearably greasy?

'There will have to be an enquiry, Walker,' he said solemnly. 'Standard procedure. Should be a mere formality, though. But we'll keep you out of the firing line for a while. You've got some leave owing. Take a holiday.'

'Sir,' she protested. 'I do not want a holiday. I want to carry on working as normal.'

I could tell what she was thinking. The stigma of an enquiry was bad enough: there were some (Quinn and his coterie, to name but a few dozen) who would delight in leaping to the wrong conclusion. But if she were actually removed from duty, the muck-spreaders would have a field-day.

'Look, Walker,' Collins said patiently. 'I don't need this. All right? I can't afford a cloud hanging over one of my officers. This job is hard enough as it is.'

I sympathised with Collins. He was a front-line cop, never happier than when at the throbbing heart of a case, leading a raid or interrogating a prime suspect. The transfer to a desk job at the Fraud Squad was anathema to him – a torture akin to the death of a thousand paper-cuts. But he had been given no option. Finally accepting the inevitable, Collins had extracted the most beneficial terms from the Commander. 'C' Squad, like the rickety office, had been specially set up for him. Now he had to make the best of it.

How much of the trap Collins had unwittingly constructed himself will probably never be known. But, as a political move, 'C' Squad was a masterstroke on the Commander's part.

Over the past few years, criticism of the Fraud Squad – and its counterpart the Serious Fraud Office – had been mounting: the momentum for wholesale change was now dangerously close to being unstoppable. Defenders of the status quo were fighting on four fronts.

The record for arrests was generally judged to be abysmal ('That good?' some critics said). For those cases that reached the courts, too few resulted in prosecutions. Even when someone was successfully prosecuted (and the verdicts not overturned on appeal), the sentences meted out were usually laughably short.

And, in the final analysis, when the sums were totted up, only a small fraction of fraudulently removed money was ever recovered. In the case of Roadex Securities, for instance, a total of ten million pounds was netted through a combination of a roll-over fraud and unauthorised overdrafts – not a penny was recovered. The perpetrator of the fraud, Ashisie Natwarhal Dhruve, received a sentence of six years (of which he would serve four, after the allowance for 'good behaviour').

The system patently wasn't working. Internal committees agreed on that. Small drunken gatherings in the Queen's Head stumbled to the same conclusion. The inescapable result was the spread of disillusionment – and of paranoia, as officers began to distrust their fellows of leaking information for a hefty backhander from the fraudster under investigation. Unless the situation could be drastically improved, SO6 was in for the biggest shake-up in its history. A reincarnation of Robespierre would be appointed as overlord, and heads would roll faster than you could say 'guillotine'.

'C' Squad was seen as the last chance.

Collins had been given a completely free hand. He could pick and choose his cases according to whatever logic or whim suited him at the time. He had first choice of any new work, and, more controversially, could take over an existing case from either of the other two squads. As long as he produced results, the powers-that-be didn't care how he did it. Justice had not only to be done but *to be seen to be done.* It was the only way the detractors could be silenced.

For Collins, it was a hiding-to-nothing job. If he succeeded, it would be the radical move itself, the imagination and creativity of the policy-makers, that would be applauded.

And if he failed, then they could claim that they had tried every which way. Collins, already tethered as scapegoat, was expendable.

'Walker,' he said wearily. 'I know that working for me was the last thing you...'

'Sir,' she interrupted. It was a pointless attempt at a denial that we all knew would lack conviction. The consensus of opinion was that 'C' Squad was the kiss of death. Wave goodbye to any promotion – maybe even any career in the force. When the revolution came, Collins and his officers would be the first to be lined up against the wall.

'I asked for you, Walker, because you're good. Very good.' He smiled at her without condescension. Collins doesn't crack his face very often. When he does, it's worth the wait. 'Trust me,' he said. 'In a couple of weeks this will all have blown over. If it's any consolation,' he added conspiratorially, 'there's plenty who will feel that today's little fiasco still counts as a result. No-one really cares what happened to Redmond. And, after all, you can't get a more effective punishment – or deterrent. A little collateral damage among the bad guys might be just what we need to make them stop and think.'

Collins registered our shocked expressions. Even through the armadillo hide that passed for his skin, he quickly realised he'd made a big mistake.

For my part, I didn't much care for the euphemism. The Americans had been its inventor. Cursed with the inheritance of the often too-expressive English language, they couldn't stop themselves from tinkering to make it more palatable. Instead of an employee being sacked, for example, he was 'an integral part of a downsizing operation'. And, in war, their troops didn't get killed any more. They merely suffered 'collateral damage'. Very convenient. Very easy to shrug off. Doesn't stop a general sleeping at night.

Walker, I suspected, wasn't grappling with the niceties of language. She'd decoded the other part of Collins's message. *If you did push Redmond out the window, then it's all right in my book.*

What had suddenly become of all the talk of justice?

Poor Walker, I thought. She was stuck with Collins. My own situation, on the other hand, was entirely different – in theory, at least.

I was on 'secondment', which was just another way of saying dumped here. It suited my employers, Jameson Browns, an image-conscious firm of chartered accountants, to pay my salary –

another misnomer, pittance was more like it – and have me out of the way. I was their instrument of atonement for past sins, a series of frauds that had gone unreported for years by the old regime. And never let it be said that, as the one who had lifted the stone to reveal the maggots crawling about underneath, my presence within the firm was an embarrassment.

Hell – I'd been getting bored with counting beans anyway.

So, unlike Walker, I was a free agent. Could wave goodbye with two fingers whenever I wanted. As a member of the Fraud Investigations Group – a loose-knit pool of legal and financial experts who assist on the more complex cases – I had no formal contract. My commitment was zero, if you discounted the not insignificant fact that Collins had once saved my life.

'Now, don't get me wrong,' Collins said, swinging his feet back to the floor. He intertwined his fingers and placed them on the desktop in an unconvincing gesture of deep concern.

'Oh, I think you've made yourself abundantly clear, Mr Collins,' I said. 'Let's get a couple of things straight, shall we? First, Walker acted impeccably: she did not intimidate Redmond; she did not push him, literally or metaphorically; she could not have stopped him jumping. Second, I for one would feel a whole lot happier if the code of ethics didn't go flying out of the window along with Redmond.'

Collins leaned across the desk, his face red with temper.

'Walker,' he said abruptly. 'Lose yourself, will

you? Go write a statement or something.'

'Worried about offending my delicate ears all of a sudden, sir?' she said.

'Sod off, Walker,' he retorted. 'Before your mouth lands you in more trouble.'

It was good advice, and reluctantly she took it. Didn't stop her from slamming the door behind her, though. A shock-wave ran through the partitions.

'If you've got something to say to me in future, Shannon,' Collins said in his best man-of-steel voice, 'then you say it in private. Not in front of one of my officers. Understand?' He stabbed a nicotine-stained finger in my direction. 'And let's get one last thing *straight,* shall we? You owe me. Remember? One more bullet and you would have finished up on a slab in the morgue. If it wasn't for me, you wouldn't be sitting here now bloody criticising.'

'Just when are you going to let me forget it?' I said. 'What do I have to do to pay off the debt?'

'I thought you'd never ask,' he replied.

So it was the sucker punch after all. And, despite my suspicions, I'd still walked straight into it. But I got up from the canvas and slugged it out with him.

I don't know how long the shouting match would have lasted if the bell had not spared us.

Collins grabbed the telephone angrily. 'Yes,' he shouted at the poor wretch whose misfortune it was to be the source of interruption. He glanced across at me and said 'Yes' again. There was a long pause while the caller spoke and Collins frowned. Grudgingly, he handed me the receiver.

It was Norman, one-time cell-mate and now temporary flat-mate. 'Get over here as quick as you can,' he said. 'Arlene's here. She needs you.'

Arlene. In the past – and that was how the relationship had seemed till now – an unquestioning helper. Rock of support, whether across the bridge table or simply by listening to me explain the choices available, knowing that my mind was already set on one particular course of action.

Arlene. Lover. And, very nearly, wife.

If she had come all the way from New England without so much as a warning phone call then she must be in big trouble.

I didn't care any more about Collins's threats. Or the most unsavoury piece of blackmail I'd ever come across. Arlene had first priority. Let Collins do his worst.

'No,' I said forcefully, rising from the chair. 'No way. Never. It's not my job. You've no right to ask me. Find someone else. Count me out.'

You would have thought that was pretty explicit, wouldn't you? Not much room for misunderstanding there, eh?

'I'll take that as a "maybe" then,' he said casually, tapping his fingers on the file on the desk. 'Go to Arlene. She's special. Look after her. Take some time to sort out whatever problems she has.'

Just as I thought I was off the hook, his voice became stern again.

'Then you'd better accept my proposition.'

Collins didn't bother to add 'or else'. He'd spelt

out that option in no uncertain terms. Refuse –
and suffer the consequences.

He had me backed into a corner.

I knew it.

And his parting smile told me he knew it too.

CHAPTER THREE

On leaving Collins, I wasted a couple of precious
minutes in a fruitless search for Walker. Her desk,
pressed tight against the thin wash of pale green
emulsion on Collins's chipboard, was empty. I
cast an enquiring glance round the wide open
spaces of this aircraft-hangar office, which
housed the operational personnel (the backroom
boffins of 'Support' were on a higher level).
Hooded eyes above lazily shrugged shoulders
made it clear that no-one knew – or cared –
where she was. I penned a brief note. Told her
simply that I'd be out of action for a while.
Wished her luck with the Redmond enquiry.
Promised to prepare a statement on the morning's events and post it as soon as possible.

The rest of 'C' Squad had wisely gone to
ground, so I made a lonely exit past 'A' and 'B'
Squads. There was no gauntlet of singing or
tactless jokes to run this time. Just an uneasy
silence as heads bowed over a job-lot of cheap
self-assembly desks in an abnormal fascination
with paperwork.

I always had the same effect on them.

No-one knew quite what to make of me.

Especially today.

The officers could not have helped but overhear the shouting match with Collins. That, in itself, would generally be enough to place me in the pigeonhole marked 'Friend' rather than 'Foe'. But Collins, for all his faults, was one of them – a serving policeman. And I was an outsider. Loyalty to the force had priority, surely? Reinforce the barriers, lads.

To add to their confusion, there was the problem of my background. The natural reaction to someone who had spent seven years in prison was condemnation and suspicion. But I had served my time behind bars for the mercy killing of my sister, Susie, after some unknown hit-and-run driver had transformed her in an instant from a carefree sixteen-year-old into a pathetic paraplegic – her boyfriend, killed outright, had been spared that undignified fate. So maybe I wasn't a real criminal after all? And yet my closest friends were ex-cons, including a 'heavy' and a swindler. Where would *my* loyalties lie, if they were ever tested?

What the hell! No matter how much I wanted to, I could not change the past. I had to live with it every day. Tote round the emotional baggage that I'd collected along the way. Confront the restless ghosts that demanded justice and would not let me sleep easy at night until it had been delivered.

Quinn and the rest of the bunch could think what they liked. What did I care? And perhaps, I told myself, their unease was well founded. To them I was a flesh-and-blood example of the uncertainties of life. There was not one of them who could say, hand on heart, exactly how they would react under similar circumstances.

I drove home more quickly than was wise, carving a path through the lunchtime traffic with that erratic combination of accelerator and brake beloved by London cabbies. I would like to think that my reckless haste was due solely to a natural anxiety to see Arlene, but a seething anger at Collins was as much the spur. He had abused a friendship and the power of his position. I was unreservedly determined to stand up to him. To refuse his demands. But a sixth sense told me he wasn't bluffing. If I pushed him, he'd go through with his threats. He was not the sort of man who makes decisions on the basis of a rational cost-benefit analysis. Cost was unimportant – it was winning that counted.

It took nearly thirty minutes to reach the house in what was mendaciously termed by estate agents as 'Hampstead/Highgate environs' but was actually 'grotty old Archway'. I parked outside. Switched off the engine. Sat there for a while, trying to clear my mind so that I could devote it fully to Arlene.

Norman, attuned to the singular roar of the Lancia's geriatric engine, already had the door open when I walked along the corridor to our ground-floor flat. It wasn't a palace, granted, but I'd known worse – and worse is what I would have had without Norman's share of the rent. Two bedrooms, double for me – ever the optimist – and single for Norman; large living/dining room; kitchen and bathroom. The furniture was old, but still serviceable. The flat fulfilled our needs, which, fortunately, were few.

Norman, embezzler of exactly one million pounds, had been my cell-mate in Chelmsford. If some enlightened university ever introduces a degree course in Financial Manipulation then Norman would be automatic choice for Head of Faculty. What he didn't know about fraud could be written on the back of a postage stamp – in copperplate. Having no heirs, Norman had made me the beneficiary of his wealth of knowledge. He was staying with me for a while (not too long, mind you, or he might jeopardise his tax-exile status), keeping a watchful eye over his new restaurant venture. Don't ask where he got the money.

'Better prepare yourself,' he said in a grave whisper, before letting me enter. 'She's in a bad way.'

Arlene was slumped against one corner of the old sofa. The tartan car-rug that I'd draped over it to conceal the worn patches of fabric was now wrapped round her shoulders. There were two tumblers half-filled with brandy on the coffee table. An ashtray overflowed with the charred butts and long, straight lines of grey ash from cigarettes she had lit but forgotten to smoke.

She had on a pair of dark glasses.

'Nick,' she cried in a soft, low whimper as she ran to meet me. She was wearing a businesslike jacket and skirt in black, with a plain white blouse. Black and white didn't suit her. Too hard. Too out of character. Just like the crumples and creases of the outfit.

'Nick, I'm so sorry. I shouldn't have come. But I didn't know where else to turn.'

Arlene threw herself into my waiting arms, nearly knocking me over with the force of her desperate rush for comfort. I pressed her tightly against me, one hand on her tousled hair, the other on her back. I could feel her body shaking uncontrollably.

She buried her face against my cheek. A warm, sticky stream of tears ran down onto my neck. I gently raised her head. Removed the sunglasses to wipe her eyes with the tips of my fingers. Felt a mixture of sympathy, horror and fury as I saw the dark brown, blood-caked cuts and the ugly black bruises that had been hiding underneath.

Arlene lived on Cape Cod, an anglicised haven for tourists, who flock there during the warm summers or pass fleetingly through in the fall as part of the 'leaf-peeping' Grand Tour of New England. It is also the world's biggest source of cranberries – but somewhere has to be, I suppose.

From her house in the town of Redemption, halfway up the fifty-mile-long peninsula of land, it was an hour's drive to Boston and Logan International Airport. Then another five and a half hours on the plane before landing at Gatwick. Finally, train to Victoria and grubby tube to Archway.

The journey must have been a trial in itself. But when you take into account the circumstances... How had she managed to endure it? All the time keeping everything tightly bottled up inside. I admired her. And loved her deeply. For her strength in times of crisis, and for the deep-down vulnerability that caused her to put such faith in me.

It took almost an hour to quieten her. During that time she lay sobbing in my arms on the sofa. I asked no questions. Simply held her close and hoped that the shock would flow from her to be absorbed and neutralised by my body.

Norman kept discreetly out of the way, apart from plying us from time to time with fresh cups of hot, sweet tea, which accumulated untouched on the table along with the brandy.

At last I felt Arlene's breathing ease, settling into a more regular rhythm. It was either an exercise in self-control or she was about to fall asleep. I hoped it was the latter – how she must have needed it.

Abruptly, she sat up and reached for her glass. Gulped down a large slug of brandy. Choked on the unaccustomed harshness. Shuddered. Then finally spoke.

'I'm sorry,' she said again, unnecessarily. 'We haven't seen each other for two months and I show up out of the blue, looking like the challenger in the final frame of a *Rocky* movie.' Her voice quivered. I didn't know whether it was entirely due to her current predicament or influenced to some extent by the manner of our parting.

'Does Mary Jo know you're here?' I asked. I would have preferred to avoid the subject, but the practicalities of the situation dictated otherwise.

Arlene shook her head shamefully.

Arlene was thirty-seven – seven years older than I. The age difference mattered nothing to me. But it didn't please Mary Jo one little bit. Mary Jo was Arlene's eighteen-year-old daughter. The two of us got on like a stick of dynamite and a detonator. Separate, we were no danger to anyone. But put us together, and wait for the inevitable bang.

I'd spent two days over Christmas with them both. The atmosphere was warmer outside in the five inches of Massachusetts snow. You needed a lightning conductor to discharge the electricity in the house. And a chainsaw to cut the icy air. It was as if hell had frozen over.

After forty-eight hours of this merry yuletide glee, Mary Jo had declared waspishly that she'd rather go back to Boston and sit alone in her cold room at Taft University than be in the company of 'that man' one second longer. She stomped out of the house, leaving the door rattling on its hinges and Arlene in floods of tears.

Mary Jo, in my humble and, of course, totally objective opinion, was a spoilt brat of the first order. She had a customised pink Cherokee jeep, more clothes than a Bond Street fashion shop, her own charge card or six, and an over-generous allowance from Arlene that she frittered away on 'partying'. In turn, but much more subjectively, she regarded me as some form of lowlife that in the evolutionary tree had immediately preceded the leech. She had me down as a murdering, penniless gigolo who was only after her mother's money. Okay, penniless was pretty close to the mark, but as far as the rest goes I couldn't convince her that she was wrong. But then again, she wouldn't listen.

My hope was that, given more time to get over her father's death (who, according to Mary Jo, was 'Jeez, ten times' the man I would ever be), she would be able to take a more detached view. Consider her mother's feelings for a change, instead of playing Arlene's emotions for all they were worth. But Arlene, faced with the imminent prospect of losing her daughter, had called a reluctant end to our relationship.

'First you tell me exactly what has happened,' I said, 'then we ring Mary Jo. She'll be worried.' At the loss of a meal ticket, I added uncharitably to myself.

Norman, bored with serving undrunk tea, appeared with a jug of coffee and poured three steaming mugs. He looked down pointedly at his coffee and flicked his eyes towards the kitchen. I moved my head downwards to signal him to stay. He settled his spindly frame in the creaky armchair closest to the gas fire.

Arlene sipped her coffee and smiled appreciatively. I sighed with relief.

'It all started about a month ago,' she said. 'You remember the Windsor Club?'

I nodded. Arlene had taken me on a guided tour of the club on Boxing Day. There was not much to see. Just the normal landscape of a typical construction site – you know, that sort of cataclysmic chaos that makes you wonder how anything ever gets built safely or on time – only on a scale twenty times bigger. But it was a good excuse to get away from Mary Jo for an hour. In time, the Windsor Club would be the most exclusive 'luxury resort complex' on Cape Cod; two golf courses, fifteen all-weather tennis courts, riding stables, more kinds of water sports than I ever knew existed – you name it and the Windsor Club would have at least one that was larger and grander than anywhere else. Arlene was in charge of selling the traditionally styled clapboard houses and modern condominium apartments for the real-estate company for which she worked. Even by Christmas, with a year to go before the first phase of development would be completed, Arlene had taken deposits on seventy units.

'Our commission cheque bounced,' she said ominously. 'I thought it was just some stupid mistake.' Arlene reached for her cigarettes with trembling fingers.

'Carry on,' I said, taking the pack from her. Shaking out two Lucky Strikes, I lit them both and passed one to her. She drew deeply and exhaled the smoke upwards in a long grey plume before continuing.

'I drove out to the Club. The place was like a ghost-town. All that was missing was the tumble-weed blowing across the street. No construction people. No landscapers. Not a sign of activity anywhere.'

'What about the offices?' I asked with sinking heart. 'What did the staff say?'

'There weren't any staff. The offices were locked and barred. On the door was a notice – an open letter to creditors. There was a lot of legal small print that took me ten minutes to decipher. The Windsor Club had been placed in the hands of administrators. I didn't need a degree in Corporate Law to know what that meant. Down the tubes. Bust.'

Maybe it wasn't as bad as it seemed, I told myself. Who was I kidding?

'How much had you taken in down payments?' I asked.

'Close to two million,' Arlene said. 'Dollars, that is.'

'Thank Christ for that,' Norman said. 'For a moment there I thought we were talking about a lot of money.'

The remark, thankfully, floated over Arlene's head.

'Well,' she said, 'the standard deposit was twenty thousand dollars, but if a buyer paid twice that they received Founder Membership of the Club – free golf, tennis, whatever, for life. It was a good deal.'

'Not when you lose everything, it wasn't,' Norman said. 'And that's the likely outcome, I bet.' He shook his head. 'Pity the poor buyers.'

'That group includes me,' she said quietly into her coffee cup.

'Oh, Arlene,' I said, biting back a sigh of frustration. 'What do you need another property for anyway?'

'It was for us, Nick,' she replied.

That made me feel really great. I tried to console myself with the thought that Arlene could take a dent to her bank account – the late Cy had collected insurance policies rather than something as trivial as stamps (philately will get you nowhere?). But it didn't help much. Somehow I knew I would end up feeling at least partly responsible.

'I got to thinking,' she explained. 'Realised that what we had was too good to give up just like that. I hoped Mary Jo would eventually come round, you know? Learn to accept you. I thought it would be a great place for both of us to live. Sell the old house with all its memories. Make a new start. You did once say you'd move anywhere as long as we could be together.'

Norman registered my discomfort. 'What can be salvaged?' he asked pragmatically.

'Nothing,' she said dejectedly.

'Come on,' I said. 'The land must be worth something. Maybe a white knight will appear and make an offer.'

'Yeah, sure,' Arlene said, unconvinced. 'The Windsor Club sank because the parent company went under. Over-committed itself with loans for a dozen or so projects. Got swept under by the rising tide of interest rates. The Club doesn't only owe money to the buyers. It's into the bank for a development loan. And the parent company for management charges – inflated, no doubt.'

'So what's the bottom line?' I asked, preparing to conceal a wince. 'What's the total of all the debts?'

'Well,' she said, prevaricating. 'From what I understand from the bank, the best estimate seems to be ... give or take ... around twelve million dollars.'

Twelve million dollars! Eight million quid!

Now *that's* what I call collateral damage.

I glanced at Norman. He lowered his eyes. 'I get the picture,' I said, as calmly as I could, with a lump the size of a medicine ball in my throat. 'But none of what you've said so far explains the cuts and bruises on your face.'

'When the news hit the streets,' she said, 'there was a whole bunch of ugly-looking people searching round for someone to blame. Some of them – including quite a few I once considered to be my friends – took it into their heads that it was all my fault. I'd persuaded them to buy, for one thing. And maybe I'd been aware that the Club was in financial difficulties. Carried on taking deposits in a vain attempt to keep it afloat.'

I took hold of her hand and squeezed it reassuringly.

'I tried to shrug it off at first,' she continued. 'Told myself that they had to take their anger out on somebody and I just happened to be the one who was still around. I explained to them that I'd lost money too. But it made no difference. "Poetic justice," they said. "And *you* can afford it. *We* can't."'

She laid down her coffee mug and made a better effort this time at taking a deep draught from her brandy glass.

'For the last fortnight I've been put through insults and increasing abuse. Then I was completely ostracised. Jeez, I'm a non-person in my own home town! Can you believe that? There's not a single soul who will speak to me. My employers were put under a hell of a lot of pressure. So I decided to hang onto a little

37

dignity and resign before they forced me to leave. I stayed late last night to clear my desk.' She broke off to finish the remains of the brandy. 'About ten o'clock I heard a noise at the door. Like some brainless Hollywood heroine, I went to investigate. Three men in hoods had somehow got inside the office. They trashed everything in sight. Including me.'

She looked into my eyes like a little girl lost.

'I couldn't think of anywhere else to go. I drove straight to the airport and caught the first plane here. I was too afraid even to go home and pack a bag. I don't have any clothes. No cosmetics, apart from what's in my clutchbag. No tooth-brush. Nothing.'

I put my arm round her shoulder, half-walked, half-carried her into my bedroom. Undressed her tenderly until she stood naked before me. Felt my anger surge again at the sight of more bruises running in a ragged line from her right shoulder all the way down to her wrist.

I laid her on the bed. Tucked the duvet carefully around her neck. Stroked her hair. Whispered gently that I'd take care of her. She must stay as long as she liked. And when she wanted to go back, if that time ever came, then I'd go with her. Sort everything out. Put it all right.

'I promise,' I said, without any idea of how I could keep my word.

When she had drifted into a fitful sleep I picked up her clothes and returned to the sitting room.

It took Norman and me a mere five minutes of

discussion to confirm to each other that the odds on salvaging anything from the wreck of the company were close to zero. So we hid our helplessness in practicalities.

I went through the labels on Arlene's clothes and noted down the sizes, remembering in time to convert the American 12 to its British equivalent of 14. I prepared a list of basic items of make-up and clothing (writing down 'bright cheerful colours', with an exclamation mark) to keep Arlene going until she felt like venturing out in public. Norman volunteered to brave the shop assistants in the lingerie department of Marks and Spencer while I phoned Mary Jo. I'd have preferred to swap jobs. But I wouldn't have wished the task of explaining the situation to Mary Jo on my worst enemy.

Two hours later, Norman returned. My ears were still ringing from the telephonic torrents of invective – the word 'mother' frequently cropping up on Mary Jo's side of the conversation, and not always in relation to Arlene. He struggled through the door with armfuls of green carriers and a white bag brimming with food, on the off-chance that we might feel like eating supper.

I opened a bottle of red wine and we sat down opposite each other by the hissing fire, our backs to the bedroom door. Over a glass or three, I took Norman through the grisly tale of the morning 'jumper' and the aftermath in Collins's office. He shook his head at the policeman's attitude, the request made and the severity of the punishment if I didn't obey.

Behind me came a polite cough. Arlene was

standing in the doorway, wrapped in the duvet. I hoped and prayed she hadn't been there long. The last thing she needed right now was the added burden of my problems.

Before I could speak, the bell rang. Norman went to answer it. I carried the bags into the bedroom and left Arlene to freshen up and change.

'There's a very persistent young lady,' Norman announced, without bothering to mask his annoyance, 'who won't leave without seeing you.'

'I have to talk,' Walker said, brushing past him.

CHAPTER FOUR

I liked Walker. Right here and now, that put me in a minority of one. Still, I was used to that: at work, those who shared my opinion also believed that the Earth was flat and was ruled over by a Pope called Miriam Finkelstein.

Apart from intelligence, insight, determination, courage, technical knowledge and a knee-weakening beauty, Walker had little going for her. If she had been a limited company, then Walker would have been declared 'balance-sheet de-icient' – assets outweighed by the size and number of liabilities.

She was a woman in a man's world.

She'd been propelled along the graduate-entry fast track, engendering along the way a bitter resentment among those, like Quinn, whom she had overtaken.

She suffered fools badly, and openly. Her intolerance to lesser mortals – which, according to Walker, covered most of her colleagues – did not win her many votes in the popularity stakes. And woe betide anyone who made a mistake that might reflect poorly on her and jeopardise her chances of reaching the top of the career ladder. I'd rather have ten lashes of the cat-o'-nine-tails any day than one of Walker's tongue.

She was also black – political correctness, for once, permitting the use of the most accurate description. (Does PC still allow the word 'woman' nowadays? Somehow 'woperson' doesn't have quite the same ring about it. Seven years in prison and you come out to find that tiramisu has replaced Black Forest gateau in the hearts and stomachs of the nation and, more difficult to swallow, that the whole acceptable vocabulary has changed. Lou Reed certainly couldn't have got away with 'and all the coloured girls sing' in these enlightened times.) Anyway, her hair shone like jet. Her skin was a deep, dark, coffee-and-a-dash. Her lips were the colour of ripe figs, and held the same promise of mouth-watering succulence.

And, as the last cross to bear, she was saddled with the name of Cherry Walker.

She was lucky in one respect. Most of her fellow officers nicknamed her 'Street'. That, at least, was preferable to any of the more biologically inclined alternatives manufactured from her forename.

'I got your note,' she said.

41

'That *was* the point of the exercise,' I replied tetchily.

'Something tells me this isn't a good time,' she said. Her intonation was strictly middle-England, middle-class, but her voice carried an infusion of ancestral depth and richness which had the power, in me for one, to conjure up visions of molten chocolate. She stood there, tall and proud like a Nubian princess, defying me to send her away.

'Well, you're here now, Walker,' I said. 'You might as well make yourself comfortable. Red wine? I take it you're not on duty?'

'Huh,' she grunted.

I took her raincoat and hung it behind the door. She was wearing a light-tan suit woven from a preponderance of synthetic fibres, the double-breasted jacket cut to an hour-glass waist, the straight skirt brushing her knees. On anyone else its chain-store dump-bin provenance would have screamed gratingly. On Walker it whispered seductively: she could have taken Naomi Campbell's place on the catwalk (sorry, runway), strutted her stuff, and had the audience writing blank cheques for an identical outfit.

She took the glass of wine from me. Lowered herself gracefully onto the sofa. Crossed her long legs demurely at the ankle. Gazed up at me with dark brown, mesmerising eyes.

Arlene stepped into the room, joining a silent and still-sulking Norman.

I poured her a glass of wine and made the formal introductions. Arlene smiled politely, but a little awkwardly, at Cherry and sat herself down

42

opposite Norman in the other armchair. She'd quickly applied some make-up, brushed the tangles from her shoulder-length auburn hair and changed into a bright yellow blouse and dark blue skirt. I gave her a little wink to signal appreciation.

Cherry stared overlong at Arlene and Norman and, with a professional eye, tried to decide what to make of them. Arlene had hung onto the inefficient camouflage of the sunglasses: neither they nor the silky foundation could mask the dark contours of the bruises. I dreaded to think how she was being classified in Walker's mental notebook. Didn't much like the idea of Walker surreptitiously slipping Arlene the address of the nearest women's refuge. And as for Norman, face etched with lines beyond his fifty-odd age, anaemically pale now that the Spanish tan had been eroded by the wind and rain of an English winter, thin as a rake in spite of his voracious appetite, Walker was probably preparing to give him the phone number of Amnesty International.

'Have you written the statement yet?' she asked, her character judgements completed.

'Give me a chance, Walker,' I replied. 'I'll do it tomorrow. Okay?' I left the 'get off my back' unspoken.

'I'm sorry,' Walker said to Arlene. 'You must think me impolite. We had a spot of bother this morning. Nick and I...'

'No need to explain, Cherry,' Arlene interrupted. 'I know all about it.'

She must have overheard the whole conversation with Norman after all. Maybe, I rationalised with more hope than logic, concentrating on my problems would take her mind off her own.

'Did Collins give you a rough time?' Walker asked sympathetically.

'Nothing I can't handle,' I said.

'I can't believe that Collins,' Arlene said, in tones reminiscent of John McEnroe on a bad day, or should that be on an average day?

I flashed her a warning look – but she was too busy denouncing Collins to notice.

'Collins wants Nick to go undercover,' she explained to Walker. 'Won't take no for an answer. Why you, Nick? That's what I'd like to know.'

'Collins only asked me because I'm a civilian,' I said, sensing that whatever my answer Cherry would feel slighted. 'He can disown me. I'd be freelancing. No problems about being deemed to be an *agent provocateur*. If it ever came to court, that is. All he's got at the moment is a vaguely worded letter – anonymous, of course. It makes a lot of unspecified claims about fraud. Full of helpful phrases like "You wouldn't believe what's going on here." And not one concrete lead to pursue.'

I sighed with weary resignation.

'But Collins,' I continued, shaking my head, 'has made his mind up already. And you know Collins. When he has a theory fixed in his brain, the only way to get rid of it is via a lobotomy. Hell, it's probably all a storm in a teacup. Some disaffected member of staff trying to stir up trouble.'

Walker nodded understandingly.

44

'What's the name of the company he wants investigated?' she asked.

'I can't remember,' I said. 'I really wasn't interested. I've absolutely no intention of taking the job.'

'It was some security firm,' Arlene chimed in helpfully. 'Glen something, wasn't it, Nick?'

'Glenshield?' Walker said. 'That figures.'

Oh well. If the cat had escaped from the bag, then I might as well mine Walker's rich seam of knowledge.

'Why "that figures", Walker?' I asked. 'Is there something that our friend Mr Collins has omitted to tell me? Or, should I say, that he has been keeping up his soiled sleeve?'

'The head of Glenshield is a man called Kinsella. Known to everyone as "Roddy". It's a nickname.'

'As in, er...' Arlene searched for an acceptable word.

'Yes,' Walker replied, saving her the fruitless task.

'Apart from that,' I said, 'which is hardly useful, except in the case of a very extraordinary identity parade, what else can you tell me?'

'Kinsella's half Irish, half Scottish,' Walker continued unabashed.

'Half Scottish!' I said, sucking air dramatically through my teeth. 'I can see why Collins would keep that quiet. Endless conversations about haggis, kilts and goalkeepers – and how all three are unappreciated. That does it. I certainly won't take the job now.'

'It's no joke, Nick,' she admonished me. 'Be

45

serious for a change. Kinsella used to be in the force.'

'Oh,' I said. 'That's bad.'

'And it gets worse,' she said, frowning deeply. 'Kinsella was in the Drugs Squad. Detective Chief Inspector.' She paused to let the rank sink in, then continued, 'Collins was his sergeant.'

'Double "oh",' I said.

'Collins and Kinsella never saw eye-to-eye. A real chalk and cheese job, they were. Kinsella, by all accounts, is a slick operator. Silky-smooth tongue and clothes to match. That, as you can imagine, didn't exactly endear him to our boss, for a start. Then Collins got the notion that Kinsella was bent. On the take.' It was Walker's turn to sigh now. 'Nobody would listen, of course. There was never a shred of proof. In the end, Collins was transferred. Kinsella worked on for a couple of years and then took early retirement. Started Glenshield.'

'I'm surprised the Commander let Collins take the case. Wouldn't it have been better to give it to one of the other squads?'

'Collins must have more pull than we realise. Unless...' she said ominously.

'Let me save you the trouble,' I said. 'Unless they're giving Collins enough rope to hang himself.'

She nodded thoughtfully. 'And if the Good Ship Collins goes down, I don't fancy my chances of being pulled into one of the lifeboats. More like out in the cold with a terminal case of hypothermia.'

It put my future in doubt too. I didn't think the

46

partners at Jameson Browns would welcome me back with open arms – unless one of the hands held a P45 with the ink still wet. As a thirty-year-old unqualified accountant and ex-con to boot, the prospects of finding another job didn't seem particularly rosy.

'Now I understand why the case is so important to Collins,' I said. 'Do you know what he's threatening to do if I don't agree to go undercover?'

'I have a pretty shrewd guess,' she said. 'Collins is like a bulldog – once he's sunk his teeth into something, he won't let go. To get what he wants, he'll pull every trick in the book. And a few that haven't been written yet. I'd say his first position when stooping low would be the you-owe-me-your-life routine.'

'He tried that and I still refused.'

'So you forced him down to gutter level, right?'

'It seems so.'

'He threatened to get your licence revoked,' she said perceptively.

'Remind me never to cross you, Walker. I don't like the way your mind works.'

'Smart move on his part, you must admit. Got you over a barrel.'

'Can he really do it?' I asked.

'You're not an ordinary ex-con, Nick. You served time for murder. Okay, we all know the extenuating circumstances. But that doesn't change the law. Murderers can't be paroled. They can only be released under special licence issued by the Home Secretary. And that licence carries a lot of conditions. Step out of line and it gets revoked.'

'Okay,' I said. 'So Collins *could* do it. But *would* he? That's the question.'

'In spite of his attitude, Collins likes you. You're a fighter, Nick. He respects that. But in this case that won't save you. Yes,' she said, nodding her head wisely, 'he'd do it. No question.'

'Just because of an old feud with a slick ex-copper who might just possibly be bent?'

'No, Nick,' she said. 'It's more than a feud. It's a crusade. There's one last thing he didn't tell you. You know Collins is divorced, I suppose?'

'I'd assumed that his appearance wasn't the result of a dutiful wife spending all day slaving over a washing machine and ironing board.'

'Collins was married for five years. Until his wife, Louise, upped and left – stolen from him, he'd claim.' She paused reflectively. 'Five years! Can you imagine any woman putting up with Collins for that long? Doesn't bear thinking about. Still, I imagine she's happy now. As Mrs Roddy Kinsella.'

Arlene lay in bed with her back towards me.

Walker had long since departed, her feelings unrepaired by the visit. The three of us had sat round the table with an impromptu feast of taramasalata, tzatziki, black olives and pitta bread, washed down with more red wine. In the background, Fats Waller had played with customary humour. In the foreground, Norman had performed his repertoire of anecdotes and quips – mostly at my expense. The atmosphere was outwardly jovial, but there was still a tension within Arlene. In the end there was nothing to do but retreat to bed and hope that tomorrow would be a better day.

'She's very pretty,' Arlene said in the darkness.

'Yes,' I agreed. Any denial of the obvious would have sounded hollow and totally unconvincing. 'You know there's nothing between Cherry and me, Arlene.'

'I wouldn't blame you if there was. Not after everything that happened at Christmas.'

I placed my hands at the base of her neck. Began gently massaging the knotted muscles.

'I've been so stupid,' she said. 'So very stupid.'

'Don't worry.' I moved on to work on her shoulders. 'It's not terminal. I know a little cure.'

'First I let Mary Jo use emotional blackmail to make me give you up,' she said, rolling over to face me. 'Then I drop forty grand into the black hole of a bankrupt company. And finally I gave away your secret.'

Her voice was cracked with emotion. Even in the dark I knew she was crying.

'Oh, Nick. What have I done? This undercover operation was supposed to be a secret, wasn't it? I've let you down. Please forgive me.'

I kissed her tenderly. Tasted the saltiness of tears on her lips. Moved my head up to kiss her eyes lightly, then down to the bruises on her arm.

'You're forgiven, my love,' I said.

She hugged me tight and let her body relax at last.

'Now,' she said. 'This cure you mentioned.'

While she slept, I lay wide awake, silently cursing Collins.

What a fool he'd been. Why did he always have to play the hard man? We knew each other too well, were too damned alike in our faults, to make any sort of act convincing. He should have swallowed his pride and told me the whole story. It wouldn't have made any difference to my decision, of course – I owed Arlene too much to abandon her when she needed me – but at least my refusal would have been cool, calm and collected. And his response, hopefully, less extreme. Both of us could have retained a semblance of dignity; could have avoided the unseemly shouting match, which had served only to give the eavesdroppers something else to smile about.

Collins should have been able to read me better by now. Worked out a different approach. Fancy threatening *me*, holder of the 'Mr Stubborn' title for so long I'd been allowed to retain the cup: it was the last way to get my help. If he'd thought about it for one moment he might have seen that. But where Kinsella – and Louise – were concerned, it seemed he was too blind to see. And too pigheaded to think. It was a dangerous combination. For Collins, and anyone else stupid enough to get involved.

Cherry had given us the grisly details of the break-up of the marriage, and the public humiliation that both preceded and followed it.

Openly cuckolded by his boss, what could Collins do?

He'd slugged Kinsella, that's what! A beautiful

right hook, which those privileged to witness it still wax lyrical about whenever nostalgia strikes.

He had been lucky not to be busted for striking a superior officer. But there was sufficient compassion for Collins to save him. And he was 'a good copper' – everyone agreed on that point. Far too good to lose.

After the separation, and subsequent divorce, Collins had become a man driven by one obsession. All the wrath, all the bile, was directed against Kinsella. Collins could not rid himself of the absolute conviction that Kinsella was as phoney as a four-pound note.

It was his lifeline. I could imagine how his mind had worked: prove his case, put Kinsella away for a long time, and maybe Louise would come back to him. Collins had single-mindedly thrown himself into his work, and let no opportunity pass to dig into Kinsella's history. He had sustained himself on a diet of nicotine and alcohol; lost all pride in his appearance; fast become an embarrassment.

Some cynics – realists, perhaps – said that it was the sympathy vote that had landed Collins the job at 'C' Squad. A last-ditch effort at rehabilitation. Give him every chance to build a new life. Let him run the show his way. If he succeeded, then they could pat themselves on the back. If he failed, then he would have to go. But no-one could say they hadn't tried.

No-one could say they hadn't tried.

I swore at Collins under my breath. I cursed the Commander too – I was in the mood by now. He should never have let Collins take the case.

Sympathy and machiavellian manoeuvres should have given way to good old-fashioned common sense. Collins was too involved. That was blindingly obvious.

Then the thunderbolt struck me.

Did the Commander actually know?

Groaning, I went over the letter again in my mind.

There was no physical evidence to provide a trail. No fingerprints. Useless WC1 postmark on the envelope. Computer-generated label addressed personally to Collins. The letter itself was word-processed, using a standard Courier typeface that could be found on virtually every software package. It was laser-printed, so that narrowed down the source to just about every office in the country and the most advanced personal in-home systems. Christ, anyone could have written it.

And the second time around, the accusations seemed more vague, more insubstantial – didn't even reach the foothills of Mount Flimsy.

There was nothing to go on.

It would be nigh on impossible.

Wouldn't it?

CHAPTER FIVE

Chelmsford Prison – eight years earlier

I walked into the cell, ignored Norman and The Major, and collapsed onto the bottom bunk. I could have slept till the next millennium – and maybe the one after that. But the muscle cramps that ran through my body had ideas of their own. And so did my bullying cell-mate Norman.

'Five minutes,' he said. 'Then it's study time.'

'It's all right for you,' I said crossly. 'You've been lounging around all day doing bugger all.'

'It's tough at the top,' he said. 'Being a Trusty isn't exactly a piece of cake, you know.' He paused briefly. 'Not exactly. But almost.'

I had my eyes closed, but I would have laid hard-earned money that there was a stupid grin plastered all over his face.

Now that my wound had healed, and the scar had closed over the two missing fingers on my left hand – a nasty attack of what might be called 'Freddie Ronson's Revenge', far more virulent and longer-lasting than Montezuma's – the Governor had decided that the special treatment must cease. The kid gloves were off. For whatever cardinal sins I had committed, I had been assigned to the prison laundry.

Chelmsford had about 400 prisoners (cosily crammed into 232 single cells), so the laundry had to cope with 1,600 pairs of underpants, 1,200 pairs of socks, and 400 each of shirts and sheets every week, together with a more irregular influx of blankets, trousers, jumpers and overalls. It took twenty of us, working eight hours a day, five days a week, to keep abreast of the never-ending pile. I doubt if Hercules would have swapped the cleaning of the Augean stables for such a labour. Mind you, the weekly reward of three pounds might have made him think about it – for a second or two, that is.

Walking into the laundry was like entering a South American rain forest in the hours immediately before the monsoon arrives. The humidity was so high that you felt you could grab a handful of air and squeeze a pint of water from it. Within five minutes of crossing the threshold, the sweat was breaking out all over your body. It wormed its way into your eyes, where the natural defence of tears fought a losing battle against the sting of the saline onslaught. The grey, heavy, prison-issue overalls first turned black under the armpits and groin, then clung to every inch of your body like a slimy second skin. Even the simple act of breathing produced a harsh scalding sensation at the back of the throat.

The laundry was a land of steam, steam and more steam. It billowed from the vast copper vats filled with boiling water that bubbled away like cauldrons at a witches' convention. It hissed in great volcanic eruptions from the giant electric irons. It squeezed forth between the rollers of mangles so large that they could have come from a medieval torture chamber – and, knowing the prison expenditure priorities, probably did. Rising like mist from every antiquated piece of equipment, it formed swirling clouds that wafted languidly towards the inadequately narrow louvres set behind the thick bars.

If it was a good day, I would be on one of the ironing boards. This meant that I only had to pull the one-armed-bandit-style handle that forced one six-foot by two-foot slab down onto its matching base. Okay, so I had to go through this operation several hundred times a day, but it was preferable to the alternatives. At least with the iron you got a moment's break while the clothes sizzled in the press. With the mangle, the handle had to be turned constantly – a continuous stream of sodden clothes demanding to be fed from a large plastic skip on one side, through the rollers into another on the other side. Apart from the physical strain, the other problem with both the iron and mangle was retaining concentration. It was all too easy to become hypnotised by the repetitive nature of the operations: start to drift and you could finish up with a bad case of steamrollered hand – and with the iron you won a free second-degree burn too.

If it was a really bad day, it would be my turn at the vats.

Today had been a really bad day.

Armed with a pair of four-foot-long tongs, I had spent hour after hour bent double, peering into the hot vapours and dragging out the heavy, waterlogged clothes from the foaming liquid. Every now and again I pampered myself. I changed hands. Not easy in my case. But worth it.

55

The day had followed its normal pattern. It was like the singing of one of those old-fashioned rounds – 'London's Burning' or 'Ding Dong Bell'. The biceps were always first to start the tune, setting my arms on fire with pain. Next the trapezius joined in. Then the voices swelled as the agony crept inexorably down from my neck through the latissimus dorsi until it reached the base of my spine. Finally the hamstrings and calf muscles sang out loudly. If I didn't manage to fiddle a change of job soon, I would either finish up a cripple or develop the body of Arnold Schwarzenegger (or, worse still, that of a female Russian shot-putter).

'Come on,' Norman said. 'Time's up. Get yourself over here for lessons.'

'I can't move,' I complained.

'You want to pass these exams, don't you?'

'Yes,' I said, sighing.

'And you want to be the best, don't you?'

'Yes,' I said again. 'But I also want to die.'

'You can do that later,' Norman said heartlessly.

There wasn't any point in resisting. Norman could out-nag a stand-up comedian's mother-in-law.

I rolled from the bottom bunk to the floor. Hauled myself to my feet and walked the short distance to the table with all the fluidity of a badly lubricated robot. The Major vacated one of the two chairs and sat at Norman's feet like a disciple.

'All fraudsters,' Norman began proudly, 'possess the same three traits – greed, cunning and effrontery. To combat the fraudster you need a good system, good sense, adequate precautions and strong deterrents. So it's pretty much a losing battle, really!'

He looked at me, expecting some comment, if only to prove I was still alive.

I nodded my head.

The muscles in my neck screamed. I would have to remember to say 'uh huh' next time.

'Let's begin with the most common type of fraud – the long-firm fraud. When you're an accountant – and notice, my cream-crackered friend, I do not say "if" – you won't be able to do much to combat it, except forewarn your clients, so as to stop them falling into the trap.

'The long-firm fraudster sets up a little business – retailing televisions and videos, for example. It's a new, unknown business with no track record, so he has to buy his first stock for cash. Are you with me so far?'

'Uh huh,' I said. What a memory, eh?

'After a little while he tells his supplier he wants to expand. How about some credit? Just a small amount? And only thirty days? The supplier agrees – there seems little risk in it, and he's become accustomed to the extra sales and the profit they generate. When our man has established that he's a good payer, he asks for the limit to be raised, and for a longer settlement period. And here's the cheeky bit, he uses the first supplier as a reference to obtain credit from other suppliers.'

I yawned involuntarily. Christ, if I didn't get to bed soon I'd fall asleep right here in the chair.

'Nearly there,' Norman said. 'When all the suppliers have been suckered into the scam, lips a-smacking, the fraudster hits them with massive orders. And Bob's your uncle. Bish, bash, bosh! Call in Nicholas Parsons. The Sale of the Century. Flog the lot. On with the spiked shoes and into the starting blocks. Do a runner. Decamp to another area. Different name. Maybe even buy up a respectable business; use that as the new vehicle. And the circle of life repeats itself.'

'Don't they ever get caught?' The Major asked.

'Not usually,' said Norman. 'Too quick on their feet for Mr Plod. They're a thorn in the Fraud Squad's side. 'B' Squad spends most of its time in the fruitless chase – time that could be better employed combating large-scale fraud.'

'But who gets hurt?' The Major asked.

'Mostly no-one who can't afford it,' said Norman. 'Occasionally the bad debt is enough to tip a struggling supplier into liquidation. Then the owners lose their money and the employees their jobs. It's normally only the little people who suffer, more's the pity.'

I wondered at The Major's new-found interest. Maybe he was planning a career change. A bit late at his time of life, I thought.

The Major was in his early sixties. A small, dapper man with a well-trimmed moustache, he looked every inch as if he could have stood at Montgomery's right hand, if he had been born ten years earlier. He wasn't really a major, of course. But 'corporal in the Pay Corps' didn't have quite the same cachet. Not when you're a con man, that is.

The Major was a fish out of water here in prison. He didn't deserve to be behind bars. No-one – well, hardly anyone – had been hurt by his little scams. After a general grounding in 'conmanship', The Major had specialised – his *modus operandi* was to befriend wealthy widows. Selecting the weak and frail, he brought a little sunshine into the twilight of their lives. In return, they usually left The Major a large share of their estate.

The Major worked hard for his money. He needed a regular flow of income, but could not guarantee just how long each widow had to go before that great tea dance in the sky called the last waltz. So he was forced to keep a string of heavily pan-sticked women on the boil at the same time. Travelling his patch from Bournemouth to Eastbourne, his life had been an immaculately organised schedule of bandstand concerts, bridge drives, candlelit suppers, invigorating walks and coach outings. The Major must have been possessed of boundless energy and a complex computer program to cope with the demands of his chosen lifestyle.

It had all gone well until one daughter, furious at being denied her rightful inheritance, had finally pulled the plug on The Major. The police investigation revealed four current widows in tow and another sixteen over the past five years. The judge, whilst admiring The Major's stamina, had felt obliged to sentence him to a term of three years.

'Right,' Norman said. 'Just time for the

advanced fee racket and value dating – that's a real peach – before lights out.'

'Give me a break, Norman,' I pleaded. 'Not tonight, please.'

I might just as well not have bothered.

'Now the advanced fee racket is...'

Connor poked his head round the door.

I'd read a guesstimate somewhere that between one-third and two-thirds of male prisoners – and, surprisingly, eighty per cent of female prisoners – are drink- or drug-dependent. There isn't much drug-taking in Chelmsford – it's a Category C prison, low security, lots of privileges, not quite take-away curries on Saturday nights, but you know the sort of thing: the inmates aren't the desperate band of hardened criminals with nothing to lose that I'd encountered in Brixton. But what little does go on is Connor's province.

'So this is where you're hiding,' he said to The Major.

'I'm not going to do it,' The Major replied.

Puzzled, I looked at Norman. He shook his head at me.

'You can't bottle out on me now,' Connor said.

He moved across to stand over The Major. Connor was maybe five foot nine but stockily built. His legs provided the top-heavy frame with the firm foundations of tree trunks. His upper body was the type that allowed Savile Row tailors to ask, without fawning flattery for once, 'Done a bit of boxing, have we, sir?' His arms were especially heavily muscled from days spent digging the cloying clay soil of the prison garden.

Connor didn't frighten me. Well, not much. In

Brixton he would have been hard pushed to qualify as one of the also-rans: but in Chelmsford he was one of the front-runners.

He bent down, grabbed The Major by the collar and pulled him to his feet. The Major, pinned against the wall, stared at the twin tattoos of 'Love' and 'Hate' on Connor's knuckles. 'Love' was reserved for Connor himself; 'Hate' for anyone who crossed him when he was engaged in his favourite pursuit of making a fast buck.

I started to rise, but Norman put a restraining hand on my shoulder. His eyes warned, 'Don't get involved.'

'Come on,' Connor said. 'Everything's arranged. The stuff will be slipped in your hand while you're looking at the flowers. Just stick it up your sleeve, like I told you. Then go for a pony and hide it properly.'

Pony? Pony and trap! I winced as I decoded Connor's *slanguage*. The grisly picture was becoming abundantly clear. The Major was being allowed out for a funeral tomorrow. Connor couldn't let the opportunity to top up his supplies go to waste.

'No,' The Major said defiantly. 'I won't do it. It's too much of a risk. What if they body-search me? I've only got three months to go. I can't afford to lose any remission.'

Connor wasn't the world's most ardent believer in philosophical debate. The fist marked 'Hate' buried itself in The Major's stomach. A cry of pain rushed out of the old man's lips.

'That's enough,' I shouted. 'Let him go.'

That really had Connor worried.

'Hate' slammed a second time into the self-same spot.

I pushed Norman's arm aside. Stood up. Began to advance on Connor. Only then did the thought strike me. How much could I rely on my damaged left hand if Connor wouldn't back down?

Sod it, there was only one way to find out. And it was too late to worry now.

Connor released his grip. The Major slid slowly down the wall, clutching his midriff. He crouched on the floor, rocking back and forth.

'Stay out of this, Shannon,' Connor said, thrusting a warning finger in my direction. 'It's not your fight.'

'Not if you leave him alone it isn't.'

Connor laughed. If you can call it that. It was more a grinless escape of acute halitosis. But as a demonstration of contempt it was pretty effective.

So was the back-heel he delivered to The Major's chin.

The Major's head hit the wall, and my temper hit the roof. I squared up to Connor.

'Control yourself, Nick, for chrissake,' Norman shouted angrily.

I took his advice – well, partially. I put a lid on my temper, at least. When it comes to a fight, a hot head is not a clear head. Arthur, my 'heavy' cell-mate from Brixton, had drummed that much into me. Along with the basic (and I mean basic) essentials of self-defence.

I feinted with my left fist, drawing a disdainful right jab from my opponent. Sidestepping quickly to the left, 'Hate' whistled past my ear. I grabbed his wrist. Twisted his arm behind his back. Then pushed up and forwards in one fast move, letting go when I judged he had built up sufficient momentum.

Connor flew across the cell as if he was going for the header that would score the winning goal in the Cup Final. Instead of a football, the iron railing of the top bunk thudded against his forehead.

He didn't fall to the ground as I'd hoped.

He turned round slowly, swaying from side to side. Clutched onto the bunk. Steadied himself further by spreading his thick legs wide.

What was I to do? I'd learned a painful lesson in Brixton. History mustn't be given the chance to repeat itself. I couldn't allow Connor to stand there gathering what few wits he had.

Besides, it was too good a target, too good an opportunity, to miss.

I brought my foot up fast and straight. Into his groin.

His eyes rolled in their sockets. His mouth formed a perfect circle like a choirboy on Songs of Praise. A very loud, very expressive 'Ooooh' shook the air like the sonic boom of Concorde.

The cry of pain was as easy to follow as a hunting horn. The warders had their sticks in their hands as they entered the cell.

The three of us looked down at Connor and shrugged innocently.

'Slipped on a bar of soap, did he?' one of the warders asked.

'Funny you should say that,' grinned Norman.

'Governor's office, Shannon. Nine o'clock in the morning,' they said, carrying Connor from the cell.

I thought of asking, 'Why me?' but knew there was little point. Justice was rough in here.

Norman gave me his surrogate father look.

'You've done it again, haven't you?' he said, his voice weary with exasperation.

'It's not my fault,' I replied. 'I don't go looking for trouble, you know.'

'You don't have to,' he said. 'Trouble has an uncanny knack of knowing exactly where to find you.'

CHAPTER SIX

I woke up on Friday morning to find an empty space beside me in the bed. Before my mind could shrug off the after-effects of an overdose of red wine and shift into panic mode I heard the spirit-lifting sounds of laughter.

The living room had been meticulously tidied, the table set for breakfast. The air was filled with the appetising smells of fresh coffee and buttery croissants. As I entered, Arlene and Norman became unnaturally unquiet, some conspiracy brewing along with the coffee.

'About time too,' Norman said, vainly trying to secrete an inch-thick magazine down the side of the armchair. 'I'm starving. Arlene's been up for hours.'

64

'Jetlag, that's all,' she said with a reassuring smile. 'Come and sit down. I'll get breakfast. And after that I'm going to get you guys organised.'

Norman and I winced.

Arlene, arms akimbo, stared back at us defiantly.

There are some things in life you just have to take fatalistically. Resistance is futile.

She spent the rest of the day, hair bunched in an elastic band, the sleeves of one of my old shirts rolled up, in a whirlwind of activity, spring-cleaning the flat from top to bottom.

Saturday, the black of her bruises toning down to a dull grey, saw us venture out in public. We strolled on the heath, had a pub lunch and passed the afternoon revising the bridge system we had hastily cobbled together six months previously.

On Sunday we drove down to Brighton, burning the inner-city sludge off the points of the Monte Carlo. (Don't get the wrong impression about the Lancia: it sounds flash and expensive, I know, but the reality is rather different. The lines of the two-seater, mid-engined car are sleek and understatedly stylish, but it's twelve years old – a perpetual automotive battleground for the opposing forces of retreating steel and advancing rust.) We walked hand in hand along the beach, our bodies bent forwards against the wind. Cupping our hands, we lit cigarettes and sat for a while just watching the soothing peristaltic motion of the sea as it rolled back and forth across the shingle. Then, like carefree children, we tossed pebbles into the water, sending them skimming over the white-topped waves. It would have been idyllic were it not for the clouds, both physical and metaphorical, hanging over my head.

By Monday, Arlene was indistinguishable from her old self. Animated, effervescent, and eager to hit the shops. Norman, knowing I had other things on my mind, offered to act as general factotum and bag carrier.

At eleven o'clock I entered the offices of BBW – Bets By Wire Limited. I had expected a seedy little place furnished with cast-offs, staffed by pot-bellied men wearing green eyeshades, cigarettes permanently drooping from between their lips, inches of ash hanging grimly on before tumbling to the linoleum floor. I got a shock.

I was met by a good-looking woman in her early forties. She was tall, slim, professional, and intentionally intimidating. Power-dressed in an expensive red tailored jacket with the shoulder pads of a quarterback, matching pencil skirt three inches above the knee, black blouse and red stilettos. She looked me up and down, examining my cheap raincoat critically, and decided that I exactly matched her perceptions of the average policeman.

I'd telephoned earlier and was fortunate to find she could 'allocate a slot' to me within her time-managed schedule. I showed her my identification with the impressive words 'Fraud Investigation Group' emblazoned in blue above my photo. It was the sort of card that Toddy, Norman's restaurant partner and semi-retired forger, claimed he could knock up in five minutes – although I think it had actually taken him a little longer.

Ms Gray led me into her office. It was a large, gleaming-white room awash with high-tech chrome-and-glass furniture that made me wish I had borrowed Arlene's sunglasses. Along the longest wall was a one-way mirror. From her desk Ms Gray only had to glance up to observe the frenzied activities in the large amphitheatre outside. It resembled a typical dealing room in a foreign exchange firm, or the NASA control centre. When the technological shock had abated, my overriding impression was of a factory farm. Operators – at least forty of them, it seemed – sat at computer terminals in purpose-built booths, tapping away frenziedly at keyboards. Each wore a voguish headpiece that made them look like a wannabe pop megastar or an aerobics instructor.

Ms Gray sat down behind the desk and leaned back authoritatively in a huge leather chair. I perched uncomfortably on what appeared to be strips of canvas stretched over steel tubing. The screen-saver on her computer was displaying a dizzying image of a fractal spiralling in space.

'Exactly how can I help you, officer?' she asked, looking at her watch.

'As I said on the telephone, we're investigating a fraud by a Mr Redmond. I believe he was one of your customers.'

'I read about the poor man's unfortunate demise,' she said, like a defendant in the witness box. 'Tell me, what makes you think he was one of our customers?'

'We found BBWs number in his address book,'

I said. 'Don't misunderstand me, please. I'm not suggesting for a moment that your company is involved in any way. But we're trying to build up a picture of the man. And I'd be interested in any background you can give me on him – details of his betting pattern, wins and losses, that sort of thing.'

'We regard all information of that type as confidential.'

'I could come back with a warrant,' I said, bluffing my heart out.

'I was about to add that, since the man is dead, I see no reason not to co-operate.'

'I'm very grateful, Ms Gray.'

She placed a well-manicured hand over the computer's mouse. The distracting fractal disappeared and the screen displayed a menu of options.

'Redmond, you say?' she asked, already typing. 'First name?'

'Martin.'

Redmond's file flashed onto the screen.

'He opened an account six months ago. Initial credit limit of a thousand pounds.'

'How do you decide on the limit?' I asked.

She gave a small sigh. I couldn't tell whether it was due to my interruption or my frustrating lack of knowledge.

'I don't decide, Mr Shannon. Too subjective. A computer makes the decision.'

I must remember to be kinder to computers in future, I thought.

'We run a credit check through the usual agencies,' she said slowly, as if telling herself that after all I was a policeman and, therefore, needed everything spelt out in words of few syllables. 'The rating technique used is called factor analysis. It's like those questionnaires you see in magazines: you tick the boxes and add up how many As, Bs or Cs you've got and then it tells you how successful a secretary you are, or how good you are in bed – not that the two are necessarily related, you understand.'

Her lips parted in a conspicuously broad smile, just in case I hadn't appreciated that it was a joke.

Obligingly, I returned her smile.

'Anyway,' she continued matter-of-factly, her allowance of humour used up for the day, 'the program assigns a score based on the individual's payment record on utilities, credit cards, mortgage and so on, together with a range of geodemographic factors, age, occupation, post-code – that alone can give a wealth of infor-mation about the type of area in which a person lives. We are also provided with any county court judgements, outstanding debts, etc. And, if still in any doubt, we introduce the human element and insist on taking up a bank reference.'

'Was the computer right in Mr Redmond's case?'

'Of course,' she said, shocked that any doubt should exist. 'His account was always settled exactly as due.'

'So he didn't win very often then?' I asked. 'Not if he was having to pay you, rather than the other way round.'

'Mr Shannon!' she said, with an incredulous

shake of her head.

Okay, I thought. It was a bloody stupid question. No need to rub it in.

'We're the only ones that win in this game,' she said patronisingly. 'In this business, the odds are stacked in our favour. In the long run the punter – customer, I mean – always loses. There's the odd occasion when we come across a regular winner, sure, but we know in that case it must be through inside information. So we ditch them straightaway. We're not a charity, you know.'

'How much did Redmond lose?'

She examined the screen, scrolling through his record.

'In total – let me see – nearly fifteen thousand pounds.'

I whistled at the unexpectedly high figure.

'Usual pattern,' she said. 'Started off small. A few freak wins at first, then the normal run of losers. Bets increasing thereafter as he tried to make good the losses. We upped his credit limit two months ago to take account of the level of business and prompt payment record.'

'Thank you, Ms Gray. You've been most helpful.'

'I imagine his wife is the next of kin. It says here he was married.'

'I presume that's the case,' I said.

'Perhaps you could tell her to get in touch with me. There's a credit balance on his account. It seems he had a treble come up on Friday. Finally got lucky.'

'I wouldn't have put it exactly like that, Ms Gray,' I said. 'If he'd finally got lucky he would have landed on top of an open truck carrying a load of feathers.'

She actually blushed.

As I left I couldn't help thinking about the man who had fallen from the top of the Empire State Building. Unlike Redmond, he was an incurable optimist. As he passed each floor, he said, 'Well, so far so good.'

On my way to meet Gloria I stopped off at High Holborn and left an envelope containing my statement with the desk sergeant. Having no wish to bump into Collins, I borrowed the sergeant's internal phone – or infernal phone, as he termed it – and dialled Walker's number. Her telephone rang and rang before at last it was answered. 'Walker's on three weeks' leave,' Quinn informed me, laughing fit to burst.

I had arranged to meet Gloria in a wine bar off Fleet Street. I'd never been there before. And I didn't ever intend to return. That made it the perfect venue. I sat at a small, round, heavily stained table, not knowing quite where to look. Around me what seemed like half the nation's legal and media professions swilled great goblets of claret as if it was about to go on ration; directly opposite me were the acres of exposed flesh of Gloria's body.

She was sipping warily at a glass of Australian Chardonnay from the bottle I'd insisted on buying – 'Well, all right then,' she'd said 'if you're sure they haven't got Blue Nun.' There has to be some limit to what one will do in the course of duty.

71

Her eyes roved around in a predatory fashion, scanning the available talent (average age fifty-five, overweight, ruddy-complexioned, balding, grey cigar ash down the front of black pinstriped jacket). Disappointed, she turned to face me, at last tucking her legs beneath the table and spoiling the fun of those who had been ogling them. Tight around her waist was a wide elasticated belt with an ornate buckle: if the belt had been any wider, it would probably have reached past the hem of her skirt. With an accompanying shake of her shoulders, she reached inside the low-cut blouse and hitched up the straining strap of her bra. Fluttering long black lashes, she looked into my green eyes.

'What can I do for you then?' she said suggestively.

'Tell me about Martin Redmond.'

'Oh, him,' she said, as if he had already been erased from the limited memory banks of her mind in preparation for the storage of new, and more promising, material. 'Who'd have thought it, eh? I didn't think he had the guts to do something like that. I don't mean fiddling the books. But jumping. You know?'

'When did you and he, er...'

'About nine months ago,' she said. 'He was fun then. We used to go out a lot in the evenings – sometimes a few drinks, maybe a meal somewhere. Then finish off back at my place. We even wangled a weekend away once.'

'So what happened?' I asked. 'Why did he stop being fun?'

'His wife went and got herself pregnant,' she

said. 'Bloody cow.' Gloria lit a cigarette and blew a long plume of smoke up towards the ceiling. 'There was Martin all set to leave her and he finds out he's going to be a daddy. "We can't go on, Gloria," he says one night while we're in bed. He'd bleeding waited till after, mind.'

She took another deep drag from the white-tipped cigarette and let the smoke exit through her nostrils this time. 'Good riddance, I say. He was as weak as bloody dishwater, was Martin.'

'And what about the gambling? When did you find out about that?'

'I overheard him on the phone to the bookies. I thought it was just the odd tenner or so. I didn't know he was talking in hundreds. I told him he was being irresponsible. He just laughed and said it was the baby's nest-egg. Bloody fool. At least he could have stopped while he was ahead.'

Gloria paused to contemplate Martin's folly, and to drain her glass. She didn't complain when I poured a refill. 'Quite nice this,' she said, 'when you get used to it.' The sips were now becoming gulps. 'Anyway, he didn't stop. Couldn't stop, more like it. Started losing big money too.'

She wagged a red fingernail in my direction. 'So do you know what the bastard does then? Goes off to the bank and gets himself a loan. Second mortgage, I think. I know he had to use the house as collateral. Baby's bloody nest-egg! More like baby's bloody millstone. Well, what did I care,' she said, viciously stubbing out the cigarette. 'It wasn't my money – although he had the cheek to try to tap me for a hundred quid once. I tell you, I made him wish he'd never asked. When I found out he was raiding the petty cash, that was the final straw. That's when I called in you lot. Pretty sharpish, too. I'd thought for a moment about telling that dishy Stevie, our boss, what was going on. But he's always so busy, what with work and three bawling kids at home. And I didn't trust Martin any more. I didn't want *him* trying to drop *me* in it.'

'Quite right, Gloria,' I said. 'You can't be too careful.'

'Someone should have told his bloody wife that,' she said.

I realised, with relief, that this was the signal for the end of the story. I wasn't going to get any more out of her – information, that is.

'I have to be on my way now,' I said.

'What, already? We were having such a lovely chat too. Why don't we do this again sometime?'

'Love to, Gloria,' I said. 'But it's a bit tricky. We might have to call you as a witness. It wouldn't be right to meet under those circumstances.'

'I suppose not,' she said grumpily. 'Well, you best be off then. I'll just stay and finish the wine. Shame to waste it.'

Sandra Redmond's house (or, as it now seemed, the bank's house) was a neat little semi-detached a few hundred yards up a side road from the busy high street in West Ealing. I parked the Lancia behind a red Fiesta. Walked up the short path. Hesitated before ringing the bell.

Why the hell had I come?

It wasn't simply the money owing from BBW – it would have been emotionally less fraught to have telephoned or written to give her that information.

Was it perhaps some devious desire to look over both her and the house in order to help me colour in the picture on Redmond?

Or did I just want to hear her say that she didn't hold me responsible for what had happened? Who was uppermost in my mind – me or her?

She answered the door wearing blue dungarees and an expression of absolute weariness. Her right hand rested below a bulging stomach, either in support of its weight or to derive some comfort from the new life inside. In contrast to Gloria, her make-up was minimal – a hint of pale pink lipstick, a light touch of blusher, a little eye-shadow to match her hazel eyes – and her hair was neatly cut in a short, practical page-boy style.

I identified myself as a policeman and produced the bogus identity card. Still unsure of my motives, I kept my thumb over the word 'Fraud'.

'It's about your husband, Mrs Redmond. Just a few questions. If it's not convenient, it really doesn't matter.'

'Come in,' she said. 'I could do with the company, to tell the truth. Tea?'

'If you're sure it's no bother. I'd love some. Would you like me to make it?'

'Thanks for the offer,' she said. 'But I'm only pregnant. Not a complete invalid.'

I stood there uneasily, shifting my weight from foot to foot, wondering if it wouldn't be better to turn on my heels and leave. Save her from reliving the memories.

'Sorry,' she said, 'but you get a bit fed up with

people fussing all the time.' She padded off in blue socks and furry black slippers down the narrow passageway to the kitchen. Pointing to the room on the left, she said, 'Go in and have a seat. I'll bring the tea.'

The room was long and narrow. To the front of the house was a sitting area with a red velour three-piece suite, settee lined up against one wall, two chairs directly opposite: it was like being inside a plush version of a railway carriage. An archway led to the dining area at the rear. Through the French windows I could see a small patch of garden.

Everything was spotlessly clean. Cushions were plumped up. Magazines and newspapers neatly stacked away in a wooden rack. Paperback novels and hardback books on pregnancy lined up on wooden shelves like soldiers on parade, tallest to the left, shortest to the right. Not a speck of dust on the coffee table. Even the carpet bore the faint tramlines of being recently vacuumed.

A gas fire burned flickeringly in a stone hearth. I walked over and stood directly in front of it, indulgently letting my body soak up the heat. In the middle of the mantelpiece were four small circles where, I guessed, a carriage clock had once stood. On the left was a photograph of the Redmonds on their wedding day. Dry-lipped, they smiled nervously at the camera.

'Happy days, eh?' she said, making me jump.

'How long were you married?' I asked.

'It would have been eight years come August.'

Sandra shook her head and handed me a mug of tea. Lowered her body slowly and carefully into an armchair, sighing as the weight of the eight-month burden eased. Placed her swollen ankles on a padded stool.

'Do you know why he did it?' she said, catching me off guard. I'd expected a certain amount of mutual foreplay before the subject of Martin's death could be broached.

'I was about to ask you the same question,' I replied. 'As you already know he'd stolen some money from work but...'

'But not enough to account for what he did. It can't have been a great deal. I never suspected anything. He wasn't a spendthrift, certainly. And we don't have much put by. Still, as long as I have enough for the baby.'

She stared deep into her tea as if it were a crystal ball. I hoped she saw a different vision from the one I saw.

'Thank God there's the baby to think about,' she said. 'That's what I keep telling myself. The baby is what matters now. Stay calm. Don't let yourself get all churned up inside.' She looked across at me questioningly. 'That's not being heartless, is it?'

'Of course not,' I said. 'It's being sensible.' Anyway, I thought, Martin doesn't deserve your grief

She sipped her tea thoughtfully.

'Maybe it was something to do with the baby coming. The books all say that men can get a bit funny. Unsure of how it's going to change their lives. Worried about the extra responsibility. Their different role within the enlarged family unit.' It sounded as if she'd not only the read the books but learned them off by heart too. 'He did seem very tense of late,' she said. 'Nervous like. You know? Jumpy. Irritable. Quick to fly off the handle.'

'No, I don't think it was the baby,' I said. I didn't want any shadow cast on the new life. 'Maybe we'll never know.'

I wished I'd never come. This was all proving far more difficult than I'd feared. Sandra Redmond was worth five of the likes of Gloria. And I wanted to tell her so. But knew I couldn't ever let on.

I took Ms Gray's card from my wallet. Felt an inner loathing as I waved it at Sandra and said, cowardly and without explanation, 'If you give this lady a call, she has some money that was due to your husband.'

As an afterthought I took out a pen and wrote my telephone number on the back. I placed the card on the coffee table.

'If you ever need to talk,' I said, 'then just give me a ring. Thank you for your time, Mrs Redmond. And the tea.'

She walked with me to the door.

'Oh, I know what I meant to ask you,' she said. 'When you went through my husband's things, you didn't find a receipt, did you? Only Martin took the clock to be repaired. He was having my jewellery valued at the same time. Something to do with the insurance, he said. And, well, I'd like to collect it.'

'No,' I replied, shaking my head. 'I'm very sorry. We didn't find any receipt.'

Nor are we likely to, I thought angrily.

If I'd known all this about Martin Redmond when he broke that window, I think I might have been tempted to give him a helping hand.

Perhaps Collins, with his simplistic concept of punishment, hadn't been too wide of the mark, after all.

CHAPTER SEVEN

I arrived home to find the hallway barricaded.

The scene that greeted me resembled a Harrods-sponsored airdrop of 'essential supplies' to Bosnia. A convoy of taxis, it appeared, had headed north and disgorged their contents in a line along the whole length of the corridor. Originally propped against the wall, the friction-less plastic bags had slid down to advertise their designer logos across every square inch of the carpet. Some of the bags had the hooks of hangers sticking out, signalling dresses or suits – doubtless both; others showed the distinct contours of shoe boxes and handbags; the remainder rustled as I stepped gingerly past, the tissue paper within folded around the silks and satins of blouses and lingerie. When Arlene hits the shops she doesn't pull her punches.

The living room was unrecognisable – what you could see of it, that is. Norman and Arlene were surrounded by a huge pile of empty cardboard boxes. The floor was littered with those little bits of polystyrene that look like a trainee chef's first stab at prawn crackers and probably taste pretty much the same too. The dining table had been inconveniently moved closer to the centre of the room and a new desk stood in its place under the window. A computer and printer, and just about every software package that was on the market, were strewn across the desk.

'What the hell is all this, Norman?' I asked.

'This, my friend,' he said smiling proudly, 'is the white heat of technology. What you are looking at here, Nick, is a vision of the future.'

'Wow,' I said. 'And there was I thinking it was just a bloody great mess spread over every inch of the living room.'

'Bit touchy today, aren't we?' he said. 'Have we suffered a conversion on the road to Archway? Become a born-again Luddite? Is this a severe case of technophobia I see before me?'

'I think,' Arlene said, noticing the strain on my face, 'it's more the case of a man who needs a stiff drink.'

She snaked her way cautiously through the debris and went through to the kitchen.

'Sorry,' Norman said. 'Not a good time for jokes, eh?'

'I've had better days. But also a lot that have been much worse. Come on. Show me your new toy.'

'How dare you,' he said with mock hurt. 'This is no toy. This is a legitimate business expense.'

'Then show me your legitimate business expense.'

Arlene returned with a tray of drinks and found nowhere to put it down. I cleared a barely adequate rectangle of space on the table by moving more boxes onto the settee. She handed Norman an enormous Scotch and American. Gave me a large tumbler and a hug.

I took a sip of the drink.

'What do you call this?' I squeaked, my vocal chords rendered numb.

'You've heard of a Sidewinder?' she asked. 'Well, this is an Unwinder. My own special recipe. It's a very large slug of vodka poured over ice and then threatened from a distance with the tonic bottle.'

I took a larger sip this time.

'This is a real breakthrough,' I said. 'A couple of these and it's no longer necessary to join the Foreign Legion to forget.'

'You make a mean drink, Arlene,' Norman said, testing his own. 'I must remember to sell my shares in Schweppes.' He sat himself down at the desk. 'Now, come over here, you two, and watch. We're just about to have the grand switching-on ceremony.'

He pressed a button and we stood there anxiously, waiting while the machine went through a lengthy start-up procedure. Eventually the screen showed a box headed Program Manager.

'Brilliant, isn't it?' Norman said, staring at the icons. 'Pentium chip. Windows. Five hundred and forty megabytes of hard disk. Sixteen megabytes of RAM. CD-ROM. Sound Blaster. This machine has everything.'

He grinned at Arlene and me.

'Well,' he said. 'What do I do now?'

We burst out laughing.

'You mean to say you've bought all this and you don't know how to use it?'

'Computers seem to have changed a bit since my day,' he said.

'Yes. They don't have beads sliding along rods any more.'

'Damn,' he said. 'I knew there was something missing. Anyway, I thought you could give me a hand. Just so I can check what you picked up during the year you spent with Jameson Browns. Purely academic interest on the part of your old tutor, of course. Wouldn't want the firm foundation I provided to have gone to waste.' He gave a nonchalant wave of his hand. 'Unless you've got anything better to do, that is.'

Arlene winked at me.

'Come on,' Norman pleaded. 'Just get me started, will you? I have used computers before. Honest.'

The screen-saver cut in and 200 multicoloured planets zoomed at warp speed towards him.

'Bloody hell,' he said, jumping up from the chair. 'I didn't touch it.'

I sat down in his place. Found the mouse and plugged it in. Jiggled it until the box reappeared.

'What do you want to do?' I asked.

'Well, I bought it for the restaurant accounts. We need to load, or something.'

'Okay,' I said. 'Pass over the program.'

'Which one?' he asked.

'What do you mean "which one"?'

'I bought the lot. The salesman said that you never know when they might come in useful.'

'Pass me Chi-Rho,' I said. 'That's the most

common package for medium and large businesses. You have got Chi-Rho, I presume?'

'Of course,' he said. 'What do you think I am? An idiot or something?'

'Far be it for me to judge my fellow man. But...'

'Careful,' he said. 'Or I won't let you have your present.'

He dug around on the floor.

'There you are,' he said.

Now this was what I call software. Omar Sharif's Bridge.

'I'll freshen our drinks, boys,' Arlene said. 'While you play.'

Resisting the temptation to lose myself in the bridge program, I loaded Chi-Rho and gave Norman a basic tour through the menu and features.

'If we can find my briefcase amidst all this rubble, I'll show you something interesting.'

Norman cast his eyes round the room.

'You were right,' he said helplessly. 'It is a bloody mess. Sorry.'

'Try the settee,' Arlene called from the kitchen.

Norman transferred a pile of manuals from the settee to the floor and held my briefcase aloft in triumph.

I inserted one of the disks from Van Damm's.

'This is what a trial balance looks like. And this,' I said, 'is what a fiddle looks like.' I scrolled down to the petty-cash account and pointed at an entry on the screen.

'On this day Redmond paid a thousand pounds to settle his betting account. Surprise, surprise, here's the thousand pounds leaving the petty-cash account.'

'How did he balance the books?' Norman asked.

'Let's see.'

We examined the headings of the other accounts on the trial balance. One stood out like a sore thumb.

'This guy was a real amateur,' Norman said, shaking his head disbelievingly. 'He's a disgrace to my profession. Fancy putting the balancing entry into a suspense account. That's the first place an auditor would look.'

A suspense account is a kind of financial limbo for entries you're not quite sure how to classify, or problems that you can't solve at that time. It has the benefit of not affecting other accounts that you would routinely examine for purposes such as cost control. Once the position on a particular entry is clear, you transfer it from suspense to its rightful destination. Everything neat and tidy again.

'He always hoped to win enough to pay back the money,' I said, shrugging my shoulders. 'Even so, he would have had a hard job explaining his actions to any auditor worth his pay.'

In sequence, I loaded the disks for previous months and found the other occasions when Redmond had put his hand in the petty-cash till.

'There you are,' I said to Norman. 'A grand total of two thousand five hundred pounds.'

'The man's even more of a fool than I first assumed,' Norman said disdainfully. 'If you're going to embezzle, go for a "pension job". A scam that will set you up for life. Not this tuppenny-ha'penny stuff.' He pointed to the disks. 'Can I keep these? They'll be good practice. And I'd like to see what a true professional could have achieved with a bit of flair and a crooked mind.'

'Okay,' I said, interested to find out what Norman would come up with. 'I don't imagine we will ever need them as evidence.'

But I took a copy of the disks. Just in case.

An hour later, Arlene had restored order to the flat, and Norman sat happily practising his mouse control by playing Solitaire.

'How did it go today?' she asked as we finally found a place to sit.

'I could have done without seeing Redmond's wife,' I said. 'And what makes it all worse is that I'm no nearer to understanding the man. At least, I still don't know why he jumped.'

'I tell you what,' Norman chimed in. 'I'll treat us to dinner. Let's invite Arthur along too. The whole gang together again. There's nothing like a bunch of friends, a juicy steak and a few bottles of Pomerol for problem-solving.' He gave us a cheesy grin. 'Mind you, the trouble is remembering the solution afterwards.'

We sat at Norman's usual table in the far corner of the restaurant. From here he could watch the door, the faces of the customers, the black-trousered waiters and, of course, the till. One of the waiters, with a deferential nod of the head to Norman, scurried past deftly balancing four large platters: the mouth-watering aroma of char-grilled meat and fish hung in the air for a brief moment before being greedily sucked away by the air-conditioning.

Arlene looked good enough to eat in a new maroon dress with those gossamer-thin straps that for some inexplicable reason hairdressers team with a white T-shirt. It was cleverly cut for those who cannot any longer quite meet the demands of size 12: high-waisted to accentuate Arlene's ample breasts, then cunningly sweeping past her bottom in long, minimising lines till it showed a trim pair of ankles.

Arthur looked out of place in his dinner suit, clip-on bow tie and long mane of pepper-and-salt hair. On the stroke of midnight he was due on duty at a West End nightclub. A six-foot-five ex-wrestler, he worked in 'customer control' – the new job title sounded even grander than the previous one of 'door steward', and much classier than 'bouncer'.

Arthur and I had shared a cell in Brixton while I was on remand and he was finishing his sentence. In three months I had taught him how to hold his own at the card table: in return, he had drilled me in the (very) basic art of prison survival. We each laid claim to the raw end of the deal. He had the misfortune of a pupil who 'couldn't fight his bleeding way out of a paper bag'. And I had to explain the laws of probability to a man whose brain functioned as if it were perpetually trying to turn round a supertanker. It was the creaky slowness of Arthur's mental machinery that had landed him in Brixton. His boss at that time had sent him on a little errand to collect a debt – and only after being charged

86

with demanding money with menaces did the penny finally drop.

Arlene examined the room with the critical eye of a woman. I doubted it was to her taste. Everything was very masculine – if anything, bordering on the macho – with few of the soft touches she would have brought to the interior design. To complement the cooking, the décor had been kept simple. Plain, dark-wood panelling and buttery emulsion on the walls. Matt-white ceiling. Large, heavy, wooden tables with hunting-scene placemats rather than tablecloths. Navy blue napkins. Chunky cutlery. No frills or fripperies. And despite being so recently kitted out from scratch, the place had a cosy, lived-in feel. All it lacked was an open fire and you could have been in a turn-of-the-century country pub. The whole atmosphere was relaxing and re-assuring. You could almost hear the sighs of pleasure issuing from the customers as they stepped through the heavy door with its bottle-glass panes.

The restaurant was packed, as usual. Toddy, the best cook in the entire history of Chelmsford prison, took a short leave of absence from the kitchen to come over in his chef's whites to greet us.

'The sole's especially good tonight,' he said in a heavy Lancashire accent. 'And the rack of lamb,' he added. 'A few herbs, some garlic – not too much, mind – and roasted to nicely pink in the middle.'

Toddy's motto (heads of large corporate enterprises would have called it a mission statement) was 'only the very best ingredients, simply prepared'. In just a few months he had established an unequalled reputation for old-fashioned, no-nonsense, British cuisine. Lots of grills, roasts, an excellent hotpot, and a bread and butter pudding that had Gary Rhodes begging on bended knee for the recipe.

'And you must be Arlene,' he said, shaking her hand vigorously. 'I've heard a lot about you.'

She tilted her head girlishly at him and toyed with one of her drop-pearl earrings. 'And I about you,' she replied.

He looked sharply at Norman.

'You haven't been giving away trade secrets, I hope,' he said.

Toddy dealt out four menus and bustled off to the kitchen, promising to return at the end of the evening.

The conversation initially, as it should be, was light-hearted. Arlene and I recounted the story of Norman's new computer. Arthur bellowed with laughter, drawing attention from the other diners. I could see some of the older men pointing at Arthur and trying to place him. I hoped none of them would interrupt our conversation by coming over to ask for the autograph of the man Kent Walton had dubbed 'Dangerous Duggan – the terror of the ring'. Arthur had, for a while, taken it as a compliment, until finally realising that it was a comment on his inability to remember the moves he was supposed to make: too many opponents had been floored by Arthur's forearm smash when the script had called for a body-check.

Over the second bottle we settled down to problem-solving. After briefly skimming over Arlene's lost cause, I told Arthur the Redmond saga.

'What I can't understand,' I said, 'is why he jumped. He must have been petrified at the prospect of diving into thin air, seventeen floors up.'

'I've been thinking about that,' Norman said with unusual seriousness. 'Now, how can I explain it?'

He took a fifty-pence piece from his pocket and placed it in the middle of the table.

'What's that?' he asked us.

Good old Arthur fell into the trap.

'A fifty-pence piece,' he said proudly.

'Oh, that life was that simple,' Norman said with a shake of his head. 'This,' he continued slowly, fingering the coin, 'is the Coin of Fear.'

We stared at him blankly.

'It has two sides,' he explained. 'One side is bravery. The other is cowardice.'

We were still none the wiser.

'Remember your claustrophobia?' he said to me.

'Yes?' I replied uncertainly.

'And how you would panic when confronted by just the thought of a door closing on you in a confined space?'

I nodded shamefully, the memory of that lock-up in Chelmsford still embarrassingly fresh in my mind.

'And remember the time when you were faced with entering a four-foot-square lift? You were petrified then, weren't you? Yet you went into that lift.'

'Only because someone was going to shoot me if I didn't.'

'Exactly,' he said. 'The lesser of two evils. You were brave enough to conquer one fear – but only because you were more scared of the alternative.'

'So Redmond was more scared of the prospect of prison? Or owning up to his pregnant wife that he'd blown their savings and sold her jewellery?'

'Maybe,' Norman said dubiously. 'Unless there was something else.'

'And what might that be, oh wise one?' I asked with bated breath.

'I only said I'd been thinking about the problem,' he said, grinning from ear to ear. 'I didn't claim to have come up with the ultimate solution.'

A chorus of groans rose from the table.

'Well, that was all very enlightening,' I said. 'Thanks a bunch.'

'Which brings us to Problem Number Two,' he said.

'And what might that be?' I asked, toying with the heavy wine glass.

'You and Collins,' he said. 'What are you going to do?'

I picked up the coin from the table and tossed it flamboyantly in the air. Catching it in the palm of my hand, I examined the exposed face.

'It looks like I'm going to accept,' I said.

'Just like that?' Arthur asked. 'A toss of a coin?'

'Not really,' I said, mimicking one of Norman's grins. 'I never told you what a head or a tail would signify, did I?'

'So you'd already made up your mind?' Arlene asked.

'I came to a decision that very first night,' I said.

'But why, Nick?' Arlene asked, placing her hand on mine. 'Why take the risk?'

'Look at the trouble the Windsor Club has caused you. The company goes down the tubes and who suffers? The little people, that's who. It's the same with fraud. It's always the little people who get hurt. If there's something rotten in the state of Glenshield, then I have to find out about it. My conscience can cope with big institutions like the banks getting hit – Jesus, they can afford it. But not when it's ordinary, innocent folk who have sunk their savings in shares or loans, or stand to lose their jobs. Someone's got to protect their interests.'

'You're a white knight then,' she said, an angry edge to her voice. 'Is that what we're supposed to believe?'

'And under pressure from Collins, don't forget,' I pointed out. 'Let me just take a quick look. What do you say?'

She stared at me uncertainly.

I tried a winning smile.

It lost. Not a blink of reaction from Arlene.

Time for a different approach.

'After all,' I said, casually shrugging my shoulders, 'there's probably nothing behind the letter. I'll simply go through the motions for a little

91

while. Then I'm off the hook.'

'There's no point in me trying to dissuade you, is there?' she asked, sighing heavily.

I shook my head apologetically.

'Then,' she said, rounding on Norman, 'I hold you responsible. You started this. You sweet-talked Collins into seconding Nick to the Fraud Squad. If anything should happen to him...'

She left the threat unspoken – rack of Norman was my guess – and went off smiling sweetly to powder her nose.

Norman gave an exaggerated gulp.

'If anything does go wrong,' I said solemnly to both my friends, 'promise me you'll look after Arlene. She's not ready to go back to the States yet. At the first sign of any trouble, Norman, get her over to Arthur's place.'

'Don't worry,' said Arthur. 'I'll look after her.'

'I'll promise too,' Norman said slyly, 'providing you come totally clean.'

Norman knew me too well. He could tell I was holding out on him.

'I decided to go along with what Collins wants. But only for a price. The trade is that he has to swear to re-open the file on Susie's hit-and-run.'

'He can't make that kind of deal,' Norman said.

'He has to. Otherwise it's a Mexican stand-off. This is too important to Collins. He'll agree. Just wait and see.'

'Don't you think it's time you let your sister rest in peace?' Norman said.

'How can Susie rest,' I asked, staring coldly into

his eyes, 'when the bastard who crippled her is still out there somewhere, free as a bird?' Clenching my fists, I reined in my emotions. 'Look, the only reason that Collins wants me to go undercover is so he can put Kinsella behind bars. He wants justice for Kinsella stealing his wife and turning his life upside-down. In return for that, he'll have to help me get justice.'

'Just as long as you're both not confusing justice with revenge,' Norman said.

'I don't think I am,' I said.

'Justice is an end in itself,' he continued, not content to let the matter drop. 'Revenge is merely the start of more hurt – more killing even.'

'What else can I do?' I said helplessly. 'I owe it to Susie. I swore an oath as she died in my arms. Now, are you going to help me or not?'

'Of course we will, you silly sod,' Norman said. 'Our God-given role in life is digging you out of trouble. What a pointless existence we would have without you. We just want to make sure you know what you're getting into, that's all.'

But I don't, I thought.

Then again, I never have.

CHAPTER EIGHT

Chelmsford

If you are one of those people who believe that
the cards of life have been stacked ready for
dealing at the moment of birth, then you
probably also accept that the croupier has a
pretty sick sense of humour at times. Fate, or
simply the unavoidable arrival of Saturday
morning, had determined that my interview
should be with the Deputy Governor.

The Governor, as per every weekend, rain or
shine, was off duty indulging his passion for
sailing. His boat – *The Bounty*, I suspected – was
his only weakness. A strict disciplinarian with
limited imagination and Victorian values (bring
back the cat; short, sharp shock; bread and water
for a week), he was the type of man who would
support capital (not corporal) punishment in
schools. What little humour he possessed was
generally bad. So no-one – and who can blame
them – had the courage to drag him away from
some muddy Essex estuary just to sort out the
aftermath of a minor fracas.

Which was my bad luck.

Because the Governor was hard, the Deputy
Governor had to be granite-like. Anxious lest his
superior consider him guilty of the heinous sin of
leniency, he had over-compensated. My punish-

ment was seven days' loss of privileges and a lengthy extension of my posting to the penal Siberia of the laundry. Step aside, Schwarzenegger – Shannon's coming through.

Norman and I stood moodily in the queue for lunch. A dozen inmates, all slavering at the prospect of Toddy's food, were lined up in front of 'the trough' – the long counter from which the meals were dispensed. My view was blocked. But it didn't matter. A monotonous regularity meant that I could picture the scene with my eyes closed.

Immense, rectangular stainless-steel containers sunk into pits of boiling water. Lids as big as Roman shields: when removed in sequence, they released billowing clouds of steam so large that a Comanche brave on the next hilltop would have been confused – or insulted – by the unintended message. Inside the pots, depending on the day of the week or how the monthly budget was holding up, there might be the inky blackness of mushroom stalks – never the caps, mind you – or the pale orange of obscenely oversized carrots.

Thankfully, Toddy was gifted with an alchemical skill that enabled him to transform the limited range of dismal ingredients into something edible, nourishing and close to appetising. Without him, I would sooner have starved. I almost had in Brixton, come to think of it. I clenched my left fist and shuddered.

'Look at it this way,' Norman said, trying to find some good in the situation. 'With the loss of your association periods, it gives you more time for study.'

95

'Haven't you heard the old saying about "all work and no play", Norman?'

'That's for wimps and losers,' he said. 'There'll be plenty of time for play on the outside. Right now the priority is to secure you some sort of future.'

He picked up a plastic tray and examined it critically. Scratched off a piece of dried cabbage with his fingernail.

'If you leave here unemployable,' he said, waving the tray at me, 'you'll be back inside within three months. As sure as eggs is eggs. There's too many temptations out there for someone with no money and little chance of legally acquiring any. And too many wolves. People who can spot easy prey a mile off.' He shuffled two feet to the left, closing the gap that had opened up. 'Before you know it, you're running the odd little errand for one of them. Just this once, you'll tell yourself – "Tide me over till I get a proper job." But it doesn't stop there. Once you're in with the bad crowd, the direction of travel is always down. Deeper and down.'

'You really know how to paint a rosy picture,' I said.

'I've seen it happen too many times before,' he replied, clicking his tongue. 'Blokes who have left here one day filled with good intentions – and who arrive back a few weeks later with their hopes dashed and another long stretch to serve. Believe me, the only way off the prison treadmill is through hard work.'

We reached the front of the queue before I could get any more depressed.

96

'What's on the menu today, Toddy?' Norman asked.

'Catholics' casserole,' Toddy mumbled.

'And what's that?' said Norman with a burgeoning grin.

'I'm not telling you,' Toddy answered grumpily. 'You know what it is anyhow.'

'Come on,' said Norman. 'Say it. Please.'

'Only if you promise. Okay?'

'I promise,' Norman said solemnly.

'All right then,' Toddy whispered. 'It's Irish stew.'

'Sorry, what?' Norman goaded.

'Irish stew,' Toddy replied more loudly.

'All together now,' Norman called out to the assembled mass.

'Irish stew in the name of the law,' they chorused.

Norman fell about laughing.

Toddy, who had heard the joke a thousand times before, gritted his teeth and ladled a dollop into one of the compartments of Norman's tray.

We moved crabwise, still giggling, along the line. Toddy's motley crew of white-coated assistants filled other sections with cabbage, mashed swede and – in one of those revolting customs you only have the misfortune to encounter in prison or the armed services – jam sponge and custard. No matter how carefully, how immobile, you held your tray, Murphy's law dictated that at least one yellow trickle of custard would appear among the dark green shreds of cabbage, or one blob of thick brown gravy would finish up decorating the jam sponge.

I turned to follow Norman in the search for a seat. Since the prison had been designed to accommodate only sixty per cent of the current number of inmates, this was a task that rivalled the quest for the Holy Grail.

In a space originally intended for forty tables, a woefully inadequate fifty now stood. This had two consequences. First, the room was as difficult to negotiate as Hickstead on a hippopotamus. Second, since the carpenter had used the measurements of six anorexic teenage girls when working out the maximum dimensions of each table, you had to resort to rubbing backsides with those who were prepared to 'squeeze along a bit' on the benches. And some, unfortunately, were more prepared than others – positively bent over backwards in fact – to accommodate. (This was the main reason why my hair was now shorn to a wiry crew cut and why I had spent hours cultivating a gruff voice and surly expression.)

'Tally Ho!' Norman said triumphantly, gesturing with his tray towards the far corner of the room. His little body scuttled off in pursuit of the quarry of vacant places. I weaved my way more circumspectly through the tight chicane of the nearest tables. Accelerating along the straight, I was moving much too quickly to avoid the foot that shot out in my path.

I lurched forwards at forty-five degrees.

Another well-aimed foot put paid to any chance of recovering my balance.

I fell clumsily, still stupidly clutching the tray.

The stone floor rapidly came up to greet me.

The Catholics' casserole must have been blessed. A soft landing in Toddy's Irish stew saved my nose from being shattered to pieces. I picked myself up. Scraped lumps of warm, sticky meat from my eyes. Ignored the gravy dribbling down my chin. Scrutinised the nearby tables for any signs of a continuance of the assault.

From where the feet had appeared, a group of men sat with heads unnaturally buried in trays.

'Clear that up, Shannon,' one of the warders shouted unnecessarily in the resulting silence.

I wiped my face. Felt my cheeks flush, my skin burn with embarrassment as the laughter began to break out.

A Trusty arrived on cue to hand me a bucket and mop.

And a message.

'Compliments of Mr Connor,' he said. 'See you in the laundry, he says.'

'What are you going to do now?' Norman asked when we were back in the calm of our cell.

I was standing at the tiny washbasin, swabbing away with a damp flannel at the stains on my uniform. It wasn't vanity. The heady smell of meaty gravy and boiled cabbage was overpowering in such a small space.

'Not much I can do,' I said, resigned by now to the encounter with Connor. 'Apart from keep my eyes and ears open. And try to remember everything that Arthur taught me.'

'You could have a word with the Governor,' Norman suggested without much conviction.

'Come to that, I could even have a word with him.'

Norman helped out with the prison accounts. He was the one the Governor mistakenly consulted when worrying divergences from budget occurred.

'The Governor's not going to give me any special treatment,' I said. 'Not even if you were to promise to stop fiddling his books.'

Norman's mouth contorted into a butter-wouldn't-melt expression.

'And,' I continued, 'especially since, only this morning, the Deputy made it clear that I was condemned to a long stretch in the laundry.'

'Can't be seen to be going over the DG's head?' Norman said. He sucked air thoughtfully through his teeth. 'There must be something we can do. We can't just sit around like lemons waiting for Connor to strike. If only I could think of a way to get you out of that bloody laundry.'

'Don't waste your time,' I said. 'If it's not the laundry, it would only be some other place. At least this way I know the where, if not the when and how, of his plan of attack.'

I gave Norman my best brave-face smile.

'Come on,' I said. 'No sense you worrying too. And look at it this way. The laundry is my territory. I know it a whole lot better than Connor does. I'll be playing at home.'

'It's never done West Ham much good,' he said with half-hearted humour. 'But then again I don't suppose entertainment value will be your main objective when Connor has you by the balls.'

I ignored the remark before my eyes began to water at the thought. 'Don't forget,' I said, 'there'll be screws around.'

'Is Nelson still in charge down there?' Norman asked.

'Yes,' I sighed.

Norman, as usual, had found the weak spot in my argument.

Prison Officer Tony Stebbings ('Nelson' to us inmates) had acquired his nickname through an uncanny ability to turn the proverbial blind eye whenever it suited him – or, more accurately, his pocket. Nelson's palms were greasier than a car mechanic's. And the grease, more often than not, was provided by Connor.

Well, I hadn't expected Marquis of Queensberry rules. But, with Nelson as referee, there were likely to be no rules at all.

Ironic, I thought.

Not even the laundry could guarantee a clean fight.

CHAPTER NINE

When you have a bluff to make it's best to leap in with the absolute minimum of thought. Too much consideration merely exposes the weaknesses of the strategy and fatally erodes your confidence. 'Decide and act' is the golden rule.

So the following morning I arrived on cue at the Fraud Squad with my poker-face set in concrete. Collins had the winning hand – that much had been obvious all along – but, if I held my nerve, I might wring some concessions from him before finally agreeing to go undercover.

That was the theory at least. The practice is always a little more difficult.

I decided to take a quick tour of the building rather than going straight to Collins's office. Told myself it wasn't just postponing the inevitable but a useful last-minute amendment to the plan. Make Collins sweat for a while and it might improve my bargaining position. Anyway, the voice of self-doubt whispered shakily in my ear, this might be your last look.

I climbed the stairs to the tenth floor. Whiled away a couple of minutes peering into the conference room, where high-flying suspects were questioned or important confidential discussions (Senior Officer-Speak for plots and intrigues) took place. Made my way slowly down from there.

With one floor left to go, I strolled casually into SO6 Support, the nerve centre of the Fraud Squad. Idly watched the officers tapping away at computer terminals whilst engaged on intelligence-gathering, financial investigations, computer crime or manning the NCIS (National Criminal Intelligence Service) desk – a kind of post office acting as the link between the Fraud Squad and the Areas. It was here that Walker had learned her trade. I wondered what she was doing now. Sipping a *cuba libre* by a poolside in Tenerife? A brandy sour in Cyprus? Glass of retsina on Rhodes?

Did I envy her?

Of course I bloody did!

On the operational floor 'B' Squad were in the middle of a briefing. A dozen men sat on top of desks littered with plastic beakers or lounged untidily against walls. The body language signalled mounting boredom, the nervous hands a desperation for the next cigarette. Their squad leader was giving details of the target – a company suspected of defrauding charities by raising large sums on their behalf and then creaming off ninety per cent as 'administrative expenses'. Quinn spotted me, his dark, darting eyes programmed to miss nothing. They narrowed to slits, accentuating the deep curves of the bags beneath. He brought a hairy hand up to the droopy black moustache designed to camouflage the thin, weak mouth and gave a loud cough, which sounded conspicuously like my name. The Detective Superintendent stopped mid-sentence, then said something inaudible. A loud peal of laughter broke out. Quinn waved a clenched fist at his superior in a sickeningly sycophantic 'right on' gesture. The diamond of the ring on his little finger caught the light. The ice in his eyes caught mine.

I turned my back. Walked the last few yards. Finally entered the office of DS Collins.

Forty minutes later the door was flung violently open. It travelled a swift half-circle on its hinges before crashing into one of the partitions and sending a seismic tremor along the chipboard perimeter of the room.

I made an undignified exit, aided by Collins's right palm jabbing away at my chest as he forced me backwards. The angry shouts that had started in his office continued as we moved erratically along the narrow walkway between the two squads.

They must have wondered whether they were witnessing a tragedy or a comedy. Collins's face was flushed and contorted with rage; his tie was askew and his shirt tail flapped outside horizontally creased baggy trousers – he looked like Coco the Clown in mufti.

'Call this a statement?' he screamed at the top of his voice, his left hand waving the pieces of paper for all to see. 'Pack of bleeding lies is what I call it.'

'You bloody hypocrite,' I responded in kind. 'You wouldn't recognise the truth if it jumped up and bit you where you keep your brains – in your bloody backside, that is.'

He stood immobile and stared at me incredulously.

'You're scum, Shannon,' he said. 'I'll see you never work again. And, believe me, that's not a threat – it's a cast-in-stone bloody promise. Thought you could pin the blame on Walker, eh? Get out of my sight. You make me sick.'

'You won't get away with this,' I shouted ineffectually back at him.

'Oh yes, I will, Shannon,' he sneered, approaching me threateningly. I stood my ground defiantly. 'And you know what else I'll get away with?' He stepped even closer. 'This.'

His right fist smacked into my chin.

I tumbled to the floor, breaking my fall with my right elbow. Lay there staring up at him, clutching my face. A thin line of blood, carved out by his wedding ring, trickled down my cheek.

Disdainfully, Collins turned his back on me like a matador who had established complete ascendancy over the bull. He walked with a swagger to his office, revelling in the limelight.

A round of applause, spontaneous and from the heart, erupted. The battle against the outsider had been fought and won.

Collins paused at the threshold of his room. Turned to face the audience. And bowed.

I slunk away, tail between my legs.

That, hopefully, was the hardest – and most painful – part of the exercise completed.

My cover had been publicly established. Not a single officer left in any doubt that I had become *persona non grata* as far as the Fraud Squad was concerned. I was finished working there, and just about everywhere else in the country. For Collins, they knew, always kept his promises. And word of the fight would spread like wildfire throughout the force, the ripples radiating out until they touched anyone with the slightest interest in its affairs or those of its more colourful staff.

Well, that was the reasoning. Not exactly as firmly based in irrefutable logic and algorithmic intellectualism as a Bertrand Russell thesis, I have to admit. But life is more 'ifs' than 'thuses'.

The plan, flimsy though it was, had been based

on two assumptions: that Kinsella, once spread-eagled in similar fashion by my co-conspirator, probably hated Collins as much as Collins hated him; and that he wouldn't be able to resist the temptation of scoring a point over Collins or putting his nose out of joint, if the opportunity were to present itself.

I now had to present that opportunity.

There was just one problem. It had to be done in a roundabout way.

I couldn't exactly march up to Kinsella in the street, shake him by the hand and say, 'Hi there. I'm Nick Shannon. How about a job then? The Accounts Department would suit me down to the ground. Oh, and you don't mind if I dig around a bit, do you? Just to see what scams you're pulling?'

Anyone else could have invented a new name, wheedled his way into Glenshield with a false background and credentials to match. But, alas, not me. I was too well known to make that route a viable, or safe, proposition. My face had been splashed across the front pages of newspapers eight years ago when standing trial for murder. And then a second time, all too recently, over the headline-grabbing affair of the decapitated corpse. If, by any remote chance, my singular features did not ring a bell and bring the name Nick Shannon springing to mind, there were always my two missing fingers to act as the ultimate *aide-mémoire*. So no luxury of a pseudonym and well-constructed 'legend' for me. If I was going to work inside Glenshield, then the offer had to come from them.

The preamble to our little charade had been all too easy. Judge for yourself. Then tell me I'm not being paranoid.

Collins greeted me warmly, rising from his chair to shake my hand. He smiled, enquired politely about Arlene and waved a generous hand at one of the two plastic beakers of coffee that lurked amid the jumble of papers on his desk. Emptying three sachets of sugar into his coffee, he stirred it lazily with a brown plastic stick. A faint aroma of whisky rose from the beaker.

I took a quick sip of coffee to counteract the dry mouth of tension and launched into a pre-prepared exposition of the bare bones of my plan. Collins, without interruption, listened attentively. And ceded to each of my demands in turn. Maybe he was just plain desperate – or had his fingers crossed underneath the desk.

In order to protect my licence, I insisted on a note being placed on record. Something that stressed, in no uncertain terms, that I was acting under his direct orders – and if anything went wrong, he was to be ultimately responsible. 'Consider it done,' he said.

'Next, I need some cash.'

'To cover expenses? Sounds reasonable enough. How much?'

'Let's say five thousand pounds. And I need it before tonight.'

Gulping, Collins reached for a cigarette.

'Don't panic,' I said. 'Yet. With a bit of luck it'll only be a loan. But you have to be prepared to write it off.'

'Okay,' he said grudgingly. 'I'll arrange it. Somehow.'

Then I hit him with the big one – re-opening the case file on the hit-and-run. There was a lot of exaggerated tooth-sucking and tilted-headed looks of concentration before the nod came.

'Is that the lot?' he asked, exhaling smoke in an angry rush. 'Wouldn't you like the ceremonial key for the Freedom of the City of London? An OBE? Date with Elizabeth Hurley? Why don't you make my life really difficult, Shannon.'

'There is one last thing.'

Roll of eyes and long, drawn-out groan.

'Kinsella,' I said. 'It's about time you stopped holding out on me. I'm not prepared to be kept in the dark. I can't operate like that. You have to tell me everything about Kinsella and yourself. And about Louise.'

'Who's been opening their big mouth? No, don't spoil the fun. Let me have one guess. Walker!'

'She was trying to warn me that you might have a secret agenda. That your motives for taking the case might not be based entirely on cleaning up this fine metropolis of ours.' Collins looked down at the desk. 'Well?' I said.

He took a slow swig of coffee. Drew deeply on the cigarette. Blew a perfect smoke ring into the air. Watched it reflectively as it drifted up and broke into wispy clouds against the ceiling.

'Come on, Batman,' I pushed. 'Tell Robin all about it.'

He looked at me undecidedly.

'My lips are sealed,' I encouraged him. 'I won't

tell a soul. Not Arlene. Not Norman. Nobody. I promise. Okay?'

Collins reached inside his jacket for his wallet and extracted a photograph, bent and torn at the edges through constant use.

'That's Louise,' he said.

I took the photograph from him. A rather thin face, framed by a fringe and chin-length straight hair, looked up at me. The smile on the full red lips was sweet, but somewhat strained. The nose perhaps just a fraction too long for perfection. But the eyes had that certain sparkle that makes you want to explore the personality beneath and promises not to disappoint.

'Very nice,' I said.

'Is that all you can say?'

'Okay then. *Very* nice. All right?'

Collins grunted, and cast a last wistful glance at the picture before replacing it in his wallet.

'Kinsella,' he said with a sigh. 'Bloody Kinsella.'

He drained his beaker and wiped his lips with the back of his hand, a small smear of coffee finishing up on his shirt cuff.

'I was transferred to the Drugs Squad to be his number two. He'd been there two years already when I arrived. Before that, he'd made a name for himself at West London Central – worked there with the Met's most famous penpusher, bloke called O'Kane. Anyway,' he said, 'do you know something? I hated his guts from the very first moment I laid eyes on him.'

I raised my eyebrows. *'Plus ça change,'* I said. 'No-one could ever accuse you of being in-consistent. Still, I suppose taking an instant dislike to someone saves you a lot of time in the end.'

'Such a bleeding poser,' he said, not allowing the remark to interfere with his flow. 'Sort of bloke who, when he's on holiday, swims length after length of the hotel pool – butterfly stroke. So bloody smooth with it, too. Fancy suits. Silk ties. And all this "Roddy" nonsense! Kinsella was more secretive about his first name than bleeding Inspector Morse! Insisted you called him Guv at work, and Roddy in the pub. It was great self-publicity – even the villains talked about him as Roddy.'

'Maybe the "Roddy" is just a front. Covering up some basic insecurity.'

'You know that's not true, Shannon. Louise was proof of that.'

'Go on,' I said, embarrassed.

'I can see him now, strutting about like the lord of the manor, the cock of the walk. And did he love throwing his not-inconsiderable weight around? Not half, he didn't. And whenever there was any crap to clean up, guess who was on duty with the shovel?'

'I thought that was the lot of the Detective Sergeant.'

Collins ignored the interruption. 'He loaded me up with so much work I had to slave away all the hours that God sent. And we all know why that was, don't we?'

'Louise?' I said.

'Behind my back. All the time.' From the glowing tip of his cigarette, he lit another. Held it just below his lips while he contemplated the past. 'And I – silly sod – was the only one who didn't know what was going on. Kinsella had to play the big man, didn't he? Let it deliberately slip out so that everyone knew. The news was beaten out so loudly on the drums of the bush telegraph that even the most humble DC couldn't miss it. They must have laughed their socks off! I still go red – see red – whenever I think about it. And I think about it a lot. Can't help it.'

He leaned back in the chair. 'There's not even any escape from it in the Fraud Squad. Bloody Quinn,' he said vehemently. 'He was that most humble of DCs! Every time I see him, I know what he's thinking. Know the gossip he's spreading.'

Quinn. That explained it. Why the new leaf had withered on the branch; why Collins had reverted so swiftly to his old self. No wonder the fire was still raging inside him – it was being fanned daily.

'How did it start between Kinsella and Louise?'

'Christ, how should I know? I was never at home, was I? That was part of the trouble between us. We never talked. Apart from Louise nagging me to pack the job in.'

He shook his head regretfully.

'Maybe I should have listened to her. Jacked it in. Become a nine-to-five merchant. I could have been in Kinsella's shoes now. Louise, security firm and all.'

'Square peg in a round hole,' I said.

'I know that. You know that. But Louise couldn't see it. "I'm a copper," I would tell her

111

every time the subject came up – and, boy, didn't it come up frequently. "It's all I know. And all I'm good at." But she didn't understand. Thought I was just being stubborn.'

'You, stubborn?' I said. 'No.'

He shot me a look. The sort one normally imagines emanating from a head with squirming snakes instead of hair. Why is there never a mirror around when you need one?

'Do you want to hear this story or not, Shannon? Because I'd just as soon keep my own counsel.'

'Sorry,' I said. 'Force of habit. Sarcasm is an instinct with me – part of my survival mechanism. Comes as a package with cynicism and dramatic irony.'

'I don't care if it comes with a free subscription to *Which Fraudster*? Any more of it and I might enjoy slugging you.'

'Like you enjoyed slugging Kinsella?'

'Walker didn't spare the details, did she?'

'So what happened?' I asked.

'They all thought I did it because of Louise. But I still didn't suspect anything. Bloody great detective, eh?' He gave a bitter laugh and shook his head. 'No, I hit him because he was the lowest form of animal on God's Earth. A tiny speck of mould on one apple, spreading out until it contaminates all the others in the barrel. One bent copper can destroy all the good work of a thousand honest policemen. Kinsella was on the take. Where else did he get the money to splash about?'

'Not a very wise move on his part,' I said, playing devil's advocate. 'You don't spend conspicuously if you'd rather people didn't wonder where the money's coming from.'

'Anyway,' he went on, blind to logic where Kinsella was concerned. 'He slipped up, didn't he?'

So you say, I thought.

'I had a tip-off,' he explained. 'Big shipment of heroin – and I mean big, street value close to five million – due to arrive at Harwich. I knew the day, the time, the truck and the destination. The only detail I was missing was how many fried eggs the driver would have for breakfast. Couldn't have been easier. So I relay all the information to Kinsella. And he takes over the operation. Sets up the raid. But pretends it's a drill. Test of the squad's reactions, it's supposed to be. "Too big," he says to me, "to take any chances. No-one must know except us two."'

'So what went wrong?'

'Everything, that's what.' Collins drew on the cigarette introspectively. 'Lorry arrives at Harwich. Two cars follow until it reached the drop-off point. Kinsella shouts, "Go. Go. Go." And twenty officers find that the stuff has gone, gone, gone.'

'How reliable was your source?'

'Immaculate,' Collins said. 'Never let me down before.'

'Always a first time.'

Collins laughed scornfully. The smoke from the cigarette caught in his throat. A spasm of coughing resulted.

'You think so,' he said when he had recovered his breath. 'Is that why my snout was found in a quarry with a bullet between his eyes?'

'Point taken.' I tried to clear the vision from my mind. 'But no-one believed you when you accused Kinsella?'

'Waste of breath,' he said. 'It was put down to sour grapes over Louise. And, when the dust settled, I finished up with a free transfer to the third division, like some played-out footballer. Kinsella stayed on in the Premier League of the Drugs Squad.'

'Sounds like you were lucky to hang on to any sort of job in the force. Why didn't they fire you? After all, you had hit a superior officer.'

'Kinsella refused to make a complaint.'

'Can't be all bad, then.'

'Wise up, Shannon. It was a deal that Kinsella cooked up. Louise walked out on me the day I hit him. Kinsella must have telephoned her. Told her everything that had happened. That I'd been suspended, too. Her bags were already packed and lined up in the hall by the time I arrived home. It was the last straw, she said. It was then that she told me everything. And spelt out the arrangement – the accommodation – we had to reach. I was to leave her alone. Let her get on with her new life. In return, I wouldn't have to face a disciplinary board.'

Had he again put job before wife? Or had he appreciated that Louise was a lost cause? Finally seen the wisdom of damage limitation? A case of salvaging what he could from the sorry mess?

He reached again for the comfort of his cigarettes. Found that his pack was empty. Somehow it seemed like a cruel metaphor for his life.

I offered him one of mine. We both lit up. Sat there for a while silently sharing the pain of the past.

'I know it's not much consolation,' I said, 'but at least there weren't any kids caught up in the separation.'

'Thanks a bunch,' he said, grinding the butt in the ashtray. 'Well, Shannon. Are you happy now?'

'Pass me the Glenshield file,' was my answer.

'Bit of a problem,' he replied, frowning. 'I can't find it. It's probably here somewhere,' he waved a helpless hand across the desk, 'but...'

'Great,' I said angrily. 'So I have no background information on Glenshield. No company searches. No accounts. I go in there completely in the dark.'

Collins shrugged.

'I assume,' I said in pointless clarification, 'that the anonymous letter you received was in the file?'

He nodded. 'Don't fret, Shannon. It'll turn up.'

'I hope you're right,' I said anxiously. Not only was I entering Glenshield blindfolded, but also out on a limb, it seemed. With no physical evidence of the original tip-off, I was totally dependent on Collins to back me up if the situation turned sour. It wasn't a very comforting thought.

'There's nothing else I should know, I suppose?'

'What do you want, Shannon? Blood? Haven't I bared my soul enough for you?' He rocked back in the chair and stared up at the ceiling. 'No,' he said finally. 'There's nothing else I can tell you.'

Maybe I should have been more precise with my question.

Because it certainly sounded as though he was being very precise with his answer.

CHAPTER TEN

'I'm not sure how much more of this I can take,' Arlene groaned. Sleepily, she stretched out a languid hand and felt around for the button to silence the insistent beeping of the alarm. 'What time is it?' she yawned. 'Jesus, what day is it, for that matter?'

I knew how she felt. It was six o'clock on Thursday evening and my body clock was busy canvassing support from all the major organs in order to hit me with a petition demanding an immediate change of lifestyle.

The past two days had seen us struggle to make the unnatural switch from diurnal to nocturnal. Our normal (huh!) pattern since Tuesday had been to leave the flat by eight, take a minicab to Latimers, the private gambling club, then a taxi back home at four o'clock in the morning when the place closed. In between, we played bridge downstairs, took a turn at the roulette wheel and blackjack table upstairs, and generally talked a little too loudly about my misfortune – the dire need to find a job, and damn quickly too. We reserved the loudest of our conversations for the area around the cashiers' stations. On each floor a cashier in shirt-sleeves (no jacket equals fewer pockets) stood protected by a reinforced glass enclosure – and a green-uniformed Glenshield guard. From the lack of result so far, it appeared that Glenshield's recruitment policy was based on positive discrimination towards the hearing-impaired.

'One more try,' I said. 'If nothing happens to-night, then it almost certainly never will. I'll have to think of a different approach – something a lot less subtle.'

And a lot more dangerous, I thought.

'Maybe,' she suggested gingerly, rolling over to look me in the face, 'we should deliberately lose tonight. That would give you something else to complain about, wouldn't it? And make landing a job even more important?'

'I suppose so,' I said unenthusiastically.

Losing was a tactic I'd hoped to avoid. There was the problem of the stake money. I wasn't quite sure how Collins had managed to come up with the five thousand pounds – or what the consequences would be if I lost it all. Collins wasn't as skilled as the Commander in the political art of backside-covering: I couldn't guarantee that somehow it wouldn't be me who finished up as the one with egg on my face and a big fat IOU to settle.

There was another reason, of course. One that I found hard to admit even to myself. I'd lost more than enough in the last eight years – sister, parents, the chance of a PhD and a cosy life in the hallowed halls of academia lecturing in difficult sums, liberty, and two fingers – and the

117

thought of losing anything else, albeit deliberately, didn't seem right. It upset my sense of justice, threatened my pride, and created superstitious anxieties about continuing the hard-to-swallow pattern of the past into the future.

'What is it you English love saying?' Arlene asked. 'It's not winning or losing that's important. But how you play the game.'

'To paraphrase Bill Shankly,' I countered, 'bridge isn't a matter of life and death. It's more important than that.'

Arlene frowned.

'But maybe you're right,' I said, purely as a means of closing the subject. 'Let's just see what happens, shall we?' I paused and added, 'Whatever I ask of you tonight, just do it quickly and without question.'

'Sounds interesting,' she said girlishly, snuggling up against me.

'Come on,' I said. 'Time to get up.'

'Just ten minutes more,' she pleaded. 'After all, there's a lot we have to discuss.'

'Like what?'

'Like whether we have breakfast, tea or supper before we go.'

The minicab pulled off Piccadilly and dropped us alongside the discreetly anonymous brass plaque and solid steel door of Latimers. Throughout the journey Arlene had sat making minor adjustments to her hair, the midnight-blue dress and silver jewellery, all in a concerted effort to stifle a fit of giggles as the driver engaged me in unwanted conversation. She had formed the hypothesis that not one single minicab driver in the whole of London is in actuality a minicab driver. Unwittingly, each example of the singular breed that we encountered had added weight to her theory. According to these drivers it was always a purely temporary job, a frustrating intermission while they were waiting for an injury to heal before they could resume their true career (generally something like brain surgeon, opening bat for England, chairman of ICI or lead tenor in Wagner's Ring Cycle).

'Told you so,' Arlene grinned as we waited in the lobby.

'Don't be so cynical,' I said. 'For all you know he may well *be* the next Eric Clapton – it was a big plaster on his finger, you have to admit. Could have been string-burn, like he said.'

Before my face totally collapsed in laughter, Stapleton, the club's Director of Bridge and resident professional, arrived. He was immaculately dressed as ever, his jet black hair matching the dinner suit. Tall, he bent his head down to greet Arlene and his chiselled features softened into a warm smile.

'So good to see you again, Mrs Tucker. And you too, Mr Shannon. If you would both be so kind as to sign the book as my guests.'

In spite of my past service to Latimers – exposing a pair of cheats – the club could not quite bring itself to offer me membership. Not that I was unduly bothered: five thousand pounds a year was way out of my price bracket. But Stapleton, although a stickler for the rules,

119

had a charmingly old-fashioned sense of fair play. He had slipped me a wink and promised to sign me in whenever I wished.

'Which table tonight, Mr Shannon?' he enquired.

'Top?' I asked Arlene.

'Whatever you say, Nick,' she replied without the merest hint of the uncertainty she must have felt.

The bridge room at Latimers contains four tables – identical but for the stakes played at each. At the top table it was a pound a point per player (or a hundred pounds a hundred, as more usually expressed by the British). We had avoided the top table over the last two evenings in order to conserve our stake money – at a pound a point, if the cards weren't smiling on you, each member of the partnership could lose a couple of grand in the space of one quick rubber (the best of three games). Since tonight was the last shot at the original plan – and 'needs must when Collins drives' – the adrenaline-promise of the top table was irresistible. It also provided the best showcase and the biggest audience.

Stapleton swung open the double doors to the bridge room and led the way across the dark red, deep-pile carpet to the cashier. Because gambling debts are unenforceable in law – someone should have told Redmond that! – the rule at Latimers was that cash, bankers' drafts or promissory notes had to be deposited before play commenced. At the cashier's booth on the top floor, chips were given in exchange; down here in the more rarified atmosphere of the bridge room, a stamped note was handed back as proof of deposit. Arlene opened her bag and slid the bundle of cash – now increased to five thousand seven hundred pounds from our efforts over the past two nights – through the gap underneath the glass.

'This is the very last time,' she said loudly. 'You know I don't agree with this. It's irresponsible, you know? After tonight you either find yourself a job – or someone else to bankroll you.'

'Yeah, yeah,' I said sullenly, turning my back to the cashier and the guard in mock embarrassment and looking out across the room.

No wonder the membership fees were so high. The room was a stunning extravagance, never failing to take my breath away, no matter how many times I played here. At forty feet by thirty, it occupied almost half the lower floor of the Regency building – the rest being the dimly lit restaurant (secret business deals and even more secret liaisons), the plush bar (drowning of sorrows), the kitchen (tantrum-throwing French chef and cowed brigade) and a suite of administrative offices (the counting houses). The ceiling was so high that they must have needed oxygen masks to clean the four chandeliers hanging below the ornate stuccoed roses. Directly beneath each chandelier was sited one of the card tables – rich, lustrous, walnut-veneered examples of Victorian folly, four long sides where the players sat, four short sides from which small flaps could be slid out to accommodate drinks, score cards and ashtrays. There were no baize cloths at Latimers: it would have been an act of sacrilege to conceal the deep shine of the sweetly smelling beeswaxed wood. The walls were clad in the most expensive paper I had ever witnessed, thickly embossed with dark blue and maroon stripes separated by wafer-thin columns of gold. It ran up to abut the mahogany picture rail, and from there duck-egg blue paint took over, flowing into and across the ceiling.

'I wanted them to copy this room for the restaurant at the Windsor Club,' Arlene said in reverential tones, her eyes following my gaze. 'Thank goodness they didn't go along with the idea – then I really would have been responsible for it going bust.'

Taking her hand, I squeezed it gently.

'Come on,' she said with a sigh. 'Let's play.'

We walked hand-in-hand to the circle of chairs surrounding the top table and seated ourselves quietly so as not to disturb the concentration of the players.

'Who are these two pairs?' Arlene whispered.

'The pair sitting sideways on to us is Bevan and Stilgoe. More money than card sense – I doubt whether we'll be playing them. The other pair is Tomaso,' I nodded towards a swarthy man with dark, tightly curled hair, 'and Brean.' This time I moved my head in the direction of a grey-haired man in his late fifties, with a frown that seemed to have been etched onto his face.

'Tomaso,' I summarised, 'is Italian; a little too temperamental for his own good; reasonable player but impulsive; better defending, when his partner can slow the tempo, than as declarer; best of all when dummy, some say. Brean, on the other hand, is solid; knows all the percentages, and all the angles. Brean will give you nothing. Except misleading body language. Don't trust him an inch. He has a habit of hesitating to try to make you misjudge the placement of the cards. If you're missing a king and Brean sighs or plays slowly when you lead through him, then he almost certainly hasn't got it.'

Arlene rolled her eyes. 'Another one who doesn't subscribe to the theory about it being how you play the game that's important, huh?'

I shrugged. Being bracketed with Brean – if that was what Arlene had intended – wasn't a very flattering thought.

'Table up,' Brean called, as the losing pair of Bevan and Stilgoe signed the cashier's chitty and vacated their seats.

'That's our cue,' I said to Arlene. 'Remember what I told you, okay?'

'You bet,' she said huskily, lightly touching my knee and rising in one movement.

Concentrate, Shannon, I ordered myself. Think of the cards.

Tomaso spread the pack face down and we each selected a card to decide choice of seating position, colour of pack and dealer. Brean drew the highest. Superstitiously – but I would have done the same – he chose to remain where he was and to retain deal with the red pack: when you've just won with that combination, you don't for a moment contemplate changing either element.

I sat on Brean's left, lit a cigarette to quell the fluttering butterflies in my stomach, and cast a quick glance around the audience. The kibitzers were mostly familiar faces. A few were busily engaged in agreeing side-bets on the outcome of the match, and one newcomer was anxiously consulting his watch, as if eager for us to finish so that he might take our place at the table.

Arlene shuffled the cards and passed them across the table for me to cut. Brean dealt, slowly and precisely.

There are two distinct parts to the game of bridge. First comes the auction, where the partnerships exchange information through their bids and attempt to buy the contract. Contracts bid and made are scored 'below the line' and count towards game. Bonuses for overtricks, slams and winning the rubber, and penalties for failing to make the contract, are scored 'above the line'. When the bidding stage has been completed, the play commences and that is when the fun really starts.

Brean examined his cards and barked, 'One Club.' Tomaso tapped the table to alert us that this was an artificial bid: in their system it showed a strong hand, saying nothing about the club suit. (An anecdote goes that one of a pair of little old ladies opened One Club. Her partner, on being questioned as to whether the bid was natural or artificial, replied, 'Of course it's natural. If it had been artificial she would have bid *A* Club.')

Tomaso, as time was to prove to his embarrassment, overrated his cards and gave a positive response – his correct bid of One Diamond would have warned his partner he was weak. Brean finished up one trick short in a hopeless contract of Four Spades.

Just fifty points to us, but the comfort of knowing they had wasted a decent hand.

Over the course of the next two hours fortunes flowed back and forth. We took the first rubber and a net gain of fourteen hundred points; Tomaso and Brean fought back to level the match by winning a tight second rubber, recouping just six hundred points in the process.

Arlene dealt the blue pack for the first hand of the decider. Passed with alacrity. Brean opened One No Trump, Tomaso raised to Three and the first game rolled in.

The next deal was the one shown below (an 'x' indicating any card of nine or less).

Tomaso

♠ K x
♥ A J x
♦ A K Q x
♣ K Q 10 x

Me

♠ A x x x x x
♥ x x
♦ J x
♣ A x x

Arlene

♠ Q J 10 x
♥ 10 x x x x x
♦ x x x
♣ None

Brean

♠ x
♥ K Q
♦ 10 x x x
♣ J x x x x x

125

Brean dealt and passed. I opened Two Spades, in our system a 'nuisance' bid designed to hamper the opponents' communications: it showed between six and ten points (four for an ace, three for a king and so on) and a spade suit of exactly six cards.

Tomaso doubled, asking his partner to bid his best suit. Arlene correctly judged that we had to sacrifice – to buy the contract, although it was unmakeable, in order to stop our opponents getting a game and wrapping up the match. Ignoring her long but ragged heart suit, she supported my spades by jumping to Four.

Brean scowled – at least it made a change to frowning. He could work out that Tomaso was strong – Arlene and I had both shown limited hands – but had no way of knowing exactly how strong. On the principle of 'if unsure, bid one more', Brean bid Five Clubs. It was the right decision. Or would have been, had he not been playing with Tomaso.

The Italian reasoned, greedily, that if Brean could bid Five, then his hand was worth a raise to Six.

With my two aces I doubled, raising the stakes.

Everyone passed – Tomaso with a red face, Brean with a wider scowl.

'Your lead, partner,' I said quickly.

Arlene swiftly laid the queen of spades on the table.

'Director,' Brean boomed, summoning Stapleton.

'What is the problem?' Stapleton enquired.

'It should have been Shannon's lead,' Brean

replied, 'and this lady has led the queen of spades out of turn. What are my rights?'

Brean knew the rule book inside-out and back to front. Was well aware of his position. But he saw a faint glimmer of hope for his contract and needed Stapleton's authoritative ruling to stem any objections.

'Well,' said Stapleton, 'you can accept the lead if you wish, in which case your partner becomes declarer.' Brean shook his head – there was no way he was going to take the risk of Tomaso misplaying the hand. 'Or,' continued Stapleton, 'the lead reverts to Mr Shannon. If you take that option you can either insist on a spade lead or prohibit a spade lead.'

'In that case,' Brean said, 'I prohibit a spade lead.'

I played the ace of clubs, studied dummy, then gathered up the first trick. One more required to beat the small slam contract and stop them scoring a bonus of seven hundred and fifty points.

I laid the ace of spades on the table.

'You can't do that,' Brean said officiously.

'Why not?' I asked. My God. Was that a smile spreading across his face?

Brean turned to Stapleton for support.

'I'm afraid the prohibition continues to apply, since you are still on lead.'

'What do I do then?' I asked helplessly.

'You must lead another suit,' Stapleton said. 'And, I'm afraid, because you have shown the ace of spades, it becomes a major penalty card. You must leave it face up on the table and play the card at the first legal opportunity.'

The kibitzers groaned, seeing all too clearly what was about to happen.

Brean won my heart lead on the table, drew the remaining trumps and cashed the three top diamonds. On the third diamond I could not follow suit. So was forced to discard. The ace of spades.

Brean triumphantly tabled his cards, claiming the rest of the tricks.

'Small slam, game and rubber.' He scribbled a set of calculations on his scorecard. 'That's eighteen hundred and forty points in total,' he crowed.

Arlene threw her cards into the middle of the table. 'That's the last straw, Nick. For someone with no money and no prospects you sure know how to make matters a whole lot worse. I want every last cent repaid. Understand? Perhaps that will teach you some sense.' She snatched up her handbag. 'I've had just about enough of you. I'm going.'

I ran after her as she strode across the room.

'I'm sorry,' I said, catching her up as she reached the cashier's station. 'I wasn't concentrating. Too wrapped up in the problem of finding a bloody job. I should have put it out of my mind. Thought only of the cards. Maybe then I would have come up with a solution – it often works that way.' I gave a long drawn-out sigh and shook my head dejectedly. 'You can't afford to think about anything else when playing bridge.'

'Can't afford is right,' she said, handing her stamped note and scorecard to the cashier.

'I'll pay you back,' I said. 'I promise.'

'Some hope,' she said. 'We're finished, Nick.'

'Listen to me,' I pleaded. 'We could have defeated that contract. Stupid bloody rules. It's not fair.'

'Wise up, Shannon,' she said dismissively. 'Life's not fair. And it's about time you realised that. Goodnight. And goodbye.'

She scooped up the depleted pile of cash – now reduced to less than four thousand seven hundred pounds – without even looking. Turned on her heels. Marched haughtily from the room, eyes fixed firmly in front.

I shrugged my shoulders at the cashier and the Glenshield guard.

'Women,' I said. 'Who needs them?'

She was waiting outside on the pavement.

'I'm proud of you,' she said, giving me a hug.

'Huh?' I said innocently.

'"Your lead, partner." Then banging down the ace of spades.' She kissed me on the cheek. 'You knew the rules. And how Brean would insist on enforcing them. It can't have been easy to throw the match.'

'Thanks for playing your part so well,' I said. 'I'm sorry it was all in vain.'

'But it wasn't,' she said, smiling. 'This was on top of the bundle of cash.'

It was a business card. *Gerry O'Kane. Operations Director. Glenshield.* In pen had been added the instruction, '8.55 a.m. tomorrow. My office. Don't be late.'

I grabbed Arlene and danced her up the street.

129

'Accounts Department here I come,' I sang. 'Easy peasy, lemon squeezy.'

I was singing a different tune the next morning.

Well, how was I to know that someone up there had a warped sense of humour?

The bloody green uniform didn't even fit.

CHAPTER ELEVEN

Gerry O'Kane was the sort of man who regarded hyperactivity as, well, *frankly, just not good enough.*

'But I'm an accountant,' I said. For the third time.

Gerry O'Kane looked up from the three separate heaps of paper he was busily signing simultaneously. Paused for the briefest moment, frozen in time like Rodin's 'Doer' (the complementary sculpture to 'The Thinker' – never completed because the model could not keep still). He took another gulp of coffee from the polystyrene beaker that seemed to have been grafted onto his left hand. Inside his body, caffeine and adrenalin were engaged in a desperate battle for control of his system.

'You still here?' he said, blinking absentmindedly. The pen-holding hand pushed the new uniform back across the desk in my direction.

The green pile had been oscillating backwards and forwards on the desktop like a time-bomb primed to explode. I didn't want it. And he certainly had no intention of taking it back.

'Didn't I hear that you were unemployable?' he said, without looking at me, his jet-propelled pen scratching away again.

'But...'

'Then be grateful we're offering you a job at all.' O'Kane's accent was predominantly flat-vowelled North London, but I detected a lingering trace of his native Irish. I waited for the 'at all' to be repeated.

The phone rang, drawing an accusing glance from O'Kane. He snatched up the receiver. Clamped it to his ear by bending his head down and his shoulder up like some clerical equivalent of the Hunchback of Notre Dame. Still, as far as O'Kane was concerned, it was another important mission accomplished – both hands free.

This was the fourth such interruption in the last ten minutes. His responses to the calls had become predictable by now. 'I'll brief you later.' 'Tell him this afternoon – I'll talk to him then.' 'Don't do anything until I get there.' I had the mental picture of an army of people sitting at desks throughout the building (throughout the world, for all I knew) drumming their fingers in frustration. A motionless sea of employees, biding their time in anticipation of a change in the tide, and a task about to be finally delegated.

I coughed in a greedy attempt to seize more than the ten per cent of concentration he was currently allocating me.

So far, in response to the job offer, I'd been through incredulity and umbrage. I had only one other option to try.

'But it's just that you'd be wasting my talents,' I said.

'From what I've heard,' he responded, eyes focused on the desk, 'your talents seem to be disloyalty to colleagues and acting as Collins's punchbag.'

He looked at his watch, at the set of bound presentations in front of him, and then, wonder of wonders, actually at me.

'Look, Shannon,' he said. 'If you don't want the job, the door's right behind you. It makes no odds to me. On the other hand, if you deign to accept, then you have a golden opportunity to prove to us that you're more than just a run-of-the-mill bitter ex-con. Now, what is it to be?'

I picked up the pile of clothes.

'Seems I've just taken the first steps on the ladder of a whole new career,' I said. Best to take the only available opportunity until I figured out a way of engineering a transfer to Accounts. At least I was inside the company, if not exactly at what could be described as the hub of the business. 'I won't let you down, Mr O'Kane.'

'You better not,' he said. 'One slip and you're out on your ear. Clear?'

'As crystal,' I replied. 'But...'

'Jesus, can't you start a sentence without the word "but"?' he said.

'I was about to say that if I'm going to do this job efficiently, then I need to know a lot more about Glenshield.'

'You're only going to be on Reception, for chrissake. Not our bloody spokesman on corporate policy.'

'But,' I said, impishly enjoying the resulting wince, 'there's bound to be queries. I have to know what Glenshield does, and who handles what.'

'Okay,' he sighed. 'I'll get you an information pack. Will that make you happy? Can you start work then?'

I nodded brightly.

O'Kane rose from the desk and stared around.

It was a large room. You couldn't really call it an office: it was more a repository for row after row of tall, tilting towers of paper. There *were* filing cabinets, but purely ornamental it seemed – tall, three-drawer, reproduction oak affairs that matched the legs of his two desks (and, one would assume, the desktops themselves, but this was impossible to verify since not one square inch of the surface was visible to the naked eye). Even the inert computer had been used as storage space: the keyboard was covered in papers and the monitor had a Post-it sticker slap bang in the middle of the screen. O'Kane would have little time for computers. Didn't possess the patience to endure the start-up procedure. And anyway, he would probably say, if God had intended Man to use computers, he would have designed us with a neat little jackpoint behind the left ear for direct input.

O'Kane began to scurry about in a clueless treasure hunt for leaflets, brochures and other background material on Glenshield. The monoliths of stacked paper wobbled precariously with the vibrations of his hurried footsteps.

Maybe – although O'Kane's erratic movements

made me doubt it – there had once been a system here. Something Holmesian, perhaps, the chronology of each pile established by the height of its dust, or geologically determined by examination of the constituent layers in the rockface. I hoped that my clandestine activities would not necessitate a search in here. The odds on me finding anything specific seemed greater than Des O'Connor winning the *Top of the Pops* 'Best Vocalist Award' – female section.

Gerry O'Kane selected a folder here, a sheaf of paper there. All the while he was dashing about, he still somehow managed to drink his coffee.

He was making me feel dizzy. I closed my eyes. Blanked out the sight of Billy Whizz on uppers. Debated with myself as to whether, on his behalf, to call Workaholics Anonymous or the nearest hospital to put the Coronary Care Unit on stand-by.

'There you go,' he said with pride. 'Now get out of my hair.'

'Thank you for your time, Mr O'Kane,' I said, carrying the bundles of clothes and paper. 'And for the job.'

He gave a grunt – a useful addition to one's vocabulary when one's mind is perpetually locked on half a dozen other issues. I'd had my allotted time. My words bounced off an impenetrable wall.

'Merry Christmas,' I said, as I left the room.

'Yeah,' he said, scribbling away.

Two hours working at Reception and I was offering myself up to be certified brain-dead.

My official duties revolved around the constant repetition of phrases such as: *Good morning, sir. Thank you, sir. Please sign here, sir. Here's your pass, sir. Fourth floor, sir.* Still, I was kept on my toes. When a female visitor arrived, I had to substitute *madam* for *sir.* And at twelve o'clock there was the switch to *Good afternoon* to remember! And I had thought a parrot could do the job.

Unofficially my main, and more onerous, task was to sit quietly and listen to Charlie. Charlie was my superior. And a miracle cure for insomnia.

He was ex-army. Real ex-army, I mean. The sort of guy who goes into paroxysms at the sight of long hair – and orgasms at the merest whiff of blanco.

Charlie – wouldn't you know it? – had served just about everywhere. And for each place he had been posted, Charlie had an amusing little story or seven. Amusing, that is, if one is familiar with the workings of a field gun, the gear ratios of a tank or the floor plan of a Singapore brothel. I soon learned that the best tactic was to nod wisely in response to whatever he said. Without this signal to proceed, Charlie would (rightly) assume that a dismal lack of knowledge was causing me to miss the full nuances of his story – and then go on to explain the workings of a field gun, the gear ratios of a tank or the floor plan of a Singapore brothel!

As if this were not bad enough, the setting for my new job resembled a clearing in the jungles of Borneo. That wasn't just my opinion, it was Charlie's too – and he should know. Our desk was situated in the exact geometric centre of a tall atrium. The atmosphere was warm, humid and smelled as if Baby Bio were this month's special offer at the cash-and-carry. Palm trees towered above me, casting long shadows on the floor. At the edges of my field of vision, great green blobs seemed to creep stealthily, triffid-fashion, towards me. There was even a long green snake semi-concealed in the thick esparto grass. Okay, so it turned out to be just a hosepipe. It was an easy mistake to make – I didn't have Charlie's experience in these matters. Charlie said there were six important things you had to do if you ever came across a snake. Luckily, I can't remember any of them. I had learned early on that, whatever the subject, Charlie could teach you more than you ever wanted to know.

So the morning fairly flew by, what with the *Have a nice day* routine, the countless knowledgeable nods at Charlie and the odd snatched glance through the background material. From time to time I looked longingly upwards at the four floors where the real work – and whatever else – was going on. So near, and yet so annoyingly far.

During the afternoon my frustration increased exponentially. To make matters worse, it was Friday: if I didn't get a chance to snoop around upstairs today, then I would have to spend all weekend fretting over missed opportunities. And endure Norman incessantly making quips like, 'I love it when a plan comes together.'

O'Kane came and went several times in blurs reminiscent of an amateur photographer's first attempt at snapping a racing car on the straight at Brands Hatch. Even when hopping into minicabs the beaker of coffee was still in his hand. Maybe he'd been born that way, I decided – grafting it on seemed a bit extreme, after all.

At ten to five the POETS Day exodus began with a whimper, as the first dribble of employees filed out of the glass-sided lifts to scurry home.

At five to five the despatch rider arrived.

'Parcel for Mr O'Kane,' he said. 'Very urgent,' he added, to my complete non-amazement. 'Sign here, please.'

I felt like telling him he'd stolen my line, but I autographed his clipboard without comment.

'I'll take this straight up, shall I, Charlie?' I said hopefully.

He consulted his watch thoughtfully.

'As long as you don't expect to be paid over-time,' he said.

'Worth a try,' I said, picking up the parcel.

I stood up. Slid the ill-fitting trousers down onto my hips so that the bottoms came only an inch above my heavy-duty, Glenshield-issue boots. This had the comic effect of lowering the crotch by three inches: now it looked as though I had received a testicle transplant from a prize bull. Self-consciously, I crossed the wide open space of the Reception area – always be alert, Charlie had counselled, for the danger of falling coconuts – and entered the lift.

I had thought that the glass sides would make the journey more bearable. Less claustrophobic it may have been, but the sensation when travelling upwards was extremely disconcerting.

It was just about – but not quite – as reassuring as being suspended by invisible strands of dental floss from a hot-air balloon. I clung onto the side rails and hoped no-one was watching.

The first three floors followed an identical layout. A narrow walkway-cum-gallery provided a view over the atrium and innumerable access points between glass partitions to the circular open-plan work area. At tightly packed desks, perspiring men and glowing women stared hypnotically at monitors or sat hunched in concentration as they transferred sheet after sheet of paper from one tray on their left to the other on their right.

Everywhere was the proverbial hive of activity.

Except that bees are probably better organised.

O'Kane seemed to have been adopted as the role model for 80 per cent of the men and women in the building.

No-one walked here.

They darted, dashed, raced, rushed – whatever Roget lists under the word 'run', these people did it with a vengeance, if not enthusiasm. This was headless chicken country. The demon of thought had been successfully cast out of the body corporate and replaced by a living tribute to the pagan god of work-rate. It was the sort of place where, given the slightest encouragement, they would all line up on the edge of the cliff and justify their future action by chanting, 'A million lemmings can't be wrong.'

The fourth floor – directors and senior staff – was probably the same, but here the work took place behind closed doors rather than in the full glare that open-plan harshly provides. Despite the overpowering urge to hurry that the ambience bred, I sauntered along the corridor familiarising myself with the layout. I passed brushed-aluminium plates bearing impressive titles like Personnel Director, Marketing Director, Public Relations.

Then I found it.

The Accounts Department.

I knocked and entered without waiting for a reply.

'Mr O'Kane?' I said, casting my eyes round the room.

Six people looked up from their computers and regarded me pitifully.

I stepped further into the room and addressed a bespectacled man frantically inputting invoices onto the system. On his screen I recognised the template. At least, if the time ever came, I would not have any problems with the program.

'Mr O'Kane?' I repeated.

'Along the corridor,' he said with very precise diction. 'Third office on the left. You'll notice that the name-plate is slightly out of alignment.' He frowned. Peered at me over the top of his glasses. Registered the cut of my trousers, and shuddered. 'If you come to Mr Kinsella's room then you will have gone too far.'

'Sorry,' I said. 'I only started today. Confusing, isn't it?'

'Not if you read the signs on the doors it isn't.'

'Well, thanks anyway,' I said. Have a nice day seemed redundant now.

Outside, I tried to call up a mental picture of

everything I had seen. Six clerks. One man – the anal-retentive Mr Precision. Five women, one about twenty-four, pretty, auburn hair, brown eyes, good bone structure, nice figure, smart clothes – but I wasn't really paying that much attention. Connecting door to the next office, 'S. Paradine – Finance Director' in white letters on a black plastic plaque: fleeting glimpse of blue-eyed blond Adonis checking to see if any of his staff had dared to leave on time. Lots of cabling leading from the terminals – networked, without a doubt. Distinctively coloured folders, recognisable logo, for the filing of bank statements. Pinned on the walls, various schedules as reminders of payroll dates, PAYE and VAT deadlines, cheque runs and so on; a holiday planner ('Beryl to Ibiza' in big red letters with three exclamation marks at the end); and one of those omnipresent signs that had once been funny back in the Middle Ages saying, 'You don't have to be mad to work here – but it helps!'

As a reconnaissance mission behind enemy lines it wasn't exactly what might be termed 'information-rich'. But, I told myself philosophically, it was a start. There wasn't much else to show for my first day, except for a comprehensive grasp of the order in which a field gun should be stripped down.

I had just reached my legitimate destination when I saw a door begin to open along the corridor.

'Any time,' a voice said.

My blood turned to ice.

140

I'd have known that voice anywhere.

I flung open the door of O'Kane's office and burst inside.

If I'd delayed for a millisecond longer, then I would have come face-to-face with someone I did not want to meet. Someone I shouldn't – by all logic – be meeting. Not here. Not now.

It was interesting to speculate on which of us would have been more shocked by the chance encounter.

Me?

Or Cherry Walker?

Gerry O'Kane had yet to return from his latest meeting. Thank God! Otherwise my panic-stricken entry would have taken some explaining. Or perhaps he would just have assumed that I'd adapted to the Glenshield culture. Might not even have noticed, come to that.

I ran across to his desk. Deposited the parcel among the general chaos. Picked up the phone. Punched out my home number.

The engaged tone sounded in my ears.

'Come on, Norman,' I said. 'Get off the bloody phone.'

I cleared the line and stabbed at the redial button for a second attempt. Collins had to be told about Walker. And the sooner, the better, as far as I was concerned. My cover might have been blown but it was safer to stick to the agreed procedure. I needed Norman to set up a meet. A 'meet'? I was beginning to talk like someone out of *Tinker, Tailor, Soldier, Book-keeper.*

Still engaged.

I cursed Norman under my breath. Tried one more time to get through.

The handset was pressed to my ear as the door opened.

A large shape blocked out all light from the corridor.

'What do you think you're doing?'

'Won't keep you,' I said cheerily into the phone. I turned to face the shape.

'Do you know when Mr O'Kane will be back?' I asked.

'I asked you a question,' the man said.

'Just a minute,' I said to him, turning my attention back to the telephone. 'It seems no-one knows when Mr O'Kane will return. Can you try again later? Thank you very much for your patience.' I replaced the handset and smiled efficiently at my inquisitor.

'Just delivering a parcel for Mr O'Kane,' I said, pointing at the evidence. 'The phone rang. So I answered it.' I feigned a look of sudden enlightenment. 'Oh, no. A private phone call. That's what you think.'

'What's your name?' he said.

'Shannon,' I said. 'Nick Shannon. It's my first day.'

'I know. I've heard all about you.'

I groaned inwardly.

'Let me introduce myself,' he said, walking towards me. He was an inch taller than I. And built as if the whole forward row of the London Irish scrum had been welded together. He wasn't quite as big as Arthur — but then no-one's quite as big as Arthur.

142

'Kinsella,' he said, extending his hand. 'Roddy Kinsella.'

Gulp, I thought.

'My office,' he said. 'Now.'

I followed him along the corridor. He was strangely light on his feet for such a heavily built man, like the product of some bizarre genetic experiment that had built a hybrid from a combination of DNA from Geoff Capes and Wayne Sleep.

Anyway, you can guess which office was his, can't you?

Right first time.

The one Cherry Walker had so recently left.

CHAPTER TWELVE

'Are you a good servant or a bad master, Shannon?' Kinsella said.

It was a difficult question at the best of times. Even harder to answer when you can feel the residual warmth of Walker's backside rising up from the seat of the chair. And when the sweet smell of her perfume is still lingering in the air.

At least I knew to what he was referring. It is said that there are only two types of accountants – good servants, and bad masters.

'All generalisations are dangerous,' I said. 'Even this one.'

'Alexandre Dumas,' he said to my surprise. '*Fils*, that is – not the one who wrote *The Three*

143

Musketeers.' He smiled at me.

Fifteen-love.

Nimble of foot and nimble of mind, it seemed. I made a mental note not to underestimate Kinsella. This wasn't Collins I was dealing with.

'So what's the answer to my question?'

'I suppose it must be good servant,' I said. 'I wouldn't be wearing this uniform if I considered myself a master, bad or otherwise.'

'Unless it's a sign of desperation, rather than an indicator of character.'

'Maybe it's both,' I said, nodding.

'Maybe,' he said thoughtfully, raising his wide shoulders in an economical gesture of reinforcement. The material (silk?) of his light-grey hand-stitched jacket made a very faint whispering sound with the movement. His shirt was pale blue, button-down collar; the tie navy and red stripes. He looked more like a Harvard graduate – even had the drastically short, Charlie-approved haircut – than the head of a security firm. He made me feel like a dummy from the window display at Oxfam.

'So how was your first day, Shannon?' he asked. His voice, like Arthur's, was very low – I suppose it comes with the build, everything buried deep inside. But, unlike my friend's Cockney vowels, Kinsella's delivery was as polished as the rest of him. If ever a trace of the hybrid Scottish-Irish background had existed, it had been successfully neutralised over the years.

'Not the biggest intellectual challenge I've ever faced,' I said, hoping to lay the groundwork for a request to transfer to Accounts. 'Still, Charlie's a veritable mine of information. He's on Reception too,' I added helpfully.

'I know Charlie,' Kinsella said, a thin smile flitting across his lips. 'I like to get to know all my employees. But it's difficult nowadays. Price of success, eh?'

He paused. Unsure of the reply he was seeking, I thought it was my turn to shrug my shoulders. The synthetic fibres of the green uniform didn't have quite the same rich sound, though.

'Let me tell you a story, Shannon. There was once a company that was sliding down the tubes. Morale low. Staff turnover high. People off sick all the time with minor ailments that, in the past, they would have worked through quite happily. Get the picture?'

I nodded my head very slightly, mirroring his economy.

'So the Board calls in a firm of management consultants. Three months later – and a whole lot richer – they report back. "The mood of a company, Mr Chairman," they say, "stems from the very top. Your staff feel you don't care about them. That you can't even be bothered to spare the time to talk to them. What you must do is get out and about more. Communicate with your workers. Reassure them. Show them you're on the same wavelength. That, above all, you understand them." So the stuffy old Chairman embarks on a tour of his factories across the country. Still with me, Shannon?'

'Yes, Mr Kinsella,' I said, wondering where all this was leading.

'The next day the Chairman arrives at some

145

far-flung outpost of his empire. Climbs out of his chauffeur-driven Rolls-Royce and walks up to the man on the gate. "Do you know who I am," he says. "Yes, sir," the astonished worker replies. "You're the Chairman, sir." "Good man," the Chairman says. "And what's your name?" he asks. "Jenkins, sir." "Good man," the Chairman says, already struggling for conversation. "Worked here long?" he asks. "Seventeen years, sir." "Good man. Live around here, do you?" "Yes, sir. I live just out of town on the Barratt estate." "Good. Very good," the Chairman replies. "Tell me," he says with real interest, "what's the shooting like on the Barratt Estate?"'

I laughed. Not much, I admit. But it seemed the polite thing to do.

'It wasn't a joke, Shannon,' Kinsella said sternly and all too seriously. 'It was a story.'

'Sorry,' I said, confused.

'I feel a little like that Chairman, you know. We've grown so big, so quickly, I've lost touch with my people.' Kinsella sighed. 'Hell,' he said. 'You can't go back, I suppose.'

'I agree with you there, sir,' I said.

'I thought you would,' he said. 'But what would *you* do differently, if you had your time again?'

I thought with sadness of my sister. Knew I would do the same all over again under identical circumstances. Even allowing for prison.

'Not much,' I said. 'Except I would steer clear of Collins. I was beginning to put my life back together until he came along.'

'Ah, Collins,' he said.

Kinsella reached into the bottom drawer of his

desk. Took out a bottle of Bushmills finest Irish whiskey and two cut-glass tumblers. Poured a large measure for each of us.

'I don't know if I should,' I said, suspicious that this was some sort of test.

'Humour me,' he said.

'In that case,' I raised the heavy glass in salutation, 'thank you.'

'Don't thank me, Shannon. Just drink. Irish blood needs the taste of the old country every now and again. Your grandfather is Irish, isn't he?'

Kinsella had certainly done his homework. It wasn't only Walker he'd been talking to. She didn't know my ancestry, any more than my brand of toothpaste – and I had the uneasy feeling that Kinsella could tell me that, if pressed.

'He was born in Limerick,' I said. 'But he's lived most of his life in County Cork. Bantry Bay.'

'A fine place,' Kinsella said wistfully. 'Till they built the petroleum terminal.' He shook his head. 'And they call it progress.'

He sipped the whiskey, rolling it round on his tongue before swallowing.

'Now what are we going to do with you, Shannon?'

'I need this job, Mr Kinsella. Can't go back to my old firm – not after being kicked out of the Fraud Squad.'

I looked helplessly at Kinsella. Walker or not, there was no option but to bluff it out.

'I didn't do anything wrong,' I said. 'That's God's truth. On my grandfather's life.' Might as

147

well milk the Irish connection for all it was worth. 'Collins was just protecting his own. He stitched me up real tight. That's why I got so angry.'

'You had good grounds, it seems. Collins hit you too, didn't he?'

'Yes,' I said, pointing to the fading scratch on my cheek. 'This was caused by his wedding ring. I pity his wife. She must be a martyr to put up with him.'

'That's another story,' Kinsella said. 'Although maybe that one is a joke.'

He topped up our glasses. I waited for him to rise to the bait.

'Good servant?' he asked, returning to the original subject.

'Yes, sir,' I said hopefully.

'Well, let's give you a chance to prove it, shall we? We Irish must stick together,' he said, the amber liquid producing the hint of a lilt in his voice. 'Oh, what I wouldn't give to see Collins's face when he hears the news.'

There was a smile on his lips.

Christ, I'd done it!

'I'll need to speak to Paradine,' he said, thinking of the administrative arrangements. 'He's our Financial Director.'

Kinsella raised his glass pensively.

'Cheers,' he said, draining the last drops of the whiskey. 'Monday could well be your last day in uniform. The Accounts Department makes sense. It's where you should have been all along. Gerry probably had his mind on other things.'

Not probably, I thought. Definitely.

'Thanks for the whiskey,' I said. 'And for the job. You won't regret it.'

'If I do,' he said, locking steely-grey eyes on mine, 'you'll see a whole different side of me, I promise. When I'm angry, I can make Collins look like Mother Teresa.'

The twist of his lips told me he wasn't lying.

It was meant to be a smile.

In the hierarchy of smiles, this one ranked on a par with that on the face of an East End villain in the second before he nails your head to the floor.

Maybe the uniform wasn't such a bad fit after all.

Only joking.

There was a job to do.

Collins had made a promise too. We had a deal. I wasn't going to chicken out and give him any excuse to wriggle free from it.

Okay, so Kinsella could probably knock me into the middle of next week – and the one after, for that matter. But he couldn't hit as hard as the car that had smashed my sister's spine.

I left work without taking the time to change back into my suit. Stopped on the way home to make another attempt to phone Norman. Still engaged. Perhaps it was Arlene, not Norman, who was putting a smile on the face of Iain Vallance. A heart-to-heart with Mary Jo? Heart-to-purse, more like it.

When I arrived, Norman was on the computer. Again. This had all the hallmarks of an obsession in the making.

'Hi there,' he shouted over his shoulder.

'I've been trying to phone you,' I said. 'Kept getting the engaged tone.'

'Oh,' he said guiltily.

Arlene appeared from the kitchen. She gave me a welcoming hug. Then looked me up and down.

'I just love a man in uniform,' she said, giving me a playful squeeze.

'Uniform?' Norman said, intrigued enough to turn away from the screen.

'Don't say anything,' I ordered.

'Now would I?' he beamed. There was a pregnant pause while we all waited for his self-control to crumble. 'Another rousing success for strategic planning then?'

'What's with the phone?' I countered.

'Norman's acquired a new toy,' Arlene said.

'It's not a toy,' Norman said, offended.

'Yes, we've heard that before, Norman,' I said. 'Another legitimate business expense, I suppose.'

'It's a modem,' Arlene said, rolling her eyes. 'Norman has become "wired".'

I wondered if the word was an oral misprint – it is an anagram of 'weird' after all.

'When you go in for a new craze, Norman, you certainly don't bother with half-measures. Ever read *Wind in the Willows?*' I asked mischievously. 'Tell me, Mr Toad. What in heaven's name do you want with a modem?'

'Look,' he said defensively. 'Through the magic of the modem and the miracle of our telephone system, I am in touch with databases you haven't even dreamed of.'

'Wonder why that is?' I grinned.

'Ask me any question,' he said. 'I'll have the

150

answer in minutes.'

'I'd rather have a drink and the use of the phone, please.'

He sighed. 'Bloody Philistine,' he mumbled, calculatingly just loud enough for me to hear.

'I need you to make a call for me. Collins. It's very important. Otherwise I wouldn't have the temerity to spoil your fun – sorry, interrupt your work.'

Reluctantly, he logged off.

Arlene brought a bottle of white wine and three glasses.

And I told them about Walker.

'I just knew there was something about her I didn't trust,' was Arlene's reaction.

'Looks bad, I must admit,' said Norman.

'Well, you both certainly know how to cheer a man up,' I said. 'There could be a perfectly reasonable explanation.'

'Like what?' Arlene asked.

'Are you going to make that phone call, Norman?' I said.

'Thank you for answering my question,' Arlene said with self-satisfaction.

She wriggled up close to me while Norman spoke to Collins.

I sipped the wine. 'Chablis?' I asked her.

'Um,' she said seductively.

'All arranged,' Norman announced. 'You meet Collins at Walker's place tomorrow morning. Six o'clock.'

'Six o'clock!'

'Collins wants to surprise her.'

'Surprise her. At that time of the morning we'll

be lucky if she doesn't have a heart attack.'

'He also said he wanted to catch her when her defences were at their lowest.'

'Mine too,' I said.

'I must remember that,' Arlene chuckled. 'Still,' she said, 'it does give us the whole evening to ourselves. Norman has to go out.'

'Do I?' he said.

She frowned at him.

'I do,' he said. He looked at his watch. 'Well, well. Is that the time? I really must be going.'

He was out in three minutes flat. Pure cowardice, I thought. But diplomatic with it.

'Now,' said Arlene. 'Just enough time to get you out of that itchy uniform before dinner spoils.'

'What are we having then?' I asked as she unloosened my tie.

'Cold lobster!' she giggled.

CHAPTER THIRTEEN

I spotted Collins's Rover by the plumes of blue smoke exiting from the narrow slit of the driver's window. He had chosen a spot a hundred yards up the street from Walker's bedsit. As I parked the Lancia behind him, his head momentarily deflected a few degrees to the left to check me out in the rear-view mirror; then he reverted to staring straight ahead.

I climbed into the passenger seat and coughed. Not to attract his attention politely. But out of sheer necessity. The car was a passive-smoker's hell on Earth. I left the door open to enable the thick fug to clear. The ashtray was overflowing, yet somehow he managed to find enough room to stub out his latest cigarette. How many this morning, I wondered? Ten? Twenty?

'Bloody hell,' Collins said, turning his attention towards me for the first time. 'Early mornings don't flatter you, Shannon. Didn't sleep much last night?'

I nodded wearily.

'Worry, I suppose?' he said.

'Something like that.'

Distractedly, Collins flicked his hand across the trousers of his blue suit. The speck of ash he was attempting to remove spread into a three-inch line. 'So,' he said, sighing, 'tell me about Glenshield. What have you managed to learn so far?'

'Very little,' I said. It was true – up to a point. Although my main source of information had been the pack supplied by O'Kane, it had contained enough to set my devious mind whirring. But that was certainly not for Collins's consumption. Given the slightest excuse or encouragement, he would be screaming for warrants to search Glenshield. Have 'C' Squad mob-handed in there, creating more havoc than the running of the bulls in Pamplona – after taking a shortcut through the nearest Lladro shop.

'Financially speaking,' I said, playing my cards close to my chest, 'I suspect Glenshield is a roaring success – you can't squeeze every last drop from your employees and not fail to make a

153

big profit. Structurally, though, it's a house of cards – with a force-ten gale due imminently. They've simply grown too quickly. Can't handle it. Kinsella said as much himself.'

'But how have they grown so big, so quickly?' Collins asked perceptively, 'Kinsella's no Harvey-Jones. More Harvey Nicks.'

'All I've got to go on is a few brochures and press hand-outs, but it looks like you may have underestimated Kinsella.'

'Balls,' he said.

Collins – envy of the Laconians. Brief and to the point, although perhaps point is not exactly the right word, given the spherical context. Pity about the subjectivity of the reply, though.

'Look,' I said patiently, 'for one thing, Glenshield have been pretty good at finding gaps in the market. They're heavily into private policing. They pick an up-market area with plenty of money. The sort of classy estate where the residents are paranoid about burglaries, the Porsche being stolen, their daughters being got at. Then they guarantee to ring-fence it. Regular patrols, day and night, to keep out the criminal element. Successful too, if the figures are to be believed. I saw a chart on O'Kane's desk – your pen-pusher pal is Operations Director by the way.' Collins let out a loud groan, probably anticipating, as I had done earlier, the gargantuan size of any search operation. 'Anyway,' I continued, 'whenever Glenshield have taken over policing an area, the crime rate has dropped dramatically.'

'All Kinsella's doing is pushing the criminals

onto someone else's doorstep.'

'Maybe. But the people protected by Glenshield aren't going to lose any sleep over that. That's human nature. Nowadays the ruling philosophy is that of the NIMBY – Not In My Back Yard.'

'What else?' he asked hopefully.

'They're doing their bit for the country's balance of payments by exporting.'

'How can you export security, for chrissake?'

'There's plenty of countries where law and order is out of control. Glenshield ships in a battalion of security guards to take the pressure off an overstretched police force.'

'Mercenaries, eh?'

'You don't know that,' I said, my frustration mounting. 'Open your mind, will you? We're talking about newly formed Eastern European states with no experience of autonomy – been tied to Mother Russia's apron for so long that they're finding it hard to stand on their own two feet now that the strings have been cut. And South American countries trying to make some headway in the battle against the drug cartels. Places where they lack the resources or the know-how to combat crime. Probably both. Kinsella's not sending armed troops to fight civil wars in Africa.'

'You sound like his bloody Press Officer.'

I let out a sigh of exasperation. There was more to tell, but with Collins in this frame of mind there was little point. It would only provide another outlet for the venting of his spleen.

'Okay,' I said. 'I get the picture. Nothing's ever

going to change your opinion of Kinsella. But I'd like to make up my own mind. Okay?'

He shrugged his shoulders. Turned off the engine. 'All set?'

'I thought you were supposed to shout, "Go. Go. Go."'

'It is just the two of us, Shannon,' he said tetchily. 'And this is not *The Bill*.'

'Yes, Guv,' I said.

'And while we're on the subject,' he said with a wince, 'don't call me "Guv". Is that clear?'

'Early mornings aren't your strong suit either,' I commented.

'Come on,' he said. 'Let's go talk with Kinsella's mole.'

Did he say mole or moll? The more time I spent with Arlene, the more American I was becoming. Still, better that than Belgian. I yawned at the thought of it.

Quietly, we closed the car doors. The air had a bite to it. It was crisp. Ten miles up the road it would be crisp and fresh, but here in Hackney they had to make do with crisp. I zipped up my black leather jacket. Turned the collar up, James Dean-style. Silently practised the cynical 'uh huh' I would use in response to Walker's answers.

The street was almost empty, the only people up and about making their way to the hospital round the corner: the staff scanned the headlines of the newspapers they carried, while the rest wore blank expressions – only Intensive Care accepts visitors at this ungodly hour.

At ground level was a parade of shops, above which were flats and bedsits. The block had been

156

built in the early Fifties and was now owned by some anonymous landlord with short arms and long pockets. The paintwork was cracked and blistered, the guttering flaked with rust. Where a downpipe had broken, a green-black stalactite of a stain ran down the wall.

Walker's bedsit was over the baker's. The yeasty smell of bread baking drifted magnetically down the street, a sadistic, appetising cloud that made my gastric juices churn and produced a loud rumble from my stomach.

We mounted the concrete stairs two at a time, the muted sound of our tiptoeing feet waking a dozing black cat. It regarded us warily through one half-opened eye. I bent down to stroke the top of its head and it curled back into a ball, purring gently. Maybe, for its sake, I shouldn't get too friendly. The last black cat to cross my path had come to a sorry end. Finished up as an improvised door-knocker. I shuddered at the thought and moved on quickly.

On reaching Walker's door, Collins banged with his fist, policeman-style. I rang the bell. From within we heard a loud, unfeminine curse.

Two minutes later, the door opened as far as the chain would permit and Walker's face peered round the gap.

'Let us in, Walker,' Collins said.

'Do you know what time it is?' she said, quickly recovering from the shock of seeing us.

'Kinsella,' Collins said simply.

The chain slid back. The door opened wide. Walker motioned us wordlessly inside.

She was wearing a long pink wrap, tightly tied

around her narrow waist. Bare feet peeked out below the hem. Her shiny black hair, always so practically scraped back and pinned up for work, hung down to her shoulders.

We walked past the kitchen and bathroom and into the large all-purpose area that comprised the rest of the bedsit. Collins looked around professionally, making a mental inventory, and passing judgement on everything he observed. I tried to see it through his eyes, and to imagine the conclusions he would reach.

A double bed rested in one corner, the duvet thrown back to reveal a crumpled sheet. The dull red numerals of a radio-alarm clock on the bedside table blinked 6:10. In direct line of sight of the bed on the opposite wall was a portable TV on top of a square, white plastic garden table. Two cane chairs, second-hand judging by the multiplicity of scratches, their green cushions decorated with pink roses, were pointed slant-wise at the television. In between them was a round coffee table in light wood, a near-empty bottle of whisky and a lipstick-smeared glass sitting on top. The congealed remnants of a Chinese meal stuck to a plate on the bare surface of the drop-leaf dining table in the corner opposite the bed: *The Times* crossword was folded alongside the plate. Along the wall behind the door were two white melamine wardrobes and a small dressing table covered with an assortment of heavy, economy-sized jars and bottles.

Collins's eyes finally alighted on Walker. She stared back at him, arms folded across her chest.

'I thought you'd come to talk,' she said. 'Not to

research a feature for *House and Garden*.'

'Very good, Walker,' he replied. 'We've seen you can play the injured innocent. Now why don't we get straight down to the it's-a-fair-cop routine.'

'So what am I supposed to have done?' she said, the fig-coloured lips now as bitter and acid as a lemon.

'What were you doing at Glenshield yesterday?' he asked.

Walker rounded on me. 'You changed your bloody mind about going undercover, didn't you?' she said. 'And they say women are fickle! Why the hell didn't you tell me?'

'For one thing, you were supposed to be on holiday, remember?' I said, omitting the second, more important and more delicate, reason. Trust. Or the slight problem of a lack of it.

'Glenshield,' Collins said tenaciously in best bulldog fashion.

'I work there,' she said. 'Temping in the Personnel Department.'

'Yeah?' he said. 'Since when?'

'Since you told me to lose myself, that's when.'

'Need the money, Walker, do you?' he asked. 'A bit of extra cash wouldn't come amiss, eh?'

'No, sir,' she said.

Collins let his eyes rove ostentatiously round the room again.

'I like living this way,' she said, her voice a semitone higher and a decibel louder. 'All right?'

She breathed deeply: a controlled sigh or a sigh of control, I couldn't decide which.

'What's the point,' she said, 'of having a big place with loads of furniture. It's just more to

159

clean, that's all. And in our job, how much time do we get to spend at home, anyway? You for one should appreciate that, sir.'

'Maybe,' he said. 'But why moonlight at Glenshield if it's not for the money?'

'It's for you, if you must know!'

'Well, thanks Walker. Going to make a secret donation to my pension fund, were you? My early retirement suit you, would it?'

'Don't raise my hopes,' she said. 'But what chance is there of you ever retiring? There's only two ways you'll leave the force – on a stretcher in a body bag, or at the end of the Commander's boot. From your recent actions it seemed to me that you're dead set on going for the latter. I couldn't stand by and watch you commit professional suicide. So, Mr Kamikaze Collins, I decided to try to help you hang onto your job instead.'

Collins looked puzzled. He really didn't understand Walker. I knew what she was going to say, even if I still wasn't sure whether to believe her or not.

'Look, it's all very simple,' she said. 'I can explain everything.'

'I'm all ears,' Collins said.

'The problem, sir,' she said coolly, 'is that sometimes there's not much in the space between them.'

Collins shook his head at her. 'You've still got such a lot to learn, Walker. You're in enough trouble as it is. Don't make it even worse. Lesson number one: when you're in a hole, stop digging. Remember that in future.'

'You wanted the truth, sir. What's the matter? Can't you take it?'

'This isn't getting us anywhere,' I said, in an effort to unlock their horns. 'Can we cut the character analysis and just stick to the facts?' I smiled at Walker, screwed up my lips, and spoke in my best Joe Friday voice. 'Just give me the facts, ma'am,' I drawled.

She looked at me with a mixture of youthful bewilderment and well-matured scorn. I should have stuck to 'uh huh' after all.

'Shannon!' she said, the accompanying sigh drawn out until she was eventually forced to take a breath. She turned to Collins. 'And you wonder why I chose to get myself into Glenshield?'

He raised his eyebrows in reply.

Thanks a bundle, Collins, I thought. You are allowed to disagree with her, you know. Being a referee is a hard life.

'I learned from Nick,' she continued, 'or rather from his American mother-figure' – miaow – 'what you were planning. That you'd asked him to go undercover in Glenshield. And, in my humble opinion, sir, I thought it was a lunatic idea.'

Collins shook his head slowly from side to side. 'Lesson number two, Walker,' he said. 'The past performance of the Fraud Squad should have taught you one thing at least. We are reactive, not proactive. What we are good at is the painstaking job of gathering the evidence once we're aware that a fraud has been committed. What we're pretty hopeless at is uncovering the fraud in the first place. That's where Shannon comes into his own.'

'I beg to differ, sir,' she said, unrelenting.

'Beg as much as you like, Walker,' he retorted. 'But history's on my side.'

'Uh huh,' she said.

Damn. She'd beaten me to it.

'Did you ever stop to think, sir, just how much you were going out on a limb by pursuing this wafer-thin, anonymous tip-off about Glenshield? How much you were putting your job on the line? And all for the sake of a personal vendetta against Kinsella? Because that's what it looks like to me. And that's what it would look like to any jury.'

Collins opened his mouth, but Walker, Thatcherlike, was just pausing for breath.

'When Nick said he'd decided not to go along with your scheme, I knew you wouldn't abandon the idea. So I decided that if I couldn't stop you, then I had better help you. That's when I enrolled with an employment agency and got the temp job with Glenshield.'

'Very altruistic of you, Walker,' Collins said. I could almost see his tongue poking through his cheek. Perhaps he was starting to understand her after all. 'And you got a job,' he said, clicking his fingers, 'just like that?'

'Yes,' she said. 'Just like that. The staff turnover at Glenshield is astronomic. People join, find they can't stand the pace, and leave pretty damn smartish. There's more holes in the organisation than in a trainspotter's string vest. Glenshield is always crying out for temps to plug the gaps.'

'Sounds reasonable,' I said to Collins. 'It fits with my first impressions of the place. The company is dangerously close to reaching critical mass. Every nut and bolt in its corporate machinery appears to be strained to the limit. Any more stress and the whole operation will explode like a nuclear bomb.'

'It's not only temporary staff in the office either,' Walker added. 'They're even sub-contracting some of the security operations. Using guards from a number of small firms and just re-badging them – sticking them in Glenshield uniforms. All kept very hush-hush on both sides. Glenshield doesn't want it to leak out. And it's a nice, regular little earner for the sub-contractors.'

Something started to nag at my mind. Something I couldn't quite put my finger on.

'Tell me, Walker,' I said, hoping that the subconscious thought would rise to the surface, given a little time, 'what was the name of this employment agency you used?'

'Bishops,' she said with a puzzled expression. 'Why do you want to know?'

'Purely for future reference,' I answered, fingering the healing itch of the cut caused by Collins's ring. 'And Walker,' I said, carefully watching her face, 'what were you doing in Kinsella's office?'

She inclined her head to one side and frowned. 'You don't miss much, do you, Nick?'

'You're not easy to miss, Cherry.'

'I was simply doing my job, that's all. Taking in some forms for Kinsella to sign. Come to think of it,' she said, 'why haven't I seen any paperwork on you? All new employees – temporary or otherwise – are supposed to fill out a form with basic details.'

'Friday was my first day. I assume O'Kane is handling the admin.'

'In that case, the paperwork will probably arrive the day after you leave.'

'When you came out of Kinsella's office,' I pressed her, 'you said, "Any time". What did that mean?'

'Jesus!' she said, shaking her head sadly. 'What is it with you? Why can't you trust me? It was just one of those things you say, that's all. He thanked me for taking the forms in, I said, "That's all right. Any time." It was no big deal. I don't fancy him, if that's what you're thinking.'

No, that wasn't what Collins and I were thinking. At least not top-of-mind.

Collins looked at me questioningly. I raised my eyes in reply.

'I could do with some coffee,' Collins said to Walker. 'Why don't you take some clothes into the bathroom and get dressed. Then maybe you could make us all a cup?'

'I suppose you'd both like ground coffee?' she said. 'Takes longer, doesn't it?'

Collins nodded.

Walker grabbed a pair of faded blue jeans and a white sweatshirt from one of the wardrobes, a pair of briefs from the drawer of the dressing table, and left the room in a sulk. Collins closed the door after her.

'What are we going to do?' I asked, moving across to the table to check her success with the crossword.

'Do we believe her?' Collins asked straightforwardly. 'That's the only issue.'

'She's ambitious,' I said, with a wave of my hand. 'Burningly so. It's the sort of action she would take to safeguard her career. She's well aware that if you get terminally hauled over the coals, then the rest of us in 'C' Squad go up in flames with you.' I paused for thought. Picked up the crossword, revealing a half-inch thick computer print-out of unrecognised names and meaningless numbers. Smiled inwardly. She'd only managed about half a dozen clues. 'And you must admit,' I said, turning my attention back to Collins, 'it's not the smartest move you've ever made. She's right, you know. You should never have taken this job.'

'Look who's talking,' he said accusingly. 'This is the man who only agreed to help if I promised to re-open the file on an eight-year-old hit-and-run. Don't lecture me on letting sleeping dogs lie.'

Point taken.

'Why the hell did you let it slip about Glenshield, Shannon? All this could have been avoided.'

'Sorry, sir,' I said in formal apology.

For a moment there I'd almost said 'Guv'. Wanted, in order to demonstrate my sincerity, to call him 'Chris', but that was an even bigger taboo for his subordinates.

'Unfortunately,' I said, 'we can't turn back the clock. We have to analyse the situation we're stuck with. Go forward from there.'

'Okay,' he said. 'What have we got? Let's recap. Examine the Fraud Squad's record and what do you find? Look at the proportion of arrests, prosecutions and money recovered. We can't be that bloody inefficient, surely? It beggars even your low opinion of the police force. No. Someone, somewhere is on the take. Sounding the warning bells. Tipping off the villains before we move in. Giving them the chance to get rid of the evidence. Or, if it's a lost cause, at least enabling them to salt away the money where we can't lay our hands on it.'

'So who's the rotten apple in the barrel, eh?' I shook my head. 'I've worked with Walker for two months now. Somehow I can't believe it's her.'

'Can't believe?' he said, 'or don't want to believe?'

'Both, I suppose. In the end, what difference does it make? What have you got to lose by trusting her? If Walker is playing both sides, if she's blown my cover, then it's my head on the block. The worst – hopefully – that can happen is that I waste a few weeks digging around for evidence that no longer exists. And, don't forget, so far we can only link Walker with Kinsella. That makes one more assumption – that Kinsella is the villain of the piece.'

'He is,' Collins said. 'There's no doubt in my mind.'

'I would have passed out with shock if you'd said otherwise. But it's bricks without straw, sir. You'd love Kinsella to be up to his big, thick neck in something illegal, but – face the facts – there's nothing against him.'

'With Kinsella,' he said, running his hand over his lips, 'there never is.'

'My vote goes for trusting her. Let her stay on

at Glenshield. You never know, she may prove useful.'

'As you say, Shannon,' he said helplessly, 'what do I have to lose? But, just in case you are wrong about her' – what happened to 'we' all of a sudden? – 'let's play it tight. Strictly need-to-know basis where she's concerned. Agreed?'

'Agreed.' I'd already reached the same conclusion. No sense taking too many unnecessary risks.

'Well?' asked Cherry, when she brought in the coffee. 'Have you reached a verdict? Guilty? Or innocent?'

More like not proven, I thought.

'You stay on at Glenshield,' said Collins, avoiding the question.

'Good,' Walker said. She sat herself down on the bed and drank some coffee, holding the mug in both hands. 'So what have you found out, Nick?'

I dragged over one of the uncomfortable cane chairs and sat opposite her.

'Not much so far.'

'Tell me about Accounts. How does it seem? Any possible suspects?'

'Well,' I said. 'I'm not actually in Accounts yet.'

'And where are you – actually?' she asked.

'Reception,' I mumbled.

'Bloody great!' she laughed. 'If it's a minicab swindle, then you're in exactly the right place.'

'I'm working on it, Walker. Don't worry, I should be in Accounts on Monday.'

'Uh huh,' she said.

She'd done it again!

'Finish your coffee, Shannon,' Collins said. 'We've got business elsewhere.'

'It's good coffee,' I said, annoyed at being rushed. 'Can't I have a moment or two to linger over the rich aroma and smooth taste of my favourite arabica beans.' I was overplaying it, I knew: the brew had that thin, insipid aftertaste that comes only from staleness. But it was hot and sweet. And at this time of the morning I wasn't about to complain.

'I'll just use the bathroom,' he said. 'Then we go. Okay?'

At the door to the room he paused. 'Now behave yourselves, you two.'

I smiled. He meant me. This time, keep your mouth shut, Shannon.

'What do you want me to do, Guv?' she asked.

I frowned at her.

'Well, it seems you're in the driving seat for a change.'

'We could make a good team, Walker. Let's give each other a chance, shall we?'

She rose from the bed and stood in front of me.

'Okay,' she said. 'It's a deal. Shake on it?'

I took her hand in mine. It was soft and warm.

'Sorry,' she said. 'For what I said about Arlene.'

'Forgiven,' I said.

'Friends?' she asked.

'Friends,' I said.

She kissed me on the cheek.

'Careful,' I said. 'What would Collins think?'

'Collins can only think about Kinsella.'

'I heard that,' he said from the doorway.

'You were meant to,' she said, unabashed.

168

'Let's go, Shannon.'

'See you Monday, Cherry,' I said. 'At the sweatshop. Keep your eyes and ears open. Okay?'

'Yes, Nick.'

'I hope you know what you're doing, Shannon,' Collins said as we descended the stairs, carefully stepping over my catnapping friend.

'Why do you say that?'

'I'm having a re-think about Walker. Do you know what I found in the bathroom cabinet? A can of shaving foam.'

'She's a pretty girl, for chrissake' I said. 'You didn't expect celibacy, did you?'

'No,' he said moodily. 'But I'd feel a whole lot happier if Kinsella had a beard.'

CHAPTER FOURTEEN

'What are you doing this weekend?' I asked Arthur innocently over the telephone. It was nine o'clock by now. Arlene was still in bed. Norman, swaddled in a beige dressing gown, was already superglued to his beloved computer.

'Nothing much,' he said, his gruff voice rising an octave in anticipation.

'Good,' I said. 'Will you do me a favour?'

'I walked right into that one, didn't I? Okay, hit me with it. What do you want?'

'First...' I said.

'What do you mean *first?*' he interrupted. 'I thought this was *a* favour. Not a whole bleeding shopping list.'

'Just one favour this weekend. Then one at your leisure next week.'

I explained the immediate problem and slowly dictated Walker's address.

'Thanks a bunch,' he said. 'And if you think of anything else that's more boring, don't hesitate to ask.'

'Come over for dinner tomorrow,' I said in an effort to placate him. Even if he'd refused the favour (which I knew he wouldn't – friends like Arthur never let you down), the invitation would have been extended.

'Well, how about that,' he said sarcastically. 'Only just joined the payroll and you're giving me time off already. That's very generous, boss. Do I have to wait until this Walker is safely tucked up in bed, or can I knock off early?'

'How about eight?'

'I'll arrive hungry,' he warned.

'You always do,' I replied. 'Thanks, Arthur. I owe you one.'

'No,' he said. 'You'll owe me two.'

I put the phone down and stood there staring out of the window, lost in thought. The small patch of communal garden was a mess, unweeded nettle and thistle having run riot in the borders surrounding the so-called lawn – now simply clumps of straggly grass of varying heights produced by the plant equivalent of the hormone surge of spring.

Norman, after a while, registered the silence and turned towards me. 'What's on your mind?' he asked.

'Collins, Kinsella, Louise, Glenshield, Sandra Redmond, Arlene and Walker.'

'Bloody hell,' he said, releasing his grip on the mouse. 'Where do you want to start?'

'How about Walker,' I said. I debriefed Norman on the meeting at her bedsit, topping and tailing my account with the bare bones of the conversation in Collins's smoke-filled car and his later discovery of the shaving foam.

'So you're suffering a crisis of conscience over Walker,' he said, at the end of the story. 'For all manner of reasons, I take it.'

I nodded thoughtfully.

'You tell the girl that you trust her, then you make a pact with Collins to tell her nothing. And, if I'm not mistaken from hearing your side of the telephone conversation, you compound the felony by asking Arthur to tail her. See where she goes? Who she meets?'

'Yes,' I said quietly, and shamefully.

'Well, do you know what I think?' he said. 'I think it makes a refreshing change that you're actually being careful for once. Thinking ahead. Covering the angles. Instead of diving head first into the unknown, like you usually do. If I were you, Nick, I'd try to forget it. Okay? You've got enough on your plate at the moment.'

'Thanks, Norman,' I said. I couldn't tell if he truly meant all he had said, but it made me feel better. For that I was grateful.

'What was the other favour?' Norman asked.

'Nothing much,' I said. 'Just something to keep Arlene occupied next week. Make her feel useful. Part of the team. She's getting more restless each

171

day. It won't be long before she wants to return home. And I promised to go with her. I can't break that promise. So I need to stall her till this Glenshield business is out of the way.'

'How long do you reckon that will take?'

'It depends,' I said, considering the many problems. 'On whether I'm successful in landing a job in Accounts on Monday, and how complex their system turns out to be. And how much time I manage to spend on extra-curricula activities. The way they work their staff, the opportunities for uninterrupted snooping are going to be few and far between. Might have to risk making a sneaky copy of the accounting disks and bringing them home.' I waved my hand vaguely in the air to emphasise the complete guess to come. 'Could take two weeks. Maybe even four. I really don't know. If, in fact, no fraud has taken place, then I'd say four at least. A negative is always harder to prove than a positive. Especially when Collins is the one you have to convince.'

'I see the problem,' he said. 'Any ideas at present?'

'Not really,' I replied. I explained to Norman what little I knew. The culture of Glenshield, the exports, the private policing.

'A couple of bits of niche-marketing,' he said cynically, 'can't account for such rapid growth.'

'I'd say only about one-third of the growth was organic, stemming from within the company itself. The major part would seem to be through acquisitions. Each year Glenshield has taken over at least two of the smaller security firms.'

'No wonder the place is creaking at the seams,'

Norman said. 'Where did the finance come from?'

'That's one of the areas I have to delve into. I doubt that Kinsella's police pension would stretch to one acquisition, let alone half a dozen. I need to suss out their Financial Director, see how sharp he is. They may have simply traded paper.'

'Bought the smaller companies with Glenshield shares? Sounds like a long-term recipe for loss of control to me. The original shareholders see their percentage ownership diluted with each new acquisition. Still, it depends whether Kinsella is happier with a big slice of a small cake, or a small slice of a big cake. Some people think that size is all-important. Satisfies their egos.'

'Hell,' I said, suddenly dejected by the number of 'ifs' and unknowns in the insoluble Boolean equation. 'There's no point speculating at the moment. Let's hope that next week brings some hard data to work on. All I really have right now is impressions.'

'Two bits of advice,' Norman said with un-natural seriousness. 'Don't deny your instincts. And don't trust Kinsella. From what Collins says, Kinsella must be considered guilty until proven innocent.'

'Okay,' I said. 'Just one last thing. Arlene has already learned from Walker about the drug-bust that went wrong. What she's not aware of is that Collins's snout finished up at the bottom of a quarry. Let's not have any mention of that while she's around. She'd only worry.'

'And rightly so, it seems. But, I agree, it makes

173

sense to keep it to ourselves.'

'So how are you getting on with your new ... acquisition?' I asked, only just stopping short of calling it a toy again.

'This is a whole new world, Nick,' he said with a sigh of religious intensity. 'So much information at one's fingertips.'

'Still messing around with – sorry, practising on – the Van Damm accounts,' I said, pointing to the screen. 'Don't suppose you've found anything else of interest?'

'No. Apart from Redmond's paltry fraud, the accounts are whiter than white. I can guarantee that fact. One hundred per cent.' He smiled at me proudly. 'I know this system like the back of my hand. Van Damm is squeaky-clean. Take my word for it.'

He scrolled through the purchase ledger until he found the point he wanted. 'Did you know they use Glenshield for transporting their shipments of diamonds in and out of the country?'

'I guessed as much,' I said. 'I saw one of the guards in the corridor outside their offices when Walker and I went to make the arrest. But there's nothing unusual in using Glenshield. It's a coincidence. Not a connection.'

Norman nodded and looked back at the screen. He gave a wistful smile. 'What I couldn't do with a company like this.'

'You're retired, don't forget,' I warned him. 'This new computer is purely and simply for the restaurant business. Don't get any other ideas. Got that?'

'Of course, Nick,' he said. 'But you must admit,

it's tempting, isn't it?'

'Then resist it,' I said sternly. 'You're too old to go back to jail.'

'And too smart,' he added with a grin.

'That smells good.' Arthur licked his lips. 'I'm so hungry I could eat a horse.'

'You'll just have to settle for lamb on this occasion,' Arlene said. 'We'll see what we can do next time.'

Arthur regarded her with horror.

'Just a joke, Arthur,' she grinned, taking hold of his hands and leading him towards the dining table.

The pair of them made a pretty picture – Beauty and the Beast. Arthur was swathed within a brown leather jacket so large and heavy it could have been made from the dyed hide of at least two elephants. Arlene's body was being caressed by the product of a thousand silkworms – a delicate dark blue 'pants suit' of loose-fitting trousers and jacket. By comparison with his boots, her shoes seemed as fragile as glass slippers. His hair was thick and comb-resistant; thin strands of her hair had been drawn away from her ears and swept into a jewelled clip, revealing a simple pair of pearl studs. I smiled proudly at her. Grinned warmly up at him. And thanked fate for leavening its load by bringing them both into my life.

Arlene stood possessively before the table, released her grip on Arthur and waved a hand ceremoniously. 'Do sit down,' she said, beaming with self-satisfaction.

Arthur stared at her handiwork with appropriate wonder. Creasefree pink tablecloth with a pattern of cornflowers covering the years of abuse that the oak table had suffered at the hands of itinerant tenants. Four matching napkins, folded origami-style into perfect cones. Wine glasses polished to the point where you needed sunglasses to shield your eyes from the dazzling sparkle. Cutlery, mirror-shine, reflecting the flickering light of the two apple-scented candles in pink and blue pottery dishes.

'Someone's been busy,' Arthur commented, to her obvious pleasure.

'Nothing's too much trouble for my chauffeur,' she beamed.

Arthur gave me a puzzled look. But then, that wasn't an unusual experience.

'My other favour,' I explained. 'Would you take Arlene to Ealing tomorrow and then on a tour of our lovely British countryside?'

'That's not a favour,' he said. 'That's a pleasure. By rights I should pay you for the privilege of escorting this beautiful young lady.'

'Flattery will get you everywhere,' Arlene said. She punched him playfully, then winced at the contact with his rock-hard muscles. 'Red wine, Arthur?'

'It's not that Chilean plonk again, is it?' he asked suspiciously, his selective memory blaming country of origin for a past downfall. 'I don't think I can survive another headache like that one.'

'You did drink rather a lot of it, if you remember – which I don't expect you do. And it was in a good cause,' I said, recalling the turning point in the case of John Weston. 'But, no. It's not Chilean. It's from Cyprus.'

'Bubble and squeak?' he said incredulously.

'No,' I sighed. 'Not Greek – Cypriot. And it's to go with the *kleftiko.*'

'I thought you said we were having lamb.'

'Don't panic, Arthur,' I soothed. 'All will be revealed in the fullness of time. And don't forget, you did say it smelt good.'

'That was before I knew it was Greek,' he muttered unadventurously.

'Put him out of his misery,' Norman said. 'Bring it in. Let's eat.'

Arlene poured the Othello, while I went to the kitchen to do my weightlifting act with the heavy clay oven.

'This wine's all right,' Arthur said, when I returned.

'You're supposed to say "wheelbarrows of rich, ripe, blackcurrants". But from you, Arthur,' I said smiling, 'I'll take "all right" as a big compliment.'

I whisked off the lid of the pot, posh restaurant-style, releasing the trapped aroma of lamb, herbs and wine. Arlene and I had prepared the dish on Saturday evening, let it cook for four hours and then stand overnight. After skimming off the hardened layer of milky fat, we had only to pop it back in the oven this afternoon. It was the sort of meal that could cope with the late arrival of Arthur, if he was delayed on the Walker front. The preparations also gave Arlene and me plenty of opportunity to talk, and for me to request her assistance in the coming week.

I placed a huge chunk of lamb on the middle of Arthur's plate and spooned the potatoes and onions round the outside. Passed it to him. Served the others, whilst waiting expectantly for a reaction.

He sat there politely – dubiously? – until we were all ready to start. Then he popped the first tentative forkful into his mouth.

'Umm. This is okay,' he said.

'What greater reward do we need, Arlene?' I said. 'The wine's all right, the food's okay. Cheers.'

We clinked our glasses.

'So,' I said to Arthur, 'how did you get on?'

'Not now,' he said. 'Not while I'm eating.'

'He's right,' Norman said. 'Pleasure before business.'

An hour – and three helpings – later, Arthur leaned back in the chair and rubbed his stomach appreciatively. Arlene refilled his wine glass, and we waited.

'Well?' I asked.

'It was good,' he said. 'For foreign stuff.'

'No,' I said impatiently. 'I meant Walker, not the *kleftiko*.'

'Oh yes,' he said. 'Walker.'

'Arthur,' Arlene said in a high-pitched voice, 'I shall scream if you don't tell us what happened.'

'She's a good-looker,' Arthur said.

'I think I will scream.'

'Sorry,' Arthur went on. 'The upshot is that nothing happened. Waste of bleeding time.'

'Come on, Arthur,' I said, 'she must have done

something. She can't have stayed in her bedsit for two whole days. She would have gone bananas with boredom.'

'Saturday, she goes shopping. Dalston market. Some fruit and veg. Bunch of flowers. Oh, and a bottle of booze from the off-licence. Then the rest of the day indoors. On her own. No visitors.'

'And today?' I asked.

'She appeared about ten o'clock. Dressed smartish-like. Frock and high heels, you know?'

It wasn't quite as detailed a description as you would have been provided with by *The Clothes Show*, but the level of interest and suspicion around the table rose like a barometer with a heatwave due.

'Goes round the back to get her car. Heads off north.'

'And you follow, I hope,' I said. 'At a distance?'

'Of course.' He sounded offended. 'All the way to bloody Northampton.'

'Cobblers,' I said inconsequentially.

'No, it's true,' said Arthur, sounding even more offended.

'Northampton,' I said, shaking my head. 'Old centre of the shoemaking industry.' Thank goodness she hadn't gone to a town famous for the manufacture of spray cans – I dread to think what Arthur's reaction would have been if I'd said 'aerosols'. 'Sorry, Arthur. Stupid digression. Go on.'

'She drives straight to a private address. Nice little housing estate. Then stays for four bloody hours. Having roast beef, by the smell of it. Agony, it was. Anyway, then she drives straight

179

back home again.'

'Whom did she visit?' I asked. 'Did you get a look at anybody?'

'Sure. Mother and kid sister came to the door to wave her off.'

'Like you said, Arthur,' I sighed, 'all innocent enough. But thanks, anyway. It wasn't a waste of time. It's some comfort to know she didn't meet with Kinsella or anyone else at Glenshield.'

'So that's it, is it?' Arlene said challengingly.

The three of us looked at her and shrugged our shoulders.

'Men!' she said. 'Impossible!'

She focused her rapt attention on Arthur. Norman and I, relieved, shrank back into our chairs and kept a low profile.

'Tell me, Arthur,' she said sweetly. 'Was she carrying anything with her when she went on this little trip of hers?'

'The flowers she bought in the market,' he said. 'Nice gesture, I thought. Oh, and a big present, all wrapped up in fancy paper.'

'And,' Arlene said with emphasis, 'how old was this kid sister?'

'Christ, that's a tricky one. Six. Seven, maybe.'

'How's your maths, Nick?' she said. 'How old is Walker?'

'University till the age of twenty-one,' I said, calculating. 'Two years on the beat. Another in CID. Three years in the Fraud Squad. That would make her about twenty-seven, I suppose.'

The penny dropped as I finished the sentence.

'So,' Arlene said. 'Twenty years after giving birth to darling Cherry, her mother decides to go in for another little bundle of joy. Unlikely, wouldn't you agree? Wise up, boys. It wasn't Walker's kid sister. It was her daughter.'

'No,' Arthur said unwisely. 'Why conceal a kid? Abandon a kid, for that matter. It doesn't make sense.'

It was time for one of Arlene's withering looks: she wasn't quite as good at it as Walker but, then again, she didn't get the practice.

'A love-child, Arthur,' she said patiently, 'doesn't look very good on your curriculum vitae. Especially when you're after a job with the police force.' Arlene looked at me with triumph in her eyes. 'And you did say she was ambitious, didn't you?'

'At least we know why she lives in a crummy bedsit in Hackney,' I said. 'Why she doesn't spend much money. Probably sends it all to her mother to look after the kid.'

'Yes,' said Arlene. 'Now you know *why* she needs money. The question, dear Nick, is *how desperately* does she need it?'

CHAPTER FIFTEEN

I arrived at Glenshield an hour before my shift was due to start. Not through diligence. But through expediency.

I had spent a restless night brooding about Walker and her daughter. Each time I came close to falling asleep, my mind prodded me awake

181

with a sharp-fingered intensity that was impossible to ignore. You think you know someone, Shannon, it lectured me in the dark. And then along comes some new piece of information that eats away at the very foundations of their persona. Suddenly every assumption, every belief, is challenged. Where once there was certainty, only doubt remains. After my crisis of conscience, I was now suffering a crisis of faith.

A gentle light filtered through the glass of the atrium, creating long, cool shadows in the lee of the plants. The sound of my shoes on the marble floor produced rebuking echoes from the silence. At this time of morning the building was dormant, a chrysalis with an hour remaining before metamorphosis. There was no clamour of voices. No rush of feet. No manic scurrying about in a supercharged atmosphere. It was a blissful interlude before normal chaos resumed.

I headed first for the drinks machine. The thin brown liquid reminded me vaguely of coffee. It also reminded me vaguely of tea, ersatz cola and oxtail soup. Ingenious, I thought. Whichever button you press, it makes no difference – the same liquid pours into your cup. Saves on pipework and the amount of stock that needs to be held. I tipped the coloured water down the gaping mouth of the drainhole beneath the dispensing nozzle. 'You drink it,' I said to the machine. 'See how much *you* like it.'

Back in Reception, I picked up the *Financial Times* from the marble coffee table in the area where visitors sat and took it over to the desk.

'If you want to go,' I said to the only man on

182

duty at this hour, 'I don't mind starting early.'

It had the same effect as shouting 'fire'. He was gone in a flash, pausing only to pack his copy of the *Sun* into a small holdall. I noticed a thermos flask in the bottom of the bag and marked him down as a wise man who had learned from bitter experience.

I spread the *FT* over the desk. Stared down at it with what I hoped was a mixture of intense concentration and deep wisdom. Okay, it was ostentatious. But it was a little more subtle than putting up a placard reading, 'I'm an accountant – please transfer me.'

After a while, a large round woman in the lime-green overalls of the cleaning staff walked towards me with that rolling gait that brings pound signs to the eyes of chiropodists.

'Pass me the sheet, luv,' she said, placing a heavy bag on the counter.

I looked at her blankly.

'"Earlies and Lates", dear,' she said cryptically. 'Yellow sheet. Reg keeps it on a clipboard.'

I passed it to her. She placed her initials in a column beside her name and squinted up at the clock on the wall behind me. She wrote 8.45 in the next column. I looked at my watch. It said 8.30.

'Well,' she said challengingly, handing the clipboard back to me, 'I'm not missing out on fifteen minutes' pay just because Mr O'Kane never lets me into his office. Reg and I have *an arrangement.*'

Obligingly, I added my initials next to the time. She smiled at me.

'How are you off for soap?' she said, unzipping her shopping bag. 'Here. Stick these in your pocket.'

Her eyes swivelled from side to side, establishing that the coast was clear, and she dropped two heavy green bricks over the counter. Then off she waddled to the door.

I put the giant economy-sized bars of soap in the drawer, where the strong smell of carbolic could lie in wait to savage unsuspecting nostrils. Flicking back over the last three sheets, I saw that O'Kane had been in for four hours on Sunday and a further six on Saturday. On Friday he had left the building at midnight. I wondered why he didn't go the whole hog and erect a camp bed in his office. Then realised what a stupid thought that was – he would never be able to resist the temptation to pile papers on top of it.

'Christ, you're keen, aren't you?' Charlie said, causing me to jump.

Not much of a security guard, was I?

'All ready for another week?' he asked, sitting down next to me.

'Absolutely awash with lethargy at the prospect,' I replied.

He gave me a puzzled look, and paused to contemplate my response. 'Good,' he said, eventually.

He opened the desk drawer. 'My God,' he said, reeling back. 'Rosie's made her rounds, then.'

With the swift reactions of a man who has experienced life under fire, Charlie made a grab for a red leather book, threw it on the desk and slammed the drawer shut.

'You haven't marked up the Visitors' Book,' he said accusingly, once he had his breath back. 'First one here does the book. Always has. Always will.'

He slid it across the desk and handed me a ruler and ballpoint pen.

I flicked back to Friday to check the layout. It was then that the name hit me in the eyes.

David Yates.

I shuddered.

The name, for me at least, was synonymous with trouble.

We had never actually met, but our paths had crossed in the past.

David Montgomery Yates – millionaire, politician, more friends in high places than God himself, and fast-breeder reactor for jealousy and envy. A few months ago he had been on the verge of being appointed Chancellor of the Exchequer. Then, at the eleventh hour, his public image had taken a nosedive.

The timing of the story was too much of a coincidence to be anything other than a well-engineered exercise in media manipulation. Afraid that the imminent elevation of Yates was merely a stepping stone to the true goal of Prime Minister, one of his rivals had started a whispering campaign. A few members of the public, concerned only for the moral well-being of our country – never let it be said that they were in any way motivated by the huge sums of money that the tabloids were offering – had come forward to set the record straight.

It had all happened, so the 'ladies' had said, a

long time ago.

But mud sticks.

And so, it was alleged, does strawberry jam to the body of David Montgomery Yates.

'Chivers' – as he had been dubbed by the tabloid press and the Opposition alike – had been forced to resign from the Cabinet. Not content with the retrograde role of a backbencher, he was now carving out a new and lucrative sideline as a non-executive director. He had three positions – the ladies had said that too! – already. It looked as if Glenshield might be making an offer of a fourth. According to the Visitors' Book, Yates had spent two hours with Kinsella on Friday night.

'Sit up straight,' Charlie whispered, interrupting my speculation as to what possible use Yates could be to a security firm (used to coping with sticky situations?). 'And look busy,' he hissed.

A tall woman approached the desk and registered the open *FT*.

'You must be Shannon,' she said. 'I've heard all about you.'

'Give me their names,' I said, 'and I'll have my lawyers issue writs for slander immediately.'

Beside me, Charlie winced.

'Come up and see me in ten minutes.'

'Yes, miss,' I said, as if back in school.

'Ma'am,' Charlie hissed under his breath.

'Sorry. Yes, ma'am. Ten minutes. I'll be there.' With a copy of *The Beano* stuffed down the back of my trousers.

She turned on a pair of shapely ankles and made her way to the lift.

'Bloody hell,' Charlie said. 'You push your luck, don't you? Got a death-wish or something? Going for a new world record for the shortest time spent as a Glenshield employee?'

'All right,' I said. 'Don't go on. Just put me out of my misery. Who is she?'

'Only the Head of Personnel,' he said in a voice laden with awe. 'Not to mention the fact that she's the boss's wife!'

She rose from her chair and stepped round the desk to greet me.

'Louise Kinsella,' she said as we shook hands. There was no stress on the surname. It was an introduction, pure and simple, not an attempt at a demonstration of power.

'Sorry about being so flippant earlier,' I said, screwing up my face in an attempt at gross embarrassment.

'It doesn't matter,' she said with a warm smile. 'Really it doesn't. It's nice to meet someone with a sense of humour for a change. We have a tendency here to take everything too seriously. Do sit down. Coffee?'

I thought of the ghastly brew from the machine. Was this some convoluted psychological test? If I refused, would I be damned as impolite? If I accepted, then condemned as having less taste than a tongueless Philistine?

'It is fresh,' she said, freeing me from the self-imposed dilemma.

'How could I resist? Thank you.'

She crossed the room to a pine sideboard that could have graced a country kitchen. Picked up a silver tray where cups, sugar, cream and a china jug of coffee sat on a linen doily.

My eyes drifted up from the black patent shoes with T-bar strap across the instep. Registered the expensive cut of the navy-blue suit, short feminine jacket, pleated skirt with hem resting on shapely knees. The softness of the scallop-neck, white Irish linen blouse. The chestnut hair woven into a plait, so long and wide that it evoked visions of the tail of a sleekly groomed dressage horse: it bounced between her shoulder-blades as she walked.

I cleared a space on the desk for the tray by moving a long-stemmed vase containing a small bunch of freesias. The sweet, heady aroma, coupled with her presence, hit me like some mind-altering drug. I gazed up at her while she stood before me pouring the coffee. Studied her face with pleasure. Sparkling green eyes. Rose-pink lips. Cutely sculptured nose. She was so different, so much more attractive, than in the photograph – it was no wonder I hadn't recognised her. Maybe the picture had been taken on bad day. Or she'd changed a lot. I don't know. But I understood now why Collins was filled with such fanatical fire, why he so desperately wanted her back.

Only when the cup, sugar bowl and cream were in front of me did she sit down.

I helped myself to sugar, flirting with the idea of taking three Collins-sized heaped spoonfuls just to see her reaction.

From the little laughter lines at the corners of her eyes, I put her at thirty-five or so. Although, in view of her history, that could have been deceptive – marriage with Collins was probably a dog's life, one year equalling seven in the normal ageing process.

'Roddy tells me,' she said, sounding genuinely concerned, 'that my ex-husband has made life a little difficult for you.'

'Master of the understatement, is Mr Kinsella?' I asked with raised eyebrow. 'Impossible would be a better way of putting it.'

'That sounds more like Chris,' she said. 'So it's time for a change, is it? A fresh start?'

'It's a long story,' I said, stirring the coffee distractedly. 'You know I've been in prison, I suppose?'

'Yes. Roddy told me. Besides, I remember the case. Normally we wouldn't even contemplate employing anyone with a criminal record. Not the right image for a security company, you understand.' She shook her head, the plait swinging like a pendulum in response. 'But, bearing in mind your circumstances, I'm – we're – prepared to make an exception. You seem the sort of man who deserves a second chance. How can somebody be expected to rehabilitate if no-one is prepared to extend a helping hand? Or show a little trust?'

She took an official-looking wad of paper from her desk drawer and handed it to me. 'You'll need to fill out this application form. For our records.'

I turned over the pages – all eight of them. Then folded the form and put it in my pocket. I had no intention of spending hours writing a potted autobiography detailing my 'previous experience' in the laundry at Chelmsford and other such responsible positions. Nor, for that matter, of having my address on file. Even at the Fraud Squad, because of the recent move to Archway, my current residence was a secret known only to Collins and Walker.

'Thank you,' I said. 'I'm grateful for any opportunity. But, to be perfectly honest, I'd prefer something that allows me to hang onto some self-respect. Mr Kinsella did say he would try to find a slot in Accounts.'

'That's already been arranged,' she replied, giving me another of those sweet, disarming smiles.

'Then thank you very much,' I said.

'Don't get too excited,' she warned. 'The job is nothing grand, I'm afraid. Just routine book-keeping. And it's only temporary. On trial, shall we say? Until Mr Paradine has seen what you can do.'

Or, with a bit of luck, I thought, *not seen* what I can do.

Tricia led me to a vacant chair and switched on the terminal on the desk. I had evidently hit a lucky streak.

A transfer to Accounts.

The auburn-haired beauty as my personal tutor.

And, instead of carbolic, the fragrant smell of jasmine drifting up to tantalise my nose.

'You'll be handling Beryl's work while she's on holiday,' Tricia said, leaning over me. 'It's ever so simple. I'll talk you through it the first time.'

The opening menu popped up. I placed my hands on the keyboard.

Tricia paused.

I looked up at her. She blushed.

'It's okay,' I said reassuringly. 'I understand. It's a natural reaction. I'm used to it. I can cope. Do go on.'

But the sight of my left hand with its two missing fingers had distracted her.

'Nick Shannon!' she said. 'I thought the name rang a bell. Aren't you the one who...'

'Yes,' I said. 'But let's keep it quiet, shall we? Someone else will eventually make the connection. But, till then, let's make it our secret.'

'Of course,' she said, touching her lower lip. 'Our secret.'

Tricia tried to return my smile, but a tear had already formed in one of those deep brown eyes. She shook her head. Despair? An effort to pull herself together? Whatever, I just concentrated on the patterns of light as it caught her long hair with the movement. This was supposed to be my lucky day, not an enforced trip down the dark alley of Memory Lane.

'I'm so sorry,' she said. She blushed a second time. 'About your sister, I mean. It must have been so horrible for you.'

'It was a long time ago,' I said, trying to keep the chill from my voice. 'But thanks anyway. It means a lot. Really.' I forced another smile. 'Come on, Tricia. Show me around your system. Otherwise we'll have everyone talking.'

'They'll do that in any case,' she said. 'Work like

slaves and gossip like midwives. They're the only two things people do around here.'

'Well,' I said. 'Let's get the work out of the way, then later you can tell me all the gossip.'

She looked at me uncertainly.

'We'll see,' she said. 'Now, Beryl handles the purchases. Select that option.'

The screen requested a password.

'Just type in "Beryl",' Tricia instructed.

I did as she said and the next menu for the bought ledger appeared on the screen.

'Do you all use your names as passwords?' I asked, wearing my auditor's hat.

'I don't know about Mr Paradine or Mr Kinsella. But most of us do. When the system was first installed, people were always forgetting their passwords. It caused a lot of problems – we're not allowed to write them down, you know. So we switched to our names. Even Beryl can't forget her name.'

Tricia laughed, whetting my appetite for the meeting with Beryl when she returned from Ibiza. She dragged a pile of invoices about a foot high across the desk to my right-hand side. 'Choose "Data Entry",' she said ominously.

A template filled the screen. The cursor flashed on a space where the name of the supplier demanded to be filled in.

'So all you have to do now,' she said brightly, 'is key in the information against the appropriate field – name, date, amount, VAT code, job number and so on.'

'Piece of cake,' I replied. I had in mind not lip-smacking Death by Chocolate, but a plain, boring, un-iced, un-jammed Victoria sponge.

'Give me a shout if you need any help,' she said, moving across to her desk. I took one last look at her before burying myself in the tower of paperwork. The vernal aroma of her perfume was complemented by a mid-calf-length dress with a floral print of whites, pinks and light blues. A navy belt gathered the dress around her trim waist. On her tiny feet she wore navy shoes, low-heeled and slingback. Around her left wrist was a thin gold chain. There was an engagement ring on her finger. Some man is very lucky, I thought.

For the next hour I keyed in invoice after invoice, hoping to whittle down the pile sufficiently to give myself a little time to sneak a peek at other parts of the system. Just as I was beginning to congratulate myself on my progress, Mr Precision appeared at my shoulder. He peered at me over the top of his glasses. And smiled!

'Today's post,' he said, placing another thirty or so invoices on top of the pile. It was now higher than when I had started. I was beginning to understand how O'Kane felt. Working here was like bailing out a leaking ship with the aid of a sieve.

Ten minutes later came the next setback.

'Tricia,' I called helplessly.

She stepped to my aid, the dress floating around her legs as she crossed the room.

'The computer won't accept this invoice,' I said.

She studied the screen.

'You haven't entered the job number, silly,' she

sighed. 'Every invoice we receive must have an authorising signature and a job number before it can be passed for payment. Without a job number we can't allocate the invoice against a specific job. Cost control would be impossible. We wouldn't know what profit we're making on any particular job. That's why the computer insists on a job number.'

I fought back the impulse to tell her that I understood that much. Instead, I examined the invoice again in case I had missed something. 'But there isn't one,' I said, handing the evidence to her.

'Oh, well,' she said, as if addressing a small child. 'This is one of Mr O'Kane's.'

That was meant to explain everything, was it? I gave her a puzzled look.

'Mr O'Kane,' she confided, 'is hopeless at filling in job numbers. Just key in Q123 and the system will accept it.'

'I'm sorry,' I said. 'I don't quite understand.'

'Well, if we waited for Mr O'Kane, we would never get around to inputting half his work. So we set up a dummy code – Q123. It allows us to process an invoice without knowing the job number. That way the cost at least goes onto the purchase ledger and appears on the monthly accounts. And the suppliers get paid on time, too. Saves us all those embarrassing phone calls demanding payment.'

She picked up a rubber stamp from the desk. Pressed it onto a red inkpad. Thumped it down onto the invoice. JOB NUMBER PLEASE! stared up accusingly.

'What you do,' she said, 'is pass this back to Mr O'Kane. In a few weeks – if you're lucky – it will land back on your desk with a job number this time. Then you just return to your original entry and change the code as if it were a mistake. That credits Q123 and debits whatever job was the right one in the first place.'

Brilliant, I thought. I couldn't wait to get home and tell Norman. Christian names as passwords. Dummy codes. In an effort to cope with the trials and tribulations of the real world they had found ways to compromise the security of the system that had never occurred to the straight-line-thinking programmers. I still did not know if there were any truth in the accusations contained in the letter that Collins had received. But there damn well ought to be. If someone wasn't on the fiddle here, then it was through a deficiency of courage, rather than a lack of imagination or opportunity.

I looked up at Tricia innocently, and chose my words well.

'Is no-one worried,' I said slowly, 'about a supplier being paid in error?'

'No,' she said, brushing the question aside. 'I don't think that can happen. We take at least three months' credit, you see. Mr O'Kane usually gives us the information by then.'

Usually, she had said. Not always.

'So every supplier has to wait at least three months for their money?'

'Some even longer.' She pointed to the screen. 'You see this code here?'

Her pink nail rested on the field that asked for

supplier code number.

'Yes,' I said, my curiosity mounting.

'The supplier code cross-references the invoice to the part of the system that deals with the actual payment. There is a database of information on all suppliers. Along with basic details, like bank account and so on, it also contains a code for the credit period – three months, four months, whatever. We take the maximum period we can get away with. Helps cash flow, Mr Paradine says. We earn interest on the money while the suppliers are waiting to be paid. Anyway, at the end of the specified period, the supplier's bank account receives a credit through BACS – the Bankers' Automated Clearing System, that is.'

Each year an increasing number of companies switched to using BACS – mostly because bank charges were substantially lower than if cheques were used (reflecting, but not equalling of course, the administrative savings for the banks themselves). The non-monetary advantages were that there were no postal delays or losses and the three-day cycle of clearing cheques was replaced by the instantaneous electronic transfer between payer and payee. Professionally – or maybe I was just old-fashioned – I still preferred a piece of paper that I could hold and see to the intangible and invisible computer transaction.

'The suppliers,' Tricia concluded, 'may not like hanging about for their money, but at least with value dating they know exactly when it will arrive in their account.'

It was the typically arrogant attitude of big

businesses. They earned interest while, in turn, the suppliers paid it on the money they had to borrow to finance the running of their operations. And if the suppliers did not like the arrangement, what could they do? There was nowhere to run: all their large customers operated on the same one-sided basis. I had heard of huge international companies that rubbed their hands together each time the base rate rose – it simply meant they raked in more money in interest. Some firms produced more profit from these pseudo-banking operations than they did from actually selling their goods or services.

'Must be some database,' I said.

'Yes, I should think so,' she said. 'I've never actually seen it. You need a special password to access it. It's the same with the payroll.'

That made sense, I thought. At least there were some parts of the system that had decent controls built in.

'So who does have access, Tricia?'

'You do ask a lot of questions, don't you?' she said. 'The directors can all access the full system on a read-only basis. Mr Paradine handles input to the supplier database, although Mr Kinsella has to counter-authorise any changes. Mrs Kinsella's responsibility is the payroll.' Tricia glanced meaningfully at the never-decreasing pile on my desk. 'Back to the grindstone,' she said. 'You'll be here till Doomsday unless you get a move on.'

'I was thinking of working through lunch to catch up,' I said.

'Me too,' she said. 'You can share my sandwiches.'

I'd rather be left on my own, I thought. Much though I would otherwise have enjoyed her company.

'Thanks,' I said, as she returned to her desk.

For the next two hours I laboured. By now the process of inputting the data was becoming automatic. My brain had switched to autopilot. I could almost make the repetitive keystrokes with my eyes shut. Occasionally I would glance across at Tricia, or over towards the back of the room where her three female colleagues were grouped. In contrast to young, pretty Tricia, they looked as if they had been cloned from genes specially selected for their low boredom threshold. All three were in their early fifties, wore skirts and twin-sets, had pairs of spectacles with cords hung round their necks and tightly permed hair. It was like some bizarre, triple-vision version of a very bad dream set in the Mothers' Union. To relieve the confusion to my optic nerves, I craned my neck to view Mr Precision.

It was one o'clock. On the dot. He sat back in his chair. Took a plastic box from his drawer. Laid a paper napkin on the desk. Tucked another into the collar of his crisp white shirt. Carefully arranged two rounds of sandwiches (neatly cut along the diagonals to make four triangles) in the exact centre of the first napkin, so that the edges of both sandwich and napkin were pleasingly parallel. He stared down and, as the tension mounted within me, paused in silent debate with himself as to which triangle to eat first.

I could see his problem. Whichever one he chose would have the unsightly effect of spoiling the three-dimensional symmetry.

Eventually, his head gave a barely perceptible nod that indicated he had made his decision. He took a bite from the corner of the selected triangle. A dribble of salad cream ran down his chin. He dabbed it away quickly and self-consciously looked around the room. My eyes returned to the screen just in time.

With three triangles still to be consumed by him, it seemed a good time to take a surreptitious trip through the accounts. I saved my work to the hard disk. Made a copy onto a back-up floppy. And prepared to return to the main menu in order to gain entry to the sales ledger. There was a little matter of exports that was preying on my mind.

'Egg mayonnaise all right?' Tricia asked.

Christ, couldn't a man have a moment to himself to do the odd bit of spying?

'Lovely,' I said, sounding like an advertisement for cream cheese.

And so the day progressed.

If I was the paranoid type, I would have suspected a well-engineered conspiracy. The mere thought of snooping only had to cross my mind for someone to appear magically at my shoulder. Tricia checked my progress from time to time. The three clones jointly decided to mother me: according to some secret rota, they took it in turns to march over in their sensible shoes and offer me boiled sweets (Clone 1 – Marjorie, I think), toffees (Clone 2 – or was that Marjorie?)

or fruit gums (Clone 3 – I give up!). I accepted each titbit gratefully and waited patiently for another clandestine chance to present itself – and for my teeth to drop out. Even Mr Precision came across to prattle on about how absolutely imperative it was that the invoices I had processed should be placed neatly in the tray marked 'Filing'.

'I hope, Nick,' he whispered after the lecture, 'that you will prove to be *de-pend-able.*' The word was drawn out with reverence. 'Fit into our little team. We all have our part to play if the department is to run smoothly. That is my responsibility, you understand? Mr Paradine,' he said with awe, the accompanying anxious frown magnified by his glasses, 'has so many other duties that he has charged me with all matters relating to the staff.'

'I'm sorry if I've been thrust upon you,' I said. 'I expect you usually handle the recruitment personally?'

'Permanent and temporary,' he replied with pride.

'I suppose you use Bishops for temporary staff?' I asked.

'Bishops?' he said. 'No, no, no. Skilled accounting staff are beyond their domain. Bishops are purely clerical.'

He smiled at me. Gave a little wink for good measure. It took a while to sink in. I wasn't expecting it from him. Bishops. Purely clerical. He had made a joke!

Except that I found it hard to see the funny side.

Walker had landed her job through Bishops.

Or so she'd claimed.

If she really wanted to investigate possible fraud at Glenshield, then why on earth had she chosen an agency that didn't handle accounting staff?

It just didn't add up.

I worried away at the problem for the rest of the afternoon without coming even remotely close to a solution. Nothing made sense. But one thing was for sure. I wasn't going to lose any more sleep on crises of conscience or faith. Walker had used up her quota of my trust.

At half past five, screens were switched off around me, bags packed and coats gathered from the rack behind the door.

'I'll just carry on for another half-hour,' I declared to the fleeing department. 'Clear the decks for tomorrow.'

Mr Precision (or Arnold, as I was instructed to call him) smiled approvingly at this proof of conscientious *de-pend-ability*. Tricia waved a cheery goodbye. The three maternal clones nodded in unison.

Alone at last.

The sales ledger was on the screen in less time than it takes a man with a nervous tick to blink his eye.

I scrolled through the list of customers, searching for the countries themselves or the names of foreign-sounding organisations. Had just found the first when the door opened.

Kinsella entered the room.

I switched off the computer as he walked towards me. Sat back in the chair with sweaty palms and an innocent smile. Tidied papers with the sigh of satisfaction of a man who had just completed an honest day's work in return for a fair day's pay.

'Thought I might still find you here, Shannon,' he said.

'Just about to leave,' I replied, rising from my seat and stretching my shoulders.

'Perhaps we can detain you a little longer,' he said.

I wish ex-policemen wouldn't use the word *detain*. It always sounds as if the handcuffs are already out of their pockets.

'Why don't you join us in the boardroom.'

It was not a question. It was an order.

And a strange one at that.

CHAPTER SIXTEEN

As I entered the boardroom, Louise flashed me a smile. Its warmth was overwhelmed by the chill in the atmosphere.

O'Kane did not even bother to look up. Sulkily, he busied himself with compiling a list of things he would rather be doing and simultaneously examining his diary for irritatingly unfilled 'time windows'.

'You know Louise and Gerry, of course,' Kinsella said.

Louise! Gerry! Two days at the firm and here I was on first-name terms with the directors already. I mentally raised my guard.

'And this is Stephen Paradine. Your boss.'

I nodded a formal pleased-to-meet-you, which he returned with an economical curl of his lip. Paradine was wearing a grey suit, blue shirt and red and blue spotted tie. In a crowd you would not have given him a second glance – were it not for his baby-blue eyes and long blond hair. He examined me with the sort of look that, if mass-produced, could have saved the National Health Service a fistful of money on X-ray machines.

'Do sit down, Nick,' Louise said. 'Roddy. Perhaps a drink would oil the wheels for us all.'

Kinsella nodded. 'Good idea, Lou.'

Jesus, I thought. How could anyone take a perfectly acceptable name like Louise and shorten it to a euphemism for a lavatory? Oh well, he is married to her after all. I suppose he knows what he's doing.

Kinsella walked balletically in his loafers to a row of teak units built along one wall of the room. The motor of a refrigerator hummed, acting as a homing beacon for the thirsty. I chose a chair at the foot of the table, where I would be facing Kinsella. On my right was Louise. On my left was O'Kane and alongside him, sitting opposite the Head of Personnel, was Paradine. There was a large gap between the two men, unwarranted by the size of the meeting. Hurry up with drinks, I thought. And whatever they choose, make them large ones.

Kinsella began to place a range of different glasses and bottles on the table. Wise man. The chances of everybody agreeing to the same drink seemed about as low as Arthur winning Mastermind.

I glanced round to take my mind off the oppressive silence. The room occupied a corner position on the fourth floor. Vertical blinds were drawn across both sets of windows, blocking out the natural light and prohibiting a view of the narrow, grubby streets leading off either side of Shaftesbury Avenue. The walls were covered in beige hessian. Here and there hung framed photographs portraying Kinsella's progress from raw recruit at Hendon to retirement presentation of gold watch from the Commander. Recessed spotlights shone down on the large rectangular table, producing alternating pools of glaring light and patches of contrasting gloom.

Kinsella placed three ice cubes in a tall glass and topped it up with tonic water for his wife. Half-filled a heavy tumbler with whiskey for himself. 'Help yourself,' he said grumpily to the rest of us.

Louise frowned. 'Nick,' she said. 'What can I get you?'

'White wine, please.'

She poured a glass for me and a weak gin and tonic for a still-silent Paradine. O'Kane stretched across for the whiskey bottle. He looked at Kinsella, then pointedly as his watch.

'A question, Nick,' said Kinsella.

You've been rumbled, Shannon, my guilty conscience whispered.

Everyone turned to face me. Yes, even O'Kane dragged his eyes away from his note pad. Paradine interlocked his fingers and rested his hands on the table.

'What would you do,' Kinsella asked, 'if you were Governor of a prison?'

'Resign immediately,' I said, smiling.

O'Kane rolled his eyes at Kinsella. For all the subtlety of the non-verbal communication, he might just as well have spoken out loud – *Told you so, waste of bloody time*.

'It was a serious question, Shannon,' Paradine rebuked me. 'We were rather hoping for a serious answer.'

The man could speak after all. Not just sit there looking stern but pretty. His voice was pure public school: plummy vowels, meticulous pronunciation and an intonation honed to perfection through years of sneering at the socially disadvantaged.

'Terribly sorry, old chap,' I said. Kinsella placed his hand over his mouth to hide the smile that was forming. 'It was just that the concept appeared to be stretching reality somewhat.'

'Perhaps,' Louise said, 'if we explain the context of the question, Nick might give us a straight opinion.'

'Tomorrow,' Kinsella announced, 'you will read in the newspapers that Glenshield has been asked to tender for a large government contract. To purchase HMP Strathmoor in Scotland and turn it into what the media will undoubtedly christen Supermax – the country's first privately run maximum-security prison.'

So this was how Yates fitted into the picture. A little inside information from his days at the Home Office.

'We thought,' Kinsella continued, 'we might pick your brains. Take advantage of your inside (pun intended) knowledge. What tips do you have for us?'

'It depends,' I said.

O'Kane sighed audibly.

'It depends,' I repeated unswervingly, 'on your objectives. Your philosophy. What is the purpose of prison? Punishment, pure and simple? A way of keeping offenders safely locked away, so as to protect society? Or an opportunity to convert the ungodly to the straight-and-narrow path of right-eousness?'

'We were thinking,' Paradine said, 'more along the lines of how to minimise costs while maximising control.'

Silly me, I thought. Fancy complicating the issue by suggesting that the perspective of the prisoners came into the equation.

'Pardon me for asking,' I said, 'but isn't this a mammoth undertaking for a company the size of Glenshield? Strathmoor, from what I hear, makes the Bastille look like Buck House. It's sure to cost millions to finance the purchase of the building and make all the necessary alterations – rein-forcing externally and refurbishing internally – to bring it up to the required standard. Then there's the recruitment and training of staff. And I don't expect the government will pay a penny until the first cell is occupied.'

'The finance is not a problem,' Paradine said dismissively.

'Stephen here,' Kinsella said, 'represents the interests of a venture-capital company called

Prospekt Holdings. Glenshield is only one of his many responsibilities. Prospekt has been involved with us since Louise and I first set up the company. As Stephen says, the investment is no problem. Prospekt will provide all the capital we need.'

At least the question of how Glenshield had financed their acquisitions had been solved. Kinsella owned only a proportion of the shares, the venture-capital company had the rest – probably the majority, I was willing to bet, in view of all it must have pumped into Glenshield.

'Okay,' I said. 'Are you familiar with the Principle of Proportionality?'

Heads shook around the table. And the interest level rose.

'It's the theory behind how you solve the dilemma of cost and security. What it says is that each individual prisoner – or, less ideally, each category of prisoner – is allocated a level of security determined by the individual element of risk, bearing in mind that some basic rules of humanity must be followed. You can't keep someone sedated all the time, confined in a strait-jacket, or break their will through demeaning conditions or a brutal regime, that sort of thing.'

I sipped the wine to give the complex concept a chance to sink in.

'The higher the level of security, the more it costs. So, proportionality says, each prisoner must be assessed and given the minimum amount of security that his risk warrants.'

'Sounds promising,' Paradine said.

'The only trouble,' I said, 'is that it doesn't work. No-one has ever been able to put it into practice.'

'Why?' Kinsella asked.

'Because it only really works at an individual level. You need staff capable of evaluating each prisoner. For instance, no two murderers pose the same threat to fellow inmates, or to the general public if they were to escape.'

'But you,' Kinsella said, 'spent most of your time in Chelmsford. That's usually for Category C prisoners only.'

'All right,' I said. 'Bad example, perhaps. But I had the benefit of a powerful media lobby behind me. A lot of people felt that the sentence was harsh. That I should never have gone to prison in the first place. Something had to be done in mitigation. Cases like mine are rare. The principle still stands. No two prisoners are completely alike. It's so much easier to treat, say, all armed robbers the same. And so much safer to elect for a system that overdoes the level of security. It's the Rank Xerox syndrome. Nobody ever lost their job by deciding to buy Rank Xerox. And no governor ever lost his job for being too cautious. But let a murderer escape and...'

'I think we could make it work,' O'Kane piped up enthusiastically. I imagined his mind already designing complex questionnaires for psychologically profiling each new inmate – some criminological variant of BBW's credit-rating system.

'Look, you're both ex-policemen,' I said,

instantly cursing myself for the slip of the tongue. There was nothing to do but plough quickly on in the hope that, if the comment had registered, they would assume that a member of staff had told me about O'Kane's background. 'You know the criminal mind. How devious it can be. Take my word for it, whatever you're thinking, it won't work. The only theory that holds true as far as prison management is concerned is Murphy's Law – if something can go wrong, it will.' I looked at each of them in turn. Showed them just how serious I was, for a change. 'If you want my advice, forget the whole scheme. There must be easier ways of making money.'

'Leave the corporate strategy to us, Shannon,' Paradine sneered.

'Look,' I said. 'Why do you think the government is doing this? It's not just because of the money generated by the sale, or the savings to be made through a private contract. It's also a way of off-loading the worst element of the prison population. You'll be lumbered with the hardest, meanest, most difficult, most dangerous prisoners.'

Kinsella's eyes ran down a print-out on the desk and his head gave a little nod.

'But we can take that into our calculations,' O'Kane pointed out enthusiastically. 'Knowing the prisoners in advance means...'

'Thank you, Shannon,' Paradine interrupted. 'I think we need to discuss this matter among ourselves.'

I shrugged my shoulders and walked to the door.

'Don't forget the image angle,' I said, determined to have the last word. 'If things go wrong and prisoners do escape, then Glenshield could become a laughing stock. That would have a knock-on effect on all parts of your business.'

'Thank you, Shannon,' Paradine said again, this time with a prolonged sigh.

I closed the door behind me.

And stood with my ear pressed against it.

'I agree with Shannon,' I heard Kinsella say.

'It's too late for second thoughts,' Paradine said. 'We're committed now. No turning back.'

That much I understood.

It was the story of my life.

CHAPTER SEVENTEEN

Chelmsford

Monday dawned and the laundry beckoned with all the appeal of spending a day in a locked room full of tarantulas.

I sat in the canteen opposite Norman and pushed porridge moodily around the plastic bowl. Yes, they really do serve porridge in prison. And it's just as awful as you imagine. Grey as dish-water. Frugally thin. But with hidden depths – lumps as big as cherry stones. If you wanted to know what the future had in store, you could fish them out and lay them on the rim of the bowl, then count off 'tinker, tailor, soldier...'

Toddy, unfortunately, did not cook breakfast. Even at this early hour he was already heavily involved in the preparations for lunch – the sort of meat he had to work with demanded more stewing than an angler's waders. A specially recruited team of dedicated sadists were responsible for the state of the porridge. This had two consequences. We had the fattest pigs of any prison smallholding in the country. And 400 men started the day as mean as hell.

I thrust the bowl away from me.

'Not to your liking, Goldilocks?' Norman said.

I grunted.

'Don't blame you,' he said. 'What I wouldn't give for a decent bacon sandwich. What happens to the bleeding pigs from the farm, anyway? How come we never see any pork?' He looked at me thoughtfully. 'You know,' he said, 'if there's ever a riot in here, it won't be because of pitiful wages, inadequate association or exercise periods, brutal warders even. Porridge! That'll be the cause.' He raised his voice to rouse the other inmates. 'When the revolution comes, brothers, we'll line every prison governor up against the wall and shovel great ladles of porridge down their throats.'

I stared down at the slice of bread that lay un-appealingly on the table (there were no compartmentalised trays at breakfast, too much washing-up – you juggled your way back from the serving counter with an enamel mug of tea, the dreaded bowl and a slice or two of bread and spread). Today's thin smearing was red. Strawberry? Raspberry? Plum? Impossible to tell, even on close inspection. Tasting it didn't provide any clues either. The stuff – well, you couldn't dignify it with the name jam – arrived in tins the size of Olympic podia, with labels that probably proclaimed proudly, 'Ideal for consumption by convicts and preserving wrought iron from the injurious effects of rust.'

Hunger persuaded me to take a bite. Christ, the bread was stale even on Monday mornings.

A heated argument was gaining momentum at a nearby table. 'It's damson, I tell you,' someone said, to the derision of his peers.

'Let's go, Norman,' I said.

Back in the cell I donned my overalls and waited for the bell. Ask not for whom the bell tolls, Shannon.

'How stupid we've been,' Norman said, smacking his forehead.

'Why's that?' I asked innocently.

'Well, here you are worried about being attacked by Connor and we pass up the golden opportunity of filling a sock full of porridge lumps. Still, I suppose you didn't want to get charged with possession of a deadly weapon.'

'Such a comfort, Norman.'

'What are you going to do?' he asked, his humour evaporating with each passing second.

'Just try to remember everything that Arthur taught me, I suppose.'

'Anything specific that might reassure an old man?'

'Back in Brixton,' I said, 'when I first asked Arthur to tutor me in the rudiments of his art, do you know what he did?'

'Pass,' Norman said. 'It's not my specialist subject.'

'He took one look at me and said I would never survive by fighting fair. He would just have to teach me how to fight dirty instead.'

'Fight dirty?' Norman said. 'In a laundry?'

The bell made us both jump.

'Good luck, Nick,' he said. 'See you later.'

'Yes,' I said, as we walked from the cell. 'See you later.'

In the corridor, men scurried to their respective places of work with that special brand of enthusiasm born out of pure boredom. The metal stairs quivered and rang out discordantly as heavy boots thumped downwards. At the bottom, Norman turned right to join the élite few on the way to the cushy jobs in administration. I turned left with the masses.

The only good point about Mondays is that it takes a little time for the steam to build up in the laundry. After two empty, unheated, workless days the walls glistened with condensation. In an hour the heat from the various appliances would cause every last drop to vaporise, producing the first quantum leap in the level of humidity. But for a while it would be cool and bearable.

Stebbings, size 12 boots and IQ to match, stood at the door like a demonic equivalent of St Peter at the gates of hell. As we filed through, he issued each of us with our allotted task for the day.

'Shannon,' he said through twisted lips, mock contemplation on his bloated face. 'Tongs, I think.'

Gee, thanks, Nelson. Do the same for you one day, if ever that beautiful occasion arises.

I picked up the four-foot-long tongs from the table and took my place at one of the copper vats. The water was just coming to the boil, the clothes beneath disappearing from sight as the bubbles increased in number and danced erratically outwards from the middle. The familiar yellow-grey scum was beginning to form on top of the liquid. My stomach thanked me for my consideration in deciding against breakfast.

The last few stragglers sloped through the doorway. Connor gave me a sick smile. There was a red mark across his thick skull from the collision with the bunk – and a gratifying bow to his legs. He walked, cowboy-fashion, to one of the irons.

'Come on, Shannon,' Nelson barked. 'Stir it up a little.'

I plunged the tongs into the vat and whirled the witch's brew around with an experienced bare minimum of effort. The resulting cloud of steam hit me in the face and the first beads of perspiration of the day burst onto my forehead. From now on it was sweat all the way.

Within an hour the usual array of aches and pains were tormenting my body. Only today there was a new addition to the catalogue – a crick in my neck from craning round to keep one eye on Connor.

As we worked, Nelson and his two associates made regular tours urging us on with constant lashings from the whips of their tongues. At least it made a change from the sounds of hissing and bubbling. Apart from the warders, no-one talked here. No-one sang. No-one whistled. No-one had the heart for anything, except watching the minute hand of the clock make its slow progress around the dial.

A quarter to eleven. The mouths of the screws were salivating with thoughts of coffee and biscuits. What a life! Christ, I'd almost forgotten what a biscuit looked like. Warder number one took the first break. Nelson and his sole colleague circulated among us more quickly to compensate for the diminished manpower.

Ten to eleven. Warder number two left ten minutes early, and my heart sank. 'Early' and 'late' are not words that have any place in the prison vocabulary. Strict adherence to the clock is one of the major commandments in here – it comes just below not coveting your neighbour's cache of snout and drinking up your bromide-laced tea. It's what makes prison tick. This break with routine was ominous. A knot formed in my belly.

Nine minutes to eleven. 'Call of nature,' Nelson announced, heading quickly for the door. 'Behave yourselves while I'm gone.'

The knot tightened. Adrenalin primed my system. My throat became desert-dry. I wiped sweating palms down the seams of my overalls. Looked across at Connor. He grinned. Abandoned his post at the iron. Walked slowly, awkwardly, menacingly, towards me.

I was ready for him.

But not for the other two.

I should have guessed that Connor would want

215

the odds stacked in his favour. The purposeful movements of two fugitives from *Planet of the Apes* told me I'd been right about Marquis of Queensberry rules. Somehow prescience wasn't much of a consolation, right now.

'Time to settle our score,' Connor said, keeping a distance of fifteen feet between us. He didn't have to make his move yet. His two simian partners in crime were closing in from left and right.

'You don't frighten me,' I lied, turning my back with feigned nonchalance to stir the boiling liquid and drag a shirt towards the surface. The show of bravado didn't accomplish much. The smaller of the two flankers slowed in his tracks, but the larger, hairier gorilla on the left continued unfalteringly.

Now or never, Shannon.

I whirled round from the vat, swinging the heavy tongs in an arc. Thank God for laundry muscles!

I released the tension on the teeth of the tongs as Gorilla drew near. The scalding hot shirt flew through the air. It made a dull slapping sound as it connected with his head. The forward momentum transferred to the tail. The shirt wrapped itself around his face.

He screamed, the animal wail muted by the enveloping material. As he clutched and ripped at the shirt in a frenzied effort to free himself, I threw a straight left into his stomach. His body buckled and hit the floor.

The odds against me were down to two to one.

I turned my attention to the man on the right.

He eyed me warily. But frustratingly stood his ground.

There was no point standing there like the proverbial contents of half a bra in a trance – time was definitely not on my side. I had no way of knowing how long Hot Cheeks Gorilla would stay down. Swinging the tongs to and fro like a cudgel, I advanced on the man playing right wing. He backed away while his brain worked on the unexpected situation: this wasn't the way it was supposed to happen – it should have been me, not him, on the defensive.

From behind me I heard the weary whine of Connor's voice.

'If you want a bloody job done properly in this place, you have to do it your bleeding self.'

I ran towards the standing apeman. Wasn't much of a strategy, but at least it increased the distance from Connor. I shouted at the top of my voice as I ran. Can't remember what I shouted. The words were designed to invoke fear and panic in him, not to strike up a meaningful communication between the two of us.

He stepped further back. Found he was up against the mangle. Having no alternative, he squared up to me, fists raised just below his chin.

Boxing match with you, I thought? No way.

So, at the last moment, my full-pitched charge became a flying leap. The instep of my boots caught him an inch below the knee and scraped down his shins. He let out a long screech. And fell forwards with the impact.

Right on top of me.

The air rushed from my lungs with the weight

of his body. The tongs slipped from my grasp. Clattered on the concrete. Bounced out of reach.

From my position pinned to the floor, I could see an upside-down Connor coming closer and closer.

I pushed up with all my strength.

It was no good.

The injured, and now very angry, thug was too heavy for me. He placed two hairy hands on my shoulders and pressed down to hold me prisoner.

As hard as I tried, I couldn't budge him.

Well, I thought, if I can't move him, then he'll just have to move himself I wriggled my left arm, threatening to break loose. As he concentrated on countering this movement, I jerked my right arm free. Sent my elbow crashing into his nose.

A howl filled the air.

And he rolled off me.

Good old Arthur. Hit someone on the nose, he'd said, and it has two effects. It hurts like bloody hell. And it has the advantage of making their eyes water so hard they can't see. Remember that, Nick.

I sprang to my feet the very instant I was free.

But still too late to avoid Connor's hand clamping down on the back of my collar.

He dragged me backwards. Swung me around like a rag doll. Then let go.

I went spinning across the room and thudded into the nearest of the copper vats. It wobbled. Boiling hot water sloshed over the rim and ran down my shoulders. It was my turn to scream now.

Connor hit me in the solar plexus. Grinned as

I jack-knifed in agony. Cackled loudly as he grabbed me by the lapels and hoisted me in the air.

Then he simply pushed me backwards.

The hard metal edge of the vat dug into the scalded flesh of my shoulders. The pain was intolerable. A red mist swam in front of my eyes. I realised, sickeningly, that my system was nearing the point where the automatic self-defence mechanism of unconsciousness would cut in and I would be rendered helpless.

I thrust with all my might against his shoulders. But it was useless. His strength was just too great. The weight of his body pinned my arms.

Connor forced me further back. And further down.

Steam seared the back of my neck as it dipped towards the foaming liquid. I could even hear the bubbles bursting as they broke the surface.

'Bye-bye, Shannon,' Connor said. 'Hello, Phantom of the Opera.'

His face was so close now that I was splattered with globules of his saliva as he spat the words at me. I fought the instinctive revulsion that made me want to move my head away – which would only have resulted in a premature appointment with the water below.

Savouring my fate, he grinned at me one last time.

I did the only thing I could. Brought the top of my head up with all the force left in my body. Smacked it into his nose.

He staggered back, dazed and temporarily blinded.

I sprang to the side, away from the boiling vat. Leaping to the nearest mangle, I grabbed one of the wheeled containers standing by its side. Swivelling it round on its castors, I ran forwards, using the container as an improvised battering ram.

Connor took the full impact on his chest. Lost his footing in a pool of spilt water. Tumbled to the ground.

I knew I had to finish this once and for all.

I retrieved the tongs. Placed one foot on Connor's neck. And the pincers of the tongs on his tender testicles.

I squeezed with just enough force to hold the grip. And for him to appreciate what was about to happen.

He squirmed and wriggled in pain.

A circle of other inmates formed. 'Squeeze 'em. Squeeze 'em,' they chanted, a primitive bloodlust filling their minds. Some cowardly soul with a grudge to settle kicked Connor in the ribs. A second boot followed.

'That's enough,' I shouted angrily.

'Now,' I said to Connor. 'What's it to be? We can either declare a truce. Or I can let the mob have you. Or maybe you'd prefer to start practising singing "Ave Maria".'

I increased the pressure of my grip, and twisted the tongs at the same time.

'Christ,' he shouted. 'No more. For God's sake, no more.'

I eased off slightly.

'Well?' I said. 'Say it. Nice and loud. In front of everybody.'

'You win,' he replied through gritted teeth. 'A truce. Whatever you want. Just let go.'

The following day I stood at the counter in the canteen.

Serving.

When Nelson had finally put in an appearance, we had a cosy chat about rotas for coffee breaks and inconvenient bladder problems. As a result of which he kindly escorted me to the surgery for the scalds on my shoulders to be dressed. And then to the Governor's office. Where he explained the unfortunate accident that had occurred. And that, in his opinion, I was unsuited for the work in the laundry. 'Transfer in order, sir?' he said.

I'm sure the Governor suspected something. But he would not budge on my request for the library. Would have made too much sense to put an educated person in charge of the library. Where would we all be if prisons ran on logic? Jesus, anything might happen then.

Still, the kitchen had its advantages. I could learn a lot from Toddy – about time I was able to boil an egg without turning it into a small ovoid cricket ball. Probably wouldn't feel as hungry in future, either.

And I could hold Connor to his word.

Otherwise he would always be wondering whether he could chance eating what I dished out for him.

And, on top of all that, it couldn't make the porridge any worse, could it?

CHAPTER EIGHTEEN

Arlene greeted me with a tired smile as I stepped through the door. She was sitting (dozing?) in one of the armchairs, Count Basie playing quietly in the background. She was still wearing the long, deep pink, straight-cut jacket which, with the black skirt, gave her an air of easy elegance and natural class. By the fireplace her stiletto shoes lay, heels together, where she had kicked them off. A large, untouched drink sat on the floor by her right hand.

I walked over to her, kissed her on the cheek and perched on the arm of her chair.

'Hard day?' I asked, putting my arm around her.

'We did Surrey today,' she said.

'What, all of it?'

'It sure felt that way.' She picked up the drink and passed it to me. It was one of her special Unwinders. 'You know,' she said, looking up at me, 'I must have seen about a dozen houses over the course of the day. And you know the worst part?'

'Tell me,' I said.

'All that tea I had to drink. Earl Grey, China, Assam, Ceylon, orange pekoe. You name it, I've drunk it. Do you British never stop drinking tea?'

'Only when we're asleep,' I said. 'But we're working on that. Intravenous drips seem the best solution, but they have the disadvantage of limiting your mobility in bed.'

'Then we won't invest in one, huh?'

I bent down and kissed her on the lips.

'I love you,' she said.

'You too.'

We kissed longer and more passionately this time, our eyes closed and the world shut out.

'Sorry,' Norman said. He stood in the doorway, unsure whether to cross the threshold. 'I could go out again if you want. Take a walk round the block. Or, by the looks of things, around the M25.'

'Come in, you old fool,' I said. 'Where have you been anyway?'

'I had to get some new glasses. All this staring at the screen made me realise how much my eyesight had deteriorated.' He dug into a carrier bag and produced a spectacle case. 'Look at these,' he said, popping on a pair of tortoiseshell glasses. 'They've got an anti-glare coating, specially for working with computers.'

'Wonderful,' I said unenthusiastically. I was wondering what the next computer-related purchase would be. Wall-mounted mirror, so that he could see what was happening behind him without having to turn away from the screen? Two-fingered leather glove for non-slip manipulation of the mouse? Anti-static carpet slippers?

'You look very distinguished,' Arlene said.

'Thank you, my dear,' he said stuffily, adopting the new persona that the glasses had bestowed on him. 'What can I get you?'

She raised the glass. 'Maybe freshen this? Just

ice and vodka, okay? And one for Nick, of course.'

'Your wish is my command. Anything for a person with such discerning taste.'

'Don't be hard on him,' Arlene said to me, while Norman was out of the room. 'Another few weeks and he'll probably lose interest in all this computer stuff. Humour him, huh?'

Norman returned with the drinks and sat down opposite us.

'How was Sandra Redmond?' he asked Arlene.

'That is one hell of a gutsy lady,' she said. 'Sure, she cried – we both cried, dammit – when she told me the full story, but this mess would have destroyed most people. Her whole life is disappearing down the tubes, but she's hanging on in there. Jeez, I hope nothing happens to the baby. The prospect of the child is the only thing that's keeping her sane.'

Arlene took a deep draught from her glass. Not for refreshment, but out of a desperate need for the soothing numbness of alcohol.

'Sandra was spring-cleaning when I arrived. Excuse to throw out her husband's stuff, I reckon. There were boxes of clothes, books, a whole mass of old newspapers, all piled up for the garbage. I made her some coffee. Forced her to sit down for a while. And, talk. And boy, did she need to talk.'

Norman and I were silent, knowing that Sandra had passed some of the burden to Arlene and that she, in turn, had to share the load.

'She blames herself, you know,' Arlene said. 'Not for the gambling itself. But for not recognising what was going on. And putting a stop to it. She can see now that all the signs were there – Martin became increasingly restless, nervy, snapped at her for no reason, couldn't sleep nights.' Arlene rummaged in her bag for a cigarette. Lit it, hands shaking with rage. 'Hell, I told her, it wasn't her damn fault. Martin was addicted. It didn't matter what Sandra did. The ball was in his court. Unless he truly wanted to stop, there was nothing that could be done. Only he could save himself.'

I nodded my agreement. Without commitment, without conviction, personal change is impossible.

'The guilt would be bad enough on its own,' Arlene said. 'But when you add the financial pressures. He'd cleared out their savings. Sold her jewellery. Used his credit cards to the limit. Even had an overdraft at the bank. The five grand he won on the day he died will be swallowed up clearing the debts.' She took a frantic puff at the cigarette. 'The insurance companies won't pay out. The policies don't cover suicide, it seems.'

I had learned that fact from my own bitter experience. I wished that I had not been so hasty in writing my statement. Then, perhaps, I could have colluded with Walker. Cooked up some story about his death being an accident. How Redmond was threatening us with the chair and lost his footing. Chair goes through the window, Redmond overbalances and follows it. But it was too late now.

'It looks like the house will be repossessed too,' Arlene said sadly. 'Sandra can't meet the payments. She'll probably lose everything. Not a terrific start in life for a new baby. They hadn't even bought anything for the kid – not a cot, clothes, diapers, nothing. That damned husband of hers had said it might be bad luck! I hope he rots in hell.'

She frowned and shook her head. 'Poor girl. I feel so sorry for her. The only thing in life she has to look forward to is that beautiful moment when the midwife hands the baby to you for the very first time and you feel its warmth against your body. For Sandra, it's all downhill from there.'

Tears began to form in Arlene's eyes. I put my arm around her. Squeezed her tight. Racked my brains for something positive to say. Anything to make her feel better.

'I just wish there was something we could do,' Arlene pleaded, staring into my eyes through a curtain of tears.

'Hit the shops, Arlene,' I said. 'Buy Sandra the whole works. Whatever it is you need – however weird and wonderful – when you have a kid, just get it. Hand her the receipts too. Tell her that way it's not bad luck. And that, in any case, she's had her lifetime's share of that.'

'Thanks, Nick,' she said. 'I probably would have done it anyway, but it makes me feel better knowing I have your support.'

'And mine,' chipped in Norman. 'Three-way split, okay?'

'You got it,' Arlene said, smiling at last.

'Well, Nick,' said Norman, anxious to change the subject before Arlene's enthusiasm drew us into the impossible task of helping her draw up a shopping list, 'how did you get on today? A success, I presume. I don't see any evidence of the dropped-crotch green uniform.'

'I did it,' I said. 'Finally landed a job in Accounts. And what an eye-opener it was.'

'You managed to check on the exports then?'

'No, not yet,' I said, cocking my head at him. 'You are a crafty bugger, Norman. You never let on about the exports, but you had a hunch about them too.'

'Who taught you everything you know, Glasshopper?' he said proudly, his eyes staring blindly into the middle distance. 'Did you think my memory was deteriorating faster than my eyesight? Even if that were the case, my olfactory glands are still as good as they ever were.'

'What are you two on about?' asked Arlene.

'A nose for fraud,' I said. 'Something doesn't smell right. Let me explain the hunch.' Norman leaned back, tutor-fashion, ready to assess the performance of his pupil. 'Glenshield are stretched to the limit. They've even had to resort to sub-contracting labour from other security firms. Agreed?'

'Yep,' she said, with encouragement, not en-lightenment.

'Well,' I said, 'exporting doesn't make much sense. As your fellow Americans would phrase it – exporting is one hell of a pain in the butt. Endless paperwork. Foreign languages. Alien cultures. Communications nightmare – postal delays, time differences, inadequate phone networks in many countries. By and large, companies only export under two circumstances:

when they're desperate for business, or when the home market is so sewn up that there's nowhere else to go for expansion. Neither circumstance applies to Glenshield.'

'So what's the scam?' Arlene asked. 'That is what you're implying, isn't it? Something – as your fellow Englishmen would say – *terribly fishy* going on.'

'*Touché*,' I said smiling. 'Yes, that's my guess. You see, it's the countries themselves that bother me. Three newly formed Eastern European states and a near-bankrupt South American republic. They all have a common link, you see.'

'All but one,' Norman corrected.

'Okay,' I admitted, 'all but one.'

'And what is this common link?' Arlene asked. 'Apart from the fact that they are all places I wouldn't visit if you paid me.'

'They all have very fragile economies,' I said. 'So fragile in fact that they have been forced to impose strict currency regulations.'

'And where,' Norman explained, 'you have strict regulations on the amount of money that can flow out of a country, you invariably find a thriving black market in the currency.'

Arlene sipped her drink thoughtfully. 'I still don't get it,' she said. 'How can this possibly benefit Glenshield?'

'It's only a theory,' I said, realising the risk of building bricks without straw.

'But one that has been practised to good effect in the past by many a fraudster,' Norman added.

'What happens with one of these economies is this.' I spoke slowly, searching carefully for a simple explanation. 'The government, in order to protect their currency, limits its outflow. Otherwise everyone would exchange their inflation-hit home currency for stable hard currencies – dollars, pounds, marks, for example. Money, therefore, can only be taken out of the country with the permission of the central bank. Are you with me so far?'

'Kind of,' she said, taking a bigger swig of her drink.

'Now these countries have to trade overseas. They have to sell whatever goods they make – raffia espadrilles, cabbage vodka, I don't know.'

'Cabbage vodka!' Arlene interrupted, wrinkling her nose. 'Yuk!'

'And, more to the point,' I continued, 'they also need to import. Modern equipment for their factories. Food for their people. Levis for the fashion-conscious. Whatever.'

Arlene nodded. 'Got you.'

'But no-one will trade with them unless there is a guarantee of the value of the money involved. So the country has to fix an official exchange rate for all trade. That way, if I sell – let's call the currency canoosras – a million canoosras' worth of machinery, and the official exchange rate is one canoosra equals one pound, then I'm *guaranteed* to get a million pounds when they are exchanged at my bank in England. I'm protected against inflation and any possible future depreciation or devaluation of the currency.'

'Seems logical,' Arlene said. 'Both the buyer and the seller know exactly what they are in for. So what's the scam?'

'One canoosra equals one pound, right?' Norman said.

'Right.'

'No,' he said, grinning broadly. 'Wrong.'

'But you just said...'

'You have to forgive Norman,' I said to her. 'He likes playing these games. You should hear his "what's one plus one?" routine. What he means is that the official rate might be one to one. But the black-market rate is probably more like five whatever it was...'

'Canoosras,' Arlene said. 'See, I was paying attention.'

'...five canoosras to one pound. Everyone in the country is so desperate to get rid of these damned canoosras that they will give five of them for one pound. That's the scam.' I paused to take a long, slow mouthful of vodka. I could see that Norman was straining at the leash.

'So what you do,' he jumped in, 'what we're reckoning an enterprising company like Glenshield is doing, is obtain a contract for goods or services worth, say, two hundred thousand canoosras. Your contact at the buying agency signs the official forms but, for a consideration, changes the total – authorises the central bank to release the sum of one million canoosras. You then go along to the black market and purchase the difference of eight hundred thousand canoosras for the princely sum of just one hundred and sixty thousand pounds. You pop it into your bank account in the foreign country, along with the legitimate two hundred thousand canoosras from the contract. Then, when you transfer the lot back to this country, you have a million pounds. And a very juicy profit. Even if you sell your goods or services at cost, you have multiplied your money five times through your purchase on the black market.'

'Wow,' said Arlene. 'Some scam.'

'I still have to prove it,' I reminded them both.

'And then will that be the end of it?' Arlene asked. 'You can drag Collins in to arrest them?'

'Unfortunately not,' I said.

'Come on, Nick,' Norman said. 'You know what they're up to.'

I flashed him a warning. Not in front of Arlene. No need to worry her at this stage.

'The problem, Arlene,' I said, 'is that what Glenshield is doing – or rather, what we suspect they are doing – is not actually illegal. Not in this country, at least. Sharp practice, maybe. But they haven't broken English law. I don't know what the foreign countries could do, mind, but as far as Collins is concerned, he would be powerless to act.'

'So what are you going to do?' she asked.

'First of all I want to prove it. To do that I have to examine the sales value and the costs of each of the contracts, and establish that the profit is too high to be the result of legitimate trade.'

'And then?' she asked.

'Then I have to try to find something else to satisfy Collins's hunger for revenge.'

'So it looks like I spend the rest of the week touring the countryside. And drinking more tea.' She screwed up her face. 'You know,' she said, 'the idea of cabbage vodka is beginning to sound

231

more appealing with every minute.'

Apart from the hunch about the export scam, my other theory – triggered by the impressive graph in the briefing pack handed to me by O'Kane – was that Glenshield had been drumming up their own business: targetting potential areas for private policing and doing a spot of burglary, vandalism, car theft, whatever. After six months or so of hitting an area, the local residents would be falling over themselves to sign up with Glenshield. The crime rate, according to the graph, then dropped sharply. Not because Glenshield made their day and night patrols – although that might deter the real criminals – but due to calling a halt to their own nefarious activities. Arlene's role, her *raison d'être* for the next week, was to talk to estate agents and house owners. Posing as your stereotypical New Yorker, paranoid about crime, she could naturally broach the subject of the safety of the area. Try to gather hearsay evidence to support my theory.

'What was their accounting system like?' Norman asked.

'If you don't mind,' Arlene said wearily, 'I'll leave you boys to the technical jazz and fix us something to eat.'

'Not for me,' Norman said. 'I'm at Toddy's this evening.'

Arlene's eyes twinkled.

'Something light perhaps then, Arlene,' I said.

'You bet,' she replied with a grin. 'Another drink, Nick? Norman?'

We both nodded greedily.

Over the second drink I told Norman all about

232

my day in Accounts. The intricacies of the system. The ingenuity of the staff, and how they had managed to override certain elements of the security controls. The BACS direct-settlement method for paying suppliers; the long credit period taken.

'What about bank statements?' he asked.

'I haven't had a chance to look yet. But, if Tricia's right about the tight cash control, and given Glenshield's appetite for receiving the maximum amount of interest, I would expect statements to arrive each morning. I imagine they shunt money into and out of their deposit account on a day-by-day basis, only ever keeping the absolute minimum balance on current account. After all, that's part of the principle of value-dating the payments – instructing the bank today to pay suppliers at a future specified date.'

'I am not your grandmother,' Norman said haughtily. 'You do not have to teach me how to suck eggs. Have you forgotten Chelmsford? My seminal – definitive, I like to think – exposition on the subject of value-dating?'

'Sorry,' I said. 'Got carried away. Hey, you'll never guess what Glenshield are planning next?'

'If I'll never guess, you had better tell me.'

'Private prisons! They are putting in a tender to take over Strathmoor and run it as a maximum-security prison.'

'Bloody hell. Is there no limit to what this company won't do? Have they got more money than sense?'

'Apparently so. They're backed by a bunch of

venture-capitalists. Never heard of them before. Prospekt.'

'Shit,' said Norman under his breath.

'You've heard of them?'

'I've seen the name. Come on,' he said, moving over to the computer. 'I'll show you.'

He sat down. Switched on the computer. Tapped his fingers with mounting impatience. Cast a nervous glance at the kitchen door. Placed one finger against his lips.

The screen blinked into life. Norman deftly manoeuvred the mouse onto one of the icons. Double-clicked. Slipped in a floppy disk. Summoned up a file. Scrolled rapidly down the screen until he found the heading he was seeking.

There it was:

31st December.

Prospekt Holdings.

Recipients of the sum of one hundred thousand pounds.

Dividend payments. On their shareholding in Van Damm Limited, Diamond Merchants.

Norman exited from Chi-Rho and called up the word-processing package. He typed just four words.

'The Coin of Fear'

Then he added a questionmark.

CHAPTER NINETEEN

The sound of the front door closing woke me. It was a relief. I'd been having the same dream again – Susie, my sister, smiling up at me while I pumped the lethal dose of morphine into her broken body. Her blue-tinged lips parting to speak the words I wanted so much to hear, but which never materialised. I shivered. Not through cold. But with the unwelcome presence of the dead.

The digits of the alarm clock glowed red as hell. It was a little after one in the morning – Norman's usual time for arriving home when he had been on duty at the restaurant. I turned over onto my side, assumed a subconscious foetal position and cuddled up close to Arlene, one knee over her leg, one hand on her ribs. She stirred – as perhaps I had intended – and I moved my hand up to her breast. Her fingers came to life and began a slow wandering journey up and down my spine.

By half past one we were asleep again.

At four o'clock I awoke to a crash, and a curse.

My whole system jumped to red alert. Something was wrong. Norman. Was he all right? Stubbornly he still refused to consult a doctor – maybe I would have done the same in his place, I don't know. He ate like a horse and was as thin as a sparrow. It was an ominous sign that he chose to ignore, and none of his friends – including me – had the heart to comment, or any desire to dwell on it.

Easing my arm from under Arlene's shoulder, I slid noiselessly from the bed and grabbed a pair of jeans from the overspill wardrobe that was the chair. Carefully zipping them up (well, this wasn't the time to go scrabbling about on the floor for my underpants), I padded across the room. Silently, my breath held, I turned the handle of the bedroom door. Peeked through the narrow gap.

Norman was kneeling on the floor.

I entered the sitting room, quietly closing the door behind me so as not to disturb Arlene for a second time that night.

'What's the matter?' I whispered.

Norman spun round.

'Christ,' he said. 'You made me jump. Don't do that again in a hurry. Not unless you want me to have a heart attack.'

'Sorry,' I said. His face was white, but purely as a result of the start I had given him. My fears about his welfare receded to the back-burner.

Like a mother who has just seen her son escape being run over in the road, anger, brushing aside relief, welled up inside me.

'Hang on a minute,' I said. '*You* were the one to wake me. What am I apologising for? Don't you know what time it is? What the hell are you up to?'

'Right at this moment,' he said, 'I'm mopping up a whole bloody potful of coffee. Why don't you make yourself useful and give me a hand?

Then I'll tell you why I haven't been to bed yet.'

'Give me that,' I said, pointing to the tea towel in his hand. 'Go get a bowl of warm water. And a clean cloth.'

He trooped off petulantly to the kitchen.

Just what I need, I thought, my mood becoming blacker by the minute. The middle of the bloody night and here I am, down on my hands and knees, doing Mrs Mop impersonations. To make matters worse, Norman's computer was switched on. The printer was churning out page after page of God knows what. The time had finally come. Norman and I were going to have a serious talk. Whether he liked it or not.

He placed the bowl on the floor and I worked away at the brown mess on the carpet. He walked across to check the printer! Thank you very much, Norman.

'Turn that off,' I said. 'I have had just about enough of that damned computer. This is the last straw.'

'No,' he said. 'I won't turn it off.'

I finished swabbing down the carpet and stood up, looking him straight in the eye.

'Norman,' I said quietly. 'If it wasn't for the fact that Arlene is asleep, I would be shouting at you so loud they would hear me in Charing Cross. Turn that thing off this very minute, and let's all get to bed.'

'Do you think I want to be up at this bloody hour? Why not give me the benefit of the doubt. How about letting me explain, eh? Just ten minutes?' He gave me a winning smile, which weakened my resolve. 'That's all I ask. At the end of that time, if you still feel the same, I'll get rid of the computer for good. Is that a deal?'

'Okay,' I said eagerly. This should be interesting. How was he going to talk himself out of this hole? And that promise.

'I got to thinking,' he said slowly. 'While I was at Toddy's.'

Having aroused my curiosity, he made himself comfortable in the chair by the computer. This had every appearance of being a long story. Resigned to my fate, I walked over to the settee. My bare feet squelched on the wet patch of carpet. Ugh!

'And the more I thought,' he continued, frowning deeply, 'the more worried I became. This connection between Prospekt and Van Damm. It puts a whole new complexion on everything. Redmond. Glenshield. The export scam. Every hunch that has been tickling the backs of our necks now seems more likely.'

'Didn't we establish that earlier this evening?' I said, shrugging my shoulders. 'The Coin of Fear. Granted, this ownership link adds a new dimension. But it doesn't take us any closer to solving the problem of Glenshield. We need proof. Proof of some crime. And, somehow or other,' I said, with more determination than confidence, 'I'll get that proof.'

'I don't think you should.'

'Come on, Norman,' I said irritably, 'you know I can't drop this case. Collins would never let me, for one thing. Remember his threat – his promise – about getting my licence revoked?'

'And we mustn't forget your side of the bargain, must we?' he said sharply. 'Re-open the case on your sister's hit-and-run.' He made a visible effort to compose himself. 'Let it drop, Nick. For your sake – for everybody's sake. The ball game has changed.'

'Then I'll just have to learn the new rules,' I said.

'That's the problem. I'm not sure there are any.'

He picked up a sheaf of papers from the printer's output tray. Waved them at me in frustration.

'I've been doing some checking,' he said. 'Knew I wouldn't be able to get any sleep. Thought I might as well use the time profitably. So I started to dig around for information on Prospekt.'

'It's not possible,' I said. 'Not at this time of the morning.'

'It *is* possible. Through the power of the computer. And the modem. This,' he said, wiggling a wire at the back of the computer, 'allows me access to any database – at any time. Computers don't close down for eight hours' kip a night. Information-providers are open for business twenty-four hours a day.'

'Okay,' I said grudgingly. 'So what have you found?'

'I started by dialling up a database of company accounts. Set up a search on Prospekt. Guess where they are registered?'

'If we follow through the export scam to its ultimate conclusion, then they will be registered somewhere offshore.' I went through the list in

239

my mind. Discounted Grand Cayman and Bermuda – their veil of secrecy can be lifted if there is a good reason to believe an account contains the proceeds of crime. There were so many possibilities. A myriad of countries where the banking system was still unshakeable and the golden rule was to disclose absolutely nothing – not even a client's existence. 'Bahamas?' I said. 'British Virgin Isles? Liechtenstein?'

'Got it in three,' he said. 'Liechtenstein.' Norman wagged a finger at me. His eyes locked onto mine. 'If Prospekt is not an *anstalt*, my brave but stupid friend, I'll eat my collection of floppy disks.'

I could see now why Norman was in such a panic. I had managed to suppress my suspicion earlier. Used Arlene as an easy excuse when Norman had tried to raise the matter. I could not continue to bury my head in the sand any longer. An *anstalt*, dammit!

Since the creation of *anstalts* in Liechtenstein in the Twenties, they had been one of the favourite vehicles of the rich for sheltering their money. *Anstalts* were single-shareholder companies. They enjoyed tax-free profit distribution, reduced capital tax, absence of supervision and examination by the tax administration, absolute tax and banking secrecy. They were cheap to set up. And ensured complete anonymity to the provider of the capital and their beneficiaries – there was no way on earth of establishing who owned an *anstalt*, how much money was involved, where it came from, or where it went.

'It looks bad,' I said.

'*It looks bad!*' he repeated, having trouble keeping his voice down. 'It doesn't look bad, it looks bleeding terrible!' He shook his head at me. 'Well,' he challenged, 'are you going to say it? Or shall I?'

'All right,' I said, waving my hands vaguely in the air, 'there is a possibility...' Norman frowned, 'a probability...' he rolled his eyes. 'Okay, I give in. It's almost a dead-cert then.' I could not prevaricate any further. 'Prospekt has only one purpose. The laundering of drug money.'

'Thank you,' he said. 'At last.'

'But–' I started to say.

'Exactly what I was going to say,' he interrupted. 'But that is not all. After checking on Prospekt, I initiated a search on their share-holdings. Databases are wonderful things, you know. What would have taken days – weeks even – at Companies House can now be achieved in a matter of minutes in the comfort of your own home. Prospekt has a controlling stake in seventeen companies, most of them in some way involved in the import-export business. This isn't some tuppenny-ha'penny drugs dealer we're talking about. This is one of the big boys. Christ, it may be a whole bunch of drug barons operating in concert, for all we know.'

I sighed helplessly. I could not disagree with Norman. The stakes had been raised to the height of the ionosphere. And yet...?

'One last thing,' Norman said, his face grim. 'Then we contact Collins. Don't look at me like that, Nick. This is too big now. It's way over our heads. If you don't call in Collins, then I promise

241

you I will.'

'What's the one last thing?' I asked, intrigued.

'Finally,' he said with an air of triumph, 'I dialled into a press-cuttings service. Typed in the names of Prospekt and its seventeen companies and waited to see what they had on them. Most of it was pretty boring stuff from the financial pages – regurgitated press releases and the like. But not all.'

He sorted through the stack of paper and passed three pages across to me.

The first cutting was over two years old: 15th August – bang in the middle of the silly season, when newspapers are desperate for any story to fill their pages. A drunken driver had crashed. And sailed over a cliff on the south coast. He was, the story said, an accountant. For a company that – according to Norman's research – was owned by Prospekt.

I felt a chill run down my spine.

The second cutting, eighteen months ago, concerned a young wages clerk. She had been raped, and then murdered.

The chill reached hypothermia level.

The third was less than six months old. The chief executive of an engineering company, and his wife, had been found dead in their home. Bound. Gagged. And repeatedly stabbed.

'Whoever they are,' I said, my blood temperature down to absolute zero, 'they don't mess around, these people, do they?'

'That's my point,' Norman said.

'So, somehow,' I said, avoiding the immediate issue, 'Redmond had made the connection between these three deaths. That's why he preferred to jump rather than wait around for the inevitable, and bloody, retribution.'

'My theory,' Norman said, 'is that, for some reason, Redmond checked up on Prospekt. Perhaps his pension is in some group scheme – controlled by Prospekt. Perhaps he'd read about dodgy dealing in pension funds. And don't forget he would have known about Prospekt being Liechtenstein-registered, their dividend payments being paid into their *anstalt* account. Redmond wants to reassure himself that his retirement money is in good hands – or, less charitably, he's thinking about asking for some of his contributions back in order to finance his gambling habit.'

I nodded. My money was on the latter too.

'Whatever the reason,' Norman shrugged, 'he digs around for information on Prospekt. Sees the disparate nature of the companies they own – a diamond merchant, a security firm, an engineering company, and so on – and wonders at the lack of a pattern, the absence of any obvious corporate strategy. He does some checking. And the more he finds out, the more suspicious – and scared – he gets. Maybe that would explain all the newspapers that Sandra was clearing out. Anyway, somehow he uncovers the stories of the deaths, and enters the land of perpetual brown trousers. Starts to panic. Stakes more and more, in a last-ditch attempt to pay back the money before someone finds out it's missing.'

'And then Walker and I arrive,' I sighed.

'And Redmond's heart sinks like the *Titanic*. He realises that the game is up.' Norman's hand ran across his mouth in contemplation. 'Perhaps – in the end – Redmond tossed the Coin of Fear and it landed with the brave face uppermost. He jumps out of the window, just in case Sandra got caught up in Prospekt's revenge.' Norman waved his hands helplessly in the air. 'What do you think?'

'I think it's a hell of a position in which to find oneself.'

'Correction: it's a hell of a position in which to find *ourselves*. You, me, Arlene, Arthur and Walker – always assuming that she's on our side. So, which of us calls Collins? You? Or me?'

'You can,' I said. 'But not yet.'

'And what do you mean by that?'

'Give me to the end of the week, eh? That way Collins can't claim that I've chickened out at the first opportunity. Surely that will count in my favour when he decides my fate. And,' I said, looking at Norman imploringly, 'I have to feel I've given it my best shot. I promised Collins justice. Let me have a few more days to see if I can deliver. Please.'

'You're bloody hooked, aren't you?' he said, staring at me incredulously. 'I thought it was just fear of Collins taking away your liberty. Or depriving you of a slim chance of finding the hit-and-run driver. Maybe even some sympathy for Collins. But there's more to it, isn't there? You can't quit, can you? Not until you know exactly what's going on. Who are the villains, who are the heroes? As much as anything else, that's what's driving you on.'

'It's the way I am, Norman. You should know that.' I heaved a sigh. 'It seems to me that whatever I do in life, trouble is always waiting just round the corner. The one thing I've learned over the years is that I can't avoid it. The only way out is to confront trouble face-to-face. So, if there's no point running away, then there's no alternative but to fight. Anyway,' I said, 'if this is all about laundering drug money, then someone has to stop them. Think of all the kids that have bought season tickets on the drug barons' gravy train. The lives ruined.' I looked at him beseechingly. 'Just a few more days, please. I'll be careful. Honest.'

'What about the rest of us?' he asked.

It was a good sign. The battle was half-won. His argument had switched from the basic principle to points of detail. If I could counter these objections, then I had bought my time.

'We minimise every risk from now on. First off, we stop Arlene and Arthur making their tour of estate agents. It was a long shot after all. We can afford to drop that line of enquiry.'

'Okay,' Norman said, weakening. 'What about Walker? If she's on our side, what are you going to do about her?'

'She's up to something, for sure. So, on our principle of not taking any unnecessary chances, we pull her out. Phone Collins for me. Say nothing about what you've discovered – or what we suspect. Just tell him I'm not prepared to work with Walker any more. I'll speak to her tomorrow – today, I mean – and make it clear she's off the case. If she complains to Collins, then it won't do her any good. He'll back me up.'

'The end of the week, you say?'

'That's all,' I agreed. 'If I haven't uncovered any evidence by then, I'll pull out. Collins will either have to drop the case or make it official. But he can have no complaints about my commitment. That I haven't given it my best shot.'

'Okay,' Norman said, to my relief. 'I suppose it was me who landed you on secondment to Collins. You've got your precious time. But when it is used up, that's the end of it. All right? No more compromises. No little extensions. When you arrive back from Glenshield on Friday, I pull the plug. If Collins won't see sense, I'll go over his head. Is that clear?'

'Perfectly,' I said. 'Thanks, Norman.'

'One more thing,' he said. 'At the first sign of any trouble, you call on Arthur. Don't try to fight single-handed. Okay?'

'Promise,' I said.

I had bought myself four days. Not much perhaps, but better than nothing.

From now on, I would need to move fast. And if I could not find time to examine the accounts at the office, then I would just have to take one risk – copy the files, and bring everything home.

All I needed was a bit of luck.

Surely that wasn't too much to ask.

CHAPTER TWENTY

'Good morning,' Tricia said, full of the joys of spring. The three clones smiled maternally in my direction and reached for their bags of sweets. Arnold tutted. Paradine humourlessly mimicked a Covent Garden mime artiste: in slow motion, he raised the face of his watch to his baby-blue eyes and effected an exaggerated expression of total shock.

'Sorry,' I said with a helpless shrug of my shoulders.

I was fifty minutes late, the result of explaining the change of plan to Arlene and soothing her melancholy mood – presumably a bout of homesickness made worse by depriving her of a role in the investigation of Glenshield. In the end I had promised to take her home at Easter – the end of next week. It would give us a chance to see if the hostility towards her had abated in her absence. And for me to recommence my sparring match with Mary Jo. Depending on how the wind was blowing (or the hurricane in Mary Jo's case), we could then make our plans for the future.

'Man threw himself under the train at Archway,' I lied.

'Remember you're on trial, Shannon,' Paradine warned. 'Make sure it doesn't happen again.'

I tried not to give him a puzzled look. Made the

assumption it was a comment on my time-keeping – rather than an instruction to spend my free time patrolling the London Underground like some peripatetic Samaritan.

'I'll stay on tonight to make up the time,' I said contritely. Arnold nodded approvingly.

I hated being late – all part of the baggage on my back from prison, the realisation that time is a very precious commodity that should on no account be squandered. But if you're going to be late, then you might as well be *really* late. A few minutes behind time merely demonstrates that you're absent-minded or disorganised. But fifty minutes is a different matter. It could only be put down to some mega-disaster occurring (and the more bizarre your excuse, the more credence it acquires: Cruise missile stuck in the tunnel on the Central Line, the wrong sort of snow on the railway lines – after all, who in their right minds would make up something like that?). Of course the other, and more generally applicable, alternative is that you simply don't give two hoots. In my case ... well, it suited me to work on after everyone else had left.

I smiled across at Tricia. Switched on the computer. Impersonated Beryl by using her password. Picked up the first invoice of the day. Typed in the data – slowly. The last thing I wanted, was to get through the pile before half past five.

I need not have worried. The morning's post was already sorted and laid out in neat stacks on Arnold's desk. Along with the expected bank statements, it brought, as on the previous day, a fresh batch of fodder for repetitive strain injury. The vast majority of the invoices were marked optimistically 'Terms strictly thirty days net!' There were several from sub-contractors, re-inforcing my view of the fragility of Glenshield's personnel resources.

At one o'clock I nipped across the road for a sandwich and rushed back to eat it at Tricia's desk. We chatted about her boyfriend (Gary), her wedding plans (August, church, white dress, reception with finger buffet and two types of sherry, disco, the works), the house they were buying (three-bedroomed terrace in Willesden), even the wallpaper for the nursery (Snow White). Then, when she was nicely relaxed, I asked my favour.

'There's this girl in Personnel,' I said wistfully. 'I'd really love to get to know her.' I twisted my fingers together nervously. 'I don't suppose, Tricia...? No. It's too much to ask. Forget it.'

She placed her hand on mine. 'You mustn't be so shy,' she said, giving me a little shake.

'It's just ... you know ... prison and all that,' I mumbled.

'You want me to arrange a date?'

'Would you?' My face lit up. 'I don't even know her name. But you can't miss her. She's tall and black. And oh, so very beautiful.' I shook my head despondently. 'No, it's silly of me.'

Tricia stood up. Addressed me firmly. 'What do you want me to ask her?'

'Perhaps – if she's not already doing something, that is – we might go for a drink after work. Could she come down here at half past six?'

'Consider it as good as done,' she said, leaving her desk. 'Won't be long.'

Ten minutes later Tricia returned. She bent down and whispered in my ear.

'All arranged,' she said with a smile of triumph. 'You're right. She is very beautiful. I'm surprised some of the other bees haven't been swarming around the honey pot.' Tricia blushed. 'Sorry,' she said, flustered. 'I didn't mean … it's just … Well, they're all at it here. If you believe the gossip, that is. They even say–'

Paradine – the spoil-sport – walked into the room just as it was getting interesting. He frowned. I typed away madly. Something told me this was not my day for making good impressions.

The afternoon passed uneventfully. (Apart from one major breakthrough, that is – I learned to distinguish between the three clones: Marjorie was into knitting, and measured me for a sweater; Molly – green fingers – asked if I would like some cuttings from her garden; Stella, who had an unexpected artistic streak, presented me with a pencil sketch of myself at the keyboard.) I ate more assorted sweets and a cream slice – it was Marjorie's birthday and cakes all round. Tricia became more excited about my forthcoming liaison. Paradine went off to oversee some other dubious corner of the Prospekt empire. And Arnold urged us on like the manager of a struggling third-division football team that was heading for relegation unless we pulled our socks up. He reminded us of the days about to be lost over Easter. And, to make matters worse – tut, tut – Maundy Thursday fell inconveniently on the last day of March and so coincided with the end of the month accounts, including (special nod to Nick Shannon) the payments run. Wow, the pressure was really mounting now. Reach for the Librium, staff.

At half past five everyone collected their coats and headed for the door. My three surrogate mothers gave me sympathetic looks that unmistakably said, 'Ah, poor boy.' Arnold, already preparing for the following morning, tidied his desk and set his pencils in a neat row at right-angles to his ruler. Tricia wished me good luck with a giggle, a nervous rise and fall of her shoulders and a quick clutch at her heart.

Throughout the afternoon I had worked at a deliberate pace. There were now sufficient numbers of invoices on the pile to look impressive, but not so many that they could not be cleared within a short time. For the next quarter of an hour I typed furiously. And then settled down to the real task.

From my briefcase I took out a box of formatted disks – thirteen in total, allowing me to go back just over a year for comparative purposes – and set about copying the necessary files from the hard disk onto the floppies. Once I had finished, I could then study the accounts at home without fear of interruption. I still hadn't cracked how to access all the material – there was the problem of passwords for the higher levels of the system – but that bridge could be crossed when, and if, it proved necessary.

It was a slow task. The hard disk was packed to

the gunwales with files going back to the very start of the company; it laboured ponderously over the execution of each 'copy' command. And I had to label every individual floppy methodically so that I knew which month's accounts were on which disk.

I was on the last one when Walker arrived. She poked her head round the door and, when satisfied that the coast was clear, walked over to my desk. She was a knockout, as usual. Beige linen suit. Dark yellow blouse. Black mid-height shoes scuffed at the heels through driving. Her hair was scraped off her face and secured at the back with a wooden clip in the shape of a pussycat. I sat there appreciating the view while Cherry eyed the mess that was the result of my labours.

'You're taking a chance, aren't you?' she said scornfully.

'A calculated risk,' I said. 'We're pulling out. This is your last day.'

'Thanks for letting me have so much warning,' she grunted. 'I'm surprised you didn't ask Little Miss Homemaker to give me the message.' She paused to make sure I had registered her annoyance. It wasn't necessary. 'Anyway,' she said, 'who says we're pulling out? Why didn't Collins telephone me?'

'Perhaps he thought you'd succumb more easily to my fatal charms.'

'Huh!' She placed her hands on her hips and glowered at me with eyes capable of reducing any man to jelly. I stood up to hide a quiver.

'I don't suppose you've found out anything

useful?' I asked.

'Your faith in me is so touching, Shannon.'

'Well,' I said probingly, 'Personnel is not exactly the first choice of location for a fraud investigation.'

'I have access to the staff records,' she said dismissively.

'And?'

'And you're right. Satisfied? There's nothing that is germane to our cause. Is that what you wanted to hear?'

'This is not a competition, Cherry,' I said. 'I'm not in this for the glory. If there's any kudos going at the end of the day, then you are free to take it. It's you who wants promotion.'

'Don't tell me a successful result here won't do you any harm. One smile from the Commander is worth a hundred threats from Collins when it comes to any talk about having your licence revoked.'

'Live long and prosper, Walker,' I said, giving her the Vulcan sign of peace.

'Oh, Shannon,' she said. 'Why do we always argue?'

'Do we always argue?' I asked provocatively.

'Hah, bloody hah,' she said. 'So, tell me, what has Mastersleuth found?'

'Not much,' I said guardedly. 'There's never a spare moment to dig around in the accounts. That's why I'm copying the files.'

'So you haven't achieved anything either?'

I shrugged.

'Right bloody pair, aren't we?' she said with a shake of her head. 'I did hear some interesting gossip, mind you.'

'Don't tell me. The place is a hotbed of seething passions and carnal lust?'

'Right from the top, so they say.'

'Roddy by name and Roddy by nature, eh?'

Walker never got a chance to answer.

The handle of the door turned with a squeak.

I moved in front of the desk to block the view of the disks still scattered across its surface. Grabbed Cherry by the shoulders. Jerked her against me and imprisoned her in an inescapably tight embrace. Felt the warmth of her body as she struggled. Placed my lips against hers. Her tongue...

'What the hell's going on?'

Speak of the devil and he's sure to appear.

Hurriedly, guiltily, we broke apart. Kinsella stared at us, a red thundercloud of anger spreading across his face.

'I ... we...' I stammered.

'Christ, what are you up to, Shannon?' Kinsella said. I had hoped that would be plain enough for the most naïve observer, let alone good old Roddy. 'Haven't you heard about sexual harassment?'

'Ask the lady if she's being harassed,' I said calmly.

Kinsella turned his attention to Cherry.

'It's not a problem,' she said, an embarrassed smile on her wet lips. 'We were just... You know?'

'No problem, eh?' Kinsella said. The expression on his face suddenly, and worryingly, changed. Anger left his eyes: enlightenment took the vacated place. 'I bet it's not a problem.'

He walked purposefully across to a phone.

'Sit down, both of you,' he ordered. Kinsella, his eyes never straying from us, punched out a number with long, thick fingers.

'Kinsella,' he announced to the person at the other end of the line. 'Yeah. Yeah. Don't mention it. Look, I need some information. The girl,' he said, 'Pussy Galore. Describe her.'

Kinsella listened attentively while staring at Cherry. His eyes moved over her body, and his brain ticked off the items on the checklist. The long legs. The slim hips. The tight waist. He nodded to himself as his eyes passed her breasts and finally settled on her face. 'Thanks,' he said. 'Yeah. I'll bell you. Okay?'

'Well,' he said, lips tightly clenched. 'What a bloody fool I've been.'

He looked at the pair of us and shook his head in disbelief.

'One of you might well have been coincidence. But not two.' He pointed an accusing finger at Cherry. 'You're Walker, aren't you?' He didn't bother to wait for an answer. 'And this is a set-up, isn't it? All a bloody set-up. From the word "go". The fight with Collins in full view of the Fraud Squad. Your performance at the gambling club, whining all the time about being desperate for a job. I must have been blind not to see it sooner. This is an official bloody investigation.'

The game, as they say, was well and truly up. Quinn – from the nickname used, it just had to be Quinn whom Kinsella had telephoned – had landed both of us up the creek. Always assuming that Walker was on my side – Kinsella could be acting out his own little charade for all I knew. The best I could hope for now was damage limitation – something with which to paddle through the proverbial to the safety of the shore.

'Yes, Mr Kinsella,' I said formally. 'This is an official investigation. It would be easier for all concerned if you co-operate. But...'

'Of course I'll bloody co-operate,' he said, screamed almost. 'If there's a fraud going down here, I want to know all about it. And I want whoever's involved punished.'

Kinsella was either in the clear, or he was a very cool customer.

I wasn't about to gamble any money on it. I'd staked enough already on the bluff I was playing. There was still that niggling doubt in my mind about how much, if anything, the Commander knew about this case. I owed Collins a shot at saving him from being nailed to the cross.

'I suggest, sir,' I said, 'that we move to your office. We have some questions to ask.' Just at this very moment I didn't know what the hell they were, but I hoped inspiration would strike me before we sat down at opposite sides of his desk.

I also hoped he had some of his whiskey left. I couldn't speak for Walker, but I, for one, certainly needed a large drink.

I gave an involuntary shudder as we followed Kinsella from the room. If he turned out to fit the latter of the two options – was actually Mr Cool Customer, after all – then it was not only Collins who was due for crucifixion.

I would be up there at his side.

Unless, that is, Prospekt's boundless imagination came up with another, more contemporary, method of disposal.

CHAPTER TWENTY-ONE

Kinsella, silent and broody, ushered us into his office and gestured at the chairs. As we sat down, I heard the click of the lock turning in the door. Great! Just about the only thing guaranteed to make me more nervous.

The hair on the back of my neck prickled. Beads of perspiration broke out on my forehead. Nightmare flashbacks of prison were forming a beach-head in my mind prior to the launch of a full-scale invasion. I clenched my fists and dug my nails into sweaty palms in order to concentrate on the present. As trade-offs go, it was like swapping vivid memories of the fire for the actuality of the frying pan. Locked in a room with a fifteen-stone slab of possibly desperate criminal wasn't exactly top of my list of the ten most fun things to do on a Tuesday evening. I looked at Walker and she rolled her eyes at me, as if to say, 'Another fine mess you've got me into, Shannon.' It was a good sign – if she wasn't playacting.

Kinsella switched on the anglepoise lamp that was clamped to his desk, and killed the main lights. Hang on a minute, I thought. Who is supposed to be interrogating whom?

'Collins is behind this, I presume?' Kinsella asked, sitting himself down and reaching for the whiskey bottle in one smooth movement.

It was a full bottle. Some heavy drinking had gone on in here since our last cosy chat reminiscing about the old country. He waved the bottle in my direction.

I nodded approvingly.

'Not when I'm on duty,' Walker said, po-faced, making me feel like a lush.

Kinsella shrugged his shoulders and waited for me to answer his question.

So did I!

The problem, in essence, was simple. Well, at least simple to define: it was the solution that was the difficult part. In carrying through the bluff, what should be revealed (to make him believe I knew more than I did) and what concealed (to make him think I knew less – about Prospekt's role especially)?

I decided to tap-dance – to play it by ear.

Which is just another way of saying I had absolutely no bloody idea.

'Mr Collins is in charge of the investigation,' I said formally. 'But we have been acting on information received.'

I decided to plunge in and go straight for the kill. If Kinsella could be persuaded to confess, then I would be spared the embarrassment of admitting that all I had to go on was a hunch or two.

'I think it would save us all a lot of trouble,' I said with the weariness of someone seeking confirmation, 'if you told us everything you know.'

'Okay,' he said.

My spirits rose.

'I know nothing,' he continued.

Down to earth again. Oh well, it had been worth a shot. Back to the age-old art of bluffing.

'I find that very hard to believe,' I said, knocking the ball over the net to land at his feet.

'I bet you do,' he said, sipping the whiskey. 'Especially if you've been listening to Collins. I can imagine what he's told you about me. Must be a pretty black picture. It's about time someone put the record straight.'

Kinsella loosened his tie. Topped up our glasses. Leaned back in his chair. Put his hands behind his neck. This had all the signs of being a long story.

Painful too, by the look of him.

In the harsh glare of the lamp, his skin had bleached to a ghostly shade of rancid white. He seemed to have aged ten years in the last ten minutes. The fancy silk suit and shirt did not flatter him any more – just gave him the mutton-dressed-as-lamb appearance of a fifty-something clinging by his fingertips to the crumbling cliff-face of youth.

He turned his head to study me. There were deep furrows of strain on his brow. And a faraway melancholic look in his eyes.

'I stole his wife?' Kinsella said, frowning. 'That's what Collins said, eh?'

I raised my eyebrows in a non-committal gesture that fooled no-one.

259

'Well, don't you believe it, Shannon. Collins had lost Louise long before I came on the scene.'

Beside me, Walker fidgeted. Eager to press for the confession? Curious to hear Kinsella's side of the story? Or just plain anxious as to how much he would reveal?

'Their marriage was dead,' he said. 'Collins killed it. Bloody fool.' Kinsella ran a hand through the stubble of his hair in contemplation. 'He put the job before Louise. Started early, worked late. Day after bloody day. By the time he got home, he was too exhausted to talk to her, let alone do anything else. It's not an uncommon situation in the force. The divorce rate for coppers is higher than inflation in Mexico. That's why Louise urged me to leave the Drugs Squad. Start up Glenshield. We didn't want history to repeat itself.'

He gulped down a large slug of whiskey. This wasn't the occasion for sipping slowly and rolling the amber liquid around the tongue while dreaming nostalgically of peat bogs and sham-rocks. Numb the brain and ease the pain – that was why he was drinking.

'Louise did everything she could to change him. In spite of her instincts, she made one last-ditch effort to save the marriage. She pressurised Collins till he agreed to take a holiday. Second honeymoon. Then she got herself pregnant.'

Walker changed her mind about the whiskey. Poured herself a large measure. Swallowed a mouthful without it touching the sides of her mouth.

'Bloody stupid thing to do,' Kinsella said with a

shake of his head. 'You can't change people, you know. No matter how hard you try. It just won't work. All you can ever do is push the faults below the surface. But you can't drown them. Sooner or later they bob back up again, large as life.'

Kinsella refilled his glass. If he carried on drinking like this, then any confession, even if coherent, would be worthless.

'She was seven months gone,' Kinsella went on, a tear glistening in his eye. 'Fell down the bloody stairs at home. At seven o'clock in the evening.' He wiped the tear away and took a deep breath. 'Collins didn't arrive home till midnight. She was still lying there. She lost the baby. And Collins lost Louise. For good.'

Kinsella leaned closer and fixed me with a piercing stare.

'He never told you that, did he? Not fine, upstanding Mr Collins. Instead he cast me as the villain of the piece.'

'He doesn't talk much about himself,' I said lamely.

'Of course he bloody doesn't,' he said. 'Would you?'

It was shrug-time again. It wasn't typing that would give me repetitive strain injury – it would be all this bloody shrugging.

'Louise rang me one day. Totally out of the blue – I'd met her once or twice at the odd police bash, that was all. She simply wanted someone to talk to. Nothing more. The poor girl was so churned up inside. Had nowhere to turn. In the beginning I just let her spill it out – acted as an escape valve. Then we used to meet as friends.

261

Finally we realised there was more than just friendship between us. We fell in love.'

Very touching, I thought cynically. It was hard to erase the fixed stereotype of 'Roddy' from my brain and replace it with the newly discovered image of a caring psychoanalyst who had fallen head over heels for one of his patients.

'Collins had to shift the blame onto somebody,' Kinsella said understandingly. 'He couldn't shoulder the burden of being responsible for a failed marriage *and* the loss of their unborn child. I was an easy target. I was even prepared to act out the role. He was a good copper, for chrissake – I didn't want him going suicidal on me.' Kinsella sighed. 'And then he started making those stupid accusations. Pure bloody invention. Our attitude to bent coppers was about the only time the two of us saw eye-to-eye. I suppose it was the last act of a desperate man.'

I nodded wisely and sympathetically. It seemed the thing to do. And it saved a shrug.

'Okay,' I said. 'You're a wronged man. History's been rewritten.' I paused. 'But what about the present? The fraud?'

'Look,' he said, with a helpless wave of his hands, 'I really don't know what you're talking about. But I'll tell you this much, if there's something going on here, I'm not entirely surprised. It's all gone wrong.'

His hand reached out for the whiskey bottle. Then he thought better of it. Placed his fingertips together. Raised them pensively to his lips.

'Glenshield was never meant to grow this big. It's got out of control. Sometimes it seems that

O'Kane and I spend every waking moment in these damned offices. And we still can't get to grips with what is happening. Jesus, I work longer hours now than I ever did in the force.' Kinsella gazed into his glass for inspiration. 'It can't go on,' he said loudly, a determined look on his face. He thumped the desk with his fist. The anglepoise shook, the pool of light quivered. 'We have to go back to our roots. Change now before it's too late.' He gazed pleadingly into my eyes, 'Help me, Shannon.'

'What exactly are you asking?' Walker said.

'I'm a simple man,' Kinsella replied. 'I'm not a wife-stealing philanderer. Or someone who takes bribes to make sure a drugs raid goes wrong. All I want in life is to earn enough to live in a bit of style, and to spend time with Louise. Tell me what is going on. Who the culprits are. Help me clean up Glenshield. Then I'll go to Prospekt and explain the position. That I'm not prepared to take the pressure any longer. One way or another, it has to be a fresh start. Either Glenshield is allowed to shrink to manageable proportions, or I want nothing more to do with it in the future.'

Rather you than me, I thought. Threatening Prospekt would come way down on my schedule of 'things to do today' – or any day for that matter. A fresh start might well turn out to be a dead end. There's more than one way to wipe a slate clean.

'I imagine Prospekt would listen to what you say,' I said poker-faced. 'I don't know anything about them, but your argument makes pretty good sense to me.'

I hoped Kinsella was paying attention. I couldn't put it more plainly without seeming to protest too much. Prospekt? Great company. Involved in drugs? Never. You could knock me down with a feather.

'I'll be honest with you,' I said. Christ knows why, but it's the sort of corny spiel you fall back on when you're ad-libbing. 'I have several lines to follow to prove my suspicions. You help me. I'll help you.'

'It's a deal,' he said, extending his hand. 'What an alliance, eh? We'll show 'em, Nick.'

Walker coughed politely.

Kinsella looked at her, smiled briefly and condescendingly, then turned back to me. 'What do you want me to do?'

'I already have copies of your accounts files going back more than a year. I need some time to study them at home.'

'Go sick,' he said with a casual wave of his hand. 'I'll cover for you with Paradine. Flu, shall we say?'

'I also need a password,' I said. 'There are parts of the system I can't access without one.'

'Then have mine.' Kinsella took a slip of paper from the box on his desk. Wrote down his password. Slid the paper across to me.

I read the password and looked at Kinsella questioningly.

His face actually flushed with embarrassment.

'It's Lou's pet name for me,' he mumbled.

I took out my wallet and concentrated on placing the piece of paper inside. It was better than giggling.

'Do you know Paradine's password?' I asked, as inconsequentially as possible.

'It's not him, is it?' Kinsella asked, stunned. 'No. I can't believe that.'

'I just wondered, that's all. From what I've seen of your employees, you might as well type out everyone's passwords and pin them up on the company noticeboard, for all the difference it would make to the security of the system.'

Kinsella shook his head gravely. 'The first thing we must do is change every bloody password.'

'No,' I said quickly. 'The first thing we must do is act normal. Let's not ring any warning bells.'

Kinsella nodded his head in agreement.

'So,' I continued, returning to my unanswered question. 'Do you know Paradine's code?'

'No,' Kinsella said. 'He and I think the same way about security. I don't know his code. He doesn't know mine. If we did, then the payments schedule would be totally compromised.' He shook his head, thinking of the consequences. 'It would be like leaving a book of blank pre-signed cheques lying about. In order to authorise the payments run, or even to make a change to the supplier database, we both have to type in our codes independently. To commit a fraud that way could only be done by Paradine and me acting in concert.'

It wouldn't be the first time a scam had been pulled in that fashion. Or the last. That's for certain. But it was good to hear that at least someone in Glenshield took secrecy seriously. After all it was a security firm.

'One last thing,' I said. 'You were studying a

265

print-out the other day. When we were discussing Supermax. May I have a quick look, please?'

'But that's not relevant,' he said.

'Let me be the judge of that.'

Kinsella shrugged his shoulders, unlocked a two-drawer filing cabinet by the side of his desk and pulled out the thick set of continuous paper. Handed it to me with a puzzled frown.

It was the same print-out I had discovered underneath the crossword in Walker's bedsit. The names still didn't mean anything. But the numbers, given the context of the discussion, now did.

'These are the prisoners earmarked as the first intake for Supermax?'

He nodded. 'And you were right,' he said. 'They are the pick of the bunch. The worst the system has to offer. I should know. I was responsible for putting some of them behind bars in the first place.'

I didn't ask him how he had come by the list.

But he felt the need to tell me anyway.

'We acquired the print-out legitimately,' he protested. 'Part of the tender documents supplied by the Home Office. Making it absolutely clear what we were in for. Just so there could be no comebacks.'

'Right,' I said to Walker. 'We have work to do. Thank you for being so frank, Mr Kinsella.'

'Call me Roddy,' he said. 'I told you that before. And now we're a team, eh?'

I stood up. Kinsella held out his hand again. Pumped mine vigorously. Any moment now I expected him to take a penknife from his pocket and go through the blood-brothers ritual.

'Let's crack this one, Nick,' he said. 'Get me a result. And if there's any damned thing you need, you only have to ask.'

'Thanks,' I said. I bit the bullet and added, 'Roddy.'

Where would it end? Who knows? If our friendship carried on accelerating at this pace, he might even let me call him by his pet name. I mentally placed two fingers at the back of my throat.

CHAPTER TWENTY-TWO

'What did you make of that?' asked Walker, sipping at a Scotch and American. 'Do you believe Kinsella's story?'

'It's certainly food for thought,' I said. It wasn't so much that I did not want to commit myself: I had other things on my mind. Walker, to be precise.

We were sitting in a smoke-filled underground cavern that had been converted at minimal expense into a 'typical English pub'. A great concept: its elements were warm beer, sullen service, dingy lighting and, presumably, freedom from prosecution under the Trade Descriptions Act. The place was a regular stopping-off point on the tourist trail – head porters received monthly backhanders from the management to send along unsuspecting foreigners for fleecing.

Apart from the prices, the service and the ambience, it was an ideal spot for a confidential discussion – Walker and I were the only ones speaking English.

I watched a gullible Japanese businessman pay five pounds for the dubious privilege of having a Polaroid of himself taken with the resident foul-beaked mynah bird. From my limited knowledge of foreign tongues it seemed that the creature could issue croaky insults in at least five different languages – if the day ever came when the bird lost its voice, I was willing to bet the landlord would teach it how to make V-signs with the tip of its wing. The flash of the camera froze the scene – another tribute to the victory of alcohol over dignity – and the resulting picture was pinned up, along with the man's hieroglyphic business card, above the bar for posterity or three weeks, whichever was the sooner. I sighed and turned my attention back to Walker.

'What are we going to do?' she asked, raising her voice above the sound of motor drives and multilingual, hacking coughs. Why is it that only the British and the Americans feel such guilt, such *angst*, about smoking?

I lit a cigarette to help me think. If you can't beat 'em, you may as well join 'em.

'*We're* not going to do anything, Walker,' I said. 'You're off the case, remember?'

'Still don't trust me, Nick?'

'And rightly so, it seems,' I replied, frowning. 'Just what sort of game are you playing, Walker?'

She gave me an ingenuous (ingenious?) look. Furrowed her brows to enact puzzlement. Tried the age-old routine of locking her beautiful brown eyes onto mine.

'It won't work, Walker,' I said resolutely. 'Not this time.'

She sat back and folded her arms across her chest. Her eyes smouldered.

'Why choose Bishops?' I asked, hoping she would come clean and save me the trouble of a step-by-step exposure. 'When you must have been aware that they don't handle accounts staff?'

'A simple mistake, that's all. We all make them, Shannon. You should know that.'

'Bullshit,' I said, disappointed in her.

'I don't have to take this, Shannon.' She picked up her bag from the spit-and-sawdust floor. Rose to leave.

'Running off to tell tales to the Commander?' I said.

She stopped in her tracks. Glared at me.

'Sit back down, Walker. You've got some explaining to do.'

'Okay,' she said, 'you sussed me out. The Commander put me into Glenshield. He pulled some strings in Bishops. Someone there owed him a favour. That's how I landed the temporary job so easily. And Personnel was where I was supposed to be.'

'To check on Glenshield's employees? See if any of them had a record? Or any links with the proposed first intake for Supermax?'

She nodded. 'All three companies tendering are undergoing the same secret scrutiny. Supermax is the key to the government's strategy of privatising the whole prison service. The Home Office can't afford for it to fail – that's why they're not prepared to take any chances. Only those companies that pass the screening will be considered for the contract.'

'And I don't suppose the old buddy system comes into it, eh, Walker? A recommendation from the Commander might tip the balance in Glenshield's – Kinsella's – favour.'

'I wouldn't know about that. I'm just doing my job.'

'And the rest, Walker.'

'What are you implying, Shannon? I've told you the truth. Why aren't you satisfied?'

'Because it's only half the truth.' I said. 'It's a good job you're a woman, Walker. You've had your feet spread so widely in both camps that any man would have done himself permanent damage by now.' I shook my head in an overt gesture of sadness and disillusionment. 'Why do you expect me to trust you? When you've been the Commander's mole all along. Spying on Collins. Ear pressed up against the thin partition wall. Reporting back everything that's done or said. Passing on files too, I suspect. That *is* what happened to the missing Glenshield file?'

I think she blushed. It was impossible to tell, of course, but she lowered her eyes. Stared at the drink. Fingered the dripmat. Hiding her shame? I bloody hoped so.

'That was the reason,' I continued, 'why *you* were chosen to check out Glenshield – and not one of countless other officers in the Met. Because it allowed you to keep an eye on the fraud investigation too. Even if I had not taken the job, you – and the Commander – knew that Collins wouldn't give up on Kinsella; that he'd browbeat someone else into doing the dirty work. Jesus, Walker, is there nothing you won't do to get to the top?'

'You've had your say, Shannon. Feel better now, do you? I bet you do. Tell me,' she said, 'what's it like up there on your cloud, looking down on the rest of us mortals?'

'Sickening,' I replied.

'Then welcome to the real world,' she said bitterly. 'And, in case it hasn't occurred to you, that's a world where a Commander outranks a Superintendent. I'm staying on this case. And there's sod all you can do about it.'

'I could tell Collins you've been playing both sides against the middle.'

'Then he'd have to explain to the Commander why, given his personal involvement, he's kept quiet about Glenshield. And then the case would pass to one of the other squads. I don't think he'd risk that. Revenge is sweet, remember? And Collins is a three-sugar man.'

'To think I defended you, Walker. When Collins's instincts told him not to trust you.' I sighed heavily. 'And now, believe it or not, I still have your best interests at heart. Take it from me, you're better off out of this. Accept the inevitable. Bow out of the case gracefully.'

'What if I don't?' she asked, looking me challengingly in the eyes. 'What if I go to Collins and threaten to spill the beans on Louise and the baby unless I'm reinstated? Contributory

271

negligence, some might say. That won't do his sympathy rating – or his tenuous hold on his job – much good. Well, Shannon, what would you do then?'

'I'd give him an address in Northampton, that's what.'

'You bastard,' she said loudly, and with feeling. Not a soul in the bar flinched. They all thought it was the mynah bird. 'And hypocrite. *You've* been spying on *me*.'

'Due diligence,' I said. 'Something I learned the hard way. There are times when you just can't be too careful.'

She sat there silently, fingers locked tightly together. A tear in her eye.

I looked away. Walker – damn her – had found my weak spot. I can't bear to see a woman cry. Maybe she was right. Maybe I was a bastard. You can't get much lower than blackmail, after all.

'Look, Cherry,' I said softly, 'maybe it was wrong of me to go behind your back. I'm sorry. Okay? But what I'm doing now is for your sake. And your daughter's. The less you know, the safer you'll both be.'

'I told you before, Shannon. It's not your job to protect me.'

'Agreed,' I said. 'But I'm going to do it all the same.'

'You're one hell of a stubborn sod,' she said.

'Nosey too. Tell me about the girl.'

'Why should I?' she asked, eyes aflame.

'Because it would show that you trust me.'

'Looks like I don't have much choice,' she said sullenly. 'How about taking out a mortgage and

272

buying me another drink while I think about it?'

I smiled at her and prepared to fight my way to the bar.

'Now don't get talking to anyone while I'm gone.'

'Fat chance,' she said, forcing her lips into the weakest of smiles. 'The only Japanese I know is *konichiwa, anjinsan*. So unless Richard Chamberlain walks in, I'm a bit stuck for an opening line.'

Five minutes later – and eight quid the poorer – I returned with two large 'gold watches', as the barman insisted on dubbing them. The local colour was worth every penny. If I'd tipped him, he might even have called me 'Squire'.

Cherry took a long, reflective swallow from her drink.

'My dad was a policeman,' she said. 'Not here. Barbados. That's where I lived until I was five. Until Dad died, that is.'

'I'm sorry.'

'Not half as sorry as I was,' Cherry said bitterly. 'You know, there's hardly any crime on Barbados. Being a policeman there means you're about as busy as a hot-dog salesman in a synagogue.' She gave a nervous giggle. 'My dad was unlucky, I suppose. Tried to stop a fight between two kids high on ganja. Got a knife in the heart for his trouble.'

She paused. I lit another cigarette so that I didn't have to watch the tears forming again.

'My mum brought me to England – she had family over here. Land of golden opportunity it was supposed to be! Still, it didn't matter. Without my dad any place was hell.'

273

'It's a rotten age to lose your father,' I said.

'Yeah,' she said reflectively. 'Do you know what I remember most about Barbados now? Not the sun, the sea, the sand. The bloody funeral, that's what. Must have been close on two hundred people turned up to pay their respects. I think that was when I decided I was going to be a police officer too.'

'Not a bad reason,' I said. 'Although it's often a hard path to tread, to follow in your father's footsteps.'

She nodded her head slowly. 'As I grew older I didn't just want to join the police. I wanted to be the leader of a crusade. The first black woman to make Chief Constable.'

I wish I could have raised my eyebrows. But somehow it didn't surprise me.

'I went through university,' she said, 'on a Metropolitan Police bursary. It meant my mum didn't have to find any money towards the grant. And a job was guaranteed on graduation. It couldn't have been simpler. The whole future mapped out. Then I had to get pregnant!'

'The best laid plans and all that,' I said sympathetically.

'I didn't have a clue what to do. Didn't want to marry the father – it was just one-night stand stuff. Couldn't bring myself to have an abortion. Or to admit to my prospective employers the state I was in. I was afraid the job would go out the window and I'd have to repay the money I'd received over the three years of my course. Luckily, the baby wasn't due until a month after my graduation. And I carried her well. Just looked like I'd put on a bit of weight, that's all. I sat the exams, passed and went home to Northampton to have Sarah. As far as the Met was concerned I was simply taking a well-deserved break before starting work.'

'So your mother took care of Sarah and you carried on as if nothing had happened?'

'Don't think I'm proud of what I've done, Shannon,' she said angrily. 'Don't kid yourself I have no regrets. Because, believe me, I do. But I'm not the maternal type, that's all.'

And anyway, I thought, there was the crusade, the driving ambition, to be considered.

'I love Sarah,' she said, sensing my approbation. 'Don't get me wrong. I send my mother nearly all my salary each month so that Sarah wants for nothing.'

'Nothing?' I chided.

'Sarah has a mother's love, if that's what's going through that moralistic bloody head of yours. She thinks I'm her sister. She doesn't know the truth. And what she doesn't know can't hurt her.'

'Exactly my point, Walker,' I said. 'What you don't know can't hurt you, either.'

'Then do it all on your own, Shannon, for all I care.' She pushed her chair back. Stood up to go, eyes blazing down at me. 'But don't expect any help from me in the future. When this is over, you find yourself a new partner. Is that clear?'

I nodded. 'If that's the way you want it.'

'Too right I do.'

'Then goodbye, Walker,' I said. 'Look after yourself, won't you?'

I don't know if I meant it the way she took it.

Probably did, with hindsight.

So maybe I deserved the slap across the face.

But pouring the best part of four quid's worth of Scotch and American over my head was going a bit over the top.

Still, if I ever went to Japan I was bound to get a sympathetic reception. I smiled as the flashes popped around me.

'Silly sod,' the mynah bird squawked.

Foul-beaked it might be. But it was a bloody good judge of character.

CHAPTER TWENTY-THREE

I phoned Connor.

Not because I was a member of the RSPCA and liked to give mynah birds a sense of self-satisfaction. But because there was no alternative.

I had arrived home the previous evening smelling as if I'd just come from a stag party in Glasgow. My brain, preferring the state of anaesthesia to confusion, wished that I had. After what Kinsella had said in his office, my heroes and villains were in danger of becoming en-tangled, if not as yet actually swapping places. I needed a second opinion on Collins and Kin-sella, an outside view on informers and drugs raids that went wrong. Connor, unfortunately, was the only person I knew who might have the contacts to throw light on the story.

Using Norman as a taciturn go-between with

Collins, I had obtained Connor's telephone number from his police file. It took a little persuasion – and a lot of economising in the truth department – but I finally extracted a pessimistic promise from Connor that he would 'bell a few blokes'. From his return call to set up a meeting it seemed as though his pessimism had been misplaced.

Or perhaps ...

I brushed the thought from my mind. Spent the morning, Norman at my shoulder, concentrating on my first real look at the Glenshield accounts. We started with the sales ledger and set about examining the export contracts one by one, compiling a spreadsheet of the amount invoiced each month. When this had been completed, we would turn to the purchase ledger and add the associated cost per month. Then see what profit Glenshield was making on each contract.

It was a slow process, completely stalled for a while by the return of a jubilant Arlene.

'I've got the tickets,' she said, an ear-to-ear smile lighting up her face. 'Gatwick to Logan. First flight out on Good Friday.' The smile faded a degree. 'I made them both open-ended returns. I hope that's fine with you? After all, you never know. You may not want to hurry back.'

'Good idea,' I said, trying to blot out the spectre of Mary Jo from my mind. 'What is there here that's worth rushing back for?'

'Thanks a bunch,' Norman said with a grin.

Lost in her own thoughts, the interruption didn't register with Arlene. 'I can't wait to see Mary Jo,' she said wistfully.

277

My poker face slipped. I must be out of practice.

'Come on, Nick,' Arlene said, frowning. 'She just needs a little time, that's all.'

Yes, I thought. About forty years.

I gave Arlene a broad smile, at the same time hoping that she would not be too disappointed – either with her daughter or the reactions of the so-called friends who had treated her as a leper.

'Can you carry on with this while I'm meeting Connor?' I asked Norman.

'No problem,' he replied. 'Glad to help. Remind me,' he said innocently, 'what was Kinsella's password again?'

'You're winding me up, aren't you?' I said. 'You know very well.'

'Say it one more time,' he said, barely controlling himself, 'Please. I won't laugh.'

'I remember you making the same promise to Toddy once. Irish stew, if I'm not mistaken. Just get on with it, eh?'

You couldn't miss Connor's club. One o'clock in the afternoon and the neon lights were flashing. The 'Ee-Zee Club' blinked on and off in a fittingly bile-coloured fluorescent yellow. Other signs in lurid red and electric blue advertised, in an economic shorthand that communicated perfectly with the target audience, the wonders to be beheld inside.

I didn't hang about on the pavement trying to work out the meaning of 'Lez Girls' or studying the pictures of the 'Ten Gorgeous Lovelies' (tautology, surely?) with their strategically placed blacked-out rectangles – it was the sort of place (either tragically sad or ludicrously funny) where the *News of the World* has a photographer on permanent posting, hoping to catch the high and mighty at their leisure pursuits.

The greasy tout on duty escorted me to a tiny desk where the exacting formalities of membership were completed with the passing over of a twenty-pound note. I signed my name (well, Robert Brown) below that of Michael Mouse and walked through the red curtain.

My first impression was of an enveloping blanket of blackness. My second, hardly mellowing with time, was of the same black blanket but with a tiny circle of light at the other end of a long, narrow room. Within this circle a rather large woman in a rather small costume lethargically completed what seemed like her twentieth strip of the day to the dying chords of 'Lady in Red' ('Lady Not in Red' would have been more appropriate, but I doubted if the music mattered much – not given the lamentable standard of the choreography). From the small audience came the hollow sound of someone – possessor of a Masters degree in Irony? – clapping.

The lights flickered briefly as one act left and another entered. I turned my head away from the stage, and from the girl wearing only a pair of stiletto-heeled thigh boots and a wrap-around snake. Let my eyes become accustomed to the darkness. In front of me a bar magically appeared out of the gloom; to my right a row of discretely screened cubicles housing faceless men and topless women. From every direction came the

279

smell of cheap scent and nervous perspiration. My nose had difficulty deciding which was worse.

I felt a hand on my arm. It belonged to a helpful female employee of forty-five who introduced herself as 'Chelsea'. I wondered whimsically if she lived in the London Borough of Sharon. Misreading my grin, she enquired politely whether I would like a drink. Hers, she informed me, was a gin sling. Resisting the temptation to tell her to gin sling her hook, I simply said, 'Connor'.

Chelsea relaxed her clawlike grip on my arm, shrugged bony shoulders and pointed a black-painted talon in the direction of a door with an unilluminated red light-bulb outside. Navigating by Braille, I walked slowly to the door, knocked and entered.

'Long time no see,' Connor said from behind his desk. He waved the hand with 'Love' tattooed on it; 'Hate' was out of sight – for now, at least. 'Sit yourself down, Shannon.'

I crossed the room. Lowered myself gingerly into a leather chair so stained it magnetically repelled my fingertips. Looked up pleadingly at the four televisions mounted on the wall. Connor flicked some switches on a long and complicated console to his right: two screens showing 'private' rooms went blank, and the sound was muted on the remaining two.

'What have you got for me?' I asked, getting straight down to business. Well, there wasn't much point in going through a nice-to-see-you, how-you-diddling routine – a relationship based on mutual loathing can be a real inhibitor in the conversation stakes.

280

He smiled at me.

God, how I hated that smile. It was always a precursor to trouble.

'Good question,' he said teasingly.

'Come on,' I said. 'You owe me. Don't forget the tongs. I could have made you a candidate for the job of chief eunuch, remember? Or simply walked away and let the others practise penalty kicks.'

'Tough,' he said coldly. 'If you'd been the one on the floor, I wouldn't have given it a second thought. But then you never were much good at finishing someone off.'

'Look,' I said, my voice rising in anger – at Connor for his ingratitude, and at myself for so stupidly expecting anything different – 'like I told you on the phone, I work with the police now. There might come a time when you need a favour. Alternatively,' I paused and let my hands draw vague circles in the air, 'I could make life very difficult for you. Won't be good for business if there's Mr Plod at your door day and night. I could even arrange for the word to be spread that you're really on our side. Topping up your income by acting as snout.'

'That's better, Shannon,' he said grinning. 'You're learning at last. Good to see the world has dragged you down to my level.'

Connor leaned casually back in the chair. Swivelled smugly from side to side. And laughed.

My system, already on yellow alert from the sight of his first smile, pressed the higher button to signal red.

Connor, against the odds, was still a force to be

reckoned with. Unlike most ex-cons, who go on a permanent hedonistic, gut-swelling, brain-deadening binge when released, Connor had managed to keep himself in shape. Not a shape I would have wanted but... Above the collar of his black shirt his neck was as broad as a bull's. Where his rolled-up sleeves exposed hairy fore-arms, you could watch – if you had a strong stomach – taut, hard muscles expanding and contracting with each movement of his squat body.

'You were right,' he said, nodding his head. 'It was a tip-off. They – no names, eh, it's safer that way – were able to switch trucks at the last moment. The boys in blue followed the wrong set of wheels.'

'How good is your source?'

'Can't get better,' Connor said. 'He was right there in the room when the phone call came through. Everyone fell about at the thought of making the Drugs Squad look like a bunch of idiots.'

'So Kinsella was bent after all?'

'Kinsella?' Connor said. He stared at me. Collapsed into a paralysing fit of violent laughter.

'Whoever told you it was Kinsella,' he said, composing himself with extreme difficulty, 'has been pulling your plonker. Kinsella couldn't be bought. Everyone knows that.'

Oh no.

I didn't want to hear any more.

But I had to ask.

'Okay,' I said. 'If it wasn't Kinsella, then who was it?'

'Does the name Collins ring any bells?'

My stomach fell to my boots. I closed my eyes and nodded.

'There must be some mistake,' I said. 'It can't be Collins.'

'No mistake,' he said. 'My source heard the name real clear. I told you, he was in the same room as the telephone.' Connor grinned at me, revelling in my discomfort. 'Wasn't the first time either. There'd been tip-offs before.'

'But why?' I asked, still struggling to take it all in. 'Why would he do it?'

'Can't you guess?' Connor said.

'Money?'

'Nah, you berk. Blackmail.'

'What did they have on him?'

'He was a user. A snowman.'

'Cocaine?' I asked, just to confirm that my understanding of the slang was correct.

'Regular as clockwork.'

Booze and cigarettes, yes. But cocaine? Was it the only way to suppress the guilt? To blot out the vision of Louise at the bottom of the stairs, the baby dead inside her?

'They had some photos apparently,' Connor interrupted my thoughts. 'Collins buying. After that it was a simple trade. Information or else. Plus a free supply, of course. Hooked, every which way.'

'Who's your source?' I asked. I felt like a man who'd just been told by the consultant that he has a terminal illness. After the second opinion I now wanted a third.

Connor fiddled with the console.

'No way,' he said. Slowly. Defiantly. And very confidently.

From behind me I heard the squeak of hinges, the muffled tread of footsteps on the carpet.

Turning, I saw two men framed in the doorway against the background of blackness. The red light outside the room was glowing brightly.

Connor's henchmen entered. Closed the door ominously. Blocked the exit. Stood there immobile, legs spread apart, arms folded across their chests, like Egyptian sentries guarding the Pharaoh's tomb.

They were both wearing dark suits – perfect camouflage for lurking unseen in the bar. The taller of the two was aged about forty: he had a broken nose and a pallid complexion – neither of which was surprising, given his line of work. The other had the thick set and swarthy appearance of Mediterranean ancestry. Italian, I wondered? Or Maltese, perhaps? Shannon, my brain admonished. What the hell does it matter?

'Now,' Connor said, 'it's my turn for some information.'

I gave him a genuinely puzzled look.

'Norman Timpkins,' he said. 'Your old cellmate. See anything of him, do you?'

'Why?'

'Good,' Connor said with another smile.

Perhaps, I thought too late, 'No' would have been a better answer.

'Seems he's been a naughty boy.' Connor sighed dramatically. 'Poking his nose into matters that don't concern him. Making enquiries. By computer, I hear.'

I shrugged evasively. Not easy when you're trying to blot out a vision of an alarm sounding on a database as the name Prospekt is repeatedly typed in.

'Some associates of mine,' Connor said vaguely, 'checked out our mutual friend. Saw that him and me had been in the slammer together. Asked me to do them a little favour. Have a word in his shell-like. But, seeing as you were kind enough to pop round, I thought you might save me the trouble of seeing him personally.'

'I'll pass on the message,' I said, rising from the chair.

'You must understand, Shannon,' Connor said, screwing up his lips in an advance apology rendered meaningless by the accompanying grin, 'that this is business. Not pleasure. No, not a bit.' He nodded his head at the sentries. 'Give Shannon the message, lads.'

The adrenalin – instinctive flight or fight response to danger – flooded through my body. My brain issued three orders: analyse the situation; think about your reaction; then repeat after me, 'Our Father...'

The Italian – his arms were too long for a Maltese, I'd concluded – moved first. He crossed the room with quick strides of his short legs. I kicked out at the chair, sent it on an unavoidable collision course with his kneecaps. It postponed the immediate problem only for a few seconds but, as he threw the chair aside, I had the consolation that at least he might catch something horrible and lingering from it in the fullness of time.

Mr Pallor came to the aid of his pal. Then they both advanced. The Italian drew an ivory-handled flick-knife from his pocket. Pressed a button to click open the blade.

'Put it away,' Connor shouted angrily. 'We're not supposed to kill him, stupid. He's as good as being a cop. All hell will break loose. Just rough him up a bit, for chrissake.'

You're too kind, Connor. Wouldn't like to define 'a bit', would you?

Mr Pallor dipped into his suit and pulled out a cosh.

'That's better,' I heard Connor say in clarification.

Then it all happened fast.

The Italian threw a wide-arced right hook at my head.

Mr Pallor swung the cosh at my neck.

And the door burst open.

'About bloody time,' I shouted to Arthur, at the same time ducking below the hook – and into the path of the swinging cosh.

The blow glanced off the top of my head. I swung round to the desk. Ripped the heavy console free from its restraining wires. Swung it from side to side like a double-handed sword in an effort to keep the two henchmen at bay.

Arthur's outsize fist landed on the Italian's collar. Jerked him backwards, spun him round. Into exactly the right position for a forearm smash across the windpipe. The Italian let out a strangled cry of pain. Thankfully, it didn't last long. Under the force of the blow he plummeted to the floor, hit his head and slipped silently into unconsciousness.

Arthur turned to face his next adversary.

'Dangerous Duggan!' Mr Pallor said, as recognition and the console hit him simultaneously. 'Oh,' he groaned loudly. Or it may have been 'Ooh'. I wouldn't swear to it, mind – it was a little indistinct for there to be a complete absence of doubt. Then he dropped like a sack of potatoes and joined his pal in an untidy heap on the carpet.

'One each,' Arthur said, shaking my hand.

'If you had been any later it would have been one-nil. To them, that is.'

'Sorry,' he grunted. 'But you should have seen what that girl was doing with the snake.'

'Save it,' I said.

'I suppose she was,' he replied. 'But it was a bloody funny way to give mouth-to-mouth resuscitation.'

'Arthur!'

'Well, then,' he said, his gaze transferring threateningly to Connor. 'What do you want me do with this one?'

'We're old friends, Connor and I. Give him a hug for me, Arthur.'

Connor stood up. Stared up. Into Arthur's smiling eyes.

I could hardly bear to look. But forced myself, you understand.

Arthur wrapped his arms around Connor. And squeezed. And squeezed.

'Who's your source?' I said, raising my voice above the background noise of loud moans.

Connor shook his head.

'The hand lock,' I said to Arthur. 'You know the one? Where you stand behind him, draw his arm between his legs and let him scratch the back of his neck.'

'Rawlinson,' Connor said quickly and decisively.

'And where do I find him?'

'You don't,' Connor said.

Arthur sighed, released his bear hug and took hold of Connor's arm.

'He's in Wandsworth,' Connor screamed in panic. 'The prison. Where you can't get at him.'

Arthur looked at me enquiringly. I nodded. He dropped Connor back into the chair.

'Bye,' I said to Connor as we left the room.

'Ciao,' I called back to the Italian.

The door slammed shut behind us. The lock clicked. A bolt thudded into place.

'You never bloody learn, do you, Shannon?' came the muffled shout.

I looked at Arthur and gave a sheepish grin.

Sheepish or not, the sound of laughter from inside the room soon wiped it off my face.

CHAPTER TWENTY-FOUR

Norman was as high as I was low. My knowledge of the theory of entropy was a little rusty – and, frankly, I had never understood it all that well in the first place – but I was pretty sure that when we talked, the net effect would be to drag him down to my level rather than raise me up to his.

'Ah,' he said, judging my mood with the experienced eyes of an ex-cell-mate. 'Let me guess. Drooping shoulders, creased brow. I have it, Holmes. You didn't get quite the answer you wanted?'

I realised now why Sherlock kept a violin – he could lock himself in his room, bow away madly for an hour like Stephane Grappelli on speed and not have to answer awkward questions. I resorted to a doleful shake of my head. And then spilled it all out to Norman. How does the saying go? A problem shared is ... twice the number of people with a problem.

'They say a little knowledge is a dangerous thing,' Norman concluded. 'Sometimes a surfeit of knowledge is even more dangerous.'

I couldn't tell whether he was referring to the trouble that his searches had unleashed, or to the dilemma Collins now posed. Both seemed to fit the bill.

'Ignorance is bliss, eh? Since when have you been a member of the Homespun Philosophy Society?'

'Since I came across the name of Prospekt.'

A heavy doom-laden silence settled in the room.

Norman shrugged his bony shoulders. I shrugged my drooping ones. Then we both got our act together and shrugged simultaneously.

'I don't suppose,' he asked, thinking out loud, 'you have any clues as to who sent the anonymous letter? The one that opened up this particular can of worms.'

'No,' I admitted. 'It could be anyone at

Glenshield for all I know – from what I hear, gossip is the necessary lubricant that keeps the machinery turning. Maybe someone picked up a vague whisper about fraud. Wrote the letter to settle an old score, or just to throw a spanner in the works.'

'Or,' Norman said, leaving the sentence hanging in the air.

'Or,' I said, 'there is another, more sinister, possibility. That's what you're thinking, isn't it?'

Norman didn't answer. Instead, he screwed up his face and tilted his head to one side. He'd had enough of shoulder-shrugging for a while.

'It could have been Collins himself,' I said, filling in the gap. 'At best, an attempt to exact a degree of revenge on Kinsella. At the absolute worst, if we discover Kinsella is up to no good, then Collins's word is suddenly a lot more reliable than Kinsella's. Collins's version of the story about the drug raid gains credibility. And Kinsella, not Collins, becomes the prime candidate for the Rotten Apple award.'

'It would make sense,' Norman said, fingering his lips in contemplation. He shook his head. 'To hell with it. We could spend all day going round in circles of bluff and double-bluff. Come and have a look at this.'

Norman handed me a print-out of the spreadsheet so far. The sales side was complete. Down the page were the names of each of the export contracts; across the page were the months, with the amount invoiced in the cells underneath. The contracts varied in size, the smallest being worth a little under ten thousand pounds a month and the largest close to a hundred grand – a cool three million a year when you added them all up. Fraud or not, this was big business for Glenshield.

'What about this one?' I asked, pointing to a row where the figures petered out halfway across the page.

'Remember our odd man out?' he said.

'The only one of the countries without currency restrictions?'

'It's this one,' Norman said, looking like the cat that had swallowed the cream – after a first course of minced fillet steak. 'Glenshield's contract stopped six months ago. I did some checking. At exactly that time a new President was installed. With the full military and financial backing of the United States. All previous restrictions on the exportation of currency were abolished overnight.'

'Well, isn't that a coincidence,' I said, tongue as far in cheek as it would go. My spirits were rising after all. The black-market currency scam had moved on through the hazy land of speculation and arrived in the realm of absolute certainty. Glenshield had lost interest in supplying security services the moment the potential for illicit profit had disappeared.

'Let's fill in the missing figures,' I said. 'I've got a wonderful feeling that we're almost there.' Okay, so the offences probably weren't prosecutable under English law, but there might be a chance of the countries themselves taking some form of action. From the little I knew of international law, it could well be a case of away goals counting double – the prison sentences for fraud in Singapore, for example, are about four times as great as in Britain: newly formed breakaway Russian republics might have lost their access to the salt mines, but they were probably not averse to locking up a foreign fraudster and melting down the key for tractor parts.

Norman started off the examination of the costings while I made a pot of tea and some sandwiches – a few days in Accounts and I was suffering withdrawal symptoms without a sandwich at lunchtime. Damn. There wasn't a single sweet in the flat. How was I going to make it through the afternoon?

After thirty minutes we changed places. I took over at the keyboard. Norman rested his eyes, stretched his legs and munched his way through the ham and mustard.

An hour later and we were well on the way to completing the spreadsheet. I'd called up the job costings on each project in turn and added the figures below the sales value. There were a few missing months, but I knew where to turn for this information. Good old Q123 – the dummy job file, set up to cope with O'Kane's laxity when it came to allocating job numbers.

Sure enough, the missing costs were there, suspended in an accounting limbo. I wrote the numbers on the print-out and sat back to take an overview.

'Bingo,' I shouted, deafening Norman at my side. 'Too big a profit. We've done it.'

On each job they were making a mark-up of

four or five times the costs. I could accept twice – Glenshield charging the customer double what it cost to service the contract wouldn't have been unusual in a business that was basically selling people's time. But no way did this magnitude of profit stack up. Or, rather, not legitimately it didn't.

'Put the champagne on ice,' I said to Norman.

'Sorry,' he said. 'What did you just say? I wasn't concentrating.'

His eyes were glued to the screen.

'There's something wrong here,' he said.

'I'll say there is.'

'No. I don't mean the currency scam. Look at this. And this. And this.'

He pointed at several places on the screen. Scrolled down to the next page of the vast Q123 file. Pointed again. And again.

'It's just O'Kane being sloppy,' I said.

'No. It's a whole lot more than that. This supplier here. I know where these costs should go.'

'And where's that?' I asked. My heart was beating faster, feeding off Norman's increasing excitement.

'The cancelled contract,' he said.

'But,' I said, 'we have all the costs for that contract. Don't you remember? You did that while I was in the kitchen.'

Then the penny finally dropped.

Or, to be more accurate, the twenty thousand pounds per month.

'We've got 'em!' I screamed with joy. 'Put two bottles of champagne on ice. Come to think of it, make that a whole bloody case.'

Six months ago the contract had been cancelled. But the invoices from the sub-contracted supplier had kept on arriving, regular as clockwork. And, equally regularly I presumed, had still been paid. At bloody last! A fraud that the English courts could pursue.

Hang on a minute, Shannon, I told myself. Don't get too carried away. This sort of thing is not unknown. You know how it goes. Some accounts clerk at the sub-contractors is programmed to produce the same invoice month after month. No-one tells him that the contract from Glenshield has stopped. So he carries on as normal.

'Let's check the payments schedule just to make sure,' I said.

'I suppose you're right. But I'll lay a pound to a penny these invoices have been paid.'

'That's a bet I'm not taking,' I said. This had all the signs of being a bigger odds-on favourite than the West Indies against Durham – second eleven.

And so it proved to be.

Each invoice had been passed for payment, albeit through the unwitting avenue of the dreaded Q123. For the first three months the money had actually been transmitted: the other invoices were still in the system, racking up interest for Glenshield while waiting to be paid.

'Okay,' Norman said, thinking aloud. 'We can put the currency scam down to Prospekt – probably even a bit of drumming up their own business, given the criminal connections. But this fraud is *against* them, not by them. It's an inside job. Someone within Glenshield lining their own pockets.' He ran out of steam, sucked at his teeth in helplessness. 'But who?' he asked. 'Who is on the fiddle? That's the question.'

'What if it goes like this,' I said, theorising. 'Glenshield pulls out of the contract when the country releases its strict exchange controls. Someone – and my money is on O'Kane – is supposed to tell the Accounts Department. Maybe he forgets. Maybe he sends a memo and it is intercepted. Beryl, blissfully ignorant, possibly even daydreaming of the four S's in Ibiza, continues to pass the phoney invoices.'

'Still doesn't answer the question,' Norman said. 'Who is the one in Glenshield with his hand in the till? Who is colluding with the sub-contractor? The only way we're going to find that out is if the sub-contractor spills the beans. And they may well decide to brazen it out. Claim it's been a genuine mistake. "Sorry, Glenshield. Here's your money back. Won't happen again."'

'Until now, Norman,' I said in reprimand mode, 'you've been doing a pretty good job of cheering me up. Don't spoil it, please.'

'Well,' he said. 'It's the defence I'd take.'

'No, you wouldn't,' I said. 'You would have found a far cleverer way of skimming twenty grand a month out of Glenshield. This sort of scam couldn't go on forever. Someone – Paradine, Kinsella, O'Kane – would have spotted it eventually. No, you would have taken a much more subtle route.'

Norman looked at me, his eyes shining as bright as signal beacons.

I stared at him.

We shouted the words in unison.

'The supplier database!'

If we hadn't been mentally chained to the computer we would have danced round the room.

Then he shook his head.

'No,' he said. 'I hate to think of anyone being as smart as Norman Timpkins.'

'Only one way to find out,' I said.

I made a swift exit to the opening menu. Selected the option for the supplier database. Typed in Kinsella's codeword to gain access.

The payments schedule used the code of GUAl to identify the details for Guardex Limited, the sub-contractor concerned.

First I went back seven months. Alongside GUAl was the name Guardex and all the associated details. I noted down the bank sort code and account number. Then I called up the same file for the last month.

Nothing matched.

Granted, the name was close – Guardrex, this time – but the bank details were totally different.

The sub-contractor was in the clear.

Someone – and the options were narrowing by the minute – had set up a similar-sounding company. Sent a phoney invoice each month. And changed the supplier database so that payments were made to the account of the new company. Anyone checking such a large database would almost certainly skim over the extra 'r' in the name; and as for the chances of spotting the change in the bank details, they were minute.

My pulse was racing. We were so close now.

'Time for you to show me the miracles of modems and on-line sources of information,' I said to Norman. 'Find out who controls this Guardrex and we have them by the short and curlies. With a four-foot set of tongs.'

I changed seats with Norman and watched as the computer followed his instructions and automatically dialled the number.

I drummed my fingers impatiently on the table. It was the thought of this sort of moment that had enticed me to take up Collins's offer of joining the Fraud Investigation Group.

'Whoever is involved,' Norman said gravely as he typed in the search request, 'I don't fancy their chances when Prospekt get to hear the news.'

He ran a finger across his throat to emphasise his point.

I gulped.

For a brief while the omnipresent threat of Prospekt – indisputable launderers of drugs money through their anonymous *anstalt* – had faded from my thoughts. I'd been enjoying myself too.

'Come on,' I said irritably to the computer.

'Won't be long now,' Norman said soothingly. 'Ah, here we are. Guardrex. Certificate of In-corporation. Memorandum and Articles. Direc-tors and shareholders.'

'Oh, no,' I said, as the names popped up. 'They're not going to like this.'

'Who?' Norman asked.

'Everybody,' I replied. 'Collins. Kinsella. Not forgetting the culprits themselves.'

'To be precise,' Norman said, reading from the screen, 'Stephen Anthony Paradine and Louise Rosemary Kinsella.'

'Idiot,' I said, for the fifth time.

I was addressing myself

Apart from who had actually sent the letter – and somehow that didn't seem so important any more – all the other pieces of the jigsaw were slotting rapidly into place as if a deft octopus were at work. The picture was virtually complete.

'I should have listened more closely to Walker,' I said to Norman. 'The gossip. "Everybody's at it. From the top," she'd said.' I shook my head in sheer frustration at myself. 'I took that to mean Kinsella – Christ, with a name like Roddy, it was an easy conclusion to draw. But if Walker had been referring to Kinsella, she would have said "from the very top". Louise and Paradine – that's who she was talking about.'

I paused to think it all through. 'And it takes two passwords to change the supplier database – Paradine's and Kinsella's. Louise knew Kinsella's password, she was in on the joke the whole time. Had the last laugh.'

I shook my head in despair.

Oh well, may as well go for a round half-dozen.

'Idiot,' I said again. 'Damned idiot.'

Blast, I was up to seven now. I added another three 'Idiots' for good measure. After all, ten is a rounder number than six.

CHAPTER TWENTY-FIVE

'Well, Shannon?' Walker asked as she drove out of the gates of Wandsworth Prison, flipping down the visor to screen the low, slanting rays of the early morning sun. 'Was it worth it?'

'Yes,' I said broodily. 'Without a shadow of a doubt. It was worth it.'

I didn't say it to reward her for the trouble she'd taken. For persuading the Commander to request the Visiting Order without which no-one, not even a police officer, is allowed into a prison. For getting the VO made out in the names of Walker and Quinn. For 'borrowing' Quinn's warrant card from the jacket slung over the back of his chair while he was down the Queen's Head enjoying a swift pint. (I couldn't enter Wandsworth under my own name. As an ex-con, the likelihood of being granted a visit at all was low: the chance of a visit at a few hours' notice absolutely zero. And there was Prospekt to consider too – better, safer, all round if my name wasn't bandied around in connection with asking awkward questions about drugs raids.)

Nor, for that matter, did I mean that we had been successful in achieving our original goal – banishing uncertainty by hearing about Collins the Informer straight from the horse's mouth.

The reason for my words, and current melancholy, was more basic. And entirely personal.

When we had arrived at the gatehouse we had been greeted by a uniformed officer wearing a name badge. Since my days behind bars, HM Prison Service had embraced the Citizen's Charter. Badges were part of the new commitment. Once past the gatehouse it became clear that badges were the sum total of the new commitment. Nothing else in the system seemed to have changed.

Forget Boot Camps, Mr Home Secretary. The best deterrent to potential young offenders is a guided tour of Wandsworth Prison.

Looking at the prison from the outside – and that, in both senses, was what I was able to do – it was hard to credit that the inside could be more depressing. Built in 1851 in the Victorian radial style, the shabby collection of cellular wings leading off the central administration block and the separate block (J wing), originally designed for women prisoners, had not weathered well. Visually, metaphorically, Wandsworth was one huge black stain on the prison landscape.

Unable (unwilling?) to move towards the beckoning finger of the twenty-first century, it is the only prison in the country to have a working set of gallows.

Ronnie Biggs escaped from here in 1965. It probably wasn't freedom as such, with its concomitant life on the run, that he craved: he just couldn't stand a moment longer the penal dustbin that was Wandsworth. Difficult prisoners (and staff too) from all across the country were transferred here in a felons' equivalent of the stalag in the *Great Escape,* to suffer what was infamous as at best an austere, and at worst a brutal, regime. The present Governor, so they say, was dragging Wandsworth in a more enlightened direction. Christ, he needed to.

Rawlinson was lucky – relatively speaking. He was in D wing, the most modern – integral sanitation and light switches (but no power points). The other seven wings, two of which were now mercifully closed, could be generously described as 'squalid'.

I listened to Rawlinson complain about the canteen/shop, which stocked one brand of cigarettes and eight different varieties of Afro hair gel. Was reminded of the five hours a day (three at weekends), including exercise and slopping out, that were spent out-of-cell. And of the petty rules and regulations that make a prison tick and an impotent inmate shake his head in dismay: to be allowed, among your possessions, one flannel – any colour but red (no DIY 'Trusty' armbands); to be able to bring in a birdcage, but not bird seed – that had to be purchased from your prison earnings; and to know that the only letters not opened and censored were those addressed to the Samaritans.

I'd survived prison once. Come out minus two fingers and with a memory softened by the unbreakable bonds of friendship forged with Arthur and Norman. Wandsworth kicked pitilessly at my rose-tinted glasses. Prison, the heavy boots reminded me as the lenses shattered, wasn't about camaraderie and times spent laughing at jokes about Catholics' casserole.

301

Prison was days of sweat, whether caused by hard physical work or the constant fear of a mindless and violent attack from someone who has nothing to lose. And prison was about nights too – nights of silent, self-pitying tears soaking your pillow.

Shannon, Wandsworth counselled, it's time you made something of this botched-up existence of yours.

So I nodded wisely to myself as we crossed the river – my Rubicon.

There could be no going back.

I resolved to break free from the past.

And a present that was no better than a halfway house in a twilight world where I was forced into contact with the dark, threatening shapes of Collins on the one hand and Prospekt on the other.

Neither of them would claim me. I would not permit them to rob me of my freedom, and with it my sanity or my life.

Yes, Walker. It was worth it.

CHAPTER TWENTY-SIX

I don't know what surprised the desk sergeant more. Six foot five of Arthur loitering inside the door, hands thrust deep in pockets, huge boots nervously kicking away at the carpet, exuding all the confidence of a guilty schoolboy waiting outside the headmaster's study. Or my presence back at Holborn police station. Probably Arthur, I suspected – the sergeant, with many years of experience under his belt, must have been used to bad pennies turning up by now.

Eyebrows raised, he telephoned Collins. Held the receiver away from his car as a curt reply barked its way down the telephone wires.

'You're expected, it seems,' he said, poking his damaged ear with the tip of an inky finger. 'There's supposed to be three of you, though.'

'He'll be here any minute. We'll wait.'

The desk sergeant shrugged to show his indifference.

'Whatever,' he said. 'DS Collins says he'll meet you in the conference room, tenth floor.' He narrowed his eyes and peered enquiringly at me. 'Do I take it this is kiss-and-make-up time? Back on the payroll, are you?'

'I was never off it, sergeant,' I boasted, my pride glowing like the aurora borealis.

Okay, so it wasn't very subtle. But it felt good to be legitimate again. The prodigal son had returned. An undercover operation under his belt, too. Surely, when everyone learned the full story, the cloak of suspicion would be removed from my shoulders and I would be accepted within the closed ranks.

Kinsella walked through the door just as the sergeant's eyebrows were about to revert to their normal position. They jumped up another notch. Any more surprises and they would finish up above his receding hairline.

'Well, well,' the sergeant said, smiling warmly. 'Good to see you, sir.'

'And you too, Sid,' Kinsella replied, beaming back and pumping Sid's hand as if drawing water from a deep well. 'How's the wife? Still making those great slabs of bread pudding?'

'Every Sunday, regular as clockwork,' Sid said, patting his spreading waistline as incontrovertible evidence.

'I hate to spoil this gastronomic trip down Memory Lane,' I said tetchily, 'but–'

My interruption wasn't prompted by a prison-induced neurotic penchant for punctuality. I was annoyed at the easy comradeship of the old-boy network. Who had I been kidding? Walker hadn't been accepted after five years in the force. With my background it would take me twenty years –and I didn't intend to stay a fraction of that time. Once Collins and I had settled our debts (and I'd found another job, of course) I was off.

'Time we went up,' Kinsella said. 'Mustn't keep DS Collins waiting, eh? Don't want to ruffle his feathers.' He grinned at the desk sergeant and winked conspiratorially. 'See you later, Sid. Have a pint or two, maybe?'

'Yes, sir,' came the quick reply. 'I'd like that very much, sir.'

'You can drop the sir, Sid,' Kinsella said, waving a hand for me to lead the way. 'It's just plain Roddy now.'

Once inside the lift, I lost no time in making the necessary introductions. The two titans shook hands, both reluctant to be the first to release the grip, then circumspectly sized each other up. Neither of them, I imagined, would see the similarities of height, build and powerful physical presence – the 'there but for fortune' twist of nurture over nature: it was the differences that would be going through their minds. Sure enough, Arthur's eyes roved over Kinsella's perfectly cut, lightweight grey suit, dwelt a while on the blue tab-collared shirt and red silk tie, settled on the hand-made loafers; Kinsella, in turn, took in Arthur's battered brown leather jacket, creased khaki cords and heavy utilitarian boots.

'Thug' would be the word running through Kinsella's mind; 'ponce' through Arthur's.

'Why all the mystery?' Kinsella asked me.

In a brief telephone call to arrange the meeting, all I had said was not to tell anyone. I'd laid heavy stress on the last word.

'If it's any consolation,' I replied, 'Collins knows even less than you.'

'It's your show, I suppose,' Kinsella replied with a casual heave of his broad shoulders. 'Play it whichever way suits you best.'

But it wasn't that easy.

The truth was that I had no idea how I was going to play it. Because I could not predict how each of them would react.

After the visit to Wandsworth, I'd spent the remainder of the previous day checking and double-checking the accounts, killing time as much as reassuring myself that nothing had been missed. Over dinner I had used Arlene, Norman and Arthur as sounding-posts. Arlene had been as supportive and trusting as ever, but ended up saying pretty much the same as Kinsella. Norman had been intensely thoughtful, but to no effect. Arthur had shaken that great head of his and nearly choked on his wine when I had asked him to come along to the meeting. 'A police station?' he'd said, his voice trembling with horror, as if he were being invited to attend the Gay Liberation Movement annual dinner dance.

So here it was, Friday morning, one minute to eleven, and I still didn't have a clue. I took a deep breath and willed the lift doors to open. Then led the way along the corridor to the conference room.

Collins's eyes brightened when he saw Kinsella. I knew what he must be thinking. In line with the probable next revision of PACE – the ever-softening procedures for handling suspects – he would be getting ready to take the chill off the handcuffs.

The oval table sat six, in theory – but what did the theorists know of the existence of beings like Arthur and Kinsella. This was going to be all too close for comfort.

Collins sat at the head, Kinsella took up the expected confrontational position directly opposite. Arthur, as instructed, bisected them. Walker, hair pinned back, wearing a chalk-striped suit and a worried frown, joined me along the spare side. The vanilla sweetness of her perfume drifted up from her graceful neck and tickled at my nose. We were close enough to rub knees. Hardly likely, though. Our uneasy alliance was based purely and simply on a mutual ability to make life difficult for each other.

The windows were open. A warm breeze drifted into the room. In response, the slats of the vertical blinds swayed rhythmically from side to side, causing an ever-changing pattern of sun and shade to dance hypnotically along the plain white walls. There was a faint smell of whisky in the air. Maybe that was why the windows had been opened – to blow away the heady fumes of a late-night meeting. The cynic in me, however, put a questionmark against Collins's breath as being the more probable source. Not a very comforting thought.

'Well?' said Collins, rubbing his hands together.

'It's a long story,' I said.

'Take all the time you like,' he went on. 'Just as long as it has a happy ending.'

I avoided his eyes. Engaged in some necessary displacement activity. Took a pack of cigarettes from my pocket. Extracted one after lengthy consideration of the identical options. Tapped the end on the table. Lit it very slowly. Drew in inspiration along with the smoke.

'Our anonymous informant was right,' I said. 'There is fraud going on at Glenshield. More than one, in fact.'

'I knew it,' Collins declared triumphantly.

'Let's nail the bastards,' Kinsella said.

Collins sneered across at him. Arthur's fingers, tensely flexed, gripped the edge of the table.

'Let's take it step by step, shall we?' I said. 'First there's a currency swindle.'

Collins leaned forward with mounting interest. Ran his tongue over his bottom lip in anticipation. Then listened attentively as I explained the details of the foreign contracts and the mechanics of the resulting black-market currency scam. Kinsella's eyes opened wider.

'So who is behind it?' Kinsella asked.

'Paradine is my guess,' I said. 'I'll tell you why later.'

Collins frowned. 'But we can't prosecute? Is that what you're saying?'

'Not in this country, no. But there'll be some foreign governments who will be only too happy to oblige.'

Collins grunted with dissatisfaction. His job was to obtain lengthy sentences. Passing the buck to some *foreign* (i.e. *suspect*) judge didn't exactly fill him to the brim with confidence.

'But,' I said, 'there is another fraud for which we might prosecute.'

'There's no *might* about it,' Collins said, his voice raised in determination.

Kinsella agreed. A competitive decibel more loudly too.

'It's a variant on the old phoney invoice scam,' I said, trying to ignore the stereo eardrum injury. 'Glenshield has been paying twenty grand a month for non-existent services.'

'That's not possible,' Kinsella said. 'The system doesn't allow it.'

'The security of your system, Mr Kinsella,' I said firmly, 'works about as effectively as an instruction to the average hot-blooded male not to tune in to *Baywatch*. Even your best-intentioned staff ignore the dictats – out of sheer bloody necessity. Because of the pressures they operate under, they have found ways round the system.'

I explained about compromised passwords and

dummy job numbers. Kinsella shook his head gravely.

'So,' he asked, on recovering from my lecture, 'who is behind these phoney invoices? Paradine again?'

'Yes. No doubt about it this time. It's a simple fraud. The invoices come in, get allocated expediently to Q123 and consequently passed for payment. Meanwhile the supplier database has been deftly altered and the money ends up in the bank account of a company of which Paradine is a director.'

'But the database can't be changed without my password. Paradine doesn't know it. It's impossible.'

'Paradine isn't in this on his own.'

'It makes no difference who else is involved,' Kinsella said. 'No-one knows my password.'

'No-one?' I queried.

'No,' he said. Then the truth began to dawn on him. He shook his head more vigorously this time. 'No,' he repeated, the certainty gone from his voice, 'I don't believe it.'

'Come on, Shannon,' Collins said impatiently. 'Cut the bloody Poirot crap. I can only take so much of this – all of us gathered together in the locked room for the final bleeding denouement. Who the bloody hell is he?'

At my side, Walker, knowing what was to come, tensed. She looked down at the blank, crisp-white notepad in front of her, and waited expectantly.

'Not he,' I corrected. 'She. It's Louise.'

Arthur later described, for Arlene's benefit, the

resulting silence as being so quiet that you could have heard an ant break wind. It wouldn't have been my choice of phrase – or exactly his either, I suspected – but you couldn't fault the accuracy of the observation.

It was Collins's turn to echo Kinsella's words and do a near-perfect Victor Meldrew impersonation. 'I don't believe it,' he said. 'No. Not Louise.' The blood drained from his face. He lit a cigarette with shaking hands.

'I'm sorry,' I said. 'But the company sending the phoney invoices is controlled by Paradine and Louise – they're both down in black and white as directors and shareholders. There can be no doubting it.'

'But why?' Kinsella asked, shock giving way to puzzlement. 'Why Lou and Paradine?'

Walker supplied the answer. 'They've been having an affair for months now. It's common knowledge among your staff.'

'It's not true,' he said. It was pure reflex action – a self-protecting protest issued without any depth of conviction. 'There's some mistake. I would have known.'

'Would you?' Collins said.

'You're loving this, aren't you?' Kinsella snarled.

'Those who live by the sword...' Collins replied. 'Or, should we say, the rod?'

Kinsella, wild-eyed, sprang from his seat. Arthur, prepared for just this eventuality, jumped up to block his path to Collins, simultaneously placing a hefty forearm across Kinsella's chest.

'Look,' Arthur said irritably, 'I don't enjoy being in police stations – not even fancy rooms in the Fraud Squad. It makes me nervous. Understand?' He paused momentarily to let the word hang threateningly in the air. 'I'm only here for one reason. To keep you two apart. And I'll do that any way I can. Now, be a good boy and sit down.'

The two men stared at each other. It wasn't in Kinsella's nature to back down, to lose face. Out in the street he would have brawled with Arthur and, if successful, moved on to tackle Collins. But in here he was having second thoughts. Collins watched dispassionately, the news about Louise robbing him of the ability to smile at his old adversary's plight.

'I wouldn't give you the satisfaction,' Kinsella finally hissed at Collins. Sitting back down, he gazed challengingly across the length of the table. 'It would really make your day to charge me with assault on a police officer.'

'Contrary to what you're thinking, Kinsella,' Collins said, 'this situation gives me little satisfaction. I still love Louise enough not to want to see her land up in court, let alone prison.'

'What are we going to do, sir?' Walker asked. 'Prosecute them both? Or let them get off scot-free because of your personal feelings?'

'To be honest,' Collins said, 'I don't know. Let's hear the rest of Shannon's story before we decide.'

'Excuse me,' Kinsella butted in. 'But this is my company. And it's my decision whether or not to prosecute.'

Kinsella was right. There were many cases of frauds being committed, particularly in banks

311

and other financial institutions, where no charges were ever brought: the victims preferred to write off their losses rather than suffer embarrassing publicity.

'It's your company, all right,' Collins said venomously. 'That much shows.'

'And what do you mean by that?' Kinsella clenched his fists and stared into Collins's eyes.

'It's rotten to the core.'

Arthur was on his feet before Kinsella had time to react. 'I'm warning you two,' he thundered. 'Come on, Nick. Get on with it, for chrissake.'

'Let's talk about rotten to the core, shall we?' I said to Collins. 'Let me take you back. To a certain drugs raid. One that went badly wrong.'

'Because this bastard,' Collins said, stabbing an accusing finger at Kinsella, 'was on the take.'

Kinsella rolled his eyes in exasperation.

'No,' I said firmly. 'It wasn't Kinsella.'

Collins shot me a look that would have frozen the steam in the prison laundry.

'I made some enquiries,' I said. 'A very good authority gave me the name of the person responsible for the tip-off. Would you like to hear it?'

There were nods from both ends of the table.

'The name I was given,' I said, 'was "Collins".'

'I knew it all along,' Kinsella roared. 'I'll see you busted for this, you hypocritical bastard.'

'It's a lie,' Collins screamed back. 'This is a set-up. What stunt are you trying to pull, Shannon? How much is he paying you for this?'

'It's not a lie,' I said. 'I found it hard to believe myself at first. So I went right back to the original source. He assured me he'd heard the name quite clearly. Last name. And first name. Frankly, I wouldn't have been surprised if he'd said it was Roddy Kinsella – after all, even the crooks know his first name. But Collins? I doubt if even Walker is privileged with that information. So I asked him to repeat the name in full this time. "Collins," he said. "Lew Collins." He'd naturally assumed it was a bloke. But it was Louise.'

'No,' Collins protested. 'It can't be true. I never even told her about the raid.'

'But Kinsella did,' I said, turning to the other end of the table. 'Didn't you?'

He slumped in his seat, placed his elbows on the table and dropped his head into his hands. Through the gaps in his fingers I could see that his eyes were closed.

We had our answer.

'Why?' Collins asked. 'Why would she do it?'

'Blackmail,' I said.

'Come off it,' Collins retorted. 'Louise was as white as snow. The only thing she ever did wrong was to take up with that bastard. What could they possibly threaten her with?'

'I can only guess the reason,' I said, 'but Kinsella knows.'

'What a fool I've been,' he said.

'You and me both, it seems,' Collins said.

'You showed me a picture of Louise once. Remember?'

Collins gave me a puzzled look.

'When I first met her at Glenshield, I couldn't get over how much prettier she looked in the flesh. Then it dawned on me.' I turned to

Kinsella. 'Louise had a nose job. Right?' Kinsella nodded. 'And it wasn't purely cosmetic, was it? A rebuild?'

'Cocaine,' he said, the index finger of his left hand worrying away at his lips as he relived the memories. 'She used to sniff it. Was on more lines a day than a public schoolboy in perpetual detention. It eventually destroyed the lining of her nose. That's when I realised what it was she was doing. We'd been married a year by then. Christ, all those years in the Drugs Squad.' He shook his head at his own stupidity. 'I should have spotted the signs sooner. But it was the last thing I expected from my own wife.'

Kinsella paused. I didn't know if he would – could – continue. I lit another cigarette. Collins hesitated and did the same.

'She's clean now. Spent three months in a clinic. Cold turkey and then the rebuild. I swear she's not taken anything since.'

It was Kinsella's turn to point the finger at Collins. 'It wasn't her fault,' he said bitterly, 'it was his. When Lou lost the baby she went to pieces. Some well-meaning girlfriend introduced her to cocaine. Told her it would give her a lift. Lou was in such a desperate state she would have tried anything to rid herself of the hollow pain inside.' He turned to me. 'From what you've just told me, Nick, it sounds like it may have been part of a deliberate plan all along. Get her hooked. Then use her as a source of information.'

Kinsella, his eyes pleading, studied my face.

What was he searching for? Confirmation of his theory? Or simply sympathy?

I smiled enigmatically, trying to cover both options and probably succeeding in neither.

'Hell, I don't know,' he said helplessly. 'I don't know anything any more. Why didn't she tell me she was being blackmailed?'

'Because she didn't want to see two careers destroyed. My guess is she made a deal with the blackmailers. Their continued silence in return for a share of a legitimate business through which to launder some of their drugs profits. That's how you came to be lumbered with Prospekt and Paradine.'

'Oh, Jesus Christ,' he said, slumping in the chair. 'Do you mean I've spent half my life fighting the evils of drugs and I wind up running a company that's just a front for washing blood-money? What the hell am I going to do?'

I turned back to Collins. My neck was beginning to feel as if I'd watched a five-set match at Wimbledon – in the days before serve and volley, that is, when they actually had rallies. 'There's no hard evidence against Prospekt. I don't even know the identities of anyone involved with the company. They operate through an *anstalt* in Liechtenstein. There's no way we can prove anything. Except perhaps...'

'Except what?' Collins asked slowly, sensing my doubts.

'We could arrest Louise and Paradine. Try to persuade them to turn Queen's evidence. Do a deal, maybe. Spill the beans on Prospekt and, in return, we drop the charges.'

'If it's that easy,' Collins asked, 'then why do you sound so worried?'

'Because Prospekt don't pussyfoot about. If their past record is anything to go by, they're likely to kill Louise and Paradine just for daring to rip them off: Prospekt only seem to have one weapon in their armoury – and that's the ultimate deterrent.' I took a supportive drag on my cigarette. 'But if Prospekt were to find out that they're helping the police, God knows what they'd do. As I've said, subtlety is not their strong suit. You'd probably need a bomb-disposal team on permanent standby.'

I wasn't joking either.

Collins lit another cigarette from the stub of the one he was finishing. Exhaled the smoke in a long, thoughtful stream. Watched it billow and curl against the ceiling.

'Paradine and Louise are small beer. Prospekt are the big boys.' He nodded his head to himself, his mind now made up – from now on he would be locked on a fixed course. 'We have to go for them,' he said decisively, the words racing excitedly from his mouth. 'I'll need to speak to the Commander – this crosses borders that even I can't ignore – but I think he'll agree to immunity from prosecution if we can build a case against Prospekt.'

'Is there any way we can keep Lou out of this?' Kinsella asked.

It was a stupid question for anyone who knew Collins's reputation – his bulldog jaws were already clamped around the throat of Prospekt. It was a fight to the death now. Nothing, and no-one, would be allowed to get in the way.

'I wish there were,' Collins said, a genuine hint

of sadness in his voice. 'But she could be a vital witness. Anyway, once Paradine starts talking it's unlikely he won't mention Louise. He'll be too busy saving his own skin. But don't worry, I won't let any harm come to her.'

'Thanks,' Kinsella said.

'Don't thank me. I'm doing it for me, not you. I may have been wrong about you and the drugs raid, but I still hate your guts.'

'That sounds like the closest to an apology I will ever get from you.'

Collins shrugged.

'Thought so,' Kinsella said. 'Will you do me a favour?'

Collins laughed, the concept striking him as too far-fetched for any other response.

'Lend me Shannon for a few days,' Kinsella said. 'I need to plug these holes in the system. Make sure nothing like this happens again. What do you say?'

Collins looked at me and raised his eyes questioningly.

'It's fine by me,' I said. 'I'm going away at the end of next week – Good Friday – but till then I'm free. Unless you have anything else for me, sir?'

'Okay,' Collins said graciously to Kinsella. 'But just for a few days. I'll send Nick over later.' Collins let his eyes drift round the room, taking us all in one by one. 'Until we move on Paradine and Louise, no-one says anything. Is that perfectly clear?'

We all nodded.

'That goes double for you, Kinsella,' he added.

'Not one word to Louise. Understand?'

'It won't be difficult,' Kinsella grunted. 'She's away on some conference or other – at least that's what she told me. Be gone all weekend. I take it you'll have an answer from the Commander by Sunday night?'

'Just leave the Commander to me, Kinsella,' Collins said. 'And whatever you do, keep your mouth shut.'

'And a fond farewell to you too, Collins.'

Kinsella shook Arthur's hand.

'No hard feelings,' Arthur said. 'Just doing my job.'

'I'm not one to hold grudges,' Kinsella said pointedly. 'See you later, Nick.'

I nodded. Lit another cigarette. Watched the procession as the room began to clear: Kinsella gliding across the carpet; Walker, hips swaying, silent and thoughtful, already mentally preparing her report for the Commander; Arthur stomping out quickly, anxious to leave the building. I smiled at him and winked my thanks. Then turned my attention back to Collins.

We had business to discuss.

I'd delivered my part of the deal.

Now it was time for Collins to settle up.

To retract the threats. And give me the licence to start a new life.

CHAPTER TWENTY-SEVEN

'The cheque is in the post.' That's probably the most frequent lie used in business. The variation on this theme favoured by Collins seemed to be 'the file is on its way'.

He was convincing, though. You had to say that much for him. His explanation was peppered with irrefutable facts so as to leave sufficient doubt to prevent me shouting 'bullshit' at the top of my voice. I suppose that is the way with all good lies. The delicate strands of falsehood are best woven with the coarse fibres of truth, so that they become invisible within the totality of the finished fabric.

It was tricky, he'd told me, a frown of sincerity stitched on his face. The file had been closed a long time. Was buried deep within Central Records. He tried the direct route of a formal requisition. No joy. Request denied – he had no apparent need, and no authority outside fraud cases now. So he'd been forced to take a round-about route instead. Pull a few strings. Call in some favours. Even that was proving difficult. But someone would come up trumps and sneak a surreptitious photocopy through the back door. Next week, for sure. Promise. Trust me.

'Meanwhile...' he added.

God, the man had more cheek than a hydro-cephalic elephant, more brass than a colliery band.

'No,' I said firmly. 'No meanwhiles. The file doesn't matter any more. The past is behind me. I'm finished with living in its shadow. It's the future that's important.'

'Please yourself,' he said. 'But if I were you, I'd ask myself why it is so difficult for a Detective Superintendent to get hold of the file. Still, if it doesn't matter...'

Damn. He had me intrigued now. But maybe that was the intention. Don't fall for it, Shannon, I told myself. Don't let him get you hooked again.

'The future,' I said resolutely. 'I'm thinking of emigrating to America. With my record that won't be easy. But you could smooth the path. Oil the wheels for the immigration visa with a suitably glowing reference.'

He smiled.

My stomach churned. In my attempt to obtain just settlement of one deal I'd simply handed him a bargaining point for another.

'Come on, Collins. You owe me, for chrissake.'

'As I was saying. Meanwhile...'

He knew he had me over a barrel. Was determined to extract the absolute maximum from me before he delivered.

I listened. Ranted and raved a bit. Called him a few choice names – none of them new to his ears, I suspect. Then agreed to his request.

But didn't let on that I was only too happy to oblige.

'Okay,' I said finally, as if making the ultimate sacrifice, 'I'll do it. In exchange for your reference. Agreed?'

'Shake on it,' he said.

Did I trust him?

Let's just say that, as I left the room, I counted my fingers.

The sight of O'Kane in Kinsella's office – *sans* coffee, to boot – sent the needle on my gut reaction meter shooting up into the red zone marked TROUBLE.

'Take a seat, Shannon,' Kinsella said. 'Just the man we need.'

The desk was littered with computer manuals – odd fragments of paper, pens and a ruler sticking out between the pages as improvised bookmarks.

'Can I have a word with you in private?' I asked, frowning.

'We can talk in front of Gerry. He knows what's going on.'

'Jesus,' I exploded, 'didn't you bloody listen to what Collins told you? "Tell no-one." Couldn't be plainer. Words of one bloody syllable too.' I shook my head violently, a mixture of disbelief, frustration and plain unadulterated anger. 'And at the first opportunity what do you bloody do? Open your big mouth.'

'Calm down, Shannon. Gerry's an old mate. We go back a long way. I'd trust him with my life.'

'And your wife's too?' I shouted.

'Yeah.' His eyes held mine without flinching. 'I trust him with Lou's life. Anyway,' he said matter-of-factly, 'we need Gerry's help. I had to tell him.'

Had to tell him! My blood was boiling. How

could Kinsella be so stupid? If he was wrong about O'Kane, then the whole operation was blown. And Louise was as good as dead.

I clenched my fists in a grim attempt to hang onto some semblance of self-control. I felt like punching him in the face – but didn't fancy the thought of my nose appearing out of the back of my head when he hit me in return.

'Look,' Kinsella said calmly, reasonably, 'we have to restore security to the system. Think about it for a moment. The biggest priority is to lock Paradine and Louise out. Remember, Paradine can dial into the system. We can't take any risks. What if Paradine won't play ball with Collins? Say some smooth lawyer gets him released on bail for the fraud charges. The first thing Paradine will do is destroy the evidence. We have to prevent that. And from what I understand from these manuals, we need Gerry's password to change the access parameters. That's why I had to tell him.'

I shook my head again, but this time in resignation. Despite the logic of the argument, I still didn't like it. But any damage had been done now.

'Come on, Shannon,' Kinsella said soothingly. 'Give us a hand. This is over our heads. You could crack it in ten minutes.'

I sighed. 'Pass me the manuals.'

The tension eased. The two men smiled. Kinsella reached into the drawer for the opiate of the masses. 'Drink?' he asked.

I declined. Not that I wasn't tempted. A couple of fingers of Bushmills – a couple of fingers of cabbage vodka even – was just what I needed. But a clear head was the order of the day.

So they drank while I read.

The systems analysts, when designing the program, had appreciated that company personnel come and go. They had made allowances for changes to be made in the access to the most secure areas of the program. As new staff joined, they could be added to the permitted list: more critically, when staff left, access could be withdrawn, thereby preventing fraud or sabotage. The procedures were in no way as complicated as Kinsella believed. But there were problems. As ever, the boffins had not thought of everything.

'Basically,' I said, five minutes later, 'the program doesn't allow for two people to be deleted in one operation – we can only remove access from one person at a time. To delete Paradine from the list, we need the passwords of all the remaining permitted users. That means we need Louise's code as well as Mr O'Kane's.'

'It shouldn't be a problem,' Kinsella said thoughtfully. 'I have a pretty good idea of what she might have used.'

'Okay,' I said. 'Let's give it a try.'

Kinsella waved an obliging hand to offer me his chair.

I switched on his computer. Entered the accounts program. Chose the 'Parameters' option. Then 'Access Control', followed by 'Delete'. The names of the four authorised users appeared on the screen. Clicking on Paradine's name, I waited for the instructions to appear.

A new list comprising the three remaining

names flashed up. The cursor blinked on the topmost.

'Ready,' I said to Kinsella. 'Your password first.'

He typed in MULE and pressed the return key. The cursor moved down.

'Now Louise's.'

'Fingers crossed,' he said, typing in MARE.

I pushed aside – with effort, I must admit – the bawdy images conjured up by their pet-names and concentrated on watching the screen.

The computer (unhampered by imagination) accepted the password without a blink, and moved onto the final name.

'Lastly,' I said to O'Kane, 'your password, please.'

He scrabbled around in one bulging pocket after another in that I-know-it's-in-here-somewhere manner that Arlene adopted when searching her handbag for a lipstick. Mind you, in O'Kane's defence, with the amount of junk Arlene kept in there, she'd probably go through the same routine if looking for a grand piano. Eventually, and anti-climactically, he drew out a faded yellow Post-it sticker. Passed it across the desk to me.

'Why did you choose this?' I asked, reading the complex combination of letters.

'I thought that if I chose a random string of the maximum permitted number of characters, then no-one would ever guess the password.'

'The only trouble,' I said, 'is that you can't remember it yourself, can you? You had to write it down.'

'There is that drawback, I suppose,' he said

sheepishly. 'I'm the same with PIN numbers on my credit cards. I know I shouldn't, but I have to make a note of those too.'

I entered KAFWTR with a shake of my head. O'Kane should have used his imagination – on second thoughts, he probably had less imagination than the computer – to concoct a mnemonic from the letters. As a bridge player I would have thought of something like Kings, Aces Fall When Trumped, Remember.

'User Paradine Deleted,' the computer confirmed, interrupting my lateral thinking.

'Further Changes?' it requested.

'Now,' I said, sighing deeply, 'we repeat the procedure to delete Louise.'

Tapping away, I consoled myself with a variant on the American lawyer joke. What do you call 40,000 systems analysts at the bottom of the sea? A start!

'Okay,' I said, a minute later. 'All done.'

'We'd like one more change,' Kinsella said. 'We want you added to the list.'

'It's not necessary,' I replied. 'I'm only here for a few days and any other changes I need to make to your procedures don't require this level of access.'

'Gerry and I have been talking. Not just about Paradine and Lou. About the future. We've got big plans. We'd like you to be part of those. We want you to join us. Become our new Financial Director. How about it, Nick?'

If I hadn't been sitting down I think I would have dropped to the floor with the shock. I stared incredulously at Kinsella. He smiled back.

It wasn't an elaborate joke. Jesus, what was the world coming to? Someone actually offering Nick Shannon a job. Made a change from going round with the begging bowl. My mind began to race.

Think of it, Shannon. This could solve all your problems. The fresh start. The clean slate. The salary is bound to be a whole lot better than you're getting as an articled clerk. Think what you could do with it. A proper house. Decent furniture. Not having to watch every penny. Or feel guilty when Norman chipped in more than his fair share of the rent and the wine bills.

Then the negatives hit me.

What would Arlene say? Her plans were for us to live together in New England (Mary Jo – boo, hiss – permitting, of course). How would settling down in smoky old London town grab her? And what would Collins say? More expletives than the contents of a Booker Prize novel, I expect – and all tagged to the word 'traitor'.

'Thanks for the offer,' I said. 'I'm very flattered. But I couldn't.'

'If it's the money, that's no problem. How does forty grand sound?'

It sounded like a host of angels singing the Hallelujah Chorus.

'Plus a car,' Kinsella added, the music-swelling in my ears and sounding sweeter with each passing second. 'Pension too. And all the usual perks.'

'It's a good offer,' I said sadly. 'Very good. But money isn't the problem.'

'Then what is? Let's talk it through. Sort it out.

We need you, Nick.'

'It's Prospekt,' I said. 'Even if I could turn a moral blind eye to their involvement in Glenshield – which, I hasten to add, I have no intention of doing – then Collins definitely wouldn't. Whether he had proof of their drug operations or not, he'd make sure my probation officer was informed. The terms of my licence are very strict. The merest sniff of any criminal association and I would wind up back in jail.' I gave Kinsella a sorrowful smile. Reluctantly shook my head. 'I only wish I could accept. But as long as Prospekt have any link with this company, then that's out of the question.'

'Good,' Kinsella declared with a smile as broad as Galway Bay. 'You passed the test. Not that we didn't expect you to. Eh, Gerry?'

O'Kane gave a confirmatory nod – or maybe it was just an involuntary reaction to an un-accustomed deficiency of caffeine.

'We wouldn't have made you the offer in the first place,' Kinsella continued, 'if we'd thought you would say anything different. Gerry and I have come up with the solution. Come on, have that drink while we tell you all about our plans.'

'No thanks,' I said, my brain resolutely fighting the demand of my shocked system for a purely medicinal shot of alcohol.

Kinsella, it seemed, had worked fast. Wasted not a single moment since leaving Collins's office. Their plan – his plan, I suspected (for I doubted that O'Kane's contribution had extended much beyond moral support) – was not without risk. But, in the circumstances, it seemed a risk well worth taking.

Kinsella was going to make an offer (and here he used the word in the Mafia sense) to buy Prospekt's shares in Glenshield. It would be a fair (but not a particularly generous) price. One that would give them a healthy return on their capital.

His declared reason for this action? Total dissatisfaction and disillusionment with what Glenshield had become. It had grown out of all proportion, so that the resulting adult was an entirely different animal from its parent's original ambitions or wishes. The company was now an uncontrollable beast that would inexorably devour itself. The only chance of survival was a return to its roots. Smaller, leaner, fitter. More personal. More manageable.

And if Prospekt refused? Then Kinsella, and O'Kane, would resign. Simply start all over again. O'Kane had no restrictive covenants in his contract. Kinsella did, but was working on the very reasonable assumption that Prospekt would not wish to expose itself to the glaring spotlight of publicity that would shine down on any legal battle to prohibit him setting up in competition. Without Kinsella and O'Kane there was no management to speak of. Without Kinsella the client base would crumble – for Kinsella was Glenshield.

From Prospekt's point of view, if they sold, they made a profit; if they refused, the body corporate would eventually bleed to death.

And where was the money coming from to buy the shares?

I'll give you one guess.

Yes.

David Montgomery Yates. Politician. Millionaire. And – allegedly, I hasten to add – all-round sharp operator.

One phone call from Kinsella to Yates and it had been as good as promised. Yates could arrange a syndicate of his wealthy friends who would be only too willing, on his recommendation, to subscribe to a private placing of the shares. Of course, Yates wouldn't be putting in any of his own money – well, not initially, the cynic in me said – since that might create problems when Glenshield was bidding for the prison contract. In a few years' time, when the new, revamped Glenshield was growing controllably and steadily, the company would be floated on the Stock Exchange. And all the shareholders would reap the benefits of their investment. A handsome profit for everyone involved, Kinsella had said. Handsome? They'd all make a killing.

'We'll throw in some share options too,' Kinsella said when he reached the end of the exposition of his battle plan. 'How about it, Nick? This is a golden opportunity. Join us. Help us. Be part of our new family. Share in our future prosperity.'

I felt like thrusting both fists in the air and shouting, 'Yes. Yes. Bloody yes' at the top of my voice. But it wasn't a decision I could take there and then. There were others to consider and consult.

'Let me think about it,' I said cautiously. 'It's a big step. I need to talk it over with someone.'

'I don't want to push you,' Kinsella said. 'Take the weekend to mull it over. I need to know on Monday, mind. That's when I intend to speak to Prospekt.'

Clever move, I thought. The timing couldn't have been better.

By Monday, the Commander willing, Paradine would be in police custody. And Prospekt would be on the defensive. If a drugs link were to be proven, all their assets would be frozen. Any offer would sound a whole lot more attractive if they were already thinking about cashing in their chips.

'Monday will be fine,' I replied. 'Meanwhile, leave me off the access list. I wouldn't want to tempt fate.'

'Do I detect,' Kinsella said, a teasing smile on his lips, 'a female presence in the background? I'd like to meet her. If she's that close to you, she must be some girl.'

'She is,' I said proudly. 'Would you mind,' I asked, 'if we call it a day? I'm not sure I can concentrate on work at the moment. There's nothing that can't wait till Monday now.'

'You get off home, Nick. Come see me first thing on Monday morning. And,' Kinsella added, a melancholy look on his face, 'thanks for what you've done. For opening this can of worms. I won't say it hasn't been a shock. But it's better to know the worst. The future, Nick. Let's think of the future.'

I left them to their thoughts and plans, and the remains of the bottle of Bushmills. Walked along the corridor. Entered Personnel.

'Mrs Kinsella in?' I asked innocently.

'At a conference,' her young assistant replied, covering a paperback book with her forearms. 'Anything I can do?'

'I just wanted to apologise for not getting round to filling in the application form. Mrs Kinsella has been good to me. I didn't want her to think I was unreliable. Or being ungrateful.' I gave an embarrassed shrug. The girl's face took on a puzzled expression – my un-Glenshield show of concern causing her problems. She removed her reading glasses and examined me with the sort of curiosity usually reserved for the first sighting of a new species of animal. It was only natural really. She worked in Personnel, after all – what could she be expected to know about *people?*

'Anywhere nice, this conference?' I asked. 'I do hope so, for Mrs Kinsella's sake.'

'Depends how you categorise Eastbourne,' she said with the contemptuous arty-farty twist of the lips of someone who regards Brighton or Edinburgh as the only places outside London worth visiting – in a cultural emergency, that is. 'Mrs Kinsella *is* in the best hotel, if that's any consolation. But all that means is being constantly tripped up by a better class of zimmer-frame.'

I smiled understandingly.

'I'll bring the form in on Monday then,' I said, making a swift exit.

Okay, Collins, I thought. I'm doing this for you – to ease your guilty conscience. And because

Louise treated me like a person rather than an ex-con.

We agree for once.

The long arm of the law.

The longer arm of Prospekt.

Neither shall have her.

CHAPTER TWENTY-EIGHT

The Victorians, judging by their architecture, must have been schizophrenic. Wandsworth was Hyde to the Grand's Jekyll. Whereas the former epitomises the darker Gothic side of their character, the latter is a monument to the grace and glory of that era.

The Grand perches imperiously like a giant white eagle, wings outstretched, overlooking the sea. Situated at the extreme western end of the promenade at Eastbourne, it is the last hotel you come to before leaving the town. Drive on for a few miles, climbing all the while, and you arrive at Beachy Head, a landmark famous for two things: its lighthouse, which sends a beam sixteen miles across the English Channel; and the number of suicides that take place there each year. So favoured is the site by those determined to end their lives that the Samaritans have installed a telephone box near the cliff edge.

It is not that the locals – average age, it appears, as you drive along the front, about 210 – are queuing up to leap lemming-like from the top:

indeed, they cling tenaciously to life with blotched and bony, arthritic fingers. In its own morbid niche market, Beachy Head has a large catchment area – magnetically drawing the lonely and desperate from far and wide. At 534 feet above sea level there is no more sure-fire way of killing oneself. Quickly. Cleanly. No messy blood from scraping a razor blade across the wrists. No uncertainty as to how many pills to swallow. No need for a chair, rope and Boy Scout knotmanship badge.

I brought the Monte Carlo to a sedate halt – somehow it seems awfully *infra dig* to do anything other than sedately in Eastbourne – a little way back from the hotel. The car was much too distinctive to risk using the car park. I circled the building and entered by the back door.

I was working on three assumptions: that Louise was indeed attending a conference, using the invoice and the joining instructions as cover for her dirty weekend; that Paradine, tied up somewhere on Prospekt business, would not arrive till early evening; and that the hotel would have changed little since The Major's days. It was one of his favourite haunts – the back door had come in handy on more than one occasion when coincidental Whitehall farce encounters had threatened to wreck his well-laid plans. From his fund of reminiscences in prison I had a fair idea of the layout of the hotel.

Following this mental map, I marched confidently up the short flight of stairs, turned right at the end of the wood-panelled corridor and stepped into the splendour of bygone days. To my left were the bars, restaurant and the revolving doors of the front entrance: to my right, the roaring fire of the lounge where the Palm Court Orchestra had once broadcast to the nation via the miracle of steam radio. Strolling straight ahead, I came to the vast ballroom that was now used as the conference auditorium. Outside stood a sign pompously announcing 'Personnel Management – The Challenge of the Next Millennium', and a pinboard cluttered with messages for delegates.

Resisting the temptation to add a note to the board or peek through the double-doors to see if I could spot Louise, I retraced my steps towards the comfort of the fire. Disillusionment. It was gas. All show and no heat.

There were only three other people in the lounge – an old lady seated at the bureau writing postcards and two men screened by the grand piano, heads bent over maps and guidebooks. None of them gave me a second glance. Taking a seat with my back to the fire, I ordered tea and settled back to watch the comings and goings in the main walkway.

It was a big risk coming down to the Grand.

But it would have been even riskier to phone. There had to be no record of any contact with Louise; no chance of a receptionist remembering a telephone message to Mrs Kinsella from a Mr Shannon.

My favour – my very last favour – to Collins was to warn Louise. Give her the opportunity to save herself by making a run for it. Disappear without trace. A tip-off was bound to be suspected, of course. But as long as there was no connection with Collins or myself, nothing could be proved. We would both be in the clear.

Collins's task also provided me with the opportunity to satisfy my curiosity – there were questions I wanted to ask, gaps to be filled in.

I consulted my watch nervously. Inwardly shouted an impatient, 'Come on, come on' to Louise. A red-jacketed waiter placed a tray before me. The heavy, silver-plated teapot and matching hot-water jug gleamed, the cup sparkled in the light of the chandeliers. My five-pound note was just enough, with the obligatory tip, to cover the cost of this light show.

I sipped the tea. And winced.

In their effort to produce a dazzling shine to the teacup it had been rinsed in what was supposed to be a very dilute solution of water and vinegar. Someone – with shares in Sarsons? – had got the mixture wrong. I munched on a piece of short-bread to take the taste away.

Suddenly, there was a clamour of voices from the corridor.

School was out.

I moved instantly. Rose from my seat, abandoning the shortbread. As I walked away from the table I saw one of the men by the piano home in, vulture-fashion, on the plate. Waste not, want not, I imagined him saying to his companion to justify his action.

I took up a position by the lifts. Stood to one side as the procession of animated delegates, bright-orange folders tucked importantly under their arms, headed thirstily towards the bar.

Risked life and limb from what was fast becoming a stampede, by kneeling down to tie my shoelace. Peered up at the advancing sea of faces.

There, coming along the corridor, was the long plait of dark hair swinging from shoulder to shoulder in counterpoint to the movement of her hips. There was the ultra-pretty turned-up nose. The rosy-red lips. The green eyes whose sparkle put the cups in the shade.

I stood up as she came alongside, knocking the folder to the floor. We bent down together. She saw my face.

'Sorry, miss,' I said loudly, shaking my head in warning as she started to open her mouth. 'Room number?' I whispered.

Louise raised the folder to cover her mouth and whispered back the reply.

'Two minutes,' I said, already turning back to the lift.

'I've come to warn you,' I said as we entered her room. It was on the ground floor, large multi-paned French doors leading to a small paved patio and then to the outdoor swimming pool in the gardens at the front of the hotel.

'Does Roddy know?' she asked anxiously.

'Everyone knows,' I replied. 'Your secret's out.'

'Oh, God,' she whimpered, sinking into one of the pink chintz armchairs. Her face turned a ghostly white.

Thinking she was about to faint, I picked up her key from the table and opened the mini-bar. Unscrewing the cap from a miniature of brandy,

I waved the bottle under her nose. She reeled back.

I poured the contents into an unsuitably tall glass and handed it to her.

'Drink this,' I ordered.

'I suppose it can't do any harm now,' Louise said cryptically.

She took a large swallow and puckered her mouth. Her composure began to filter back as the brandy flowed through her system.

'Where did you leave your charger, Mr White Knight?' she asked, her wits returning. 'But you didn't come all this way just to tell me I'd been found out. You want to know why, I presume? Why cheat on Roddy? Why Paradine?'

They were not the most important of my questions, but if that was where she wanted to start...

'There isn't much time,' I said. 'If you don't want to talk, pack your bags and leave now. You were willing to give me a chance when I came to Glenshield. I'm simply repaying that trust.'

Louise studied me, head tilted to one side. Which would I be? Confessor? Or judge?

'It's not what you think,' she said. 'I love Roddy. Love him dearly. I wouldn't do anything to hurt him. Believe me.' Somewhere inside her a floodgate opened. Tears began to roll down her cheeks. 'It's just that I want a baby.' She was sobbing now. 'God,' she said, staring at me, 'is that so very wrong?'

I sat on the floor by her feet. Took her hands in mine. Squeezed them gently, comfortingly. 'I'm sorry,' I said quietly, 'but I don't understand.'

'I so nearly had a baby once,' she said. Her voice had a dreamy quality. But with an undertone of anger. 'I fell down the damned stairs. Lost it.'

'I know. Roddy told me.'

'Did he?' she said, dabbing at her eyes with a handkerchief 'Not like Roddy to confide secrets to strangers. He must think a lot of you.'

I nodded, glossing over his selfish reason for telling the story.

'Roddy wants kids too, you know. It isn't only me. Perhaps if...' She shook her head sadly. 'We'd been trying for a long while. But nothing happened. Month after bloody month went by. So I decided to have some tests. Thought the fall might have done some permanent damage. Or the cocaine. Did he tell you about that too?'

'I guessed,' I said. 'The new nose – unnecessary in one already so pretty and one so lacking in vanity.'

I should have left it at honesty verging on flattery. But I couldn't keep my mouth shut. Just couldn't resist proving how damned clever I was.

'And there was the tip-off on the drugs raid too,' I said.

Her eyes glazed over, staring straight ahead, unfocused. She swayed in the chair. Cursing my pride, I bent her head down between her knees. Ran to the bathroom, drenched a face flannel in cold water. Pressed the wet cloth to her forehead.

We sat there, precious seconds ticking by, for what seemed like hours but was probably only a minute or two. Until, at last, she pushed my hands away and sat back in the chair, breathing

338

deeply. While she completed her recovery, I unlocked the French doors and opened them a fraction to let in a draught of ozone-laden air.

'Does he know everything?' she said.

'Everything.'

'But not the all-important reason.'

'Tell me,' I said soothingly. 'I'll make sure he understands.'

'Yes. He will need to understand. I wouldn't want to see him hurt any more.'

Louise took a gulp of brandy. 'I had the tests,' she said, returning to the story. 'There wasn't a problem. Not with me, that is.'

Then it all made sense.

Kinsella's password.

The liaison with Paradine.

Her motive.

'The gynaecologist was ninety-nine per cent sure that the problem was Roddy. Needed to take a sperm count to be absolutely certain. One morning Roddy and I made love. After he had left for work I rushed along to the clinic.'

Louise looked into my eyes. 'How could I tell him?' she asked. 'The sperm count wasn't just low, it was non-existent. All this time Roddy had been firing blanks. The man who was known for his virility was infertile. It would have broken his heart to know that we – I – couldn't have children.'

'So you chose Paradine. To be the father of your child.'

'Stephen was the perfect choice,' Louise said, in the same matter-of-fact premeditated manner she must have used when originally making her decision. 'Good track record – three kids already. And if I weren't able to seduce him, I could threaten him with revealing the true nature of Prospekt to Roddy.'

I doubted it had ever come to that.

'Weren't you worried that Roddy would find out? Wouldn't that have destroyed his pride, rather than just denting it? Surely that was exactly what you were trying to avoid?'

'I thought we were being so discreet, so careful. We only, er, met once or twice a month. Once, theoretically, should have been enough. Twice was merely trying to improve the odds. I did my calculations thoroughly, you see. Always chose exactly the right time.'

Whoever said women were the weaker sex? The fool had obviously never encountered the likes of Louise or Walker.

Although I felt pity for her, I couldn't let her escape guilt-free. 'And, if your conscience ever began to prick, then you could always fall back on blaming Roddy. It was his fault, after all. Was that why you couldn't resist the secret gibe of calling him Mule to your Mare?'

'It just slipped out one night in bed.' She laughed – humourlessly. 'He thought I was referring to his Scottish-Irish cross-breeding – that he was like a mule, a hybrid; more muscular, more intelligent, than both parents. Or, more likely, knowing the way Roddy's mind works, believed it was a comment on the size of his... Well, you know? Anyway, he took it as a compliment! After that, the name stuck. He never realised that a mule is sterile.'

'So why the escalation in the relationship with Paradine? Whose idea was it? Who suggested becoming more than just sleeping partners?'

She gave me a puzzled expression. 'I don't know what you mean, Nick.'

Was there only so much she was prepared to confess?

A knock on the door interrupted her need to continue the lie.

'That will be Stephen,' she said.

'Get rid of him. Tell him to go to the bar. You're feeling sick, okay? You'll meet him later.' I headed towards the only hiding place – the bathroom. 'And, for chrissake,' I said sternly, 'make it convincing.'

That was the last I ever saw of Louise.

I spent five minutes with my ear pressed to the bathroom door, listening to silence, before it dawned on me that I had been too trusting. I'd blown it.

The door to the corridor was wide open. So were the French windows. My guess was that they had made their escape through the gardens.

Her handbag was gone. Everything else was as we had left it. Including my fingerprints all over the place.

I closed the bedroom door. Picked up a towel from the bathroom. Tried to remember every damned thing I had touched. Let out a loud, expressive curse at the impossibility of the task.

So I wiped every surface in the room. A male version of Lady Macbeth manically polishing everything in sight: door handles, the table, the outside and inside of the mini-bar.

Finally, I drank the remains of the brandy. Put the glass and the bottle in my pockets. Took one last, insecure look around the room. Then melted into the comforting darkness of the garden.

The exhaust of the Lancia seemed to roar my guilt to all within a ten-mile radius. I pulled away in second gear, trying to keep the revs to a minimum, and drove slowly towards the pier. Only on joining the London road did I allow myself to think about Collins.

How would he judge the bungled outcome of my intervention?

Success, in that Louise had got away? Or failure, since Paradine had slipped the net?

No choice really.

Success would let me off the hook. Failure kept me dangling.

What a bloody mess!

CHAPTER TWENTY-NINE

Collins was never one to court popularity.

He made no friends among the other tenants – in the neighbourhood, that is, not just our building – by banging on my door like a demented bull at four o'clock in the morning.

He'd been drinking.

Boy, had he been drinking.

His breath reeked of whisky. His clothes were

an abstract painting of stains, the result of the spillage when his mouth and hands had been incapable of getting their act together. His eyes were bloodshot, and seemed to move independently of each other. And he damn near fell into the room when I opened the door.

I helped him into one of the armchairs. Looked imploringly at a yawning Arlene.

'Black coffee?' she said.

'Lots of it,' I answered, with a roll of my eyes.

'What did you say to her?' he said, his words so slurred as to be barely comprehensible. 'What in fuck's name did you say to Louise?'

'I tried to warn her, that's all. Just like you asked me to.'

'Scared the bloody shit out of her, more like.' He stared up at me, eyes swivelling chameleon-fashion in their sockets. I don't know exactly how bad he felt, but it was making me dizzy just watching him. 'I'm gonna bloody kill you, Shannon. With my bare hands.'

Well, as far as the operation was concerned, it seemed that success wasn't the option on the tip of his tongue.

He lurched forward from the chair. Staggered in my general direction. Made a clumsy grab at my neck with uncoordinated hands.

His brain was at the point where it could only handle the transmission of one set of signals at a time. His hands received the sole message. Consequently his knees moved together in a last, instinctive act of support before his legs buckled beneath him. He pitched forward and crashed to the floor.

Lay there in a pathetic heap.

Sobbing his heart out.

Oh no, my brain screamed. It can't be. Tell me it isn't true.

But the sight of Collins – the state of Collins – shouted otherwise.

My stomach turned a triple somersault. I felt the sour taste of bile hit the back of my throat. 'Collateral damage,' Collins had once said, with a pitiless and economical lifting of his shoulders. Not so easy to shrug off now. Not for Collins. Or for me.

You hid in the bathroom, Shannon.

You might have saved her.

If only you'd thought for a moment. Instead of leaping to the obvious conclusion.

It hadn't been Paradine at the door. He was already in the bag.

Louise hadn't escaped, you bloody fool.

Prospekt had snatched her.

And killed her. There was no doubt in my mind about that.

It had all been for nothing, Louise. The hard years with Collins. Kicking the cocaine habit. The rehabilitation that followed. And the final deception. No baby for you, after all, Louise.

I sank to my knees.

Put my arms around Collins.

And cried with him.

It took two hours to sober him up. Would have been a whole lot longer but for Arlene's Prairie Oyster. She forced him to drink the foul concoction of raw egg, Worcester sauce and Tabasco

344

(her own special ingredient) in one swallow. It worked instantly. Any alcohol that hadn't already been absorbed into his system disappeared down the toilet bowl. After that, we poured enough coffee and iced water into him to float a small battleship.

Paradine's wreck of a car, he told us, had been found at the bottom of Beachy Head. There were two bodies inside. Burnt beyond immediate recognition – a dental records job for the forensic scientists. In the charred remains they found a gold watch. On the back was the inscription 'To Lou. With all my love. Roddy'.

If the name had been John or Tom, or anything else for that matter, it might have taken days to identify the occupants of the car – suicides are a low priority for the police, and there was only the number on the engine block from which to work. But 'Roddy' rang a bell with one of the older hands in Eastbourne CID – hadn't Roddy been that big man from the Drugs Squad who had muscled in on one of their cases about five years ago? So he phoned the Met.

Two uniformed officers were sent to give Kinsella the bad news. Then someone thought that Collins should be told too. He'd hit the bottle rather than the roof Otherwise he might have been round earlier. Made a better job of ripping my head from my shoulders.

'Someone talked,' Collins said. Sitting there on the sofa, Arlene's arm round his shoulders, he looked like death inadequately microwaved. But his brain was functioning again.

'Kinsella told O'Kane,' I said.

Collins groaned. 'And O'Kane told Prospekt?'

'Maybe,' I said, pondering. 'Or O'Kane passed on the information to someone else. The news spread like wildfire. And Prospekt gets to hear. Could even have been a leak inside the Fraud Squad, for all we know. Quinn would be my guess, if that were the case. We know he's thick as thieves with Kinsella.' I paused to consider all the possibilities. 'But O'Kane must be the favourite.'

'Then he's a corpse waiting to happen,' Collins said, his hands shaking as if practising a dry run of wrapping themselves round O'Kane's throat.

'You'll need proof first,' Norman's voice cautioned from within the deep folds of his dressing gown.

But proof was a luxury that Collins could not afford. 'And I'll tell you something else,' he said. 'Prospekt is finished. I won't rest till every last person involved with them is six foot under in an unmarked grave. I swear that. On Louise's dead body. As God is my witness.'

I looked at him. Saw the unswerving resolution etched into every feature of his haggard face. And below that, the irreplaceable loss, the unhealable wound, the pain that never goes away.

'If we can compromise on jail,' I said, 'then count me in, Chris.' I had to use his first name: nothing else could have conveyed the depth of my empathy, or my sympathy. 'I'll help you put them behind bars.'

Behind me, Norman's breath escaped in a hurricane of exasperation. 'Don't you ever learn, Nick?' he said. 'Do you have to jump in with both bloody feet all the time?'

'Nick has his reasons,' Arlene said, rallying to my defence. 'You might as well humour him. Support him. Whatever we say will make no difference. And whatever he does won't stop us loving him. Eh, Norman?'

He sighed. 'You're a lucky bloke, Nick. But don't push your luck too far. Save some for when you really need it.'

'Thanks, Norman,' I said, smiling.

'Christ,' Collins said, looking at his watch. 'I'm due to see the Commander at half-nine. And I need to call Eastbourne nick to arrange for Louise's room at the Grand to be sealed off. Get the boys from SOCO to check it out for finger-prints.'

Oh dear. Well done, Shannon aka Lady Macbeth.

'I'll come with you,' I volunteered. 'After all, I did all the leg-work. And I can help to explain all the financial intricacies. We may not need the Commander's approval on a deal with Paradine any more, but we can get his commitment to pulling out all the stops on a witch-hunt against Prospekt.'

'He can't go looking like that,' Arlene said practically. 'Sorry, Chris, but right now you wouldn't be out of place at a hoboes' convention. You'd better borrow some of Nick's clothes.'

'Have a shower and shave,' I said. 'You'll find everything you need in the bathroom cabinet – my razor, spare blades, and so on.' Then I realised it wasn't a very good idea. 'On second thoughts, you'd better borrow Norman's electric razor.'

Much safer.

The Commander came up trumps. Prospekt was to be top priority – Fraud Squad, Drugs Squad, anyone and everyone would be part of the hunt. Collins was to drop every other case. Would be given extra manpower.

'Just get me some proof,' the Commander had said. 'Any proof. Then freeze their assets. Hit them where it hurts.' Collins had nodded happily, thinking more of anatomical parts than of wallets. 'Bring them to justice.'

It was midday by the time I returned home. Norman was out at Toddy's. Arlene looked impossibly fresh, considering the disruption of the night. She was wearing a pale pink blouse, belted outside of a pair of black leggings, and knee-high black boots. When she kissed me I could smell peaches in her hair.

'Let's go to bed,' she said. 'You need some sleep.'

'I also need to talk,' I said seriously. I hadn't got round to telling her about Kinsella's job offer yet.

'Me too,' she said. 'There's no law that says you can't talk in bed. Sometimes it's the best place. Like right now, for instance.'

She took my hand and led me, willingly, to the bedroom.

'Do we sleep first, or talk,' I asked her, as we slid under the duvet. 'Or...'

'Talk,' she said, putting my arm round her and cuddling up close. 'You start.'

'Kinsella wants me to join him. Either in a Prospekt-free Glenshield or a totally new company. I'd be Financial Director. It's a very good offer.'

'Uh huh,' she said.

'Probably the best offer I'm ever likely to get.'

'How can you square it with your promise to Collins? Helping him to track down Prospekt.'

'Paradine managed to handle the job on a part-time basis. I think I could too. For a few months at least. It would mean working long hours – evenings, weekends. But there's someone in Accounts who could take more responsibility. I could shift some of the load onto her.'

'You seem to have thought of everything.'

'And decided nothing,' I said. 'It's a decision for both of us.'

'But what do *you* want, Nick?'

'I want – at least I think I want – to accept.'

My mind drifted back to the visit to Wandsworth. I shivered involuntarily. Arlene cuddled closer.

'It's a golden opportunity,' I said. 'Maybe a once-in-a-lifetime chance to shake off the tag of ex-con – and everything that goes with it. It's what I slogged my guts out for in prison. Sweating over textbooks. Forcing myself to concentrate on Norman's tutorials when all my body craved was to collapse in a heap on my bunk. Sitting in the Governor's office taking the exams while some cold-hearted screw watched over me, willing me to fail.'

'So where do I fit in? What's my role in this golden opportunity? This once-in-a-lifetime chance?'

'I want – and this time I know, not just think –

I want us to be together. That would mean you moving to England.'

'And if I weren't prepared to do that?'

'I'd turn Kinsella down.'

'I don't know if I could ask you to do that.'

'Then I'd do it without being asked. Gladly. Just give me a few months to sort out things and then I'll join you in America. New England, new life.'

'Maybe,' she said.

'Why so unsure, all of a sudden? I thought that was what you wanted.'

'That was before I knew about Walker.'

Arlene rolled off me. Moved a foot across the bed. Stared into my eyes.

'What about Walker?'

'Don't lie to me, Nick. I could tell from the first moment I saw her. The way she looked at you. The way you didn't look at her. And when Norman passed on the message from Collins – to meet him at Walker's place – he never gave you the address. And you didn't need to ask.'

I could have tried to bluff it out. Told Arlene that her female intuition was wrong. That I knew where Walker lived from some innocent drink after a long, hard day together. But I owed her the truth.

'It was a one-off,' I said sadly. 'A stupid one-night stand I've regretted ever since.' I paused to curse Walker under my breath. I'd known what she was doing all along. That I was the convenient option. Not part of the force. Self-gratification without complications. But I hadn't resisted. Jesus, what man could have? And, if I were honest with myself, I had to admit that given the same circumstances, I probably wouldn't act any differently. Except not leave a can of shaving foam lying around. Should have thrown it in the bin along with the cheap razor. Or maybe it had been a subconscious act, a Freudian slip. To leave something behind was a way of not feeling as disposable as the razor.

'I thought you and I were finished,' I said, trying to justify my actions to Arlene. 'That it was all over for good between us. That you'd chosen Mary Jo before me.' I reached out my hand for her. She neither took it nor discouraged me when I touched hers. 'If only I'd known how you felt – the future you were planning for us – then I wouldn't have let it happen. Believe me. Walker means nothing to me. I love you, Arlene.'

'And I love you too, Nick. That's what makes it so hard. Where are we going, Nick? What are we going to do?'

She rolled back onto my body. Buried her head in the crook of my shoulder. I couldn't see her face. But I could feel her tears running down my chest.

'Can you ever forgive me?' I asked.

'Of course I can forgive you, you damn fool. But that's only part of it. If the future is going to work out for us, we need to think about it more. It's not just a matter of where we live. Or the job you settle on. Don't you see? Have you forgotten Louise already?'

'That's not fair,' I said, guilt over her death forcing anger into my voice.

'I'm sorry. I didn't mean it that way. But Christ,

Nick,' she went on, her body shaking with emotion. 'I'm thirty-seven, goddamnit.'

'Strange,' I said, in a desperate effort at lightening the mood, 'I'd have guessed more like 36C.'

She pulled away from me. Propped herself, on her elbows. Looked down at me with eyes blazing. 'God, you are one impossible sonofabitch, Nick. Do you know that? Don't you understand what I'm trying to say?'

'I understand,' I said, softly. 'Time's running out.'

I put my hand in her hair. Drew her head gently down towards mine. Kissed her lips tenderly. Rolled her over onto her back.

Then broke away to look down at her. I smiled, outwardly, inwardly. My cup, it seemed, runneth over at last. I had everything I could want within my grasp.

'We'd better not waste a moment,' I said.

CHAPTER THIRTY

'Let's play bridge,' Arlene said, as if it were the most natural thing in the world.

It was three hours later. We were still in bed. Not wasting a moment.

'Are you mad?' I asked. 'At a time like this.'

'I don't mean right now, stupid,' she said. 'But you said you needed to think. Right?'

'Yes,' I agreed dubiously. 'About the job. And

about the whole Glenshield affair. There's still the question of who wrote the letter. But...'

'You also said once – and correct me if I'm wrong – that bridge was the perfect way to sort out a problem. That to play bridge well you had to give all your concentration to the cards. And while the higher levels of your mind are focused on how to bid or play the hands, your sub-conscious is working away behind the scenes at the bigger issues.'

'Do you remember everything I say?' I asked.

'You better believe it,' she said with a smile.

And I did. This smile wasn't one of Kinsella's pathetic little Galway Bay jobs. It was wide enough to span the Atlantic Ocean.

So we played bridge.

Not at Latimers. Even I couldn't delude myself into thinking my concentration would be good enough to play for money. Instead we went to the 'Ham & High' – Hampstead and Highgate, old fruit – Bridge Club for a session of duplicate.

Duplicate bridge is the form of the game that is played at championships – big or small – throughout the world. It is the game of experts. Where the luck of the cards is all but eliminated – since everybody plays the same hands.

In rubber bridge, your opponents are the people sitting at your table. In duplicate bridge, you play against the whole room. It is what *you* do with the cards, compared with the rest of the pairs who hold them, that decides how you score on each board.

It works like this. You and your partner take up

a position (either North/South or East/West) at a table. You deal and play the first hand – but instead of the cards being thrown into the middle of the table at each trick, they are played in front of each player. If your side wins the trick, the card is turned over and pointed in your direction; if your opponents win the trick, the card is pointed their way. At the end of the hand, the tricks are counted and the result agreed. Each player then gathers up his or her cards and places them in the appropriate slot (North, South, East or West) of a purpose-built board. The result of the hand is written on a scoresheet called a 'traveller' (for reasons which, hopefully, will become obvious), which is then tucked into another slot in the board.

After two or three hands, depending on the particular movement that is being played, that round is finished. The boards played are passed to another table, eventually travelling round the room. The North/South pair, normally, remains seated and the East/West pair moves on to another table.

At the end of the evening you and your partner will have played against, say, eight different pairs. The twenty-four boards (at three hands per table) will have been played eight times. Then the scores are compared. And you see how well – or badly – you did with the cards relative to all the other pairs playing in the same direction.

In rubber bridge, if you get a minus score on a hand, then that is a bad result – although there may have been nothing you could do about it because of the poor cards you were dealt. In duplicate bridge a minus score can still be good – providing you have lost less than all the other pairs who were playing those cards. Say, for instance, that you went down in a contract by one trick, losing fifty points (non-vulnerable) as a result, but all the other pairs went two down, losing a hundred points. You have done better with the cards than any other pair. This is called a 'top'. The converse, where you did worse with the cards, is called a 'bottom'.

It is not usually as cut-and-dried as that. The scoring system awards two points for every pair you outscored, and one point for each pair with which you tied. At the end of the evening you add up your scores on the twenty-four boards and see where you came in the field.

At duplicate pairs, it matters not whether you beat the rest of the pairs by a thousand points or a mere ten – it is still a top. Thus every point, every trick is vital. That is why you cannot afford to relax your concentration for one moment. And why it is probably the highest – that is to say, the most skilful – form of the game.

Ham & High, thankfully, is not a typical bridge club. It meets every day of the week, has its own premises – a terraced house on four floors including the rather claustrophobic basement, which houses the bar/café area. It is also very stuffy – one of the last bastions of Empire. Not the type of establishment where you show up in jeans and a T-shirt. Not unless you're the sort of person who enjoys the sound of thirty-odd old buffers of both sexes shouting 'Shame' in unison, as if they were fully-fledged Members of Parliament – could well be, for all I knew.

I'd only played at Ham & High twice before, each time with a scratch partner – there was always someone loitering in the bar with a 'Harry Pinkers' (pink gin) willing to make up a pair. I'd scored badly on both occasions – my respective partners' fault, of course. (That's the wonderful thing about bridge – failures belong to your partner, successes are entirely your own.) I wasn't expecting to do much better tonight, for a variety of reasons.

My mind would need to be yanked away from more important matters.

Arlene and I were an inexperienced partnership (bridgewise, I mean).

It was 'no smoking' till the halfway point, a factor militating against me retaining concentration.

And Arlene was American.

At the Ham & High they were not particularly tolerant of Johnny Foreigner (what the hell is the female equivalent – Fanny Foreigner?).

And so it proved. The sour smell of chauvinism was as rank as only the British can produce.

We performed as badly as I had feared. Bridge is rarely about esoteric coups, obscure squeeze situations, flashes of inspiration or daring plays. What brings success is not making mistakes. A series of careless slips cost us dearly.

But, in the end, there was one hand that made it all worth while.

I was sitting South, superstitiously my favoured position at the table (whenever you read a bridge book, because of the convenience of laying out the hand, South is invariably the declarer), and Arlene was in the North seat. Two gentlemen – for want of a better word – arrived at our table for the final round of the evening. West, acting the country squire, was dressed in a Norfolk jacket with leather elbow patches, baggy corduroy trousers, large chequered shirt and brown knitted tie. East, at seventy years old the junior member of the partnership, was wearing a dark blue blazer, conspicuous gold regimental crest on the front pocket, crisp white shirt and a tie whose stripes probably signified membership of some exclusive, and extreme right-wing, group.

'Good evening,' we said, observing the proprieties and introducing ourselves.

West's ears pricked up at Arlene's accent. 'From the colonies, what?' he said, taking his cards from the slot in the board.

Arlene looked at me and raised her eyebrows. I shrugged back at her, and nodded my head in the direction of the cards.

I'll spare you the bidding – and our embarrassment. Suffice it to say that we reached a contract of Four Spades, which was doubled in a booming voice by the squire on my left. Not a good omen. He obviously felt that the contract was doomed to failure and wanted to extract the maximum penalty.

He led the ace of clubs and Arlene, rather sheepishly, tabled her cards.

I thanked her politely, as custom dictates. And viewed the sorry collection of cards. This was the full hand:

North
(Arlene)

♠ 10 9 6 5 4
♥ A 6
♦ 4 2
♣ Q J 9 6

West
(Squire)

♠ Q J 2
♥ K Q 9
♦ K J 7
♣ A K 10 4

East
(Blazer)

♠ void
♥ 8 7 5 3 2
♦ 10 9 6 5
♣ 8 7 5 2

South
(Me)

♠ A K 8 7 3
♥ J 10 4
♦ A Q 8 3
♣ 3

To make my contract I could afford to lose only three tricks. It didn't look very promising. There was a certain loser in clubs, another in hearts and, from West's confident double, probably another each in spades and diamonds.

West took his ace of clubs. Went into a lengthy pause. And uncertainly fingered different cards in his hand.

Maybe it wasn't a lost cause after all. He was obviously in trouble. His discomfort, following the double, confirmed my view that he held all the important cards. In which case, his strength could also prove to be his weakness.

The queen of spades hit the table. When East could not follow suit, a loser in spades was unavoidable.

I won West's queen with my ace, and cashed the king. Then led the three of spades. West had to win this trick with his jack.

He turned to glower at me.

I smiled back at him.

The outcome was inevitable.

Since I could not afford to play the other suits without putting myself in a losing position, I had thrown him in. And he had no safe exit.

He could follow any path he chose.

But whatever he did would play into my hand.

He couldn't lead a heart without setting up a winner for me in that suit, allowing me to dispose of a diamond loser in dummy; a diamond lead would be equally fatal, since that would run round to my ace-queen and there would again be no diamond loser; and a club would eventually enable me to ditch the losing hearts in my hand.

West grudgingly conceded.

Arlene took out the score sheet. It was a top for us.

As she wrote in the score, I relived the moment. The strong hand thrown in. No exit. Did my dirty work for me. Losers effortlessly transformed into winners.

My brain suddenly made the connection. The clouds hanging over me cleared. Brilliant sunshine shone down.

I reached across the table and placed both hands on Arlene's cheeks. Pulled her towards me. Planted an enthusiastic kiss on those luscious lips. Then raised both hands in the air in triumphal salute.

'Steady on, old boy,' Country Squire said. 'Decorum, don't you know.'

'Anyway,' his partner commented, 'it wasn't that difficult a hand. I would have found the same line.'

'That's not the point,' I said, beaming from ear to ear.

'Then I fail to understand what all the fuss is about,' Country Squire barked.

'But I don't,' Arlene said jubilantly. 'You've cracked it, haven't you? You've cracked the damned sonofabitch!'

They were fit to explode.

There was only one thing left to add.

'Baby,' I said to Arlene, drawling the words in my best Boston private-eye accent, 'you bet your sweet ass.'

CHAPTER THIRTY-ONE

'Kinsella?' said Norman dismissively.

I'd seen him more impressed, I must admit.

'You descend on my private table,' he continued. 'Gobble down Toddy's finest steak sandwiches. Drink my wine.' He waved the empty bottle in the air as if presenting damning evidence to the members of the jury. A vigilant waiter, misinterpreting the gesture, hurried off to fetch a replacement. 'You have a smile on your face like you've discovered the answer to life, the universe and everything; can prove that Stephen

Hawking got it all wrong. Earth was in fact created by the great god Ronald McDonald solely as a means of disposing of a pan-galactic pickled-gherkin mountain. And what do you tell me?' Norman shook his head and looked at me as if considering a straitjacket as my next Christmas present. 'Kinsella wrote the letter.'

Immediately after the brainwave (brainstorm, Norman seemed to be thinking), Arlene and I had left Ham & High – sighs of relief from all concerned – and raced round to Toddy's. Scribbling down the bridge hand, I had tried to take Norman through my thought processes. The hand, and I – gabbling away on a tidal wave of adrenalin – were unintelligible. So I leapt straight to my conclusion.

'I don't get it,' he said. 'It doesn't make sense.'

'Who has been the one to gain?' I asked. 'Kinsella, that's who.'

'Pardon my dimness, but are we talking about the same Kinsella whose wife was so recently found at the bottom of Beachy Head? Gain,' he said pensively. 'Must buy a new dictionary. My current one is obviously seriously out of date.'

'Look at it all from Kinsella's point of view.' I sat back in the chair and took a long, slow sip of the claret. 'He marries Louise. Over the moon. Happy as a sandboy. All that stuff.' I raised the glass to my lips for a longer sip of the wine – purely as a pause for effect, you understand. 'Then he discovers she's hooked on cocaine. Probably now realises she was the one who blew the whistle on the drugs raid. But he loves her – let's at least give him credit for that. And there were extenuating circumstances – the pressures of living with Collins, the loss of the baby. So he forgives her. Helps her dry out and rehabilitate.'

Arlene nodded. Norman, abnormally, still looked puzzled.

'Then,' I said, 'he rumbles Prospekt. And another nail is hammered into Louise's coffin.' I drank some more wine while imagining what had gone through Kinsella's mind. 'Kinsella's no mug, right? At the start he's only too happy to have Prospekt involved. A bottomless pit of cash for expansion. But after a while he begins to feel just a little uncomfortable about the ease with which Glenshield is making such large profits. Especially on the foreign contracts. Maybe he has some doubts too about the ring-fencing operations – such a vast and instantaneous improvement in the crime figures. And then he asks himself, "Why Liechtenstein? Why does Prospekt cloak itself in such secrecy?" It can't have taken the former head of the Drugs Squad too long to put two and two together. And come up with a freshly laundered four.'

'And last, but by no means least,' Arlene chipped in, 'Kinsella learns that Louise is having an affair with Paradine.'

'The final nail,' I said sadly. 'Kinsella – a good cop, a straight cop, during all his years in the force – finds himself a mere pawn of the drug barons. And saddled with an adulterous wife. His whole world is crumbling about him. So what can he do? How can he rid himself of Prospekt? Of Paradine? And Louise?'

'He writes a letter,' Norman said, gazing down

at my scribbled diagram. 'But he doesn't just write a letter. He sends it to the one person who can be relied upon not to ignore it. Collins.'

'Exactly,' I said. 'He throws Collins into play. Knowing that Collins will play right back into his – Kinsella's – hand. That his old adversary would sooner roast in hell on a slowly turning spit than pass up an opportunity to dig the dirt. Collins has no exit but the one door that Kinsella has clearly marked. Kinsella sits back and waits for Collins to do his dirty work for him.'

'So Kinsella knew you were coming?' Norman asked perceptively.

'He knew Collins would send *someone* from 'C' Squad to try to infiltrate Glenshield. Probably tumbled Walker straight away – maybe Kinsella did some reconnaissance by having a beer with Quinn when Collins was appointed; Quinn's powers of graphic description would have made Walker unmissable. Then I arrive on the scene. Too big a coincidence. His plan has to be working. You've got to hand it to Kinsella,' I said, shaking my head, 'he played it superbly.'

'Louise and Paradine,' Norman said, a pained expression on his face. 'They *weren't* on the fiddle, were they?'

'No. Kinsella set them up. He sent the phoney invoices – I bet if we look again at the originals we find that they started to arrive just after Collins was transferred to the Fraud Squad. Kinsella formed the company, but named Louise and Paradine as sole directors and shareholders. Made sure the finger pointed squarely at both of them. All very neat.'

'How did he change the database to switch the payments into their account?'

'The same way I deleted Paradine and Louise from the authorisation list. Kinsella knew Louise's password. And O'Kane had his on a Post-it note stuck to his computer screen. Kinsella simply deleted Paradine. Changed the database and then reinstated him. It wasn't without risks. The next time Paradine logged onto the system it would request a password – Kinsella couldn't input one when making the re-instatement – but Paradine would more than likely put it down to some computer glitch. Apart from that, there would be no evidence that there had ever been a change.'

'And once we,' Norman said, taking his share of the credit, or the blame, whichever way you wanted to look at it, 'had discovered their fraud, all Kinsella had to do was make sure Prospekt got to hear about it.'

'Confident that they would rid him of the pair of them. And it provided added ammunition when he came to make his proposal to Prospekt to buy their shares. In one fell swoop Kinsella scoops the pool, gets everything he wanted. Control of a clean company. And gets shot of an unfaithful and embarrassing wife who had put him into a compromising position.'

'Who was it?' Norman asked. 'Who was the one to let Prospekt know about Louise and Paradine?'

'O'Kane,' I said. 'That's my guess. I don't know if he did it on his own initiative or at Kinsella's prompting. I'm pretty sure O'Kane must have been aware of the rumours that Louise and Paradine were lovers – that would account for the frosty atmosphere in the boardroom during the discussion of Supermax. Now Kinsella tells him that they are not just lovers but fraudsters too – and at the same time drops the bombshell about the real nature of Prospekt. Maybe then it was just another case of ex-coppers closing ranks to fight the outsiders. O'Kane doing Kinsella a favour – whether requested or not.'

I reached for my glass and found it empty. The bottle too. Evaporation, no doubt.

'Excuse me for a moment,' Norman said, rising from the table. 'Get another bottle while I'm gone, will you?'

I turned round to summon a waiter. Toddy, his night's work over, was propping up the bar drinking a well-deserved pint. He watched Norman's exit and scuttled over.

'You'll have to talk to him,' he said, blunt as ever. He bent down over the table, placing one hand on my shoulder. 'The stubborn old boogger won't listen to me. Just calls me an old woman. Tells me to stop my mithering. But, whatever he says, red wine and painkillers aren't the answer. He needs an operation, Nick. Been putting it off for months. If he delays any longer, it'll be too bloody late.'

I cursed myself silently. I'd been too wrapped up in my own problems to consider Norman's. Failed to appreciate the sudden deterioration in his condition. The continued weight loss. The occasional, hastily bitten-back winces of pain.

'Leave it with me, Toddy,' I said. 'I'll talk some

sense into him. Enlist the help of Arlene and Arthur too. Believe me, by the time we're finished with him, Norman will be only too glad of a stay in hospital just to get some respite from our nagging.'

Toddy nodded. 'Another bottle, then,' he said loudly, as Norman walked back across the room.

'What are we going to do?' Norman asked. 'About Kinsella. You can't be considering telling Collins?'

'Hell, no,' I said, shuddering at the thought of Collins's reaction – and likely course of action. 'He would go berserk. Pistols-at-dawn time.'

'But you can't let Kinsella get away with it,' Arlene said, appalled. 'The frigging scheming *numero uno* creep as good as murdered his wife. You have to do something, Nick.'

'How about some poetic justice?' I said.

Norman nodded in agreement, his brain whirring away. 'A dose of his own medicine.'

'So I take it,' Arlene asked, happily moving onto the next subject, 'that you won't be accepting his job offer?'

'No,' I said, smiling. 'I'll decline politely, mind you.' I reached across the table, placed my hand on hers and squeezed it lovingly. 'But I can give him a very good reason why Glenshield – and England – don't fit into my plans for the future.'

CHAPTER THIRTY-TWO

Monday morning found Glenshield in an un-characteristically subdued and sombre mood. Even the plants in the atrium – sensing the aura of gloom and doom? – seemed to droop their heads to a solemn and respectful half-mast. Charlie was wearing a black armband.

The previous day, the papers had been full of the story; and the sight of a copy of the *Sun* already lying discarded in the bin told me that the dailies had picked up where the Sundays had left off.

And who could blame them? It made fascinating reading. Kinsella had seen to that.

Appearing to take the pragmatic view that if he could not avoid the attentions of the media, then he might as well confront them *en masse*, Kinsella had given a press conference. Flashbulbs froze the tear at the corner of his eye. Microphones caught the emotional quiver in his voice. Cameras played witness to his courage and determination. The whole nation sat riveted to their TV screens as he revealed all. The crime uncovered by the Fraud Squad. Louise's affair with her co-conspirator. And how – here he had come closest to breaking down, being forced to pause and sip at a glass of water with shaking hands – the lovers had chosen to commit suicide rather than face a future apart in separate prisons.

His hypocrisy disgusted me – to the very pit of my stomach. And yet that would have to be repressed, temporarily at least, if I was to act convincingly ignorant in his presence.

'You're back then,' Charlie said, making me feel as if I had deserted a sinking ship.

'And official this time,' I said, allowing him to inspect my fake FIG card. 'Fraud Squad. I'm here to see Mr Kinsella.'

'I'm surprised you have the nerve to show your face,' Charlie grunted. 'Under the circumstances. You being responsible for everything that's happened, that is. That's why you were here, I take it – to dig the dirt? Well, I hope you're bloody satisfied.'

I shrugged. I'd had a day to grow used to shouldering my share of the blame.

'If I hear any screams from Mr Kinsella's office,' he said, 'I'll cock a deaf-un.'

As I travelled up to the fourth floor in the glass-sided lift, Charlie's eyes never left me, their dual laser beams burning holes in my body. It would have been nice to set him straight. But nice wasn't on my agenda at the moment.

On the way to Kinsella's office I stopped off briefly at Personnel. Offered my condolences to the downcast, red-eyed crew. Borrowed their equipment to print off some documents on company stationery for Kinsella.

Outside his door I took three deep breaths, the way actors are supposed to do before stepping onto the stage. Apprehensively, I knocked and entered.

He was standing by the window, staring out

into the distance.

'Nick,' he said, turning round and throwing his arms open in welcome. 'It's good to see you, my boy.'

Mentally I swallowed an anti-vomit pill and went into a manly clinch, patting Kinsella consolingly on the back. Then swiftly put some distance between us by taking a seat at the other side of the desk. Kinsella continued to stand, returning his gaze to the horizon.

'I'm so sorry to hear about Louise,' I said genuinely. 'So very sorry.'

'She was a good woman, Nick,' he said, his back towards me.

Yes, you bastard, I thought. Yes, she was. Too good for you.

'I shall miss her,' he added, sighing and turning in one manoeuvre, his face composed into a forlorn look.

'I know this isn't a good time,' I said, not giving a damn, 'but I'm afraid I've got some more bad news. I can't accept your offer of a job.'

'But why not?' His jaw dropped. His huge body flopped into the chair as if unable to support all the burdens a moment longer. 'Let's talk about it, Nick. Tell me your reasons. Maybe I can change your mind.'

I told him about Arlene. Laid it on real thick. By the shovel-load. How we were in love. Simply had to be together. But there was a daughter – poor, sweet Mary Jo – to consider. Arlene couldn't – wouldn't – abandon her. Mary Jo, young and helpless, needed a mother's guiding hand. And a father's shoulder to lean on. We

369

couldn't leave her to fend for herself. Or disrupt her life by asking her to settle in England. So it was up to me to emigrate to America.

'I understand, my boy,' he said. 'Life isn't a dress rehearsal, you know. You're only given once chance to get it right. Take *your* chance, Nick. You leave with my thanks. And with my best wishes for the future.'

'What will you do now?' I asked, rhetorically.

'I'll have to find someone else to take your place, Nick. You'll be a hard act to follow. But it's too late to change course now. The consortium's formal offer to Prospekt to buy their shares is due to be submitted at noon today. It will be a whole new life, Nick. I only wish that you and Lou could have been part of it.'

Instead of sticking my fingers down my throat, I managed to shake my head sadly.

'Can you still stay on for a while to help clear up the mess?' Kinsella asked.

I'd assumed he would make that request – someone as selfish as Kinsella was easy to predict. I was prepared – very prepared – to go along with it. But only for a limited period. There was no telling when the rage and loathing inside me would rise to the surface and show through the mask.

'Only for today, I'm afraid. There's a lot to do in a short space of time if I am to be on the flight on Friday with a clear conscience.' I smiled reassuringly at him. 'But everything's in hand. Don't worry. If you could come along to Accounts with me, I'll set the wheels in motion. You need to make some pretty fundamental changes, and I'd rather you were there to give your imprimatur when they hear the news.'

I took the papers from my briefcase and presented them to him.

'I've taken the liberty,' I said, 'of preparing a memo in your name. Setting everything down in black and white. From what's gone on in the past, it seemed best to have a permanent record. If you could just sign it, we can run off a few photocopies to hand out when I've finished talking to the staff. Oh, and here's a letter informing the bank of the changes to the Board. As far as authorising transfers of funds, payments and so on, I've put you down as sole signatory in future – I thought Gerry had more than enough on his plate without adding to his responsibilities.'

'All very sensible,' he said, when he finished reading. 'You seem to have thought of everything, Nick.'

'I hope so, Roddy.'

He smiled at me and scrawled his signature on the papers.

'Are you ready then?' I asked. Added sympathetically, 'You're sure you feel up to this?'

'Can't sit around moping all day, can I? What good would that do? Got to force myself back into harness.'

'Like the old mule you are, eh?' I said with a smile.

'You all know Nick,' Kinsella said to the glum-faced assembly of accounts staff. 'Except you, that is, Beryl.'

371

Beryl, flattered by his use of her first name, tilted her eyes a degree or two downwards and fluttered long eyelashes up at Kinsella. She looked about nineteen, going on eighty. She gave all the signs of needing a bloody good holiday – which, it seemed, was exactly what she'd had. Her tan was non-existent. The whites of her baggy eyes were tinged with the sickly shade of hepatic yellow that comes from a hard-pressed and complaining liver. She was wearing a short summer dress, still creased from the suitcase. And a scarf round her neck, under which peeked out the purple bruise of a love bite.

'Nick is not what he seems,' Kinsella continued dramatically. Tricia looked across at me anxiously. 'In fact, Nick works for the Fraud Squad.'

I flashed my identification for authenticity.

Oohs and ahs from the female brigade.

Well-I-never shake of the head from Arnold.

'During his time here, Nick has discovered certain irregularities in our accounts. He has kindly volunteered to help us rectify matters. Over to you, I think, Nick.'

'There are three things I want you to do. With Mr Kinsella's approval, of course?'

Kinsella waved his hand to dismiss the question.

'First, you must all change your passwords. And keep them absolutely secret from now on.'

Embarrassed faces turned down to study the floor.

'Second, but a much lower priority, this stupid Q123 account must be reconciled to the last penny. And then deleted for good.' I turned to

Kinsella. 'I'm sure Mr O'Kane will co-operate fully in this task.'

Kinsella nodded at the staff.

'And lastly,' I said, steeling myself for the anticipated reaction, 'I want you to re-input everything you have put on the system since the close of work last Tuesday.'

There was a collective groan. From the strength of it, England might just have lost the deciding Test Match against Australia. At the Oval. Off the last ball.

'I'm sorry,' I said sincerely. 'But Mr Kinsella allowed me to take a copy of the accounts last Tuesday evening.' I produced a disk from my briefcase and held it aloft for them all to see. 'I've been through everything most thoroughly. Removed all the illegal invoices. Altered the payments schedule. And the supplier database. What's on this disk can be guaranteed clean as a whistle. But when I load it back on the system, we lose all the work you've done over the last three days. It can't be helped, I'm afraid.'

Arnold straightened his back, puffed out his pigeon chest and addressed Kinsella.

'I'm sure I speak for all of us, sir. We'll do as Nick says. Willingly, sir. We'll make sure everything's back to normal by Thursday. The payments schedule will go to the bank, interim dividends paid, the nominal ledger closed: the end-of-month accounts will be on your desk, as per usual, five working days after that. And,' he said, raising a cupped hand to his mouth while clearing a lump from his throat, 'I'd like to add how sorry we all are. Not for being so sloppy –

that goes without saying. But about Mrs Kinsella. She was well respected. And well liked. So don't you concern yourself with things here, sir. Whatever needs doing, you can count on us.'

It was a big speech for a little man.

Even Kinsella seemed shaken. But he would, wouldn't he?

'Thank you,' he said. 'Thank you all.' He turned embarrassed eyes towards me. 'If that's all, Nick, I'll leave you to it.'

'Sorry, Roddy,' I said. 'But if Glenshield is going to turn over a new leaf as regards security, then it has to apply to everybody. When I load the disk, you ought to check the payments schedule and supplier database. I'd rather you took nothing on trust in future.'

'Good point,' he said. 'Let's get on with it.'

I took my old seat at Beryl's terminal while the accounts staff beavered about hunting for all the necessary pieces of paper to re-do their work.

I loaded the disk and called up the first of the files. Then I swapped places with Kinsella and, setting a good example, he knuckled down manfully to the laborious task of checking my work.

An hour later he rose from the chair, stretched his shoulders and extended his right hand to me.

'I have to leave now, Nick,' he said. 'Things to do. People to see. You understand? Probably won't be back today.' He took my hand and shook it vigorously. Slapped me on the arm for good measure. 'It was good to know you. You've been a great help.'

'Believe me,' I said, 'it was something I had to

374

do. Think nothing of it.'

'Goodbye,' he said, walking from the room. 'And the luck of the Irish to you.'

'Thank you,' I said.

They were a good bunch.

There were no complaints. No ostentatious glances at the clock and accompanying loud sighs. No excuses tendered for having to leave on the stroke of half past five. They all worked till late in the evening, by which time the size of the backlog seemed less daunting.

And, all the while, I never left their side. One by one, I took over at their terminals and gave them a break. Or at least a chance to relax their concentration for twenty minutes or so, for I made them sit next to me and monitor my inputs. I was the new boy, after all, I'd told them.

At one o'clock, as planned, I had nipped out for a while. Met briefly with Arlene.

'How did you get on with Sandra Redmond?' I asked.

'No problems,' Arlene said with a smile. 'She thanks us all for the gifts for the baby.'

'Didn't see it as charity?'

'Of course not,' she replied reassuringly. 'Now, stop worrying. Get back to work. Here's your shopping.'

I returned heavily laden. Dished out sandwiches and polystyrene beakers of tea or coffee.

No-one broke off for lunch. Without being asked, they typed away at their keyboards, munching and sipping intermittently, brows creased in concentration.

By nine o'clock there was no point in continuing. The work rate had slowed down markedly, and we had arrived at that counterproductive stage where tiredness dramatically increases the risk of silly mistakes.

'Time to call it a day,' I called out. 'And a very good one at that.'

As they gathered their coats and bags, I went round to each of them in turn to say my goodbyes and wish them a happy Easter with its well-earned four-day break.

To my three surrogate mothers I gave kisses on cheeks and big boxes of Belgian chocolates.

To Beryl, a bottle of pre-mixed sangria. 'Hair of the dog, Beryl,' I said with a wink.

To Arnold, a desk organiser, complete with compartments for everything and anything. Plus a card with my telephone number at the Fraud Squad, in case he needed my advice in the week ahead. 'Don't hesitate to call, Arnold. Any time. Okay?'

And to Tricia?

'Early wedding present,' I said, kissing her on the cheek. 'I hope it comes in handy – some time in the future.'

With unsuppressed excitement she tore the wrapping paper from the parcel.

'He's cute,' she said, tightly hugging the huge teddy bear.

Cute. That's how my sister, even at the age of sixteen, had talked of her battered bear. Susie would have been Tricia's age now, if...

'I'll call him Nick,' she said, throwing her arms round me.

'Doesn't sound much of a name for a bear.'

'Not the bear, silly,' she said. 'The one I'll save him for.'

I walked from the room with my heart lodged in my throat.

I had come so close.

The thickness of a playing card from achieving the ex-con's dream.

Legitimacy.

Acceptance for what I was – rather than condemnation for what I had been.

A proper job. A bloody good job, too.

Financial security.

Not to mention the people. I was really going to miss them.

Damn you, Kinsella.

CHAPTER THIRTY-THREE

'A sad, but in many ways, a very appropriate occasion,' Norman said.

'If this is the start of a speech, Norman,' I replied, wondering how many drinks he'd downed before the rest of us had arrived, 'then please make it a short one.'

It was Thursday evening, and we were gathered in Toddy's. The old gang was there – Norman, Arthur, Arlene and myself – plus, in need of cheering up, our new honorary member, Detective Superintendent Collins. The last few days had been a mad flurry of activity as the final preparations were made for Arlene's departure and my short trip to New England. At the Fraud Squad, we had started the long process of bringing Prospekt to justice: information was being gathered on every company in their stable; liaison meetings held with the other arms of the force. The heady scent of the quarry was in our nostrils.

'Today,' Norman continued, 'is Maundy Thursday. In our quaint little country, Arlene, the significance of the day is marked by the Queen giving alms – Maundy money – to the poor. Most people, I imagine, have forgotten the origins of this ritual.' Norman glanced round the table to check whether there were any sparks of enlightenment among his guests. We fiddled with our champagne flutes, like pupils hoping to avoid the teacher's eye. 'The custom dates back to the time when the sovereign washed the feet of the poor. And, in its turn, that is a mimicking of the ceremony when Christ washed the feet of the disciples. Are you with me now?'

'Aren't we a bit short of numbers for the Last Supper?' I said, hoping to nip his oration in the bud.

'Quibble not,' he said. 'This, dear friends, is indeed our last supper together.'

'Don't be so melodramatic, Norman,' Arlene said. 'I'll be back from time to time. And this is just a sort of reconnaissance mission for Nick. He'll only be gone for three days.'

'After which time,' Norman said, in the monotone of a preacher at the pulpit, 'he will return to us – born again. A man who will speak in a strange tongue of "faucets" and "leezure time" and "hold the mayo".'

Collins smiled. It certainly was a miraculous time of year.

'Gentlemen,' Norman commanded, rising to his feet, 'raise your glasses to Arlene and Nick.'

Arthur and Collins looked at each other. Shrugged helplessly. Stood up, in full view of the packed restaurant. And, embarrassed, joined in the toast.

'And may I wish you all a Happy Easter,' Norman added. 'Or – for the pagans among you – a Happy Bank Holiday.'

Norman chuckled and, to everyone's relief, sat down.

'New whistle, Mr Collins?' Arthur said, bringing the conversation down to earth.

'Demands of the job,' Collins said, not wishing to admit that he had turned over another new leaf since the death of Louise. The new suit was charcoal grey and, as yet, spotless. His ginger hair was squeaky clean, shining brightly in the light. His face freshly shaven. Even his shirt looked as if it had been ironed – well, the bits that showed, at least. 'Nick and I have been seeing some very important people lately. Got to make the right impression. And you, Arthur?' he asked with a curious frown. 'You look like a different person. New haircut?'

'Demands of the job,' Arthur grunted ill-humouredly.

'Barbers are all the same,' Collins said philosophically. 'Always go over the top. Feel unfulfilled unless they take just that little bit too much off. You'd think it would be better for business to leave it long. People would have to come back more frequently.'

'I cut it,' Arlene said curtly.

'And a fine job you've done, I was going to say,' Collins said, red-faced. 'Arthur looks so ... well...'

'I know what I look like, thank you very much,' Arthur mumbled.

'It'll grow, Arthur,' I said consolingly.

'That makes me feel a whole lot better.'

'Oh,' Collins said, clicking his fingers. He made a great show of delving inside his brand-new briefcase. 'In case I forget. Something to read on the plane – on the lonely return journey, of course. Sorry about the quality of the photo-copying, but it's all there. Just as I promised.'

He held out a large manilla envelope, about an inch thick.

The file on the hit-and-run.

You don't need this, my head told me. Don't touch it.

I listened to the impassioned pleas of my heart instead. Reached out with shaking hands and grasped the envelope. Arlene snatched it from me.

'I'll look after that, Nick,' she said firmly. 'Till we've talked it through.'

'Good idea,' I said, too afraid to open the damned envelope in any case.

I didn't know which I feared more.

Disappointment that it would contain nothing I didn't already know.

Or the path I might feel compelled to follow if it did.

Cast it from your mind, Shannon. Let Arlene own the problem. For tonight at least. Don't spoil the occasion. Enjoy.

The grilled lobster was succulent, the baron of beef pink and tender. Bottles of wine came and went with increasing frequency: Chablis with the first course, our host's favourite Pomerol following hard on its heels. The conversation, driven by the exuberantly hyped-up Norman, was good-humoured, bordering on the hysterical at times.

In short, everything was perfect.

Until the leather-clad despatch rider arrived.

A waiter brought the parcel to the table.

Without thinking, I ripped at the brown paper.

Inside was a thick layer of bubble-wrap.

Beneath that a clear plastic bag.

It contained a tea cup. On the front was the crest of the Grand Hotel. On the side, fine carbon powder delineated a fingerprint.

Puzzled – baffled – I read the accompanying note.

Tea and sympathy?
Did Louise show her appreciation?
Remember this, Shannon.
It's better to have a friend than an enemy.
A friend can do you a favour – example enclosed.
But an enemy...
Accept this peace offering.
And forget Northampton.

Thanks, Walker. Indian giver. I take your gift. And your point. The unstated one, that is. That somewhere, safely hidden no doubt, you still have a record of the find. Some little note from your friend in Forensics, confirming the fingerprint as mine.

So I forgot Northampton.

That was easy.

What proved more difficult was erasing from my brain how the cup had found its way to Louise's room. It hadn't been buttery shortbread the man was after as he left the cover of the piano for my table by the fire.

Prospekt had issued me with a second warning.

I didn't fool myself into thinking there would be a third.

CHAPTER THIRTY-FOUR

'Come on, Collins,' I said impatiently, to the empty office. 'Where are you when I need you?'

Thank God I didn't believe in reincarnation. The way my luck had been going lately, if I died I'd probably come back as myself! After three days in New England, I had returned to London not so much reborn as regressed. By nine years.

Perhaps I should have left well alone. Not raked over the ashes of the past. That was certainly Arlene's view. She'd kept a tight grip on the confiscated file, handing it back only as she kissed me goodbye at Logan airport. That was a smart move on her part. If I'd read the file on the way out, instead of on the way back, it would have ruined the long weekend.

It was still only half past seven on Tuesday morning. My nerves were a jangle of taut wires waiting to snap at any moment. I sat chain-smoking at my desk in the Fraud Squad, the contents of the file spread across its surface.

'Come on,' I repeated pointlessly. Collins, unless he'd had as bad a case of insomnia as I, wouldn't arrive for another hour or so. He must have read the file. Wasn't his style to hand it to me without studying it first. Surely he had a theory. There were so many questions I desperately wanted to ask. But they all boiled down to just one: was it a cock-up or cover-up on the part of the police?

The phone rang, loud and shrill against the backdrop of silence. My heart was beating fast as I picked up the receiver.

'Nick,' Arnold said. 'Thank heavens you're there.' Anyone else would have said 'Thank God' or 'Thank Christ' but, from Arnold, 'heavens' was enough to send prickles up the back of my neck.

'Can you come over here straight away?' he asked, his voice quivering. 'Something's wrong. Very wrong.'

Adrenalin kicked into my system.

I scooped up the papers. Stuffed them back into the file. Locked it in the desk drawer and out of my mind.

With trembling fingers I dialled Arthur's number.

'Go,' I said, sending him on his errand. To wake Connor. And to make the trade that I hoped would get Prospekt off my back.

I hurried across to Walker's desk. Placed the bottle of expensive duty-free perfume in a conspicuous position. Penned a short note.

A gift for a gift.
Join me at Glenshield.
Very, very urgent.
Truce?

In the back of the cab, I managed a smile. Arnold's call was a good omen. Today was all about timing. And Arnold 'thank heavens' – was early.

'Earlies and Lates, please,' I said to the guard on the reception desk, flashing that useful FIG card one more time.

O'Kane had signed in at six o'clock. Bloody ridiculous! He would have made an England footballer twenty years ago, when work-rate counted above such unimportant attributes as talent, skill and imagination.

Arnold had arrived at a quarter past seven. No mention of Kinsella on the sheet. Another good sign. We were ahead of the game.

The Accounts office – unheated for the four days of the Bank Holiday – was cold. Arnold had his jacket off. There were damp patches under his armpits, dark stains thrown into sharp contrast by the bright, shining metal of his elasticated armbands. Beads of perspiration glistened on his forehead. He took out a neatly folded handkerchief and dabbed nervously at his face.

'Nick,' he said, agitated. He cast his eyes down at his desk. Shook his head disbelievingly at the papers scattered there. 'Nick,' he repeated, shaking now.

'Take it easy,' I said. 'Talk me through it. In your own time. Then we can sort everything out.'

'We're still behind,' he said. 'Not in a position to close the March accounts yet. I decided to make an early start. Get a couple of hours in while it's quiet. I collected the post on the way up. Sorted out the cheques for banking. Then moved onto the bank reconciliation.' He handed me the statements for the close of business on Thursday. 'It must be a mistake. Yes?'

I looked at the statements. The figures glared out instantly.

'Jesus bloody Christ,' I said, stunned.

I felt the blood drain from my face. I pulled up a chair and collapsed into it. Lit a cigarette, heedless of the no-smoking rule – it could never have been intended to cover times like these.

'It's not a mistake, then?' Arnold said, registering my shocked expression.

I shook my head, words failing me.

'Then this is the end, isn't it?' he said, sitting down and staring into space. 'Someone's cleaned us out. Eight million pounds.'

'Yes,' I said. 'Eight million pounds.'

The greedy, scheming, cunning, crafty, underhand bastard.

It was only supposed to be eight hundred thousand!

Arnold went off to get the biggest, blackest

coffees he could find while I studied the figures.

Whatever I felt about the motive and the repercussions, I had to admire the way it had been done. But, then again, it was partly my idea. Norman had simply taken it to the very extreme.

The deposit account, swollen with funds in readiness for the normal end-of-month payments, plus the amount set aside for the interim dividends to shareholders, had been cleared. The payments schedule for March, the computer showed, had been altered – but not as planned. To allow for settlement of the additional item (the eight million pounds rather than our agreed eight hundred thousand), all the value-dated amounts that should have been transferred to the bank accounts of creditors had been cancelled. I suppose I should have been grateful that Norman had allowed the payroll to go through – at least the staff had got their money.

We had planned collateral damage.

Norman had turned it into a bloody collateral holocaust.

'I can't understand how it happened,' Arnold said, passing me the beaker of double-strength ersatz coffee/tea/cola/soup from the machine. 'After all, your man was in here on Thursday. He never spotted anything.'

'What man?' I asked, reverting to script. 'We never sent anyone.'

'You must have done,' Arnold said. 'He came in at lunchtime. Showed us his identification.'

'Did it look like this?' I asked, taking out my FIG card.

'Well, it was hard to tell,' he said, doubt

beginning to spread across his face. 'I didn't get a really good look at it. And I had my reading glasses on at the time. But it had his photo on it.'

'Oh dear,' I said solemnly. 'I think you were conned, Arnold. But you mustn't blame yourself. They are obviously very clever people.'

'They? There was only one.'

'Only one to change the schedules, yes. But whoever it was must have had detailed knowledge of the system and procedures. My guess' – guess! – 'is that this has to be an inside job. We'd better keep this to ourselves for the moment. Let's not tell anyone. Okay?'

'Apart from Mr O'Kane, you mean? I bumped into him while I was getting the coffee.'

Oh, no.

I groaned inwardly.

Don't tell me, Shannon, that your need for a caffeine fix has spoiled everything. The first thing O'Kane will do is call Kinsella. The element of surprise was important. I wanted Kinsella shell-shocked by the news. Docile as a lamb when we led him away to the tenth-floor conference room to lay the charges on him.

And then a worse thought hit me.

Don't let O'Kane ring Prospekt. They were supposed to hear only after we'd arrested Kinsella. That's why I hadn't despatched Arthur until this morning. His brief was to take his time negotiating the deal with Connor – put in a good word for me with Prospekt in exchange for the low-down on Kinsella. By the time Connor could pass on the information, I had reasoned, it would be too late for Prospekt to do anything – still a

387

brownie point for me, though.

Timing. Bloody omens! You can never trust them.

And where was Walker anyway?

I telephoned reception. Charlie was on duty now. I asked him to send Kinsella straight up to Accounts when he arrived. Then settled down to check whether Norman had deviated in any other respect from the original plan. He bloody well better had not – otherwise the Serious Fraud Office would be snapping at Collins's heels. Anything over five million pounds was technically their province rather than the Fraud Squad's, with the proviso that the fraud had to be 'terribly complex' (whatever that was supposed to mean). If Norman had kept to the simple path, then we were still in the driving seat.

It was close to nine o'clock when Walker finally put in an appearance. She looked tired. The skirt of her grey chalk-stripe suit was creased just below the waist, the result – I assumed – of a long drive back from Northampton.

'What's all the urgency, Shannon?' she asked, standing over me, hands on hips. 'This had better be good. I could have done without dashing over here. There are other cases, you know? The world doesn't begin and end with bloody Glenshield.'

'And good morning to you too, Walker. Nice weekend?'

'Does it show that much?' she asked.

'Well,' I said.

'Okay,' she said. 'Let's start again. Good morning, Shannon. Thank you for the present – and the sentiment behind it.'

'Good morning, Walker.'

'Now,' she said, 'what the bloody hell is so damned important?'

'Oh, nothing really.' Since we were a team again, albeit one built on the rocky foundations of mutual necessity rather than trust, I couldn't resist winding her up. 'Probably shouldn't have bothered you. Just a bit of money gone missing. That's all.'

'Thanks a lot,' she said, rolling her eyes. 'So, hit me with it. How much?'

'Eight million quid,' I said, with a nonchalant shrug of my shoulders.

She gulped. 'I said hit me with it – not run me over with a bloody steamroller. This had better not be one of your jokes, Shannon.'

'No joke, Cherry,' I said, serious now. 'I'm on the money trail already. Can you get Support to check on this company?'

'Why can't you do that? Too menial a job?'

'Support is where you started out in the squad. I imagine you have friends there. For you, they'll make it top priority. For me, it would go to the bottom of the pile. Anyway, you've been involved all along. You deserve to be in at the kill. And who knows, there may even be a promotion handed out for this one.'

She nodded. Ran her tongue thoughtfully over her bottom lip.

I passed her a slip of paper with the name 'Elum Holdings Limited'. Okay, I admit it wasn't very original, but Norman and I were trying to leave a trail, weren't we? And having our own private joke too, of course. At Kinsella's expense.

'And while you're on the phone, can you talk to Collins? Ask him to fix a meeting with a judge – we need to take a look at the company's bank account. Eight million quid should be grounds enough.'

In order to examine a bank account, the police have to obtain a warrant from a High Court Judge – a common-or-garden magistrate, sufficient for a normal search warrant, won't do. They need to demonstrate (good old PACE again) that 'a serious arrestable offence has taken place and serious loss or harm has been caused to any person'.

I glanced up at the wall-clock. The staff would start arriving at any moment. Arnold, Walker and I went through to the small side-office that Paradine had used on his days at Glenshield. Walker, excitedly, made the phone calls. I practised a knowledgeable, but innocent, expression.

'Fill me in,' Walker said, swivelling from, side to side in Paradine's chair. 'How was the stunt pulled?'

'It seems,' I said, from the minion's position on the other side of the desk, 'that someone came in here on Thursday impersonating a Fraud Squad officer.' I looked across at Arnold for support.

'That's right,' he said. 'Checking evidence to do with Paradine and Mrs Kinsella. Well, that's what he said.'

'I suppose he worked in here?' I prompted. 'Didn't want to disrupt the outer office?'

Arnold nodded.

'While he's out of sight,' I explained to Walker, 'he must have made all the necessary changes to

390

the accounts – input a non-existent invoice for eight million pounds, altered the payment schedule and supplier database.'

'But he would need all the codes for that,' Walker said, placing her hands behind her neck and gazing up at the ceiling. 'Wasn't that the way Paradine had operated?'

'Yes,' I said. 'You've hit the nail on the head. What do you reckon?'

'Inside job,' she said. 'Has all the signs. But who?'

I waved my hands in the air and exhaled cluelessly. 'Maybe your friends in Support can come up with a name.'

'But,' Arnold said, his brow creased in concentration, 'I printed off everything myself – the hard copy of the payments schedule and the supplier database, and the letter of authority to transfer some cash from deposit to current account. Took them along to Mr Kinsella in person for him to sign. I didn't see any changes on the print-outs. I would have noticed a sum as big as eight million pounds.'

I paused. Ran my hand over my mouth. Tapped my lips in contemplation.

'Then how...' I said.

'A switch, Shannon,' Walker said, shaking her head at my slowness. 'It's obvious. Someone substitutes a fraudulent letter of authority and copy of the schedules for the real ones.'

'Of course. You're right.' I paused a little longer this time. 'No. It wouldn't work. Not if Arnold was watching Mr Kinsella sign.'

'But I didn't,' Arnold protested. 'Mr Kinsella

391

appreciated just how busy I was. He said to leave everything with him because it had to be checked thoroughly. Told me I wasn't to be offended, but you'd been adamant he was to take nothing on trust any more.'

'So what happened to the papers?' Walker asked.

Arnold shrugged. 'Mr Kinsella said he would take them downstairs when he'd finished. Leave them with Charlie. Get him to arrange for one of the guards to take them round to the bank.'

Walker picked up the phone.

'This is Detective Sergeant Walker. Is that Charlie? Good. Cast your mind back, Charlie. To Thursday afternoon. Was there anyone hanging around reception? Right. Hang on a minute.'

She turned to Arnold. 'What did this bloke look like?'

'Average height. Thin. Sixty-ish. Hairpiece, dark brown – terrible job, stood out a mile.'

Walker relayed the description to Charlie. Listened to his lengthy reply. Nodded to herself from time to time. Looked across at me, yawned and rolled her eyes. Finally replaced the receiver.

'Charlie remembers the man. Came in before lunch claiming to be Fraud Squad. Produced identification – forged obviously.'

'Must have been,' I said.

'Anyway,' Walker went on, ignoring my interruption, 'Charlie cleared him to come up here. When the bloke eventually came back downstairs he hung around talking for a while. Told Charlie he was ex-Artillery. They seemed to have had a long conversation about the shortcomings of a badly cleaned field gun. The man left immediately after Kinsella put the envelope for the bank on the reception desk.'

'So was that when the switch was made?' I asked.

'Of course, Shannon. From my conversations with Charlie, anyone who hangs around him for longer than a second has to have an ulterior motive – or a serious personality defect.'

'Probably both,' I corrected. 'What I can't understand,' I added quickly, 'is how someone managed to get hold of Kinsella's code. I mean, a signature must be pretty easy to forge. But who would know his code? Apart from Kinsella himself, that is.'

Walker frowned.

Then smiled. And opened her lips to speak.

The ringing of the telephone delayed the inevitable.

She snatched up the receiver. Announced herself. Listened intently, her breath held. 'Make sure you tell Collins,' she said. 'And thanks, Andy. I owe you a large one.' She gave a throaty laugh into the mouthpiece. 'Really,' she said. 'That's what they all say.'

'Well?' I asked excitedly. 'What did he say?'

'Nothing I hadn't worked out already,' Walker said. 'Elum Holdings Limited is owned by... Do you want three guesses, Shannon?'

'Come on, Walker. Don't play games with me.'

'I remember you saying that once before, Shannon. Still, that's all in the past, eh? I'll put you out of your misery.'

But not immediately, it seemed.

'Collins is going to love this,' she said. 'If I don't make DI, then there's no justice in this world.'

But there is, Walker, I wanted to say. Poetic or otherwise, it all counts.

'Kinsella,' she said, raising her fist in triumph. 'Bloody Kinsella owns the company. No need to forge his signature. No need to try to work out his code. It was Kinsella all along. We've got him, Shannon. We've got the smooth-talking bastard.'

'Not yet, Cherry,' I said cautiously. 'We may have the evidence, but we don't have the man. Make another call. Put out an APB – or whatever it's called. Let's get him in the bag. I want to hear you say those magic words – "You're nicked."'

Or maybe, I thought with a grin, it should be 'You've been Nicked.'

And 'Normaned', of course.

After that, it was all action.

Walker made her phone call. The hunt for Kinsella was on.

Arnold watched as we took back-up copies of the accounts. Walker placed the disks lovingly in an envelope. Then the three of us signed our names across the seal.

Back at Holborn, Collins was dancing with delight. Parading around the offices, mentally waving two fingers at anyone who had ever doubted him.

By twelve o'clock he had the warrant from the judge. And a Mareva order to freeze Kinsella's personal assets and those of Elum Holdings.

Ten minutes later he called at the bank. Requisitioned the records. And took a statement from the manager. There could be no doubt. Kinsella's name and signature were on the bank mandate for the company. And the worried manager was able to give a very clear recollection of the pair who had opened the account: the small one, with the dark brown carpet-tile on his head, who had done most of the talking; and the giant of a man with the short haircut and the 'sort of faint Irish accent'.

By one o'clock ports and seaports had been put on alert. The country was sealed. No escape for Mr Kinsella.

Everything was going strictly to plan.

Except for one problem.

We couldn't bloody find Kinsella.

No news is good news, I told myself. But I wasn't very convinced. It was beginning to look as if Prospekt had got to him before us – the intelligence network of the underworld, un-hindered by rules and regulations and PACE, functioning more quickly than that of the police force.

When the news came, it seemed to confirm the theory.

A team of CID and uniformed officers had been detailed to accompany Walker in a search of Kinsella's home. Receiving no answer, in time-honoured fashion they had smashed the door down with jackhammers.

Of Kinsella there was no trace.

What they did find was a lot of blood.

A hell of a lot of blood.

I gave up the wait at six o'clock. Went home to

roast Norman over an open fire. Or skin him alive. I hadn't made my mind up yet. Prolonged consideration of the alternatives was part of the pleasure.

But the gruesome discovery at Kinsella's house had taken the edge off my appetite. Had blunted what should have been a mood of exhilaration and celebration. Kinsella's death had never been part of the plan.

'I want a word with you, Norman,' I said, storming through the door.

'Rather thought you might,' he replied, playfully raising his hands to his face to shield himself. 'What you have to understand, Nick, is that I'm a creative artist. I need some licence. A little scope for my imagination. I find a rigid plan much too restrictive, too undemanding, of my talents.'

'Bullshit,' I said. 'I've seen the bank records. You wanted your sticky fingers on some of the money. I'm surprised you left anything at all in the Elum account.'

'There were expenses, you know? The hair-piece, for instance. New clothes for Arthur – silk suits don't come cheap in this day and age. Especially when they have to fit someone as big as Arthur or Kinsella – that's a lot of material, you know.'

'Norman,' I said, elongating the word until it contained exactly the desired amount of menace (that is, the maximum).

The telephone burst into life.

'Saved by the bell,' Norman said, snatching up the receiver. 'It's Walker. For you.'

'We've got him,' she said, her voice trembling with emotion. 'Safely under lock and key. The blood we found wasn't his. Someone tried to kill him and bit off more than they could chew.'

'Wonderful news,' I said. 'Congratulations on your imminent promotion.'

'That's it,' she said, a little uncertainly. 'Why I rang. Chris is here at my place. The Commander has taken over the interrogation – said it wouldn't do our case any good if Chris was involved. We're having a little party. Come and join us. Please.'

There must have been a dozen good reasons to decline the invitation. Arlene wouldn't have liked it, for one. And there was Norman to attend to.

Oh, what the hell!

It was only a drink, after all.

What harm could a little drink do?

And we weren't going to be alone. Collins would be there, she'd said.

Yes.

Tonight, celebrations were in order.

I could tear strips off Norman's hide later.

CHAPTER THIRTY-FIVE

In the street outside Walker's bedsit the early morning appetising aroma of freshly baked bread had been replaced by the strong, over-rich smell of fatty lamb turning slowly on the spit of the doner kebab house. On the concrete stairs, the cat sat hunched up predator-style, busily licking away at the remnants of some unidentifiable spillage. As I approached, it watched me warily. I bent down slowly and stroked the top of its head. The cat tolerated my fingers for a while, even emitted a short, low, gutteral purr as my reward, and then returned thirstily to its lapping. I climbed up the last few stairs and knocked on Walker's door.

'Come in, Nick,' Walker shouted. 'The door's on the latch.'

I turned the handle and heard the muffled sound of music coming from the radio. Jazz FM, I assumed. The bouncy rhythm of 'Avalon'. Teddy Wilson on piano playing quiet, supportive chords in the background; Lionel Hampton up front producing a delicate and precise solo from the vibes.

I hummed along with the music – *My heart belongs to Avalon*. Took three strides down the short corridor to the main room. Pushed the door open. Stood on the threshold peering in.

The curtains were shut tight. The room was dark, save for the weak cone of light from a small table lamp by the television.

Walker was sitting on the bed, her legs drawn up under her. Her hair was loose. It tumbled over her shoulders, and hung across the side of her face so that her down-turned eyes were concealed from me.

The jacket of the chalk-stripe suit lay on the floor.

The blue blouse was partly unbuttoned, revealing a seductive hint of cleavage.

I stepped into the room.

Immediately felt the pressure of a gun between my shoulder blades.

'Welcome to the party, Shannon,' Kinsella said, pushing me forward. 'Take a seat. On the bed.'

I knelt down next to Walker and took her head in my hands. She turned her face towards me. There was an ugly red mark across her cheek and the indentations of Kinsella's fingers on her throat.

'Are you all right, Cherry?' I asked.

She nodded slowly. 'Sorry, Nick,' she said. 'There was nothing I could do.'

I drew her head carefully forward and nuzzled it tenderly against mine, my lips brushing against her ear.

'How very touching,' Kinsella said.

I turned towards him, my fists clenched in rage.

'Easy, Shannon. Sit.' The gun dipped in the direction of the bed to reinforce the order.

Kinsella reached out and pulled over one of the cane chairs. Positioned it a few yards in front of us. Sat himself down heavily. His eyes narrowed as a shock-wave of pain ran through his body. Reaching inside his black leather jacket, he clutched at his right shoulder. When he withdrew his hand, it was covered in blood. That was what the cat had been lapping.

'Happy now, Shannon?' he said, thrusting the bloody hand accusingly at me.

'What do you want, Kinsella?' I asked. 'As if I couldn't guess.'

'You set me up, Shannon. Revenge would be nice. But I'll settle for a confession.'

Walker brushed her hair aside and peered at me curiously.

'What is he on about, Nick?'

'Don't you know, my dear?' Kinsella said. 'Didn't your boyfriend tell you?'

Walker stared at Kinsella with hate in her eyes.

'Firstly, I am not *your dear*. Secondly, Nick is not my boyfriend. Now,' she said indignantly, 'would someone please tell me what is going on? In the last hour, this thug,' she stabbed an angry finger at Kinsella, 'barges into my home, grabs me by the throat, slaps me round the face and points a bloody gun at me. What the hell is happening?'

'I like 'em with a bit of spirit, don't you, Shannon?' Kinsella said with a humourless smile. The gun stiffened in his hand, the long, silenced barrel moving fractionally towards Walker.

I felt her body tense beside me.

Whether it had been my arrival, or simply the passage of time, her initial shock had worn off. I felt a sense of dread as I realised from bitter experience what was going on inside her. Adrenalin would be pumping through her veins at this very moment. It would make her impulsive, unpredictable. And put us both in even greater danger. I was reminded of what she had once said. Long ago, it now seemed. In the aftermath of Redmond's leap through the window. *It's my job to protect you.*

'Let Walker go,' I said to Kinsella. 'My car's outside. I'll take you anywhere you want. Give you anything you want. I promise. Just leave Walker out of this.'

Kinsella frowned in disbelief at my naïvety. His lips twisted into a sneer.

'You should have been a bloody comedian, Shannon. Don't make me laugh any more, please. There's a bullet in my shoulder – courtesy of your friends at Prospekt – and it doesn't like movement much.'

'Tough shit,' said Walker.

Kinsella stiffened, and winced. 'Get up, slag,' he ordered. 'Make yourself useful. Bring me that whisky bottle.'

Walker rose slowly from the bed. Moved sideways across the room like a vigilant crab, eyes never straying from Kinsella. Even when she reached the coffee table she didn't look down. Just stretched out her hand and felt around in the air until she located the bottle. She picked it up by the neck. Paused, as if judging its balance.

My heart began to beat faster. Don't do anything stupid, Walker, I prayed.

Kinsella hadn't missed her action either. 'Stand very still,' he said quietly but firmly. He swivelled the point of the gun to Walker's left. Took aim at a half-full tumbler on the coffee table. Squeezed the trigger.

The barely audible 'phut' of the gunshot wasn't very impressive. But it didn't need to be. The tumbler exploded into what seemed like a million pieces. Tiny splinters of glass burst into the air, causing Walker to leap back involuntarily. I heard her catch her breath. Saw her shocked expression as she watched a pool of whisky spread across the table.

'Have I made my point?' Kinsella said.

Walker nodded, her eyes blazing.

'Put the bottle down there,' Kinsella directed, pointing with the bloodstained toe of his loafer at a spot a little way in front of him. 'On your knees, my dear.'

Walker bit her lip, and placed the bottle precisely where indicated.

'Good girl,' he said.

She looked up at him.

Smiled.

Then spat in his face.

His leg shot out. Kicked her hard under her neck. Sent her rebounding backwards with the force of the blow. Her head hit the bedside table with a sickening thud. A heavy jar of night cream bounced upwards. The clock-radio careered across the surface and fell onto the floor. The music abruptly stopped.

I started to spring forward, at the same time grabbing the jar and propelling it at Kinsella's forehead, David-versus-Goliath-fashion.

Kinsella ducked. The jar whistled past his head and smashed into the wall behind him. But I was closing in on him.

I felt a bullet thud against the humerus bone of my left arm and rip its way out the other side.

The pain, the shock, stopped me dead in my tracks.

Kinsella didn't miss the moment. He leapt nimbly to his feet. And smacked the barrel of the gun hard across my face. I fell to the floor, joining Walker in a tangle of bodies.

'Very chivalrous, Shannon,' he said, pointing the gun between my eyes. 'And very stupid.'

I glanced away from him and examined the unconscious Walker. There was a thin trickle of blood running down her forehead.

'You're a bastard, Kinsella. An A1, solid-gold, 24-carat bastard.'

'But a bastard with a gun, Shannon. Think on that.'

I dragged Walker over the carpet. Cradled my good arm around her and somehow manhandled her inert body onto the bed. I placed her head on the pillow, and a handkerchief over the wound. There was nothing more I could do for her. It was time to attend to my own problem.

Kinsella watched with disinterest as I removed my belt and, with an awkward combination of teeth and fingers, tied it tightly above the hole in my arm. The rhythmic pumping of blood stopped.

Kinsella cast a sideways glance round the room. He walked backwards to the dining table and picked up a pad and pen. Threw one after the other at me.

'Start writing,' he commanded.

'And what if I don't?'

'Christ, I'm a patient man, Shannon. That much should be clear to you from the way I was prepared to bide my time over Paradine and Lou. Prospekt too. But even my patience is not boundless. Pick up the pen. I'll dictate.'

'Typecast as ever,' I said. 'Tell me. How did you know it was me who set you up?'

'O'Kane phoned me early this morning. Told me about the missing eight million pounds. I thought at first it was another fraud.' He laughed and shook his head. 'Then I realised where the finger would point. I was down as sole signatory at the bank – you made sure of that with that letter of yours. Then all this malarkey of checking the schedules in full view of the Accounts staff – that could only have been to put you in the clear when someone asked who could have made any changes. I'm an ex-copper, remember? Don't you think I can smell a frame-up?' His lips curled derisively. 'And you were the only person to know my password. Not even O'Kane had that information. There were only two people who could have pulled that scam – you and me. And, in spite of all the jokes about the Irish, I knew it wasn't me.'

'Shame no-one will ever believe you. Same *modus operandi* as you used to set up Paradine and Louise. Your signature on all the documents. Your unmistakable presence at the bank when you opened a new account. Tut, tut. I wonder whether Collins will put it down to carelessness or over-confidence?'

'I might have an alibi, for all you know,' Kinsella said. 'Might be able to prove I was somewhere else when the bank account was opened.'

'And what could that be, I wonder?' I asked innocently. 'Some cock-and-bull story about having to tend to a heavily pregnant woman who came over all faint in the street?'

Kinsella's eyes narrowed to slits.

'Very clever, Shannon,' he said. 'You seem to have thought of everything. Just so long as you write it all down, you can crow to your heart's content. Start writing. You're going to get me off the hook. With Collins. And Prospekt.'

In reverse order, I thought. Kinsella had always got his priorities right.

I cursed Norman. If he had stuck to the original plan, then the confession would have lacked substance, had an unconvincing, hollow ring about it. But now – and especially when phrased in the words of Kinsella – it would look pretty damning. Greed – nearly eight million pounds worth – would be my motive. There would be no mention of retribution, of Paradine or Louise.

And, of course, there would be a little post-script.

How Walker had rumbled my fraud.

How I couldn't stand the thought of going back to prison. Would rather die than suffer that fate.

Whatever I said. Whatever I did. Kinsella was going to kill us both. Then place the gun in my hand.

The least I could do was delay the inevitable.

'Get you off the hook?' I said. 'I don't think so, Roddy. After all, what can you do? I'm no use to you dead. You can't kill me.'

'Not you, stupid,' he said. 'Her.'

The barrel of the gun shifted threateningly towards the recumbent figure of Walker.

'Why do you think I lured you here? Not just because I could find out her address from the personnel records, but not yours. She's my hold over you, Shannon.' He let out a weary sigh. 'So? What's it to be? A bullet between Walker's eyes? Or a confession?'

He picked up the whisky bottle. Spun off the

top with the thumb of his left hand. It rose briefly in the air before landing at his feet. He raised the bottle to his lips, his eyes peering past it, studying me as he drank.

'What guarantee do I have?' I asked. 'That you won't simply take the confession and then kill us both?'

It was a stupid question, I admit. But it used up a little more time. And there was the outside chance that the combination of the whisky and the pain from his shoulder would make him inattentive.

'Absolutely none,' he said. 'You'll just have to trust me.'

Well, that certainly reassured me, I can tell you.

But there wasn't really any alternative.

'Okay. You win, Kinsella.'

Christ, my arm was pounding away like a pneumatic drill, blood beating incessantly against the improvised tourniquet. I shuddered as a wave of pain ran through my body.

'I suppose,' I said, eyeing the whisky bottle, 'a drink and a cigarette are out of the question?'

'Quit stalling, Shannon. Write.'

I poised the pen over the pad of paper. 'Fire away,' I said. 'Figuratively speaking, of course.'

Kinsella didn't smile. 'I, Nick Shannon,' he said.

'Being of sound mind?' I interjected.

His finger twitched on the trigger.

'Sorry,' I said, writing hastily. 'I won't interrupt again. Promise.'

There was a miaow from the corridor.

Kinsella tensed. Suddenly seemed uncertain as

to where to point the gun. Still threateningly at Walker? At me? Or at the door?

The cat padded noiselessly into the room. Sniffed the air. Sauntered in Kinsella's direction.

He raised his foot.

The cat did a smart about-face. Walked over to the bed. Rubbed its head against my legs. Purred gently.

'Sorry,' I said again. 'Must have left the front door open.'

Kinsella sighed with irritation. 'Get rid of the bloody thing,' he said, waving the gun. 'And shut the door at the same time. I want no more interruptions.'

I picked up the cat, held it tight against my stomach and rose from the bed. Kinsella took a step closer.

'No tricks, Shannon. Nice and easy. Into the hall. Real slow. Understand?'

I nodded. Extended one leg to prise open the door with my foot.

'Good boy,' Kinsella said. 'Now, one pace at a time.'

I started to walk forwards, freeze-frame-style. The front door was very slightly ajar – enough for a cat to squeeze through, but not a Shannon.

'That's far enough,' he said, when I was a yard from the door. 'Put your foot out again. Same procedure as last time. Edge the door open.'

Okay, Shannon, I thought. What do you reckon? There might never be a better opportunity, you know? Narrow corridor. Not much room for Kinsella to manoeuvre. A forward roll might take you out of the door.

But I didn't have a free hand, not with one useless and the other holding the cat. And if I managed to make it out of the door without crushing my skull or taking a bullet in the back, then the stairs were going to be a bit of a problem. Kinsella would have an easy shot from the vantage point at the top.

Sod it!

Well, cat. It looks like it's just the two of us against Kinsella.

Here goes.

I stretched out my leg. Curled the toe of my shoe around the edge of the door. Balanced myself on one foot.

The door burst open.

'Freeze,' came the urgent shout. 'Armed police.'

Two guns pointed into the corridor, one over each of my shoulders.

Two men in blue flak-jackets stared unwaveringly past me.

'Holy shit,' Kinsella said from behind me.

Too bloody right, I thought.

I heard the blood-curdling sound of a click as he cocked the trigger.

Then all hell broke out.

Blinding flashes of light.

Deafening bursts of gunfire, inches from my ears.

And a sharp pain in the very pit of my stomach.

CHAPTER THIRTY-SIX

You couldn't blame the cat.

All it wanted was to get the hell out of there.

The noise, the light, the acrid smell of cordite. The cat's natural instinct was flight. And in order to do that, it had to break free from the prison of my arm. Raking its claws along my stomach was a pretty effective way of forcing me to let go.

'Christ, you took your time, Collins,' I said, breathing heavily.

He was kneeling over Kinsella's body, checking it unnecessarily. Jesus, the guy hardly had a head, let alone a pulse.

'These things don't just arrange themselves, Shannon,' Collins said. 'And we couldn't very well come barging in, could we? What good would it have done you to be caught in cross-fire?'

His words sounded as if they were coming from the next county. My ears were still ringing. And my body still shaking.

'Wasn't that exactly what happened?' I said pedantically.

He shook his head wearily at me. Clinically, he untied the belt around my arm and eased off my jacket to examine the wound.

'You'll live,' he said. 'To fight another day.'

I gave him a long, hard look.

Which he ignored.

'Now,' he said. 'Where the bloody hell is Walker?'

Walker!

I rushed past Collins. Bent down over her. Cradled her head in my hands.

She flinched at my touch. Her eyelids flickered. She squinted up at me.

'Are you all right, Cherry?' I asked anxiously.

'I'll kill you for this, Shannon,' she replied.

She was all right.

'Well done, Walker,' Collins said. 'I'm proud of you.'

'Excuse me,' I objected. 'But don't I get a mention in despatches?'

'You had the easy part, Shannon. All you had to do was buy us a little time. It was Walker who had to use her brains. Think of a way to alert you to the danger without raising Kinsella's suspicions. You know something?' he said, grinning at me. 'I might break my own rule. In future, she can call me "Chris" whenever she likes.'

CHAPTER THIRTY-SEVEN

'It's not that I don't like grapes,' Norman said, propped up in bed, 'but it's just that I prefer them when they come in bottles.'

Arthur and I looked at each other and rolled our eyes.

It was two weeks since the shoot-out at Walker's bedsit. Norman, rather than endure my nagging

– and my harping on about his unilateral action with Glenshield's money – had taken sanctuary in the hospital.

Arthur picked a grape from the bunch and popped it in his mouth. 'Well?' he asked. 'Don't keep us in suspense. What's the news?'

'Bloody non-malignant,' Norman said, tossing his head. 'Wish I'd known.'

'I hope that means you won't take such stupid risks in the future,' I said.

'I thought you promised you wouldn't mention it again. I apologised, didn't I? And sorted out Sandra Redmond. What more can I do? No-one got hurt, did they?'

'Excuse me,' I said, pointing to the plaster protecting the chipped bone in my arm. 'But what exactly do you call this?'

Norman gave a little whimper and glanced up pointedly at the saline drip by his bedside.

'Bloody flesh wound,' he said dismissively. 'Stop complaining. It all worked out fine in the end. Even your friends at Glenshield are happier now than they've ever been. Christ,' he said wistfully, 'I wish I could have been cut in on that deal. The consortium picked up the company from the Receivers for next to nothing. Oh well,' he sighed. 'Can't have everything, I suppose.'

'I had a letter from Arlene today,' I said.

'Oh, yeah,' he grinned. 'I bet the envelope steamed itself open!'

'When are you off?' Arthur asked casually, concentrating on devouring the bunch of grapes.

'A little while yet,' I said. 'A couple of things to sort out first.'

Norman frowned. He knew what they were. A promise to Collins. And a file.

'How's that Mary Jo bird?' Arthur asked. 'What did Arlene have to say? Has she squared her?'

'Mary Jo is looking forward to seeing me again, apparently,' I said. 'Probably already practising her smile of greeting. By sucking lemons.'

'Did Arlene say anything else?' Norman asked matter-of-factly.

'Nothing much.' I picked up the following day's menu and examined the choices. 'Oh. She's got her old job back. Seems like some white knight came along and made a rescue bid for the development company. Insisted that Arlene handled the property sales.'

'That's nice,' said Norman, retrieving what remained of the grapes from Arthur's grasp.

'She sent me a cutting from the local rag - *Cape Cod Courier, Massachusetts Mercury*, something like that.'

I handed the torn-out page of the newspaper to Norman.

'Nice photo,' said Norman, with a quick glance. 'These grapes are good, Arthur. Very sweet. And juicy. What are they? Spanish?'

'I didn't think the picture was very flattering, myself,' I said.

'Oh, I don't know,' Norman said, chewing away. 'Israeli perhaps, Arthur? They produce a nice grape, do the Israelis.'

'Of course it might simply be the effect of the camera lens, I suppose.' I shrugged my shoulders. 'Or could have put on a bit of weight, for all I know. After all, it is a while now. Since I last

saw The Major.'
  Norman coughed and spluttered.
  I slapped him on the back.
  'Bloody pip,' he said, a twinkle in his eye.

The publishers hope that this book has given you enjoyable reading. Large Print Books are especially designed to be as easy to see and hold as possible. If you wish a complete list of our books please ask at your local library or write directly to:

Magna Large Print Books
Magna House, Long Preston,
Skipton, North Yorkshire.
BD23 4ND